Kate White's *Hush*

"Kate White delivers a top-notch, nail-biting thriller. . . . Lake Warren's personal complications make her a compelling character, and the nonstop action leads to a deliciously scary conclusion." —*Romantic Times*

"A stand-alone thriller that generates a real sense of jeopardy while avoiding clichés. . . . A subplot about the clinic's questionable practices adds to the tension, but doesn't detract from the main plot with its myriad twists." —*Publishers Weekly*

"Kate White places her wily heroine in a real jam, then keeps her, as well as readers, asking 'Whodunit?' right up till the gripping finale." —Sandra Brown, author of *Rainwater*

"In her first stand-alone thriller, White effectively blends mommy-lit issues with murder and suspense. . . . The mix of family pressures and murderous suspense makes this a page-turner." —*Library Journal*

"A nerve-jangling adrenaline rush! From the first sentence to the last, Kate White catapults you into a tense vortex of deceit, danger, and double-crosses, where one wrong word is all it takes to lose everything. When in doubt, hush." —Lisa Gardner, author of *The Neighbor*

"A pulse-pounding thriller. . . . Once you start reading you won't be able to stop." —Linda Fairstein, author of *Hell Gate*

"Sexy and suspenseful, Kate White's *Hush* is a true page-turner. The subtle twists and turns on the glamorous streets of New York City are going to thrill White's longtime fans and earn her a legion of brand-new readers. A clever, fast-paced thriller!" —Lisa Unger, author of *Die for You* and *Beautiful Lies*

HUSH

ALSO BY KATE WHITE

FICTION

If Looks Could Kill

A Body to Die For

'Til Death Do Us Part

Over Her Dead Body

Lethally Blond

NONFICTION

*Why Good Girls Don't Get Ahead
but Gutsy Girls Do*

*9 Secrets of Women Who Get
Everything They Want*

You on Top

KATE WHITE

HUSH

a novel

HARPER

NEW YORK • LONDON • TORONTO • SYDNEY

HARPER

A hardcover edition of this book was published in 2010 by HarperCollins Publishers.

HUSH. Copyright © 2010 by Kate White. All rights reserved. Printed in the United States of America. No part of this book may be used or reproduced in any manner whatsoever without written permission except in the case of brief quotations embodied in critical articles and reviews. For information address HarperCollins Publishers, 10 East 53rd Street, New York, NY 10022.

HarperCollins books may be purchased for educational, business, or sales promotional use. For information please write: Special Markets Department, HarperCollins Publishers, 10 East 53rd Street, New York, NY 10022.

First Harper paperback published 2011.

Designed by Ellen Cipriano

The Library of Congress has catalogued the hardcover edition as follows:

White, Kate
  Hush: a novel / Kate White. — 1st ed.
  p. cm.
  Summary: "An ordinary woman flees the scene of a murder—and realizes it's not just the law that may be coming after her"—Provided by publisher.
  ISBN: 978-0-06-157661-4
  I. Title.
  PS3623.H578H87 2010
  813'.6—dc22   2009030651

ISBN 978-0-06-157665-2 (pbk.)

11 12 13 14 15   OV/BVG   10 9 8 7 6 5 4 3 2 1

To John Searles.
Thank you for all the wisdom, fun, and joy
you've brought to my life as a writer

PAIN WOKE HER, forced open her eyes. She was lying in pitch-black darkness, and her head was throbbing, as if someone had smashed the back of it with a chair. There was a weird taste in her mouth—metallic. I've cut the inside of my mouth, she thought. She tried to find the spot with her tongue, but it was too swollen to move.

Where am I? she wondered, panic-stricken. Her heart began to pound in time with the throbbing in her head. She tried to shift her body, but she felt paralyzed.

She forced herself to take a breath. I'm in a nightmare, she told herself, one of those nightmares you can dream and see yourself in at the same time. And I'm going to wake up. As she breathed, she smelled something musty, like mildewed clothes. No, this was real. She tried again to shift her body. Her arms didn't move but she was able to twist her head a little.

A sound slid through the blackness—a long, low groan that

she didn't recognize. Her heart pounded harder. It's a motor, she thought finally.

She realized at last where she was. But why? Had she fallen? Or had someone *hit* her? Her mind was so confused, her thoughts choked like a tangle of weeds in a lake. She found the beginning and tried to go step by step from there. The last thing she recalled was trying to reach the flashlight. It must have gone out, though. How long had she been here, and why was she alone? And then suddenly she knew. She remembered everything. She let out an anguished sob at the truth.

She realized that the hum of the motor must be from the freezer she'd seen earlier, which meant the power was back on. She had to get out. She twisted her head back and forth and commanded the rest of her body to move. Her legs still felt leaden, like metal drums filled to the brim, but she was able to shift one of her arms—the right one. She flexed her right hand slowly open and closed.

Then there was another noise—from far above this time. Footsteps. And next a door opening. Terror engulfed her body, squeezing air from her lungs.

The killer was coming to get her.

"YOU'VE GOT A secret, don't you?"

"What do you mean?" Lake asked. Caught off guard by the comment, she set her wineglass down on the café table and pulled her head back slightly.

"There's a cat-that-ate-the-canary look on your face."

She knew Molly was picking up on something she herself had only realized in the past few days: the grief and guilt that had stalked her so unmercifully for four months had finally begun to retreat. She felt lighter, less oppressed, suddenly even hungry for life again. Earlier, as she'd hurried down Ninth Avenue to meet Molly for lunch in Chelsea, she'd actually felt a brief surge of joy—because of the brilliant summer sky and the work she was doing and the fact that somewhere something new and good might be waiting for her.

"Don't tell me you're seeing someone?" Molly added.

"God, no," Lake said. "I just feel like the gloom has finally lifted." She smiled. "I may even surprise you and be less than a total sad sack today."

"Just remember, it can be a real emotional roller coaster right now," Molly said, shaking out her long red hair. "What I learned the first year after my divorce was that you feel great one second and then *bam*, the blues are back—and you're in bed for the next four days with the covers pulled over your head."

"I'm not expecting any miracles," Lake said. "I'm just sick of moping around like some character in a Lifetime movie. I'm a forty-four-year-old single mother, and it won't be a breeze, but I'm ready to see it as an adventure rather than a curse. And it helps that I love working with my new client. The clinic does good stuff."

"So what's happening with the divorce? Are things moving along?"

"My lawyer has been playing telephone tag with Jack's. But he thinks the agreement should be ready to sign before the kids are back from camp. Once that's done, I'll really be able to move on."

"Then why *not* date?" Molly asked. "It would be so good for you."

"Well, I'm hardly beating men off with a stick."

"The reason no one's in hot pursuit is that you make it so hard for guys to talk to you," Molly said. "When are you going to let your guard down? You're a knockout, Lake."

That's helpful, Lake thought. Molly made her sound like a feral cat that ran and hid under the nearest porch whenever anyone approached. Sometimes she rued the day she confided in Molly about what she'd gone through when she was younger.

"I don't think I'm ready for any kind of romance, anyway."

"What about the doctor?" Molly asked, her green eyes flashing.

"*Who?*"

"That guy at the fertility clinic—the one you said was kind of flirty with you."

"Oh, Keaton," Lake said. As she said his name she pictured his face: the slate-blue eyes, the brown hair spiked a little in front, so un-doctor-y. And that soft, full mouth. "He's the type who would flirt with a coatrack," she added. "A real player, I'm sure."

"Playing has its place, you know. Why not try a little eye sex and see where it takes you?"

"Do you make these expressions up yourself, Molly?" Lake asked, smiling.

"When there's nothing suitable in the vernacular, yes."

"He lives in L.A., anyway. He's just consulting with the clinic for a few weeks. Should we check out the menu?"

Over lunch Lake did her best to steer the conversation off herself and toward her friend's latest exploits as a fashion stylist. It wasn't that she failed to appreciate Molly's concern for her. When Lake had gradually withdrawn from her two closest friends after the separation, too sick with shame to face them, Molly had persisted with her, offering herself as combination confidante and coach. Lake had eventually relented and had come to like the attention. But at times it could feel overwhelming. Maybe because Molly had always been just a casual friend, someone Lake had known professionally, and it was weird to have her in this new role. Or maybe because at heart, Lake had always been a bit of a loner.

"I'm supposed to hear about another job today," Molly said later, as their coffee arrived. "Do you mind if I check my email?"

Lake used the moment to look at her own BlackBerry. There was a missed call from her lawyer, Robert Hotchkiss. *Finally*, she thought. But as she played back the message, she felt a rush of fear, like water gushing through a garden hose. He wanted to see her right away. And his voice sounded grim.

"Look, I'd better jump in a cab and get up there," Lake said after filling Molly in. "Something's clearly come up."

She called Hotchkiss as soon as she hugged Molly goodbye and stepped onto the sidewalk. Though she didn't reach him directly, the receptionist told her he was anxious to talk—no, she didn't know why—and it was fine for Lake to drop by as soon as she could. *Now* what, she thought, as she threw her head against the backseat of the cab. Was Jack going to renege on his promise to let her and the kids keep the apartment? She'd spent a year being humiliated and hurt by him, and it made her furious to think he might have something else up his sleeve.

She was fuming by the time she arrived at Hotchkiss's midtown Manhattan suite. The receptionist, an older woman whose champagne-colored hair was curled as tight as a poodle's, didn't even announce her but simply led her down the hall.

As Lake entered Hotchkiss's office, he rose from his boat-size desk to greet her. He was about sixty, with a ruddy face and a stomach that draped over his expensive belt like a sandbag.

"Excuse the chaos, Lake," he said, gesturing toward stacks of bulging brown legal files. "I'm in the middle of a messy case."

"Well, with two kids in grade school, I know all about chaos."

Her comment sounded stupid to her own ears. What she wanted to do was skip the chitchat and shout, "What the hell is Jack up to *now*?"

"I can tell you never let it get the best of you," Hotchkiss said. "Please sit down. I appreciate your coming on such short notice."

"Is there some new development?" she asked, working to keep her voice calm.

"Yes—and I'm afraid it's not good."

"What *is* it?" she blurted out.

"Jack has filed a custody complaint," Hotchkiss said. "He's now asking for full custody rather than joint."

"*What?*" Lake exclaimed, shocked. As shabbily as her ex-husband had behaved, there'd been no hint he'd pull something like this. "That makes no sense. His business is so busy these days—he doesn't have time to take care of a fish tank, let alone two kids."

"Then it's probably a ploy for money. Maybe it's finally sunk in that besides child support and alimony, you're getting half the assets, and he's not happy. This may be a way to convince you to settle for less."

Lake's stomach began to knot in both anger and fear. Her kids were hardly babies—Will was nine and Amy eleven—but the thought of losing them sickened her. It was tough enough turning them over to Jack every other weekend.

"Does—does he have a chance?" Lake asked.

"I don't think so. From what I can determine, you've been a terrific mother. But we need to proceed carefully and guard our flank. Tell me a little more about your work—what are the hours like?"

"Because of everything with the divorce, I only have one new client right now—a private fertility clinic. I don't even work a forty-hour week."

His brows knitted in incomprehension and she realized he'd forgotten what she did for a living.

"My consulting business," she clarified. "I develop marketing strategies—for clients in the health and beauty industries."

"Yes, yes, of course. Sorry, I forgot the details. Well, that's excellent. You've scaled back. No one can accuse you of being a workaholic and turning over the care of your kids to a cadre of Jamaican nannies."

"No, no one could say that at all." Lake hesitated for a second. "Before I started my business two years ago, I *did* have a regular job—at a luxury cosmetic company. The hours weren't brutal, but I sometimes didn't get home till six-thirty or so. And I had to travel."

She felt a trickle of sweat run down her neck. She'd been

damn proud of her job back then—would Jack dare to turn that against her? From the start of their marriage he'd been so supportive, especially after Will was born and the working-mother equation became even crazier to solve. "You can't *not* work, Lake," he'd said. "You're so good at what you do." It was impossible to believe that the man she'd fallen for fourteen years ago had become this vindictive.

"How *much* travel?" Hotchkiss asked.

"Well, not every week," she said. "Not even every month. But I went to L.A. a couple of times a year. To London once a year."

He scribbled a few notes, his red face scrunched in consternation, as if she'd just announced she'd recently been in rehab for addiction to crack cocaine.

"But that's hardly out of the norm," she said. "How can that—?"

"It shouldn't present a problem," Hotchkiss said, shaking his head. "I just need to be fully informed. Do you presently spend a good amount of time with the kids?"

"Yes, of course. We do have a nanny slash housekeeper, but only part-time. She's off now because the kids are at sleepaway camp."

"When they return, you have to make them your number-one priority. When school starts, you escort them there yourself—not the nanny."

"I'd do that anyway," she said. She couldn't believe she had to defend herself this way.

Hotchkiss raised his beefy fingers to his lips steeple-style for a moment, and then lowered them.

"So you've had a little free time this summer," he said. "Have you been up to the Catskills? You kept the weekend house, right?"

"Yes, I kept the house in Roxbury," she said, wondering what that had to do with anything. "Jack wasn't interested in it anymore—he wanted a place in the Hamptons. But I actually haven't been up there at all this summer since the kids have been at camp. I've just stayed in Manhattan."

He offered a tight smile, as if waiting for the other shoe to drop.

"Are you seeing anyone right now?" he asked after a moment.

So *that's* what he'd been getting at. In her agitated state, she was briefly tempted to respond with sarcasm, to say that at age forty-four she'd discovered the thrills of being a cougar, an older woman with a taste for young hotties. But Hotchkiss wouldn't be amused. He'd probably never even heard the word *cougar* used that way.

"No, no one," she admitted.

Hotchkiss sighed. "I'm glad to hear it. Technically there's nothing wrong with dating now—or even having a sexual relationship with someone—as long as it doesn't impact negatively on the kids. But during a custody dispute you don't want to give even a hint of impropriety. This is not the time to bring a new man around the kids. *Definitely* do not bring a man into your home whether the kids are there or not. In fact, the smartest thing for you to do right now is socialize in groups."

Not that there was a slew of dates to be canceled, but here was yet another thing Jack was stealing from her.

"So how do we fight this?" she asked anxiously. She realized that they'd now be going from a no-fault divorce situation to a contested one. And the kids would be dragged through the mess.

"The court will appoint a child psychologist to make an evaluation, probably in a month or so. But if this is about money, as I suspect it is, Jack's lawyer may tip his hand before then."

"I'll being seeing Jack at the camp this Saturday—it's parents' day. What should I do?"

She wanted to hear him say "Skin him alive," but Hotchkiss simply flipped up his hands and shook his head. "Don't say a word about this. And be civil, *especially* in front of the kids."

Her brain was racing and she knew she'd soon have more questions, but she saw Hotchkiss glance at his watch. He'd obviously squeezed her in this afternoon.

"I know this is a terrible curveball," Hotchkiss said, "but I'm optimistic. The key point is not to do anything out of the ordinary. Make your life as routine as possible." He smiled. "Don't rob a bank, for instance. The worst thing is to give Jack a reason to file for temporary custody. If you lose ground, it's hard to get it back.

"Not to alarm you," he added, leading her to the door, "but it's possible Jack might even have you followed, looking for evidence."

"*Followed*," she exclaimed. "I can't believe this." Her anger seeped through her entire body, making her feel flushed. Jack had been the one to leave. He had no right to sic a private eye on her.

"Actually, we might consider something like that ourselves, considering what you told me previously. Let's think it over."

When she'd agreed to give Jack a divorce so he could start his shiny new life, she'd told Hotchkiss she thought he might be involved with someone—but, other than his total detachment, she'd never had any evidence and had come to doubt her own suspicions. But now Hotchkiss's comment brought the possibility rushing back. Was Jack planning to start a new family with a wife better suited to his hot entrepreneurial image, the kids just part of the package? Is *that* why he'd lodged the custody challenge? If Jack thought Lake was going to step aside and hand her kids over to him and a girlfriend, he was sorely mistaken.

By the time she was in a cab home, Lake nearly slumped over in exhaustion. Two hours ago she'd been relishing life again, no longer worried about seeming undone in front of the kids or her clients. She'd even started planning for the future. And now it seemed as if she'd been dragged back to square one.

As the cab hurtled north, she kicked herself for not seeing this coming—but how could she have? All of Jack's attention lately had seemed focused *away* from his old life with her and the kids. So this had to be about money. During their marriage she'd supported him, emotionally and financially, when he started his software business and she spent endless weekends alone with the kids while he was holed up at work. She'd even contributed marketing ideas. Why would he try to deny her half of their assets?

Lake couldn't wait to get home. Her place was a rambling old apartment on West End Avenue in the Eighties, bought years ago at a bargain from Jack's widowed aunt. Jack could have made a case for keeping it after the split, but in a surprising act of generosity, he had insisted it would be best for her and the kids to continue living there. Only later did it dawn on her that it was because he wanted something sleeker and hipper for his new life. *The Bachelor: Forty-six, Fabulous, and Finally Free.*

The apartment had been a refuge for her lately and she was looking forward to a quiet night at home. But when she stepped inside late that afternoon, it was hot and oppressive. The cat, Smokey, darted out to greet her and she patted his thick, black fur distractedly. After she turned on the air conditioner and poured a glass of wine, the phone rang.

"Everything okay?" It was Molly.

Lake briefly brought her friend up to speed.

"What a shithead," Molly proclaimed. "Are you sure you don't want to go out? You don't always have to keep a stiff upper lip. You know, Lake, it might do you good to blow off a little steam."

"Thanks, but I want to do some research online about custody. I need to know how bad this could get."

"What's the next step in the process?"

"An evaluation by a shrink. Till then I just wait—and keep my nose clean."

"Don't tell me men are totally verboten?"

"Apparently a woman can't lose custody just because she's had a few dates—or even because she's had sex—but my lawyer says it's smart to lay low, act like a nun, at least when the kids are around." She looked at the clock and noticed the time. "I better go. I have to fax the kids tonight, too."

The summer camp Lake had chosen for the kids allowed parents to send faxes, which were then distributed to the campers after dinner. She tried to write every day, loved coming up with things for notes, but today she had nearly run out of time. For Amy she scribbled a few lines about Smokey chasing a dust ball that morning. For Will she copied a riddle from a book she'd bought just for this purpose.

Faxes sent, she stayed in her small home office and Googled "custody battles" on her laptop. The news wasn't reassuring. Mothers rarely lost custody, but there weren't any guarantees. Judges could be unpredictable. Lake even found stories of good mothers who'd lost out and learned years later that the judge had been bribed.

The old Jack would never do something like that, but she wondered if the new one might. He seemed alien to her now, self-absorbed and greedy. It was like dealing with an animal she'd found in the wild—one that could bite her hand off without warning.

She skipped dinner—the glass of wine was all she could stomach—and undressed for bed. As she washed her face in the bathroom sink, barely concentrating, she suddenly caught her reflection in the mirror. Her father, long dead, once said that with her deep-brown hair and gray-green eyes, there was something actually *lakelike* about her appearance. She would hardly call herself a knockout like Molly had, but she knew that she looked good for her age and should just relish it. But it was difficult to let go of what she used to see in the mirror—the purply birthmark over her entire left cheek. It wasn't until the age of fifteen that she'd flown from her home in central Pennsylvania to Philadelphia for the laser treatments that had removed all but the faintest shadow of it.

After splashing cool water on her neck, she ran her hands over her breasts. Unless she counted the humorless radiology tech who'd squashed them onto the X-ray tray for Lake's routine mammogram last month, it had been nearly a year since anyone had touched them.

Lake marked the death of her marriage on the night last fall when she reached for Jack in bed, eager to make love, and he'd shrugged her hand off his shoulder. The rebuke had stung.

She knew, however, that things had begun to unravel six months before, when Jack's business had gone through the roof. He was working even harder, but also going out more—socializing with clients, playing golf, always extolling the virtues of *living large*. She had oscillated between annoyance and the need to cut him some slack. After all the stress he'd been through, maybe he deserved a little fun.

But it wasn't until he rebuffed her in bed—that first time, and then again and again—that she'd panicked. She searched his pockets and his emails, assuming an affair, but found nothing. She bought sexy lingerie and felt like a fool when he lay motionless next to her, like a hedgerow in the bed. Finally she tried to talk to him, but he claimed he was simply tired—couldn't she *see* how demanding things were for him? And then suddenly *she* was the problem. He accused her of lacking spontaneity and fun. "Where's your *passion*?" he'd ask, as if she was guilty of some moral failure. That's ironic, she'd thought, considering you won't even touch me.

His departure had had the abruptness of a prison break. He took just his clothes, some papers, and the stupid Abdominizer. She felt a kind of shame she hadn't experienced since her days with her birthmark. But another part of her had been angry as hell at his betrayal. It was hard to imagine that he was the same man who once said, "You're my rock, Lake. You saved me."

Lake put on her nightgown and paced the apartment. What

did Jack think he could use against her? Was he going to lie and make her business seem more demanding than it was? She went into Will's room and touched his toys, fighting off a sob. Above the dresser was a framed collage she'd made for him, designed with snapshots and scraps of souvenirs. Jack's face appeared twice, flashing the famous grin that had once captivated her. But it seemed satanic now. She fought the urge to smash the glass and ink out his face.

Finally, sick of thinking, she retreated to her room and slipped into bed. She'd expected to toss and turn, but, exhausted, she fell asleep within minutes.

And suddenly she was awake again—jerked out of a dream. She lay there for a few seconds, wondering why, and then heard the phone ring, for the second time, she realized. The clock on the bedside table said 2:57. As she fumbled for the phone, her mind went instantly to the kids.

"Hello," she said, her voice hoarse from sleep.

"Is this the Warren residence?" a voice asked. It was a woman, she thought, but wasn't sure. The voice sounded oddly distorted.

"Yes, who's calling?" Lake asked anxiously. The phone display read "private caller."

"Is this *Mrs.* Warren?"

"Please tell me who's calling."

"Are you the mother of William Warren?"

Her heart nearly stopped.

"Is this the camp?" she blurted out. "What's wrong?"

The person said nothing but Lake could hear breathing.

"Please, what's the matter?" she demanded.

And then there was only a dial tone.

LAKE KICKED OFF the sheet and tore down the hall to the foyer. Her purse was on the hall table and she upended it, spilling the contents. She pawed through the clutter until she found her Black-Berry and scrolled to the camp's emergency number. Five rings, then a deep hello. It was the gravelly voice of Mr. Morrison, the director.

"This is Will Warren's mother," Lake said quickly. "He's in cabin seven—um no, five, cabin five. Did someone just call me?"

"What?" he asked groggily, clearly not comprehending.

Lake explained the situation, trying to keep her voice even.

"No, it wasn't me," he said. "But let me go down to his cabin right away. I'll call you back in ten minutes."

Pacing the hallway, Lake tried to convince herself that nothing was wrong—the camp director would have *known*—but as the minutes passed without a call, her alarm ballooned. Had Will been *abducted*? Did this have something to do with Jack?

Fifteen minutes later, her BlackBerry finally rang.

"There's absolutely no reason for concern," the director said. "Will is fast asleep, and the counselor says he's been fine all night. Sounds like it must have been a wrong number."

It had to be, she thought. For one thing, Will's name was just Will, not William and someone really familiar with him wouldn't make the mistake. And why would anyone she knew call at this hour? Her mind flew back to Jack. Had *he* orchestrated it, because of his custody fight? But what would he gain from a stunt like that? After crawling back into bed, it took her over an hour to fall asleep again.

The next morning she woke feeling hungover from worry—about the phone call, about her conversation with Hotchkiss. She'd felt so giddy yesterday as she'd dashed toward lunch, and she wondered now when she'd ever summon that feeling again. It was almost a relief to be on the Eighty-sixth Street crosstown bus an hour later, headed to the offices of her new client on Park Avenue, the Advanced Fertility Center.

Her plan today was to finish up her background research about the practice. She'd been recommended for the job by Dr. Steve Salman, an associate at the clinic whose sister, Sonia, had been a friend of Lake's in college. Private fertility clinics, compared to those affiliated with hospitals and universities, had a bit of a stigma attached to them. The perception sometimes was that making money took precedence over making babies. Lake had been hired to help the clinic overcome that hurdle and to stand out among the burgeoning number of competitors.

It was a challenge she relished. The trick in marketing was to find the unique aspect of a product or company—*the unique selling position*—and optimize it. To Lake it was like studying a drawing with a hidden object and then, with a thrill, finding it. Like most fertility clinics, this one focused heavily on in vitro fertilization

(IVF), the process by which a woman's eggs are removed from the ovaries, and then, after being fertilized by sperm in a petri dish or test tube, are transferred to her uterus or frozen for future use. The clinic had been particularly successful with women over forty. Lake needed to find ways to play that fact up without turning off younger patients. In a week and a half she would present her first round of ideas to the two partners.

As much as she enjoyed her work so far at the clinic, she always felt a moment's hesitation whenf she first walked through the door. The reception area had been nicely decorated with minty green walls and plush carpeting, but to Lake the room seemed so melancholy. Though the women who sat there—some with husbands and partners, some without—hardly looked morose, Lake could sense how sad and tortured they felt underneath.

In a small way, she could relate to their anguish. Though she'd never grappled with infertility, her birthmark had created a deep sense of despair and hopelessness in her, starting in childhood. By eleven she'd become an egghead in school, caught up in endless art and history projects and pretending nothing else mattered, when all she really wanted was to be normal, to be pretty, to never again have to see that double beat of surprise and pity in people's eyes. A doctor had saved her with his laser. She knew it didn't take a psychiatrist to see why she found herself drawn to clients in the health field.

For the past two and a half weeks she had worked in the small conference room at the very back of the clinic office. Today, as usual, she made her way there through the crazy warren of short corridors—past the doctors' private offices, the nurses' station, the hushed exam rooms, the futuristic-looking embryology lab, with its sliding window to the OR, where the egg and embryo transfers were done. As she was getting started, spreading open a folder on the conference room table, one of the nurses, a dark-haired Irish girl named Maggie, passed by the open door and smiled hello. About fifteen people worked at the clinic, and Maggie had been one of the warmest to her. Along with Dr. Harry Kline, the consulting psychologist.

Alone in the conference room, Lake read through the last articles in the batch she'd collected as soon as she was hired for the job. She'd been consuming anything that had to do with the clinic: journal articles the doctors had written, press stories that featured the practice. It was often in these kinds of materials that she found nuggets that she could begin to work with and leverage as part of a marketing plan.

While she worked, she tried to keep yesterday's meeting with Hotchkiss out of her mind, but it wouldn't leave her alone. The strange phone call from last night also gnawed at her. Before she'd gotten very far with her reading, she called the camp director again. He'd checked on Will that morning, he said, and everything was fine.

About an hour later, Rory, the clinical medical assistant, poked her blond head in the door. She was about thirty, tall and pretty in an athletic way, the kind of girl who looked like she'd led her high school basketball team into the state tournament. And she was five months pregnant, which Lake realized must be tough for some of the patients to see. Rory's blue eyes were rimmed with black liner today and her blond hair was scooped up on her head in a loose bun.

"Brie hasn't been by here, has she?" she asked.

"No, I haven't seen her," Lake said. Brie, the no-nonsense, tightly wound office manager, normally ignored her. Lake assumed it was because until Lake's arrival, Brie had handled any so-called marketing for the clinic.

"Dr. Levin wanted her to give you a bio."

"I think I've got everybody's," Lake said, glancing down at one of the folders.

"Dr. Keaton's?"

"But he's just a consultant, right? Why—"

"He's decided to join the group," Rory said, smiling. "He's leaving his West Coast practice and coming in with us."

"Oh, um—okay," Lake said. To her surprise, the news flustered her.

"Is something the matter, Lake?"

"No, I just hadn't heard the news yet."

"Oh well, Brie should have mentioned it to you. You should be kept in the loop about these things."

"Not a problem," Lake said. She appreciated that Rory seemed to have picked up on Brie's passive-aggressive streak.

Rory turned to go. Lake wondered if she should try to engage her in some kind of small talk, but it often seemed that Rory preferred to focus on the next thing on her list.

"You look very nice today, by the way," Lake said. "Do you have a special night planned?"

"My husband's traveling this week," she said, smiling ruefully. "But I try to make an effort anyway. I think it's so important not to let yourself go just because you have kids in your life. I hope you don't mind my saying this, but you're such a perfect role model. When I'm your age I hope I look as good as you."

"Oh, thank you," Lake said, a little taken aback.

She chose to take Rory's comment as a compliment and got back to work. At close to eleven she realized it was time for her scheduled interview with Dr. Sherman, one of the clinic's two partners, about some of the more advanced aspects of in vitro fertilization. She had done a number of these sessions with the doctors just to familiarize herself with their work. As she picked up her pad and got ready to head down the hall, Keaton himself appeared in the doorway. She felt her pulse kick up a notch. He was wearing perfectly draped navy pants, a crisp lavender shirt and a lavender-and-purple print tie. He looked great—and she was sure he knew it.

"Have they still got you locked down back here?" he said, grinning. "That seems awfully cruel on a gorgeous day like today."

"It's not so bad," she said. "Congratulations, by the way."

"Oh, right. Thanks. I just made the decision last night, in fact.

"And actually," he added, stepping into the conference room and locking his slate-blue eyes with hers, "you're actually part of the reason I accepted."

She felt flustered by this unexpected statement. Unsure of what he meant, she just cocked her head and smiled.

"Oh, is that right?" she said.

"Yup. This is a great practice, but it only gets a C-plus in marketing. Hiring you was a *very* smart decision."

"Thanks," she said, annoyed at how instantly deflated she felt. How ridiculous, she thought. Had I really thought he was going to announce that he came on board because I'd tantalized the hell out of him?

"It doesn't seem fair," she added, all business again, "but even a practice that should win on merit has to play the game and do its best to stand out."

He stepped even closer and slid his butt onto the conference table. His tall, lean body was just inches from her now, invading her space a little. She could smell his musky cologne. She could also see a small, jagged scar above his left eye, a vestige perhaps of having been whacked hard with something like a hockey stick.

"You don't strike me as someone who tolerates a lot of game playing," he said slyly. Lake was sure he was talking on two levels now, and she didn't know how to handle it.

"Well, sometimes in business it's unavoidable," she said, thinking she should change the subject. "Will you, um, miss L.A.?"

"A bit. But I trained at Cornell and I've been anxious to get back to New York ever since." He tucked both hands in his back pants pockets, and as he did, his shirt strained against the muscles of his chest. "You know, all the great things about this city—rude waiters, packed subways . . . the smell of wet wool in the winter time."

"Maybe I should suggest that idea to one of my beauty clients as a fragrance launch," Lake said. "Manhattan Wet Wool." God, that was lame, she thought, but he laughed, his eyes not leaving her face.

"Perfect," he said. "But yes, I'll miss L.A. a little. The weather, mostly. I should tell you that the practice I'm leaving is actually pretty good at marketing."

"What kinds of things do they do?"

"Community events, glossy takeaways, interactive website."

"I'd love to hear more about it."

"When?" he asked, a little smile at the corner of his mouth. He held her eyes hard now. So this was eye sex, she thought.

"You tell me," she said. Would he suggest coffee? she wondered. No, he was the kind of guy who went straight for drinks, no pussyfooting around.

But as he started to answer, Brie barged in, the ubiquitous clipboard on her arm.

"Dr. Sherman is expecting you, Lake," she said curtly. Her thin mouth was like a slash today, painted a shade too red for her short auburn hair.

"Okay—I'll be right there."

Lake hesitated, waiting for Brie to leave but she didn't budge. Then Keaton rose from the table.

"I'll catch up with you later," he said to Lake, smiling. Lake could almost read *to be continued* in his eyes.

She ended up waiting ten minutes outside Sherman's closed-door office, and she suspected that Brie had purposely rushed her. When the door finally opened, a young couple emerged. The husband looked stricken, ashamed almost, and Lake wondered if they'd just been told their infertility issue rested with him.

Sherman was in his early sixties, and he was blunt-spoken and humorless. He had yellowed gray hair, a bulbous nose, and pale, almost translucent skin. As he rambled on imperiously, Lake took notes, trying to concentrate, but her thoughts kept being tugged away. To the meeting with Hotchkiss. And then, against her will, to Keaton. Where was she headed with this thing? she wondered. Would she really go for a drink with him?

There were all kinds of reasons why she should turn and run the other way, not least of which was the warning from Hotchkiss. Well, she didn't really have to think about locking herself up until the kids came home from camp, right? In the meantime, couldn't she enjoy the dance? Even if Keaton was one of those love-'em-and-leave-'em types—as she had no doubt he was.

"The most viable embryos survive to the fifth day of incubation," she heard Sherman say, and she made an attempt to refocus. "That's what we call the blastocyst stage. A blastocyst transfer allows us to place only one or two of the most viable embryos into the uterus. That not only improves embryo selection but it reduces the chances of multiple births. No decent doctor wants to be responsible for an 'octomom' situation. Any questions?"

"Uh, I think I'm set for now," Lake said. "I'm pretty familiar with all these procedures from the background materials you provided."

Sherman seemed as happy to end the meeting as Lake was. It was clear they weren't going to be the best of friends, but no matter—that wouldn't get in the way of Lake doing her job.

On her way back to the conference room, Lake casually looked for Keaton but didn't find him. The door to Harry Kline's office was open, though, and she peered in to say hello. She'd enjoyed the few conversations she'd had with him—he had that shrink way of seeming intrigued by every word that came out of your mouth. But he wasn't in his office.

"I heard he left early," one of the older nurses, Emily, said quietly behind her. "Some sort of personal emergency."

Lake returned to her articles in the conference room and after an hour more of reading and note taking was ready to call it quits. As she walked to the storage room to return the reading materials to the files, she kept an eye out for Keaton. There was still no sign of him. Retracing her steps, she spotted Steve in the doorway of the small conference room, obviously looking for her. It was amazing how much he resembled his sister, Sonia. They were half Belgian, half Pakistani, and both extremely attractive.

"There you are," he said. "How's it going?"

"Good," she said. "I'm really enjoying the project, Steve."

"I knew you were the perfect choice. By the way, we're having a dinner tonight in honor of Mark Keaton. How about joining us?"

"Thanks, but I should make it an early night," she said. It'd been a knee-jerk response, and part of her instantly regretted it.

"We hardly plan to push on till dawn," he said. "Come on—it'll be fun. Besides, Dr. Keaton wanted me to ask you."

She shrugged, trying to seem indifferent to his comment.

"Okay, why not," she said, smiling. "I appreciate the invitation."

They were going to Balthazar, he said. In SoHo. Eight o'clock.

As she walked up Park Avenue ten minutes later, Lake couldn't contain her excitement. In her mind she imagined sitting next to Keaton tonight, feeling those eyes trained on her again. After this miserable year, I *deserve* a night like this, she told herself. For a moment, Hotchkiss's warning flashed in her mind. But wasn't this exactly what the man had suggested? Socializing in *groups*? Plus, the kids were still away. No harm to be done.

Back home she fixed a late lunch, faxed the kids, and, because her part-time assistant was off on her honeymoon, took care of paperwork. At close to seven, she began rummaging for an outfit. She tried on and discarded black pants and a crisp white shirt; a flowy skirt and blouse; the same blouse with a denim pencil skirt.

Finally, her bed strewn with clothes, she chose a coral sundress, burnished gold sandals, and gold hoop earrings. The dress was striking with her long brown hair and showed off a little cleavage. She felt slightly wicked—like she was sixteen and had just shoplifted a lipstick from the drugstore. Before leaving, she grabbed a lightweight trench, not sure what the weather would be later on.

All the way down the West Side Highway, as the taxi's AC hummed like white noise, she replayed the scene with Keaton in the conference room, his body just inches away from her. Was he just being his flirty self or did he want to take things further? Did *she* want to take things further? The thought of what *further* meant made her blush.

As the cab exited at Canal Street, she remembered Hotchkiss's other warning—about being followed—and glanced out the back window. There were no cars behind her cab. She half-laughed at her paranoia.

She was the last of the group to arrive at Balthazar. The only seat left was at the foot of the table—next to Steve and across from Dr. Thomas Levin, the clinic's other partner. Keaton was at the opposite end, next to Steve's wife, Hilary. In between were Sherman; Dr. Catherine Hoss, the clinic's senior embryologist; Hoss's date; Matt Perkins, a doctor who'd recently joined the practice; Perkins's preppy-looking wife; and Levin's blond, Botoxed trophy bride, her arms lined with jeweled bangles. Keaton politely nodded his head in greeting, and that was it. In the cavernous French bistro with its whirring overhead fans, she couldn't even hear the conversation at his end of the table.

Lake pulled in a breath, trying to squelch her irritation. She'd imagined sitting next to Keaton, talking to him, maybe even accidentally feeling his leg against hers under the table. But it wasn't going to happen. Suddenly she had little interest in conversation with a bunch of people she barely knew. Why had she bothered to come?

But Levin soon made it easy for her. In the office he'd seemed arrogant and at times brusque, but tonight he let her see his suave, charming side. He was about the same age as Sherman and yet handsome, dashing almost—with thick gray hair, a hawklike nose, and unruly eyebrows that added a bohemian touch to the polished image. He wanted to know what had brought her to New York, where she had learned the best lessons about marketing, and what she thought really gave people an edge in business today. All the while he listened intently. Eventually Steve and Dr. Hoss's boorish date joined in. As they swapped stories, Lake let herself relax against the red banquette, luxuriating in the taste of the great Bordeaux and the breeze from the overhead fan on her bare shoulders. At one point all three men seemed to be hanging on her every word. It had been ages since she'd enjoyed that kind of experience.

As the appetizers were being served, she glanced slyly down to Keaton's end of the table, thinking she'd catch his eye. But she didn't. A few minutes later she tried again—with no luck this time either. She hated how disappointed she felt. Had he just been toying with her earlier? But then why suggest to Steve she join the group tonight? As she ate, she saw that Hilary had turned all her attention Keaton's way, cocking her head back and forth like a titmouse at a bird feeder.

After the main course, a few people asked for coffee. Lake let her eyes stray to Keaton's end of the table again. This time, to her shock, he looked directly at her. He pulled his body back in his seat and held her eyes. Desire flooded through every inch of her.

Now what? she wondered. She pretended to fumble in her purse for something but she was just trying to think. Finally she turned to Levin.

"Excuse me," she said to him. "I need to sneak to the ladies' room." It was insane, she knew, but she longed for Keaton to follow.

To her complete annoyance, Catherine Hoss got up, too. *Just perfect*, Lake thought. But rather than head for the restroom, Hoss stepped outside the restaurant. Through the paneled windows Lake saw her pull a cell phone from her purse. Lake was struck by how attractive Hoss was out of her lab coat and with her black hair loose around her shoulders rather than pinned tightly in her usual French twist.

After edging past the restaurant's zinc bar, Lake descended the stairs to a dimly lit lounge. She entered the ladies' room and patted fresh foundation over the faint trace of her birthmark. In the mirror she saw that her cheeks were deep pink, as if she'd spent the night huddled over a bonfire. She felt almost woozy with excitement from Keaton's last look.

As she tugged open the door, her mind pleaded—please let him be there. And he was. He stood in the lounge, glancing at the screen of his phone. As she emerged he looked up and smiled—as if this were just a chance meeting. God, she thought, the guy had all the moves down.

"So, how were things at your end?" he asked. "You had the pleasure of sitting next to Dr. Thomas Levin, fertility rock star."

There was an odd edge to his words.

"He's an interesting guy," Lake said. "Was he the main reason you chose this practice—because of his reputation?"

"Good question. But one that may be moot at this point."

"What do you mean?"

"There's been a little snag in the plan. This may not be the best place for me after all."

"Wait—you're not joining the clinic?" Lake asked, completely taken aback.

"You sound *sorry*," Keaton said, his voice teasing.

"Well, I'm sorry if you're in any kind of a difficult situation."

"You know what would take the sting out?" he said with a smile. She knew what was coming.

"What?" she asked quietly.

"Having a drink later with you. Without all the other revelers."

"I'd like that," she said. Her boldness surprised her.

"Why don't you come to my place," he said. "It's just around the corner—at 78 Crosby. I'll leave first and you can head over after."

A drink at his place. She could no longer have any doubts about where this was going. Her heart pounded as she thought about being with him and what it would be like to completely let go. If she didn't take advantage of this moment, who knew when she'd be able to risk something like this again. Once the kids were back home, she would have to play the nun as Hotchkiss had advised.

"All right," she replied, "sounds good."

He smiled again and slipped into the men's room without a word.

"So, Jack, how's *that* for spontaneity?" Lake thought as she started up the stairs.

3

THE COFFEE WAS being served when she returned to the table. As she took a sip of her cappuccino, Keaton slipped back into his seat. At the same moment she saw Steve give his wife a *let's-get-out-of-here* look, but Hilary pretended not to notice. The group suddenly grew quiet.

"This has been a terrific night," Keaton announced to the table. "I really appreciate your doing this in my honor."

"Well, we're thrilled to have you with us," Dr. Hoss said, her chin raised. For Hoss the comment was positively effusive. She had the manner of someone who'd grown up affluent and never felt the need to simply make nice.

"Would anyone care for an after-dinner drink?" Levin asked. He made it sound less like an invitation than a signal that the evening needed to come to an end.

"I'm afraid I should get home," Keaton said. "Would you excuse me for bolting now? I have a call to make to a patient on the West Coast."

As he stood and said goodbye, he grabbed Lake's eyes briefly, and to her dismay, she saw Hilary catch the look and weigh it. The last thing Lake wanted was any gossip. She took her time leaving, waiting until Levin paid the check and hanging back until all but Dr. Perkins and his wife remained.

"Which way are you going?" Perkins asked Lake as they walked toward the front of the restaurant with her.

"Upper West Side," she said, praying they were bound for some Jersey suburb, which would require them to head for the Holland Tunnel.

"We're on Central Park West. You're welcome to share our taxi."

"Oh, thank you, no. I need to stop at a deli."

"Well, at least let us drop you part of the way," Perkins said.

"Thank you, but you go ahead," Lake urged, ready to bite their heads off. "I have to make a call first anyway."

Lake rustled in her purse, faking a search for her cell phone. After giving them two minutes, she headed outside, her trench coat flung over her arm. Glancing at her watch, she saw that close to fifteen minutes had passed since Keaton's departure, and she suddenly felt frantic to get going.

She swung left outside the restaurant and hurried along Spring Street. It was only when she reached Broadway that she realized she'd gone the wrong way. Cursing, she dashed back to the restaurant and then up to Crosby. On a hunch, she turned left, crossing the street.

A few doors up the dark, canyon-like street she saw by the numbers that her guess had been right. Number 78 turned out to be a quarter of the way up the block, an unassuming twelve- or thirteen-story building that might have once held small factories on each floor before being converted into apartments when SoHo became fashionable to live in. The exterior was sooty with age, as if they still burned coal in New York. There was a small vestibule and beyond that, behind a locked door, was a nondescript lobby with no doorman. She looked behind her and glimpsed people walking along Spring Street. But Crosby was deserted.

As soon as she stepped inside the vestibule and saw the intercom panel, she let out a groan. She'd never asked Keaton for an apartment number. He was probably subletting and his name wouldn't be on the buzzer. Her eyes raced down the two rows of buttons. To her relief, she spotted his name next to PH2.

"Hi there," he answered after she'd pressed the button. "Come on up. Penthouse 2. On twelve."

The buzzer sounded, nearly making her jump. She pushed the door and stepped inside the lobby. One wall was mirrored, which made the space seem bigger than it was, and she glanced at her reflection. Her cheeks were less flushed but still pink. I'm really going to do this, she thought. She felt nervous but also nearly drunk with anticipation. It had been ages since she'd felt seductive or yearned for—or charged with desire.

She half-expected music to be playing (please don't let it be Barry White, she prayed), but when Keaton answered the door of his apartment—smiling, his jacket off and shirtsleeves rolled—it was absolutely silent behind him.

"I was beginning to worry that you'd opted for a crème brûlée instead of an after-dinner drink with me," he said. He was teasing her, she knew. He was the kind of guy who would never be bested by a crème brûlée. He accepted her coat and she followed him into the apartment.

The place was beyond anything she could have predicted from the lobby down below—a double-height loft with open living, dining, and kitchen areas, all decorated in whites and beiges. A staircase led up to a bookcase-lined mezzanine. And, most spectacular of all: a large terrace beyond French doors. There were a few soft lights on out there and she could see teak tables and chairs, a couple of chaise longues, and several box trees.

"This is fantastic," she said. "You must be subletting, right?" As she set her purse down at the far end of a creamy white sofa, she noticed the hallway that shot off to the left, most likely to the bedroom. Her heart knocked against her chest.

"No, I actually bought it six months ago—I knew I was coming back to New York one way or another. What would you like to drink? I've got white wine chilled. Or would you prefer cognac?"

"Cognac sounds good," she said.

Keaton laid her trench coat across the arm of the sofa and walked to the kitchen area. While he had his back to her, Lake surveyed the space. Though it was still sparsely decorated, there were a few stunning pieces. On one wall was a striking abstract painting of a man with an elongated head. She stepped closer. Below it was a sleek side table with a primitive wooden bowl sitting on top. She glanced inside the bowl. Nestled at the bottom were a few coins and an ATM slip. Also a business card from a woman named Ashley Triffin, an event planner. And a scrap of paper with the name Melanie Turnbull scrawled on it. Well, she thought, I *knew* he was a player.

"Here you go," Keaton said, walking up with their drinks. As she accepted the glass, she saw that his arms were tan, muscular, and covered with hair so light it looked like it had been bleached by sunlight. "Why don't we go out to the terrace?"

He opened one of the French doors and motioned her outside. The view was mainly north—to a dazzling, glittering midtown, endless rooftops and wooden water tanks. All set against a blue-black sky. She could hear the faint hum of traffic twelve stories below and the sporadic blare of a car horn.

"I feel like I'm looking at Oz," she said as a soft breeze lifted the back of her hair. "It seems almost unreal."

"I've practically lived out here this summer," he said. "One night I even dragged a sleeping bag onto a lounge chair and slept here."

"Is that safe? I mean, it *is* the middle of Manhattan."

"There's no access from anywhere but my apartment—though I guess Spider-Man could reach it."

She smiled and walked over to the outside wall, peering over.

"You're not afraid of heights, are you?" he asked. She smelled his musky cologne as he came up slowly behind her.

"No," she said. "Not heights."

"Ahh, but *something*?"

"A crazy little phobia. Not what you'd expect." She couldn't believe she was going to confess it. But she felt reckless with him.

"So you're true to your name, then? Still waters run deep."

"I don't know how *deep* it is." She took a sip of her cognac. "I have this weird fear of clowns."

"Clowns?" he said, looking intrigued. "Does that mean you've never taken your kids to Ringling Brothers' circus?"

"Correct. . . . But how do you know I have kids?"

"I overheard you say something about one of them to Maggie. I'm just guessing you have more than one."

"I've got two, actually. They're at sleepaway camp this month."

"And a husband?"

Had he asked her up here not knowing the answer to that?

"We . . . ended things a few months ago." She turned it over to him. "You don't have kids, do you?"

"No kids. I was married briefly in my thirties, though, to another doctor. Commuter marriage. Probably doomed from the start."

"And does it take as long as they say to recover? To feel like you haven't been flattened by a car?"

She regretted her comment instantly. The last thing she wanted was for things to turn heavy.

"Is that how it's made you feel?" Keaton asked.

"Well, in the very beginning, yes," she said, trying to sound breezy now. "But it's been about four months, and these days there are moments when I feel really good, happy."

"Because of? Evenings spent chatting with eminent fertility experts like Dr. Levin?"

"Well . . . more because of being on my own again. Not having to answer to anyone. Getting all the crumbs I want in the bed."

She couldn't believe she'd said the word *bed*. How transparent, she thought. The blood went rushing to her cheeks again.

"Sounds good," he said, holding her eyes in the dim light. "And you'll see that things will only get better from here."

"That's nice to know," she replied. Was he saying *tonight* things would only get better? She felt as if her whole body was on the verge of trembling uncontrollably.

And then he leaned down and kissed her, softly at first, and then stronger, his full mouth seeming to envelop her. A rush of desire went through her as fast as the snap of a whip. It almost hurt when he pulled away.

"If I promise to provide a bag of chips or something else nice and crumbly, can I take you to bed, then?" he asked.

It seemed like such a slick line, endless variations of it used before on other women, but she didn't give a damn.

"Yes," she said. "But the chips aren't necessary."

He kissed her again and this time he slipped his tongue into her mouth. He placed his hands at her waist and pulled her toward him. She relaxed into his body and wondered if he could feel how fast her heart was beating.

"Let's go inside," he whispered.

He guided her through the door, and took a minute to flip off the lights on the terrace and all but one light in the great room.

His bedroom was spare, Zenlike. He stopped in the middle of the room and untied the halter of her dress, then unzipped it and let it drop in a puddle on the floor. She stepped out of the dress and flicked off her sandals.

"You're beautiful," he said. That was something she hadn't been sure she'd ever hear again.

He kissed her roughly, with her breasts in his hands, and then he took her left breast in his mouth, sucking on it, flicking her nipple with his tongue. She moaned in pleasure. She reached between his legs with her hand, stroking him.

After peeling away the comforter from the bed, he laid her down on the cool sheets and slowly tugged off her underwear. Then he unbuckled his pants and slipped them off.

He found her mouth again with his, kissing her intensely and fondling her breasts, pinching the nipples so that each time, blood went rushing between her legs. As she writhed, he began to descend down her body, trailing his tongue along her abdomen, and then lower. She let out a gasp as he parted her legs with his hands and slid his tongue into her. Slowly he began to circle her clitoris with his tongue, and it was only seconds before she exploded in spasms of orgasm.

Rolling over, he stripped off his gray boxer briefs and reached toward the bedside table. In the dim light she saw him pull out a condom. After slipping it on effortlessly, he entered her. He was large, filling her up. He began to thrust but with exquisite slowness, watching her face intently with each stroke. She moaned again as another climax began to build.

She waited for him to move faster, but suddenly he pulled out of her and flipped her over, urging her up on her knees with his hands. Then he was inside her from behind, grasping her hips, and driving deeper into her. She climaxed again, letting out a cry of pure release. His chest grew damp against her back and finally he moaned with pleasure. She could feel him shudder as he climaxed inside her.

He turned over, sunk into the bed, and in the dark she could tell he was slipping off the condom. Then he pulled her into a spoon position. After a while she could hear him snoring lightly, and a few minutes later, she felt herself drift off to sleep.

She woke at around three o'clock, needing to pee. His attached bathroom was as Zenlike as the bedroom, and inside she picked up the musky scent he wore. As soon as she returned to bed she realized she wasn't going to fall back asleep. She felt wound up suddenly, off kilter from lying in this strange bedroom. She slid out of bed again and felt in the dark for her belongings that had been left strewn on the floor. After slipping on her panties and sandals and folding her rumpled dress over a small armchair, she tiptoed toward the door.

With the light still on in the great room, she spotted her glass where she'd left it on the coffee table, still with a splash of cognac. She picked it up and took a sip.

She was about to settle on the sofa when her eyes strayed to the dark terrace. She put on her trench coat, quietly opened the French doors, and snuck outside with her glass. The surrounding buildings were now dabbed with only a few lights, like the last fireflies in a field at midnight.

After allowing her eyes to adjust to the darkness, she walked over to one of the chaise longues in the far corner. Easing onto it, she took another sip of cognac and leaned back. She still felt giddy from the sex—her first time with another man since meeting Jack—and unregretful. For a few minutes her mind replayed it all. She smiled, could feel herself almost smirk.

Her eyelids felt heavy and she let them drop, just for a second, for the pleasure of allowing them to close. She saw why Keaton had camped out some nights on the terrace. It was intoxicating to lie there with the city all around her. The air was as soft as a piece of worn cloth against her skin. Soon her thoughts disintegrated and she drifted off to sleep.

She woke with a start. It took her ten seconds or so to figure out where she was. She couldn't see her watch in the darkness but she sensed she must have been sleeping for more than a few minutes. The temperature had dropped since she first came outside. She twisted her body, looking behind her toward the door. She wondered if Keaton was looking for her, curious where she'd gone.

She forced herself up, her neck stiff. She glanced up beyond the terrace wall and suddenly felt exposed, as if someone was watching her from someplace out there. Bunching her coat closed tightly, she lowered her head and hurried back inside. The clock across the room on the microwave said 5:13. She'd actually been outside for over two hours.

Though she didn't see Keaton, she could tell he'd been up. The bedroom door, which she remembered pulling halfway closed behind her, was now all the way open.

"Are you looking for me?" she called out softly.

No answer.

As she entered the bedroom, she realized he was in the bathroom. The bathroom door was open a couple of inches with light peeking through, and she heard the sound of water running softly. But when she glanced across the room toward the bed, she saw that Keaton was *there*. He was sprawled on his back with the sheet kicked down by his feet. She almost jumped when she discovered that there was something big and dark next to him—a dog, she thought. It took up the entire center of the bed. It didn't make sense, though. Where had the dog been earlier? Her head felt muddled.

She moved closer to the bed, nervous about the dog. She soon saw it wasn't a dog. It was a huge dark stain on the sheet. She glanced over at Keaton. His eyes were open but blank, and his mouth was frozen in a grimace. On his neck was a bloodied gash, rippled with muscle and gaping like a horrible grin from one end to the other.

LAKE OPENED HER mouth to scream but nothing came out. Her breath seemed dead-bolted in her chest. She knew she needed to get closer, to check if Keaton was alive. But she couldn't move.

Finally, she forced herself to lurch toward the bed, her legs lead-heavy. She stared at Keaton. In the dim light from the bathroom she saw that he was clearly dead. His body was completely limp, lifeless, with his right hand partially closed by his neck, as if he'd wanted to grasp the wound. From the size of the stain on the sheet, it looked as if half his blood had drained onto the bed. A wave of nausea crashed through her.

The sound of running water punctured her consciousness again, and she jerked her head toward the bathroom. Was someone in there? she wondered frantically. She backed up. Her butt hit hard against something and she spun around. It was the arm of the easy chair, her dress still folded on the cushion. She grabbed the dress and stumbled out of the bedroom.

Police, her mind blurted out. She had to call them. But first she had to get out. She snatched her purse from the floor at the far end of the couch and bolted toward the front door. Opening it a crack, she checked outside. The hallway was empty and deadly quiet. She nearly flung herself into the hall and instinctively pulled the door closed behind her.

The elevator was just a few feet away and she stabbed frantically at the button. She heard a whooshing sound from far below as the car began to ascend. But then, too scared to wait, she rushed toward a door with an exit sign above it and yanked it open.

She was in a stairwell, the landing lit by a single lightbulb on the wall. She looked down the long shoot of empty space to the bottom. The stairs seemed to go on forever. Lake turned back to make sure no one was behind her, and then began to careen downward, letting her hand race along the railing for support. There seemed to be two of her—one tearing down the steps, terrified, the other watching from a distance and telling her what to do.

Six or seven flights down, as she stopped to catch her breath, she heard a sound. Her entire body froze as she listened. But it was just the groan of the elevator. She began to move again. Finally, she reached the ground floor, completely breathless. She pushed the door partly open and looked into the lobby. It was empty. Outside, the street was dark and deserted. She dashed through the lobby and vestibule and nearly stumbled out of the building. Down the street, a white delivery van was stopped at the intersection of Spring. She began to run toward it. Before she'd even gotten a few feet, the driver gunned the motor and shot off.

Lake spun around, checking behind her again. There was no one there. But she still needed to get help, to call 911. She fumbled frantically in her purse. She saw that she still had her dress in her hand. As she pulled out her BlackBerry, she stuffed her dress inside her purse.

She punched three numbers. When she heard the recorded voice announce "411" she realized that in her crazed state she'd called directory assistance, not 911. With trembling fingers, she disconnected the call and started again. But right before hitting the final 1 she stopped. What am I *doing*? she screamed to herself. Hotchkiss's words replayed in her head: *Don't rob a bank*. She hadn't. But a man she'd just made love to had been murdered while she was still in his home.

Hotchkiss had said there was nothing wrong with having sex but surely he hadn't meant casual sex with a near stranger—and a client to boot. And would the cops even believe her story? She thought of the explanation she would give them. That after she and Keaton had made love, she'd gone out to the terrace alone—and fallen asleep. While she was out there, snoozing in the night air, someone had entered the apartment and butchered her bedmate without her ever hearing a thing. Even though it was true it sounded ridiculous. They'd suspect *she* had done it.

Rubbing her forehead, she tried desperately to think. What she needed to do, she decided, was to just get home. She would be safe there and could decide how to handle things once she had a clear head. After checking once more behind her, she hurried down the street and swung right onto Spring Street. There would be cabs on Broadway. But then she stopped in her tracks. Once Keaton's body was discovered, the police would surely interview everyone they could find who'd been in this area. And like she'd seen on TV crime shows, wouldn't they also go to cab companies to see what fares had been picked up around this time of night in SoHo? A cabbie might easily recall her: a woman all alone, dressed in a trench coat. The police would find out who from the clinic had been at the dinner and put two and two together.

So she had to take the subway instead—and buy a MetroCard with cash.

There was a station for the C line at Sixth Avenue and Spring, she remembered, and that would take her to Eighty-sixth and Central Park West. But subway stations had cameras. What if the cops watched the tapes to see who'd entered any station within a certain radius? She ducked into the dark doorway of a building to calm herself. She felt short of breath, like she was being smothered. *Calm down*, she told herself. The best thing to do, she realized, was to walk—for blocks and blocks. And finally, when she was far enough away, she would find a taxi.

With her head lowered, she made her way to Broadway and then turned north. She walked fast, so fast a stitch came and went in her side. But she didn't dare run—or else someone might take notice. She felt like one of those lost dogs she sometimes saw at night in the city, trotting along without ever stopping. Every half block, she checked behind her, terrified someone might be following.

For a while she saw practically no one. Sometimes a car or a delivery van would drive by and she'd duck in a doorway. At Houston Street she turned west and made her way to Seventh Avenue. Once there, she crossed the street and headed north. People began to emerge from apartment buildings, bound for work. She kept her eyes trained on the ground, not daring to make eye contact. In the east, she noticed, the sky began to grow light.

Just before six-thirty, she reached Twenty-third. Spots on her feet were raw from walking so far in her sandals, and though she was wearing only her trench coat, her back felt damp with sweat. A cab came barreling down Seventh and she hailed it, telling the driver to turn around and head to the Upper West Side. As she leaned back into the seat, tears of relief pricked her eyes.

She started to give her address and then stopped herself. The driver would have a record of it. Plus, she couldn't let her doorman see her coming in at this hour. I have to go somewhere, she thought, but *where*? The driver glanced back at her through the Plexiglas.

"You gonna give me an address?" he said.

"Yes, yes," she said. She blurted out the cross streets of a diner twenty blocks south of her apartment, where she sometimes took the kids before school. She would wait there and go home closer to eight, when the doorman would be busy hailing cabs for people.

The diner was half full. Some people sat in groups or pairs, but most were alone, reading the *Post* or *Daily News* or a paperback book. She made her way toward the back, to a table in the corner. Without thinking, she started to unbutton the top of her trench and then realized she had nothing but her panties on underneath. The thought almost made her laugh manically. She rested her head against the tips of her fingers, trying to regroup. On the table was a smudge of hardened ketchup, and the sight recalled the huge, horrible stain next to Keaton. Tears welled in her eyes again. He had touched her, made love to her. And now he was dead.

She ordered coffee, and though the taste nearly made her ill, she forced herself to drink it. She needed the caffeine, she needed to break through the dense fog of terror and *think*. For the first time she asked herself why—why was Keaton dead? Was it a burglary gone awry? There had been no sign of forced entry; the apartment hadn't looked "tossed." The murderer must be someone who knew him, Lake deduced. Keaton looked as if he'd been attacked as he slept. That meant someone had gone there with the sole purpose of slashing Keaton's throat. And if she had been in the bed with him, she would be dead now, too. She let out a gasp at the thought. Her kids—it would have ruined their lives.

For a few moments Lake fought with the idea of calling the police after all. Her failure to get in touch before now wouldn't be hard to explain—she'd fled in panic, worried that the killer had still been in the apartment. And the forensic evidence would confirm that she didn't kill Keaton.

But *would* it? What if the weapon was still in the apartment—a butcher knife, for instance—and it had been wiped clean? They'd think *she'd* wiped it clean. It wasn't hard to imagine the scenario the cops would form in their minds. A recently dumped, possibly drunk, possibly *unstable* divorcée sleeps with a hot doctor. She asks when she'll see him again, he makes it clear he isn't interested. In a drunken rage, she takes a butcher knife to him while he sleeps. Even if she weren't arrested immediately, she would be a "person of interest," like in those cop shows.

Jack would have a field day with that. He'd convince a judge to give him custody until her situation was resolved. And that's what Hotchkiss had warned her about. He'd said that it was almost impossible to regain custody once it had been lost temporarily. So even if her name was cleared, she could end up without the kids.

That meant she *couldn't* tell the police. She flashed back to Keaton's loft, making certain in her mind that she'd grabbed everything of hers. There was still evidence of her there, of course. Her bodily fluids in the bed perhaps, her fingerprints on the cognac glass. But from what little she knew, she was pretty sure that the police couldn't ask for her DNA or fingerprints unless they had legitimate reason to suspect her. And what reason could there be? She'd never spoken to Keaton at dinner and she'd left alone.

She wondered whether she should call someone—Molly, for instance—and ask for guidance. But wouldn't that put the person in some kind of legal jeopardy?

What she *did* have to do, she knew, was to go to the clinic today—as horrible as that would be. She would have to act normal and be cooperative when the police arrived—as they surely would.

She stayed in the diner for another half hour. At seven-thirty she left and just walked, back and forth along the side streets, slowly making her way home to West End Avenue and Eighty-fourth—keeping her eyes down the entire time in case someone she knew was nearby.

Half a block away from her building, she stopped and positioned herself by a parked truck, watching the front. A light drizzle had begun, which was lucky for her. She could see that Ray, the morning doorman, was busy trying to flag down a cab for someone. Having no luck, he moved farther up the street to the corner. The person waiting stood under the building's awning keeping an impatient eye on the corner. Fortunately Lake didn't recognize him and she saw her chance. She bolted to the main door and slipped inside.

Rather than chance the elevator, she took the stairs, two steps at time. When she finally slammed her apartment door behind her, she let out the strangled sob that had been lodged in her throat for hours.

In the kitchen she poured a glass of water and gulped it down, and then, as she sat at the table, she let the tears come. A man who had made love to her had been murdered. And though she'd escaped death, she wasn't safe. Everything in her life was in jeopardy now.

She showered, scrubbing her body red with a loofah, and then dressed in a white shirt and dark-blue pencil skirt for work. Staring at her reflection, she wondered ruefully if things would have gone differently last night if she'd worn something other than the sundress. Maybe she wouldn't have felt so sexy for the first time in ages, so ready to be seduced. As she remembered the sundress still in her purse, her stomach tightened. She would take it—and the trench coat, too—to the dry cleaner's on the way to work, just in case.

Lake arrived at the clinic shortly before ten. A few women sat in the waiting room, leafing listlessly through magazines. As she headed down the corridors past the nurses' station, it was clear from the easy manner of the staff that no one had heard anything yet. For the first time she recalled what Keaton had said to her in the Balthazar lounge—that he might not be joining the clinic after all. What had *that* been about?

After opening her laptop in the small conference room, Lake went to the kitchenette and fixed some tea, trying to act normal. The cup trembled in her hand as she pumped hot water into it.

"How was the dinner last night?" a female voice asked with a trace of sarcasm. Lake turned to find Brie towering in the doorway, her thin, scarlet-painted lips locked in a tight smile. Brie had obviously not been invited.

"Nice," Lake said as lightly as possible. "I got a chance to spend more time with Dr. Levin. He's a very impressive guy."

"*We* certainly think so," Brie said, snippily.

Lake took a small breath and forced herself to smile. "I'll be in the conference room making some notes—if anyone's looking for me."

"Expecting someone?" Brie asked.

"I—no. But one of the doctors might want to talk to me." She felt stupid for having stammered, for having overexplained herself. If she was going to get through the day, she told herself, she would have to compel herself to calm down.

She went back to her laptop and tried to read the file of notes she'd been taking. But really she just waited, reading the same line over and over. At eleven, she spotted Maggie in the corridor, talking to someone just out of sight.

"I've left him at least ten messages," Maggie complained. "He was supposed to be here at nine for a procedure, and Dr. Levin is fit to be tied."

Oh God, Lake thought. She had to be talking about Keaton. He was officially missing in action and soon everything would come to a head. She felt a wave of nausea and wondered if she'd be sick. She hurried to the restroom to the left of the kitchenette. After locking the door, she wet a paper towel with cold water. Sitting on the toilet seat, she pressed the towel to her face and forced herself to breathe.

When Lake stepped out of the restroom, the hall was even quieter than usual and every door was closed. Suddenly she heard a cry that sounded almost animal-like. She spun around. It had come from an exam room just down the hall, and as Lake stood frozen, Rory and Dr. Levin emerged through the doorway. Have they just heard the news? she wondered. Had Rory let out the cry? But then she saw there was a patient with them, and it was she who was crying.

"Rory will help you now," she overheard Levin say.

"Would you prefer to stay in the room for a few more minutes, Mrs. Kastner?" Rory asked the slender, spent-looking patient as Levin headed toward the front. "It might help to rest for a minute."

"No, I can't bear this," the woman said, through her sobs. "I just want to go home."

"I understand. But I'll walk you out. And I brought you some of my jams today. Come on, we'll pick them up on our way out."

This is surreal, Lake thought. People are passing out jams as Keaton's body lies rotting in his bed.

Back in the conference room, she started the horrible waiting again. The lab supervisor popped his head in at noon and announced that people were ordering lunch—would she like something? Sure, she told him, forcing a smile. Maybe they won't find Keaton today, she thought miserably as he walked away with her order. Maybe I'll have to spend another hellish day waiting.

But forty-five minutes later, as Lake picked at a sandwich, Brie appeared in the door and her face looked dark.

"Please come to the big conference room," she said, her voice strained. "There's an emergency meeting of the staff."

"Of course," Lake replied. A wave of panic crashed over her. This is it, she thought. I have to seem normal. And look as shocked as everyone else when they hear the news.

Lake was one of the last to enter the conference room and it was packed; the doctors, nurses, lab personnel, and support staff were all there—except Harry Kline, Lake noticed. There were also two men whom she guessed to be detectives. One was black, early forties, sort of beefy, with kind eyes. The other was white, shorter, with salt-and-pepper hair. His eyes weren't the least bit kind.

"I have terrible news to report," Levin said somberly as soon as everyone was quiet. "Dr. Keaton was found murdered in his apartment today."

There were exclamations of horror around the room. Lake's eyes met Steve's, and he flashed her a look of shock. Chelsea, one of the young embryologists, burst into tears, and then there was a flurry of questions.

"Please, everyone," Levin," said. "We have two detectives here and they need our cooperation."

"Folks, we're very sorry for your loss," the one with the unkind eyes said. "I'm Detective Hull and this is Detective McCarty. We're here because we need to speak to each of you privately. Until it's your turn to meet with us, just resume what you were doing. And do not discuss the case among yourselves at this time."

Levin interjected, telling everyone that all nonessential appointments were being canceled for the day and that it was critical to give the remaining patients the best care possible. He dismissed the meeting then and everyone dispersed, walking zombie-like out of the conference room.

Back in the small conference room, Lake opened one of her folders, trying not to let her hand shake. She mentally rehearsed for the meeting with the detectives, trying to guess the questions they'd ask. They'd want to know if she was at all friendly with Keaton. Grasping at straws, she thought of a marketing strategy she once read about called the Rule of Candor: *admit a negative and twist it into a positive.* She'd need to be forthcoming about talking to Keaton yesterday in the office. It would be better than having them find out about it from Brie.

Rory came in at one point to place a reference book back on the bookshelf. Her eyes were misty and she had one hand draped across her pregnant belly.

"Isn't it horrible?" she said to Lake. "He was only forty-five."

"I know," Lake said. "Who—who do you think would have wanted to kill him?"

"Oh, but they told us not to talk about the crime," Rory admonished

"I know. I just—" Lake said defensively. But Rory turned and left before she could finish.

Lake assumed the detectives were calling people one by one into the large conference room so she was startled when a short while later they entered the small conference room where she was sitting.

"Lake Warren?" McCarty, the nicer-seeming detective, asked.

"Yes." She started to rise but he motioned for her to stay seated. They slid into chairs opposite her, and McCarty flipped open a notebook.

"So you've worked here for just a few weeks?" McCarty said.

"Um, yes. Though I'm not an actual employee. I'm a freelance consultant." Her words sounded clunky, as if she were relearning how to speak.

"Did you know Dr. Keaton very well?" McCarty asked.

"No. No, I didn't. But I did chat with him a little bit yesterday."

"What'd you talk about?"

"His joining the practice, some details about his former clinic."

"And what about previously?" Hull asked, speaking for the first time.

"Previously?" she said, confused.

"Did you know him previously?" he asked, staring at her.

Her pulse jumped. Why was he asking *that*?

"No," she said as evenly as possible. "I only met him when I started working here."

McCarty scribbled a few notes in his pad and then looked back at her.

"Tell us about dinner last night. What did the two of you talk about?" he said.

"We didn't talk. To each other, that is. We were seated at opposite ends of the table."

Don't sound so defensive, she told herself. She was starting to feel ill with anxiety.

"And after dinner?"

"You mean, did I speak to him?"

"Yup."

"No—he left early. He said something about needing to call a patient. I was one of the last to leave the restaurant."

The two men swapped a look, and then Hull trained his gaze at Lake.

"And then what?" Hull said, his voice hard. "Because you didn't go home right away, did you?"

5

LAKE FELT AS if she'd been stabbed with a shot of adrenaline and instinctively she touched her cheek with her hand, to the spot where her birthmark once was. Did they know she'd gone to Keaton's? That she'd spent the night with him? She wondered suddenly if there'd been a security camera in his lobby.

But if they'd known she had been with him, they wouldn't have waited so long to interview her. They must be just toying with her, she decided, seeing what they could find out. They were probably doing the same thing with everyone who was at the dinner.

"You mean, did I go someplace else—after the dinner?" Lake asked. She tried to keep the nervousness out of her voice but it felt like trying to submerge an oar in water.

"*Did* you?" Hull prodded.

"No," she said. "I caught a cab and went home."

"Which way did you head?" he said.

Why was he asking that? she wondered anxiously.

"West—and then north. I live on the Upper West Side."

"Dr. Salman says he saw you headed east on Spring Street," Hull said. "He passed you in his car."

Oh God, she thought. Had Steve also seen her turn up Crosby? Could he have spotted her going into Keaton's building? She had to gamble and assume they didn't know.

"Well, I did walk around a little. I couldn't find a cab right away"

"Why go east, though, if you live on the Upper West Side?"

A lump formed in her throat, but she had to answer.

"I did look on Broadway first but I didn't see any cabs. So I thought I'd try farther east. When I didn't have any luck there, I went back to Broadway."

McCarty scribbled again—more words, it seemed, than she'd spoken. What was he writing down about her?

"Did you see anyone from the dinner party when you were strolling about?" Hull asked. He seemed to be mocking her.

"No, no one," she said.

"Tell us more about the dinner," Hull said. "What was the mood like?"

"Very nice," she said. She slowly let out a breath. "People seemed happy that Dr. Keaton was joining the practice."

"And were you surprised to have been included?" Hull asked.

"Uh, not really," she said. "I think the doctors here realize that it's helpful for me to spend time with them. Get to know them."

The two detectives exchanged another look. She wished she could just bolt from the room.

"All right," McCarty said, flipping to a clean page of his notebook. "Please write down your name, address, and both your home and cell phone numbers. We may need to speak to you again at some point."

She couldn't believe it was finally over. She wrote her information down quickly.

When they rose to go, she stood up too. It seemed silly, as if she were seeing them off after a social visit, but it would have been odd to just sit there. As he reached the door, Hull turned and stared at her. His small eyes were dark and deeply set.

"One more thing," he said. "What time did you arrive home?"

During all her rehearsing, she had forgotten to factor that. She stared at him blankly as her mind did a desperate calculation. At ten-fifteen she'd been at the corner of Spring and Crosby. It might have taken fifteen minutes to find a cab. Twenty minutes or so to get home.

"The time?" Hull prodded.

"Sorry, I didn't pay much attention. I guess it was around eleven."

"And did anyone see you come home? Your husband, for instance?"

Why are you asking that? "I'm not married," she said. "The doorman might have seen me. But I think he was hailing a cab for someone."

"Thank you," he said, not sounding the least bit grateful. And then they left.

As soon as they were gone, she put her head in her hands and pulled in a long deep breath. Then she replayed the interview in her mind. McCarty was decent enough but Hull had been curt, almost snarky. They'd wanted to know if anyone could verify that she arrived home at eleven. Was she actually a suspect? Or was she in their sights simply because she'd been at the dinner? Weren't the last people to see someone alive always possible suspects? Plus she was a woman. By now, Keaton's sheets—and the used condom, if Keaton had left it by the bed—had clearly given away what he'd been doing during the hours before his death.

The detectives' interest in her might have been heightened by whatever Steve had told them. He was supposed to be a friend, but he'd thrown her under the bus, and she had no clue why. If he'd driven by her last night, why not pull over and offer her a lift? Had he not stopped because he'd seen her searching for a particular building? Had he told the police that?

She glanced back down at the page open on her laptop. How was she ever going to be able to concentrate enough to pull her presentation together?

A sound in the doorway jolted her out of her thoughts, and she looked up to see Dr. Levin standing there.

"Sorry if I startled you," he said. "It seems we're all on edge at the moment."

"Yes, it's awful."

"The police tell me they're almost done, for the time being. As soon as they're gone, and I'm done with my final procedure, we should talk—you, me, and the other doctors. We need to know how to handle this from a PR standpoint."

As he spoke Lake realized that she should have been the one making this recommendation, but she'd been too crazed to think straight.

"Absolutely," she said. "I have some suggestions I can make."

He nodded soberly. "Let's say about four then."

"By the way," she said as he turned to leave. "Reporters will start to call. Until we've discussed a plan, you shouldn't talk to anyone. And tell the staff not to."

A short while later she became aware of staff moving up and down the corridor, and Lake figured the detectives had probably gone. She decided she needed to get out of the office for a few minutes, to try to calm herself before her meeting with Levin, and think of what advice she should offer. On her way out Lake saw that the receptionist was the only one in the waiting room—sitting grim-faced, twirling a strand of her hair.

Lake was halfway down Eighty-third Street, headed toward

Lexington Avenue, when she heard her name called and turned to see Steve hurrying up behind her. He was still wearing his white lab coat, as if he'd dashed out when he saw her leaving.

"You okay?" he asked when he caught up to her. His brown eyes looked worried.

"Not ideal," she said. "It's pretty upsetting."

"I know," he said. "Sorry you got stuck in the middle of this."

"Well, you haven't made it easier for me," she said. She surprised herself by her bluntness.

"What do you mean?" he asked, clearly perplexed.

"You told the police you saw me wandering around SoHo last night."

He drew a breath. "But—I don't understand—what's the problem with that?"

"They seem to find that suspicious," Lake said.

"God, Lake, I'm sorry. That wasn't my intention."

"What exactly did you tell them?"

"Just that I saw you as I was driving home. They asked when I'd last seen each person who'd attended the dinner, so I mentioned that I spotted you after we'd picked up the car."

"I was looking for a cab."

"Well, there's hardly anything wrong with that," he said.

"I'm surprised you didn't stop for me."

He sighed and glanced off to the left.

"I should have. But to be honest, I was having a pretty intense discussion with Hilary. It would have been awkward."

Lake wondered if it was about how flirty Hilary had been with Keaton during dinner.

"Is that all you told them then?" Lake asked.

"What do you mean?" Steve said. "What else would I tell them?"

"Nothing. I just don't want to be caught off guard again."

"That was it—and again, I'm sorry. Is everything all right?"

"Yes, I'm just feeling a little rattled," she said. "Because of everything. I'll be back in a little while."

It was hot out, in the mid-eighties, and the walk did nothing to calm her, only left her blouse damp and sticky with sweat. But at least she could relax with the knowledge that Steve hadn't seen her on Crosby Street, or going into Keaton's.

Upon her return, even the receptionist was now gone from the waiting area, though she found Maggie, Rory, Chelsea, and Emily bunched by the kitchenette, whispering. Clearly they'd been discussing the murder.

"Oh, there you are," Maggie said, smiling weakly.

Lake glanced at her watch. It was twenty to four.

"Was Dr. Levin looking for me?" she asked.

"No, but a man called for you. He wouldn't leave his name."

It was hard for her to imagine who it would be. Hotchkiss? Had she ever told him the name of the clinic?

She started to turn to get back to the small conference room, but caught herself. She should stay, she thought. Gossiping with these four would help keep her in the loop—though she would have to be careful of every word she spoke.

"So how's everyone doing?" she asked, forcing a sympathetic smile.

"I'm scared to death," Maggie said. "I asked my sister to spend the night with me."

"You don't think you're in danger, do you?" Lake asked.

"I just don't want to be alone," Maggie said. She turned to Rory. "What are *you* going to do? You shouldn't be under stress in your condition."

"I know—I have to think of the baby," Rory said. "Colin's going to be away for a few more days and our house is kind of secluded. I'll probably call a friend."

Emily shook her head.

"You girls are being silly. It's not like there's some serial killer out there stalking people who work at fertility clinics."

"What *do* the police think?" Lake asked. "Was it a burglary?" She'd tried to make her voice seem natural, but her words sounded stilted to her, like she was acting in a high school play.

"They asked me if I knew if he was seeing someone," Maggie whispered. "Like it might have been one of those crimes of passion."

"They asked me that, too," Rory said. And then she turned to Lake. "Did they ask you that, Lake?"

"No," Lake said. "But then again they wouldn't. They know I've just been here a short time."

"But you knew him, didn't you?"

"Keaton?" Lake said, startled. "Um, no. I only met him when I started here."

"Oh, I saw you talking to him for quite a while yesterday. I thought you might have known him from before."

Was that why the police had asked if she'd known him previously—based on something Rory had said?

"No, I didn't." She could hear a slight defensive edge in her voice. "We were just talking about work—"

"Well, speaking of work, I've got things to do," Emily said. "Can you give me a hand, Maggie?"

Good, Lake thought. She didn't want any more awkward conversation about Keaton and was glad for the excuse to leave. The group broke up and Lake walked away.

It was almost four. Before going to Levin's office, Lake returned the folders of articles she'd been reading to the storage room in the back of the clinic. She was pretty certain she'd studied every press clipping and journal article filed there, but just to be sure, she thumbed through the drawer once more. With her mind on everything but the presentation, she needed all the inspiration she could get.

Finding nothing she hadn't already seen, she pulled the lower drawer open. It seemed to contain mostly old correspondence. Just as she was about to close it, she noticed a hanging file with the word "Archer" in the tab, and Lake could see pages of a magazine peeking out. She tugged the file out of the drawer. At a glance she saw that it was an article about the fertility business. She slapped the file closed and took it with her.

By the time she arrived in Levin's office, the doctors had already gathered there—Sherman, Hoss, Steve, and Matt Perkins. Brie was there, too, perched on the windowsill.

"We've had two calls from reporters since I spoke to you," Levin said grimly to Lake as she sat down. "The *Daily News* and Channel 7."

"We should have seen something like this coming," Sherman said. "You pick someone flashy and this is what happens, isn't it?"

"Oh, for God's sake, Dan," Levin said. "The fact that he was a good-looking guy doesn't mean we should have expected he'd end up murdered."

"It's ironic, isn't it?" Sherman said. "We finally decide to get serious about marketing and we end up with a mess like this."

"It doesn't have to turn into a mess for you," Lake interjected. "But you do have to do some damage control."

"*Damage* control?" Brie asked curtly. "You make it sound as if we've done something wrong."

"That's not at all what I'm saying," Lake said. "This is an external situation beyond your control, but it has the potential to impact your business. I know a PR person who specializes in crisis management. I'd suggest bringing her onboard briefly. She—"

"But isn't that what *you're* supposed to be doing?" Brie said. "PR?"

"Please, Brie, let her finish," Levin said. Brie straightened her back, looking irritated.

"I've got a PR person on retainer as part of the marketing plan," Lake said, "but she's not an expert at handling a crisis, and neither am I. You need a real pro here. The woman I'm suggesting doesn't come cheap, but I highly recommend that you hire her."

"I think it's essential," Hoss said. "We don't have a choice."

It was agreed that Lake would make the call. After that, there was thirty more minutes of anxious talk—about dealing with patient questions, upsets to the schedule, and just getting through the next few days. Levin and Hoss dominated the discussion, while Sherman mostly shook his head in disgust. Steve and Matt Perkins looked shell-shocked and spoke up only when they were asked specific questions. Finally, Levin suggested that everyone go home and try their best to relax.

"I also recommend that you not discuss this with anyone outside your immediate families," Lake added.

Everyone streamed out of the office, and as Lake followed them to the door, Levin called to her.

"Do you think this woman can really help?" he asked, rising from the desk.

"Absolutely," Lake said. "She's handled situations far worse."

He crossed the room, buttoning his jacket. She saw him glance at the file in her hands.

"Where did you get that?" he asked sharply.

"From the file drawer in the storage room—I've been reading all the clippings."

"Well, that's not one you need," he said, grabbing the file from her hand.

6

IT WAS JUST before six when Lake finally arrived home. Following the awkward encounter with Levin, she'd returned to the small conference room and left a message for Hayden Culbreth, the crisis guru she'd recommended. Then, totally spent, she'd packed up and hailed a cab for the West Side.

After tossing down her bags, she sank into one of the armchairs in her living room. She began to sob. Sensing something was wrong, Smokey leapt into her lap. As he nuzzled her chin, Lake stroked him and blinked back tears. Her eyes swept the living room, with its comforting shelves of books and pretty landscape paintings. What she'd told Molly and Keaton was true. Though the past week or so of her life could hardly be described as blissful, she had started to feel at peace again and hopeful about her future. But that all changed in an instant. Everything in her life was in jeopardy now—her kids, her work, her future. She'd given in to a desperate hunger for approval and connection—and to her own raw desire—and because of that she might end up losing custody of her kids. There was even a chance she'd be arrested for murder.

After forcing herself up off the chair, she left a second message for Hayden. Thirty minutes later, as Lake stared at a frozen slab of vegetable lasagna, knowing she had to eat but wondering how she could summon any appetite, Hayden returned the call. Lake outlined the situation to her, and made an urgent pitch for her to come on board as a consultant.

"I'm totally swamped right now," Hayden confessed in her Alabama drawl, "but I can't turn this down. I've done damage control on everything from drug companies that sold tainted drugs to a CEO who used company funds to rent a water park for his kid's birthday—but never a *murder*. That's very, very sexy."

"So that's a yes?" Lake said.

"Yes, but we need to hit the ground running. This is going to be big and move fast—it'll probably be the plot on *Law and Order* next week. Can you arrange for me to meet everyone at eight tomorrow morning?"

Lake assured her it wouldn't be a problem. Next she phoned Levin.

"That's terrific, Lake," he said. "I'll let Dr. Sherman know. I think this first meeting should just be the senior team."

His tone was almost obsequious; she wondered if he was trying to make up for rudely grabbing the file out of her hand earlier.

Next she needed to summon the energy to write the kids. She skipped the stories and riddles and scribbled a simple message:

"I can't wait to see you both on Saturday and meet your new friends," she wrote. "I'll be there right at ten."

She wanted to add more but she was already feeling weirdly fraudulent, reminiscent of when Jack was beginning to withdraw and she'd had to act normal in front of the kids. What would she say if she were being totally honest? "Mommy may be implicated in a grisly murder, so there's a chance I won't be able to come after all"?

As she slipped the paper into the fax machine, she wondered how she was going to handle bumping into Jack at the camp. Prior to her recent conversation with Hotchkiss, she'd hardly relished seeing him there, but now the idea seemed unbearable.

She nuked the lasagna and pushed it around on a plate as she drained a glass of wine. She tried to calm herself but she kept picturing Hull and McCarty at their precinct desks, searching their notes for clues and combing through evidence reports. The crime-scene people would have lifted her fingerprints but because hers weren't in the system, there would be no match. Her DNA would be meaningless, too. But if she gave the cops any reason to truly suspect her, they could take her fingerprints and her DNA and then they would know she'd been in Keaton's bed.

Closing her eyes, she let her head drop into her hands. In her mind she could see the horrible, oozing gash from one side of Keaton's neck to the other. Whoever had slashed him must have been overwhelmed with rage. So who had Keaton managed to infuriate? Was it a woman he'd bedded and then dumped? He'd told Lake that he'd bought his place six months ago; he was likely visiting the city even before consulting with the clinic. So this fury could have been building for weeks. It was a fury that would have been directed at her, too, if she hadn't been safely asleep on the terrace. She let out a moan as she contemplated what her fate would have been.

Another question gnawed at her. How had the killer gained entry to the apartment? Had he—or she—possessed a key? Or had the person jimmied the lock somehow? Maybe Keaton actually let the person in while Lake was sleeping, perhaps even assuming that Lake had left. But if Keaton had answered the door, he wouldn't have been stabbed in his bed.

She considered Hayden's comment about how big the story would become. Lake had been so preoccupied about her own connection to the murder that she hadn't even considered the ramifications of just being employed by the clinic. Reporters might start to hound her. She wondered, in fact, whether the nameless person who'd called her at the clinic yesterday had been a reporter who'd gotten wind of her name.

Something unformed began to nudge her, but it was only later, when she was crawling into bed, that she recognized what it was: Keaton's comment to her about a snag in his plan to be a partner. During today's meeting in Levin's office, there'd been no mention of any hitch. Either Levin had chosen not to bring it up in front of the associate doctors or the snag had only occurred in Keaton's mind— and he hadn't yet shared it with Levin.

Lake anticipated hours of fitful tossing that night, but she fell into a stupor almost instantly. Twice she was jounced awake by nightmares. She couldn't remember the first one—it evaporated as soon as her eyes shot open. In the other, someone called on the phone about her children—saying their names, laughing, and then hanging up.

She woke with a start at six. For a brief moment she remembered nothing—but her stomach was knotted, as if she'd forgotten an urgent task. Then, like a tidal wave, the memory crashed against her. She hurried to retrieve the *Times* from on top of the mat outside her apartment door. The story was in the Metro section, a half-column long. It described Keaton as an L.A. ob-gyn and fertility specialist living part-time in New York. No mention of the clinic. So maybe the story wasn't going to be huge after all.

But later, at a newsstand on her way to the bus, she picked up the *Post* and cringed as she saw Keaton's photo splashed across the front page with the headline: BACHELOR DOC SLAIN DOWNTOWN. The photo was like a Hollywood red-carpet shot. He was in a tux, emerging from some event, looking handsome and cocky, like George Clooney at the Golden Globes. She forced herself to read the story. This time it included the name of the fertility clinic.

The *Daily News* had a more formal photo, the kind you'd see in a program for a medical conference. And this article had one new piece of info: Keaton's super had found the body. When Keaton hadn't shown up at the clinic yesterday, Levin had probably told Brie to try to locate him. In the course of looking for Keaton, his super had somehow been tracked down.

When Lake arrived at work, she found that the mood was an awful mix of somberness and agitation; people were both despondent and all churned up.

"Can you believe all the stories about this?" Maggie whispered to her as she set her things down in the small conference room. "I mean, it's like the Laci Peterson case or something."

"Have any reporters called you?" Lake asked.

"Not me in particular, but they've been calling here all morning."

Lake could see the strain on Maggie's face.

"How are you doing, anyway?" she asked. "Did your sister end up staying with you?"

"Yes—but it didn't do much good. I had the worst nightmares. I might ask Dr. Kline for some advice when he gets a minute today."

"Oh, he's here?" Lake asked, realizing she hadn't seen him since before all this happened.

"Yes, he was away for a few days but he's back now. He was totally shocked to hear the news."

Lake and Maggie agreed to try to get their minds off everything and get some work done. At five minutes to eight, Hayden Culbreth arrived, wearing a dazzling purple silk shift that contrasted boldly with her blond bob. As promised, she hit the ground running.

"Let's start," she said to Levin as soon as Lake had introduced them.

Sherman had joined them in Levin's office, along with Hoss and Brie, notebook and pen in hand. Brie ran her eyes up and down Hayden, her disapproval loud and clear.

"So far you've done a decent job of handling things," Hayden announced. "By that I mean no one on your staff has blabbed to the press. But they still might be tempted to. We need to implement a lock-and-load strategy."

"Good God," Sherman said. "It sounds like you're suggesting firearms."

Hayden pursed her lips and gave her head a little shake. "Of course not. But to protect the reputation of the clinic, you have to lock down communication—make sure that no one, and I mean *no one*, discusses this with the media. Let them know that their asses will be in the ringer if they do.

"But at the same time," she continued, "keep people here in the loop and give them updates on what you learn from the cops. When there's secrecy and people don't know what the hell is going on, they start buzzing—sometimes to reporters."

"I assume you'll handle all the press calls," Levin said to her.

"No, we'll let the NYPD do that."

"The *NYPD*?" Levin exclaimed. "But—"

"It's best to have the police take those calls. When the press contacts you here, the person fielding those calls—and let's designate someone smart to do it—should say that all calls are being referred to the New York City Police."

"But isn't that why we've hired *you*—to handle those calls?" said Hoss. Despite her haughtiness, she looked tired and drained, her black hair lanky, as if she hadn't bothered to wash it today. She was probably concerned, like everyone else, Lake thought, about what all this might do to her reputation.

"You've hired me to devise a *strategy*," Hayden said. "If I talk to the press and they quote me, they'll say I'm a rep for your clinic—and *name the clinic*. And you want to distance yourself from this as much as possible. We're following the same approach abortion clinics use when they've been bombed—keep the name of the clinic out of the paper by letting the cops do all the talking. Now let's talk about 'load.' That means you load me up on information. I need to know about Dr. Keaton."

Levin, who was still wincing from the abortion clinic comment, briefly went over Keaton's bio—Cornell med, a fellowship in reproductive endocrinology, the L.A. practice. Again, no hint that Keaton might have had second thoughts about coming on board. Had Keaton not had a chance to share his misgivings with Levin, Lake wondered—or was Levin keeping something to himself?

"Well, that's all nice and good," Hayden said, "but what I'm really interested in is why someone wanted to murder him. According to the papers, it doesn't sound like he was killed during a burglary."

"We really don't know much about his personal life or the people he associated with outside of the clinic," Levin said. "Up until now, he'd only worked with us on a consulting basis."

"Have the police shared any details?" Lake interjected. Desperate to know, she couldn't resist asking, and she knew the question had come out abruptly. Hoss eyed her quizzically.

"Nothing," Levin said. "All we know is what's in the papers."

"He was an attractive guy," Hayden said. "Was he gay?"

"Hardly," Sherman said.

"A womanizer, then?" Hayden asked. "Could he have been killed by a jealous lover?"

"As Dr. Levin explained already, we really only knew the man professionally," Sherman said, sounding exasperated. Lake noticed that Brie was watching smugly, as if she found the whole process positively stupid.

"There is one thing you should know," Levin said soberly, "something I had to share with the police." Everyone jerked their heads toward him in surprise. Lake held her breath in anticipation.

"Yes," Hayden coaxed.

"The afternoon before we all went to dinner, an old colleague of mine from L.A. called," Levin said "He told me he'd heard Mark was joining us and wanted me to know there were rumors circulating about him on the West Coast—that he apparently had a gambling problem."

"And we're just hearing this *now*?" Sherman said, clearly vexed.

"I hadn't had a chance to say anything yet," Levin said. "Obviously I didn't like what I heard and was going to suggest that we investigate as soon as possible. That's not the kind of person we want associated with us."

"Did you ask Keaton about it?" Sherman asked.

"Of course not," Levin snapped. "He certainly wouldn't have admitted it. The only way we would have found out was through outside inquiries."

Lake wondered if Levin *had* said something to Keaton—and that was the snag Keaton had coyly referred to.

Hayden pressed for more information about the gambling, but Levin assured her he had no details to share. She then reviewed procedures she wanted people to follow. Lake tried to concentrate on the conversation but her mind was racing over what she'd just heard. Could Keaton's killer have been a mobster or hoodlum hired by a bookie—someone who knew how to jimmy a lock?

At eight forty-five Hayden finished the briefing and Lake walked her out. Because most appointments had been rescheduled, there were only a few patients in the waiting room.

"Let's catch up later," Hayden said quietly to her.

There was really nothing more for Lake to do at the clinic—she'd finished up her research—but she hung around, thinking there might be more talk of Keaton. She craved information, anything that might help her feel less frantic. If the gambling rumor proved to be true, for instance, the police would start pursuing that particular angle. But no one was talking and the halls were deadly quiet. She suddenly just wanted to get out of there as quickly as she could.

After grabbing her things in the conference room, she turned to leave and was surprised to see Harry Kline was standing in the doorway.

"Oh, I heard you were back," she said, smiling. There was something so calm and easy about him; just setting eyes on him seemed to slow her pulse.

He smiled back. "I hadn't planned to come in today but with everything that's happened I decided it would be a good idea," he said.

"I'm sure it's a relief for everyone to have you here," she said.

"Are you doing okay?" he asked. "I heard you were with the group at dinner that night."

"It's upsetting. I mean, I barely knew him, but still . . . for him to die so horribly. You know this happens in the city, but it always seems so removed. And now . . ."

Her nerves, she knew, were making her ramble, and when she looked up, she saw Kline watching her closely. Was he using his shrink skills to read her? Did he find something odd or troubling about her manner?

"I'd be glad to talk to you about it—if you think it would help," he said.

"Oh—that's nice of you. But I'll be okay."

"Here," he said, pulling his wallet from his pants pockets. "I'll give you my card, and if you change your mind just call me. It's no bother."

She thanked him, accepting the card. She was touched by his offer, but there was no way she'd tell him a thing.

"Oh, by the way—is everything okay with *you*?" she asked.

"What do you mean?" he said, his brown eyes looking puzzled.

"They said you had a personal emergency the past few days."

"Thanks for asking; fortunately things are fine now."

She said goodbye, now desperate to get out of the office. Instead of grabbing a cab, she walked west to Madison Avenue. She thought again of the bomb that Levin had dropped. If Keaton *had* been a reckless gambler, possibly leading to his death, it might make Hull and McCarty less intrigued by her. But at the same time she could be in even greater danger than she'd imagined. The person or people who'd killed Keaton might get wind of the fact that a woman had been in the apartment that night. What if the killer *had* been in the bathroom and seen her?

Since she was close to Central Park, she decided to walk home through the park, thinking it might quell her nerves. But by the time she reached Central Park West, her feet ached and she felt bedraggled. After trudging the four long blocks to West End Avenue, she was finally home and couldn't wait to walk through her door. As she approached her building, though, she jerked to a stop.

Jack was standing under the awning. He was clearly waiting for her.

WHY THE HELL was he here? she wondered. Had he stopped by to gauge her reaction to his nasty custody gambit? All she knew for sure was that a face-to-face with him was the last thing she needed now. She started to turn, calculating how to retreat without him seeing her.

But before she had fully spun around, Jack spotted her.

"Lake," he called out, less a salutation and more of an order for her to stop. Though he usually wore business casual for work, today he was really dressed down—khaki pants, a pale yellow polo shirt, and, to her shock, flip-flops—as if he were about to split for the Hamptons that afternoon with a bunch of twenty-four-year-olds. He stuffed both hands in his pockets and strode toward her with that cocksure gait of his.

In the first weeks after his departure, she had yearned for her encounters with him—on those weekends and occasional week-nights when he'd come to pick up or drop off the kids. As betrayed as she'd felt, she missed him, literally ached for him some nights. In her mind back then he was like a person who'd gone off his meds. She believed that if she was simply patient enough, he'd straighten out and come back to her.

But it soon became clear there was no way of communicating with him. The first few times he'd brought the kids back, he'd agreed to join her for coffee in the kitchen—with Amy and Will ensconced in their bedrooms—and each time she'd experimented with a different tactic. Calm and slightly detached hadn't worked; neither had a sympathetic ear. Finally she'd resorted to pathetic imploring—please, come back, she'd begged, for the sake of the kids and their fourteen years together. He'd shrugged her off, saying that he'd made up his mind, that they didn't share the same needs and goals and that it was definitely over. Talking to him, she realized, was like driving onto a stretch of black ice on the highway and being hopelessly unable to gain traction.

So for the sake of her sanity—and self-esteem—she'd stopped the coffee klatches and instead went down to the lobby to meet him for each pickup and drop-off. She willed herself not to be so affected by his presence. Sometimes her eyes barely met Jack's during their brief exchanges.

But her reaction this morning was totally different. The sight of him, in light of the recent lob via his lawyer, nearly made her sick.

"Have you got a minute?" he asked as he approached.

"Now's not a good time," she said coolly.

"I just need a few papers from the apartment."

When Jack had conceded that it made sense for Lake and the kids to keep the apartment, they had agreed that he'd be able to store some clothes and papers there until his sublet was up and he bought a place of his own. He usually picked up items he needed when he brought the kids home. This out-of-the-blue request seemed odd, suspicious even.

She knew she couldn't let him go upstairs. He might pick up a hint that something was terribly wrong in her life.

"I'm not even going up right now," she said. "I just realized I left a folder at a client's and I need to go back for it."

"Look, I really need those papers today."

Damn, she thought, if I don't say yes, he'll tell the psychologist I'm uncooperative.

"All right," she said, keeping her voice flat. "Why don't you tell me where the papers are and I'll bring them down."

He grimaced and shook his head.

"I'm not exactly sure where I left them. I'm going to have to come up and hunt around a little."

She took a deep breath.

"For God's sake, Lake, I'm not going to *bite*," he said. "It'll take all of five minutes."

She felt a sudden urge to shove him down on the sidewalk.

"Fine," she conceded.

They rode up the elevator in silence. Now that she was standing closer to him, she could see that Jack's slightly round, boyish face was more tanned than it had been in years, and his dark blond hair was coarse—the kind of coarseness that comes from lots of sun and salt water. Obviously he'd been true to his pledge to live large this summer, to—how had he put it?—*go big or go home*. She felt a wave of disgust. He might in fact feel entitled to his new major-player lifestyle, but the deep tan and flip-flops came across to her as desperation.

"I'm just curious," she finally said to him, still trying to keep her voice even. "Were you just going to wait outside the building until I came home?"

"You mean was I *stalking* you, Lake—is that what you're asking?" There was anger in his voice.

"Of course not. But it seems like an awful waste of time."

"You didn't pick up your cell phone so I called that clinic where you work. They said you'd just left so I took a chance and came over here."

"Did you call me there yesterday, too?" she asked, startled by the revelation.

"Yes—is that a problem?"

So Jack was the mystery caller. "I'm just wondering how you got the number," she said.

"I decided to blow a buck and called 411."

"I meant, how did you know the name of the clinic?"

"You mentioned it at one point when we were talking about the kids."

She didn't remember ever doing so, but she couldn't be sure and decided it was best to drop it. Jack seemed hyped up now, irritated, and she sensed that her smartest strategy was to avoid pushing any buttons with him.

She opened the apartment door, with Jack right behind her. Smokey had obviously heard the key in the lock and was waiting in the foyer. He curled his body around Lake's calves and then Jack's.

"Hey, Smokes," Jack said distractedly without bothering to pet the cat.

"Most of your stuff is still in Will's closet," Lake said. "Except your black suitcase—that's in the back of the closet in our room."

Our room. She couldn't believe she'd called it that.

"What I need is in the suitcase," Jack said. "I'll just head back there, okay? It shouldn't take more than a minute."

His tone had changed slightly. He sounded friendlier, less confrontational, which made her more suspicious. As he strode down the hall toward the master bedroom, she wondered if she should follow him, check out exactly what he was doing. Was this whole "I need a few papers" thing actually a ruse to *snoop*, to try to spot something he could use against her? Maybe that's why he'd suddenly sounded friendlier—to throw her off her guard. She felt her anger begin to rise.

As she started down the hall behind him, the phone rang. She wanted to keep tabs on Jack, but if she didn't answer it, Jack would hear the message on the answering machine. She stepped quickly into the kitchen and grabbed the phone. Her hello seemed to echo through the quiet apartment.

"Don't tell me that guy who was murdered is Dr. McSteamy from the clinic?"

It was Molly. At full throttle.

"Yes—it was him," Lake said, lowering her voice.

"Why are you whispering?"

"Jack's here. Picking up some papers. Or so he says."

"What do you mean, 'Or so he says'?"

"I'll have to tell you later."

"Okay, so back to McSteamy. I can't believe you didn't tell me."

"I was going to but it's been crazy. Can we talk later? I need to get off."

"Call me, okay? 'Bye."

"Something the matter?" Jack said from behind her, nearly making her jump. With the phone still in her hand, Lake spun around to see him standing in the doorway to the kitchen, two folders under his arm, his head cocked in curiosity.

"As I told you—I'm busy today. Do you have what you need?"

"Yup. Thanks. And, by the way, I'm closing on my new apartment next week, so I'll be getting the rest of my stuff out of here really soon."

"All right," she said, leading him down the long hallway toward the front door. Did he expect her to gush with gratitude?

"Are you planning to attend parents' day at the camp tomorrow?" he asked.

"Of course," she said, incredulous at his question. She could feel her blood begin to boil. "Did you assume I'd spend the day at Barneys along with the other neglectful mommies?"

She regretted the remark as soon as it had shot from her mouth. It was the kind of sniping Hotchkiss had warned her against.

"You shouldn't take everything so personally, Lake," he said, stopping in the foyer. "Are you just driving up for the day or are you going to be using the house this weekend?"

Now what? she wondered. "Why?" she asked.

"If you're not going to use the house, I'd like to stay there tonight. I have to go on to Boston from the camp and it'd be nice not to have to make two long trips in one day."

"Actually I *am* using the house this weekend," she lied.

He studied her face, though she couldn't tell what he was looking for. A sign that she'd just fibbed? She wished he'd just leave already.

"Okay, then," he said coolly after a moment. He reached for the door handle—and then hesitated. "Are you coming?"

"What do you mean?" she asked. It was as if his whole visit was some mind game meant to drive her nuts.

"You said you had to go back to your clients'."

She remembered her earlier lie. "I do. But I have a call to return first."

After he'd left, she leaned for a moment in relief against the foyer wall. Then she hurried down to her bedroom and swung open the closet door. His old black suitcase was exactly where it had been, though slightly askew from having been put back haphazardly. She surveyed the room. She'd totally changed the bedroom a month ago, making it all white and spare, far different from what it had been when Jack had shared the space with her. But it was less than tidy today, with a few items scattered on the low dresser—a Starbucks receipt, a clipping she'd torn from the *Wall Street Journal.* She walked over and glanced at them. She was pretty sure they had been moved. Jack *had* snooped around.

Kicking off her shoes, she fell back onto the bed. Everything right now seemed Kafkaesque to her—Jack's behavior, Keaton's death. She thought of her lie about using the house in the Catskills. The kids' camp was only twenty-five minutes from the house, but her plan had been to drive all the way to the camp from Manhattan and return to the city later that day. She had avoided going to the house all summer, mainly because of what was happening with Jack—she was afraid of memories. But maybe it would do her good to be there. The house had always been a refuge for her, and it might be exactly what she needed right now. Nothing there could conjure up Keaton and the horrible mess she was in. It would be great for Smokey to poke around outdoors. And there was no reason she couldn't leave right now.

It took her only a half hour to pull everything together for the trip. She gathered her folders and her laptop, with the hope of working on her presentation at some point during the weekend. She packed the cooler with a small steak from her freezer and a fresh head of lettuce. As usual, Smokey resisted the carrying case, so she spent a few minutes gently easing him inside.

"You're gonna get to be outside tonight, Smokey boy," she told him. "Won't that be nice?"

Ten minutes later, as she waited for the garage attendant to bring her car around, she considered how escaping the city would put her out of the loop with people at the clinic, who'd be among the first to hear news about the murder investigation. Cell service was spotty where she was headed, so if someone decided to call her, it might be impossible to get through. After pondering this for a few minutes, she called the clinic and asked for Maggie.

"I just wanted to let you know that I'm going to be at my house in the Catskills this weekend," Lake told her. "The cell service around Roxbury is bad so I thought I'd give you my number up there—in case you want to reach me."

"Is one of the doctors supposed to call you?" Maggie asked.

"Um, no—I just thought it would be good for you to have it. You know, in case someone needed me."

"Okay," she said obligingly. "But I'm sure it won't be necessary. Since we have no transfers today, Dr. Levin is sending everyone home at lunchtime. He thought we all needed the break."

Lake also left a message on Molly's voice mail, telling her about her plans and that she would catch up with her later.

The traffic north was heavy and aggravating, though Lake managed to make the first part of the trip in just over two hours. When she finally pulled off the highway for the last leg—along several rural highways up through the Catskill Mountains—she felt a rush of pleasure override her anxiety. In her mind there had never been a better word to describe the landscape up there than *piney*—endless fir trees hugging the mountains that rose steeply from the road. The temperature was seven or eight degrees cooler here than in the city, and she rolled down the window to breathe in the mountain air.

Nothing had changed in the months since she'd last been here, but then again it never did. The small towns she passed through, with their general stores, painted clapboard houses, and weathered steel bridges, seemed untouched since the 1950s. She and Jack had bought the weekend house here ten years ago based mostly on the affordability of the area, but she'd come to love the region—it reminded her of parts of the Pennsylvania landscape where she'd been raised.

Jack, however, had eventually grown bored of it. "Every other restaurant is made from an old caboose," he'd said snidely during a drive up just a few months before their split. It had been no surprise when he'd told her she could keep the house.

Just outside of Roxbury she stopped at a farm stand to pick up fresh tomatoes and fruit. When she pulled into the town a few minutes later, it seemed deadly quiet, and there was the usual dustiness the town always seemed to wear in August as the summer wound down.

Her house was at the far end of town. When she and Jack had gone house hunting they hadn't been able to afford a place with lots of land, so they settled on a lovely center-hall colonial in a short row of houses across from what was called the village green, but what was really a smidgen of park with a few tired benches. The house didn't provide much privacy, but the backyard was spacious enough for the kids to romp around in. And she loved her next-door neighbors, David and Yvon, gay partners in their fifties.

It felt strange but good to set eyes on the house again. As she parked in the driveway and unloaded her bags, she heard someone's long strides behind her. She turned to see David approaching the car.

"Hey, stranger," he said, embracing her. "We've missed you like crazy."

"Same here. And I so appreciate you keeping an eye on the house for me. You guys have been wonderful."

"We weren't expecting you this weekend. Does this mean you're going to start coming up again?"

"Yes, I really plan to—though this trip turned out to be just a spur-of-the-moment thing. I'm going to parents' day at the camp tomorrow. How about a drink tonight before dinner?"

She'd originally planned to hibernate for the evening, but she suddenly felt the need to have Yvon and David chattering on her back porch.

"I can't think of anything I'd like to do more, but we just heard that Yvon's mother is in the hospital. It's probably just another kidney stone but we've got to head back to the city right now."

She felt a rush of disappointment. "Well, we'll do it another time. I just hope she's okay."

"She's fine, I'm sure, though I don't know if *I'll* be okay after spending the weekend at Mt. Sinai, waiting for the damn thing to pass. What about you? How are you doing these days?"

"Better, much better, really."

"And you'll be all right here all by yourself?"

"Of course," she said. "I've been up here plenty of times without Jack."

"It's going to be kind of quiet around here—Jean didn't come up this weekend and the Perrys are at a wedding in Dallas apparently." He gave her a smile. "Well, I'd better dash. We don't want to make Momma Bear cross."

He sprinted back across her front yard and up the steps of his house. Next door, Lake saw that Jean Oran's house was locked up tight, and so was the Perrys'. Lake glanced over to the green across the street. Usually there were a few kids kicking a ball on the grass, or people lounging on the weathered benches, but today it looked totally forlorn. Except for a pair of ratty squirrels scampering after each other, there wasn't any sign of life.

Please, Lake thought as she unlocked the door to the house, don't tell me I've been a fool to come all the way up here alone.

THE HOUSE SMELLED both musty and lemony at the same time—it was likely that the cleaning lady Lake had kept on through the summer had dusted every surface but never cracked open a window. Lake set the cooler down on the kitchen table and went back to the car for her duffel bag and the cat.

"Okay, Smokey, here you go," she said, unzipping the front of the carrying case. "Freedom . . . country air." The cat crept cautiously out into the kitchen, reacquainting himself with the space. For a minute he just slunk around the room, peering and sniffing, and then, with a sudden burst of bravado, pushed through the pet flap in the side door of the kitchen and disappeared. She'd been nervous when they'd first experimented with letting Smokey go outside, but there'd never been any problems, other than the occasional dead mouse or bird he triumphantly brought back with him.

After unpacking the cooler and wrenching open a few first-floor windows, Lake prowled through the rooms, taking stock.

Though the house had come fairly cheap, it had wonderful bones and had cleaned up beautifully. To the left of the center hall was a long, wide living room with a fireplace. On the other side were a small library and a dining room. The kitchen was at the back, and though not huge, it had what real estate agents like to call "country charm." Flowing from it was a tiny den with a TV. Her favorite part of the house was the screened porch that ran along the back. Whenever she read or just daydreamed in one of the black wicker rockers out there, it brought her instantly back to her grandmother's house in central Pennsylvania.

It had been four whole months since she'd last been at the house. Though she'd been avoiding coming up here because she feared her grief was still too raw, it wasn't sadness that she experienced today. It was *discomfort*. The house felt foreign to her, as if she were in a dream and everything that should be familiar was slightly off, out of place. Give it a few minutes, she told herself. You love this place and it's just going to take time to feel at home here again.

She poured a glass of water from the tap in the kitchen sink. There was a small purple stain in the porcelain sink. What was it from, she wondered. Blueberries? She couldn't even remember now.

With the glass still in hand, she carried her duffel bag upstairs. The stairs creaked and groaned, disturbed by the sudden weight. When she neared the entrance to the master bedroom she felt a pit begin to form in her stomach. It was this room, far more than her bedroom in New York, that she associated with the death of her marriage. Because it was here, on weekends, that she and Jack most often had sex—and it was here where he had first shrugged her hand away.

She stepped into the room. As she saw the bed, with its pale-blue spread, she caught her breath. It made her think not of Jack but of Keaton. She could see his butchered body all over again, lying in the bloodied sheets.

Why did I come here? she felt like screaming as she stood frozen in place.

She needed a plan, she told herself, something to keep her from going crazy. She turned around and walked across the hall to the guest room. This will be my room now, she decided as she laid her duffel bag on the wooden luggage rack. She would organize the room and later tackle the garden. And next it would be time for dinner and then for bed. When she felt calmer tomorrow, she would work on the presentation.

After changing the bedding in the guest room and dragging in some of her possessions, she put on shorts, a T-shirt, and a pair of wilted gardening gloves. As she stepped onto the porch, the phone rang, making her jump. It can't be the police, she thought, scolding herself for being so skittish. They had no idea she was here—unless of course they talked to Maggie.

She let out a small sigh of relief when she heard Molly's voice on the other end of the line.

"So I'm sitting here on pins and needles," Molly said. "Tell me what's going on."

"You don't sound as if you're on pins and needles," Lake said. "You sound as if you're in a car."

"I'm just driving up to the fish market on Ninth Avenue. I'm doing a dinner tomorrow night. So tell me about Jack's little visit. What was that all about?"

"He claimed he needed to get some papers—but it seemed odd to me."

"Odd how?"

"Like he was looking for an excuse to come by."

"Like he wants to get back together?"

"You're kidding, right?"

"Actually, no. How did he act toward you?"

"Molly, you can't be serious. The guy just filed for full custody. That's hardly a strategy for wooing me back."

"Guys rarely behave logically when it comes to women."

"Trust me, that's not it. Here's what *I* think—that his coming by for the papers was a ruse so he could snoop around the apartment to see what I've been up to."

"You mean, like he's trying to find incriminating evidence?"

"Maybe. God, I don't know. He's like a complete stranger to me now and it's impossible to read him."

"What if he *did* want to get back together? Would you?"

A month ago she might have answered yes, but she realized now that Jack's custody bid had burned off the last feelings of love she felt for him.

"No. Not in a million years."

"Okay, then. So tell me about the murder. The *Post* said the cops don't have a clue who did it. Is that true?"

Lake wished she didn't have to talk about Keaton.

"I have no idea. The police interviewed everyone at the clinic, but it's not like they're letting us in on anything."

For a brief moment, she ached to confess everything to Molly. By coming clean she could ask for guidance, and potentially soothe the twisted, tortured feelings inside her. Yet she couldn't. Her friendship with Molly was still relatively new, and she didn't know if she could totally trust her. She also couldn't put Molly at risk legally.

"Are you upset about it?" Molly asked. "It must be so weird for you."

"Uh—yeah, the staff seems fairly freaked out by it."

"But what about *you* personally? The guy was getting pretty flirty with you. It must be upsetting."

"It's not like I *knew* him," Lake said, hearing the defensiveness in her voice. "And would you please drop the 'He was getting flirty with you' stuff. That's the last thing I need going around."

"You're not a suspect, are you?"

"No—*of course* not. But the situation is a mess."

Suddenly she wanted nothing more than to get off the phone. Talking to Molly was churning everything up again.

"Look, I better get going," Lake said abruptly. "There's stuff I need to do while I'm up here."

"Are you okay up there by yourself? You're not scared, are you?"

God, she thought, this is going from bad to worse.

"No, I'm fine. I've stayed up here many times without Jack. I mean, the kids have always been with me, but I've never felt unsafe."

"And Smokey's an attack cat, right? I'm sure he'll protect you if necessary."

"The only thing he's interested in right now is taking down some poor little sparrow. I should go. I'll give you a call tomorrow, okay?"

As soon as she hung up, she regretted how curt she'd sounded at the end, but the conversation had been vexing. She wondered if there was any chance the police would contact her friends as part of the investigation. In her imagination she heard Molly describing to Detective Hull how she'd suggested Lake engage in eye sex with Keaton. Wouldn't *that* be great?

For the next couple of hours she worked in the garden out back, digging up weeds, dividing a few plants here and there. At one point Smokey appeared and slid his body along her bare calves. She realized that touch of his silky black fur was the only comfort she'd experienced in the past two days.

"Are you happy to be back here, Smokey?" she asked him.

He let out a soft meow and then slunk away, snaking through a row of deadheaded foxgloves.

She went back to the weeds, trying to focus, but her mind kept coming back to Keaton and the police. Would it make any sense, she wondered, to contact a criminal lawyer to see what advice *they* would offer her under the protection of client confidentiality? But weren't lawyers obligated to report a crime—and hadn't she committed one by not going to the police?

The sun was getting low in the sky. She returned to the house and showered in the guest bath. If they just catch the killer everything will be okay, she thought as she scrubbed at her dirty nails. And it won't matter who Keaton had been in bed with that night. She glanced at her watch through the ribbons of water. It was almost six. The house had satellite TV and she would be able to catch the local news in New York. Maybe there would be some kind of update. After throwing on a robe, she hurried downstairs and turned on the TV in the little den.

A four-car collision on the Tappan Zee Bridge was the top story, but the Keaton murder was next. The anchors went live to a young redheaded reporter outside the apartment building on Crosby. Lake grimaced at the familiar sight.

"It's been over two days since prominent fertility doctor Mark Keaton was found brutally murdered in his SoHo loft," the reporter announced, "but police still haven't made an arrest. There are no known suspects at this time."

Before the story even ended, Lake regretted turning it on. She told herself that the kids needed her tomorrow, that she had to find a way to seem normal for them. She leaned back against the loveseat, closed her eyes, and tried to drive Keaton and Hull and McCarty all from her mind.

Later, after getting dressed, she dragged the grill from the small garage next to the house and set it up in the backyard. She lit the coals and waited for the flames to die down. The smell of the burning briquettes usually brought Smokey running, but he was obviously too busy to be bothered. Lake let her eyes wander toward the far end of the yard, to the western sky above the maple trees. The sun had set and the sky was the smooth, milky-blue color you find on the inside of a scallop shell. On nights like these, she and Jack and the kids used to sit in the backyard and watch the stars and fireflies come out one by one. Her heart ached from the memory of it.

When the coals were ready, she laid the steak on the grill. Next she sliced tomatoes and set a place for herself at the table on the porch. There had been many times when she'd sat alone at that table—times when Jack had stayed in the city working and the kids had gone to bed—and the loner part of her had relished it. But tonight the solitude held no appeal.

She *had* been a fool to come here alone, she realized, especially because it was mainly to spite Jack. And how could she have thought that being alone in the country would make her feel less rattled? At least in the city she would have had the option of grabbing lunch with Molly or going to a movie. There was no way, she decided, she was staying here Saturday night. Once she was finished with the parents' day activities, she would come back, pick up Smokey, and drive straight back to the city.

She ate her steak and salad with a glass of wine, tasting none of it. After clearing the table, she chopped up a piece of steak for Smokey and left it on a small plate on the floor of the porch with the screened door propped open.

"Here, Smokey," she called out into the now utter blackness of the yard. "Come on now."

He'd always had an instinct about when leftovers were being served, and she expected to see him dart through the darkness at any second. But he didn't come, even after she called twice more.

She went inside and poured herself another glass of wine and returned to her chair on the porch. The crickets and katydids had begun to chirp in a loud, cacophonous concert. Still no sign of Smokey. That damn cat, she thought. His refusal to return was probably payback for having been denied the country for so long.

By the time she had finished her wine, her annoyance had morphed into worry. It had been four hours since she'd laid eyes on Smokey in the garden, she realized, and he had never before stayed away this long, even when he was being obnoxious. Was he lost? Or, worse, injured? She let out a jagged sigh. She had no choice but to search for him.

After digging out a flashlight from a kitchen drawer, she started out across her backyard, training the light first toward the trees in the rear, and then into the black hedge that formed the border between her house and Yvon and David's. The night was moonless but stars twinkled across the sky.

"Come on, Smokey, come *on*," she called in irritation.

She listened, hoping for a meow, but none came. From the street behind her yard, she heard a car door slam and a motor turn over. After the car drove away it was only the crickets and katydids again.

Great, she thought. This is the last thing I need.

She passed through a small break in the hedge into David and Yvon's yard, letting the beam of light dance over the lawn. Nothing but rows of coneflowers and black-eyed Susans. From there she cut through into Jean Oran's yard, and then into the Perrys'. A small light came on suddenly, one attached to the Perry house. She realized it was triggered by a motion sensor.

She had never felt anything ominous about the darkness up here before, but she didn't like it now—especially with all her neighbors gone. She was about to turn and head back when she heard a rustling in the bushes at the far end of the Perrys' yard. She whirled around and pointed the beam of light down there.

There was another rustle, loud enough to make her think it was being caused by something bigger than a cat. She held her breath. A raccoon suddenly lumbered out of the bushes, making her jump. Quickly she retraced her steps back to her house.

"I'm going to shoot you, Smokey," she muttered to herself, but she was really worried now. There was the possibility the cat had been hit by a car. After grabbing her keys, she headed out to the driveway. She drove up the street and circled the green several times, looking back and forth. She also drove along the side street that ran behind her house, and then the one behind that. There was no sign of the cat, no sign of *anyone* for that matter—though in several houses she could see the blue light of a TV pulsing through a window. A half hour later she let herself back in the side door of her kitchen, praying Smokey had returned. But he hadn't. It felt like everything was starting to crash down on her.

At the kitchen table she held her hands over her eyes and tried to come up with a strategy. If the cat hadn't returned by morning, she would drive around before she left for the camp, maybe even stick up a few signs. If she still didn't find him, she would have to come back after the parents' day activities and resume her search.

Please, please be okay, Smokey, she pleaded half out loud.

She locked up for the night and poured a glass of milk to take to bed with her. Before she went upstairs, she glanced at one of the kitchen windows, its screen the only barrier between her and the outdoors. They'd always left the ground floor windows open at night, but now the idea made her uneasy. One by one she lowered and locked them. As she shoved the final one closed, she heard the haunting call of a whip-poor-will, a sound that on any other night would have filled her with joy. Tonight it only intensified her misery.

Upstairs she changed into a cotton nightgown and crawled into her new bed. She'd brought a novel up with her, but her eyes kept sliding over the words. Every minute or so she'd set the book down and lean forward, listening, hoping for the sound of Smokey coming through the pet flap. Just once she caught a noise from outside— riffs of laughter from what she thought must be adolescent boys. At midnight she went back downstairs again, thinking Smokey may have slunk in, guilty as sin, but there was no sign of him.

And then, just before one, as she was turning out her bedside light, she heard Smokey meow from the floor below. In utter relief, she slipped out of bed, flicked on the hall light, and rushed downstairs.

The meowing seemed to be coming from the kitchen and it had a plaintive feel, as if signaling distress. It became more frantic-sounding, almost growing to a screech. As she reached the bottom of the stairs, she heard the cat dart into the living room. Great, she thought. He's dragged a half-dead animal in with him and he doesn't know what to do with it.

"Come here, Smokey," she called out as she stepped closer. The hall light only spilled into the entrance of the room, and she couldn't see him. It was silent for a few seconds, but then the cat let out a wail from the far end of the room. Lake fumbled with the switch on a table lamp and when the light came on, she searched the space with her eyes. There was no sign of him.

"Smokey, what's the matter?" she said, taking tentative steps down the length of the room.

Without warning, the cat sprang out from behind an armchair, and Lake's hand flew to her mouth in shock. In the dim light she could see that the fur on his body was now a different color—a pale gray instead of black. As he wedged himself into a corner, though, she was horrified to see that it wasn't fur she was looking at—but skin. Except for his head, tail, and legs, the hair on his body was gone.

HER FIRST THOUGHT was that Smokey had been attacked by an animal, but as she edged toward him, she saw that all his fur was missing, not just chunks of it. And he had no wounds, not even a scratch mark. It couldn't have been done by a dog or a raccoon.

"It's okay, Smokey," she said softly. He had pressed himself into the corner and she could see he was trembling. As she took another step toward him, Smokey bolted back behind the armchair and began to wail. She'd been able to get a closer look, though. There were row marks on his body. He'd been shaved, with what must have been an electric razor. A person had done this to him.

Flushed with fear, she turned quickly to face the two large windows on either side of the fireplace. They looked out at the narrow side lawn and border garden between her house and David and Yvon's, but right now all she could see was pitch-blackness. Was the person who'd done this still out there, perhaps even spying on her to see her reaction? She rushed toward the nearest window and yanked the long yellow drapes closed and then did the same with the other windows in the room. With Smokey still wailing under the chair, she double-checked that the front door of the house was locked as well as the two doors off the kitchen.

Who could have done this? It was clearly a prank of some kind, a mean, nasty one. Suddenly she recalled the adolescent laughter she had heard waft through her bedroom window not long before Smokey returned. She felt more than scared now. She felt enraged.

I've got to call the police, she thought, hurrying back to the living room. But as soon as those words flashed across her mind she knew that she couldn't. There would be a record of her call, and through some inter-network of police, Hull and McCarty might learn of it, which would not be good. She couldn't afford to be on their radar any more than she already was. She couldn't let her life seem anything less than perfectly normal.

Smokey had stopped wailing, though he was still behind the armchair. Lake decided to try to get a blanket around him to calm and contain him.

After grabbing a chenille throw from the arm of the sofa, she bent down on one knee and tried to coax him out with her voice. Smokey let out a soft, mournful cry, as if eager for contact. But when she reached one hand behind the chair, he scratched at her with his paw, drawing three thin red lines along the top of her hand.

"Damn," she muttered. She stood up and pulled the chair forward with both hands, forcing Smokey out of hiding. As he shot across the living room again, she tossed the blanket over him. Trapped, he squirmed frantically beneath it. She scooped him up and fell on the couch, holding him as firmly to her chest as possible.

"There, there, little boy," she whispered, pulling the blanket back from his head. He writhed in her arms, trying to escape her grasp, but eventually he began to relax, as if from pure exhaustion.

She held him like that for at least ten minutes, purring softly to comfort him. All the while, though, she kept one ear cocked, listening for sounds from outdoors. If she heard anyone moving out there, she would have no choice but to call the police.

When Smokey finally seemed calm, she carried him into the kitchen and slipped him into the carrying case. She figured he'd sleep better that way and it would allow her to keep watch over him.

As for herself, she knew there was little chance of her falling asleep, especially upstairs. Better to stay on the couch, she thought, so she'd be able to detect if anyone was prowling around outside. She scurried upstairs to grab a pillow, blanket, and an alarm clock. There was an animal clinic that opened early about twenty minutes away and she would take Smokey there first thing in the morning to make certain he wasn't injured.

For the next few hours, she lay on the couch with one lamp burning and Smokey in his case on the floor by her head. In her mind she replayed her search through the backyards. Had the teenagers who'd done this—if she was right in her assumption—been watching her, then? she wondered. Had she been in any kind of danger?

Some time before dawn, just as the light began to seep through the cracks between the drapes, she finally managed to fall asleep, though it was a restless, sweaty sleep that did her little good. An hour and a half later, Smokey woke her. He was meowing at least, no longer wailing. After struggling up, Lake let him out of the case to eat and use the litter box. She blocked the pet flap with a wastebasket—though it was hard to imagine him ever wanting to go outside again. By seven she had him back in the carrying case and next to her in the front of the car.

There was only one car in the parking lot, so she wasn't surprised to find the animal clinic empty except for a man sitting on the edge of the reception desk, drinking coffee from a cardboard cup. When she entered he looked up from the magazine he was reading and nodded. He was no older than thirty with a pleasant, slightly doughy face.

"Morning," he said warmly. "I'm Dr. Jennings. How can I help?"

"Someone's done something awful to my cat," Lake said. "They—they shaved most of his fur off. He—his name's Smokey. He's calmed down now, but I wanted to make sure he wasn't injured."

The vet wrinkled his face in surprise and concern.

"Okay, why don't you bring him back this way," he said, cocking his head toward the back. He picked up a clipboard from the desk. "You'll need to fill this form out—the receptionist doesn't come in for an hour."

She followed the vet down the hallway to a small exam room with a stainless-steel table that dropped from the wall. Jennings set the carrying case down on the table.

"Okay, Smokey," he said softly, unzipping the front of the case. The cat snarled and tried to claw him, but the vet expertly scooped him up and held him in a way that was instantly calming.

"My God," he said, glancing at Lake. "Who did this to him?"

His voice seemed cooler now, and she wondered if he was suspicious of her.

"I think it might have been teenage boys," she said quickly. "I thought I heard a few of them laughing near the house just before Smokey came in. They may have been out cruising, looking for trouble."

"You've called the police?"

"Um, no, not yet—no. But I will, of course."

Jennings looked back down at Smokey and began to run his hands over him carefully, feeling for any kind of fracture perhaps. His eyes followed his hands. Finally he looked back up at Lake.

"I think you're wrong," he said soberly.

She froze, confused. Was he challenging her, suggesting that she was lying?

"What do you mean?"

"It's too complicated a job for teen boys. You could never shave a cat this smoothly unless it was sedated first. The cat would freak out and you'd never get it to stay still."

"Are you—? You're saying this was calculated?"

"That's my guess. I hate to say this, but do you have any enemies? I mean, has one of your neighbors been complaining about the cat lately? People do awful stuff to other people's pets if they're annoyed by them. They poison them, set them on fire."

Lake's body sagged in dismay. "All my neighbors are friendly," she said. "And they're not even here this weekend."

But her mind had begun to catch up with the truth: this was no random prank. Someone had planned this out. And the goal had been to scare the bejesus out of her.

"How could the person have tranquilized him?" she asked.

Jennings shrugged. "He could have left some food outside with a sedative in it." He glanced at Smokey again and ran his fingers over the cat's body. "Oh, wow."

"*What?*" Lake said.

"Here," he said, pressing his finger just in front of a red dot on Smokey's upper back. "It looks like he's been given an injection."

Lake caught her breath.

"Look, I've clearly scared you," the vet said. "Would you like me to call the police?"

"No, no," Lake said. "I appreciate it but I know the cops in my town. I'll do it when I get home."

"Okay, if that's what you want." He glanced back at the cat. "Let me just finish my exam and make sure that Smokey's okay."

After grabbing an instrument from its holder on the wall, he looked into Smokey's eyes. Lake sat down on the small stool behind him, her mind racing.

If this was planned, she thought—and surely it must have been because you don't just happen to show up in someone's backyard with a hypodermic needle and an electric razor—then it meant that someone was doing their damnedest to rattle her. Did it have to do with Keaton's death? Her heart sank. Maybe the killer knew she'd been with Keaton—and had followed her to Roxbury. She thought back on the drive yesterday. She didn't recall any one car following her for any length of time, but she'd been lost in her thoughts much of the time—she probably wouldn't have noticed.

But that wasn't the only possibility, of course. She remembered her call to Maggie yesterday. She'd told her that she was coming up here, even given the name of the town, and had asked Maggie to let people at the clinic know. Maggie had also pointed out that the clinic was closing early that day. Anyone with a car could have checked her address with directory assistance and found the house. She'd mentioned to at least a few people at the clinic that she had a cat.

And what about her kids? she wondered frantically. Could they be in any danger? She had to get to the camp and make certain they were okay.

"But don't exceed two a day."

She looked up, startled. Dr. Jennings was holding out a small white packet to her.

"I'm sorry," she said. "Can you repeat that?"

"If he acts stressed again, you can give him one of these, but don't exceed two a day."

A few minutes later she was headed back to Roxbury, her mind spinning. She wished she could just pack up everything at the house and not have to come back, but she couldn't take Smokey to the camp with her. Not only would it be cruel to leave him in his carrier all day, but she also couldn't risk the kids getting a look at him.

She pulled the car into the driveway and scanned all around the outside of the house. Not seeing anything out of the ordinary, she left Smokey in the kitchen with food and a fresh bowl of water, and then raced back out to the car.

She was now running ten minutes late. She tried to make up the time by driving as fast as possible, but her foot kept easing off the accelerator as her mind attempted to fathom this new twist to her nightmare. If someone from the clinic had done this, *why*? Because the person had murdered Keaton and knew she was with him that night?

But if the killer knew she'd been in the apartment, why did it matter so much? Obviously because he—or she—assumed Lake suspected who it was. But if Lake was a supposed threat, why harm her cat and not her? It must be a warning, she decided. "I know you were there and you better shut up—or you'll be next." There was no way she could ever let Hull and McCarty find out about Smokey. They would suspect instantly that something was up with her.

Just before she made the second-to-last turn for the camp, she checked her rearview mirror for what seemed to be the hundredth time. No one was behind her.

As she pulled into the overflowing parking lot of the camp, she realized that she'd been so preoccupied with what had happened to Smokey that she hadn't mentally prepared for seeing Jack today. Jack, who, she suddenly realized, had also known she would be at the house this weekend. Maybe the scare with Smokey wasn't related at all to Keaton's death, but to the custody situation. Jack trying to scare her so she'd come unhinged. Could he have done this? Opening the car door, she realized how this thought would have been impossible with the old Jack. But she knew nothing about what the new Jack was capable of.

She heard her daughter before she saw her—as the word *Mom* rang out from the grassy slope just above the parking lot. It was just like Amy to be waiting excitedly for her arrival—and Lake felt a surge of relief.

"Hey, sweetie," Lake called, waving broadly and forcing a big smile. Amy was with another girl about the same size, both in their khaki shorts and hunter-green shirts stamped with the camp logo, and they bounded toward Lake as if she were an ice cream truck pulling up on a sweltering hot afternoon. Lake hurried to meet them. Though Amy possessed Jack's tall, athletic build, she had Lake's coloring—the brown hair and gray-green eyes—and people always knew instantly they were mother and daughter. Amy, however, was self-possessed in a way that Lake hadn't been at her age—because of the birthmark she was deeply ashamed of.

As the two girls reached her, Amy threw her arms around her mother's waist.

"Wow, it's so good to see you," Lake said, hugging her back and kissing the top of her head.

"Mom, Mom, this is Lauren," Amy said, smiling at the red-haired girl with braces standing next to her. "She's from Buffalo. We've been there, right?"

"Yes, on our way to Niagara Falls. Hi, Lauren. It's very nice to meet you."

"Well, it's really a suburb," Lauren said. "Amherst. Have you ever heard of it?"

"Yes, of course," Lake said. "So tell me about the plan today, girls. The swimming races are first?"

"Yes, and then lunch and then we're doing a talent show," said

Amy. "Lauren and I are singing. Will is doing an animal dance—he's a skunk."

"A skunk—perfect! So where is he?" Lake needed to set eyes on him as soon as she could.

"He's playing soccer, I think," Amy said. "He's probably already filthy. I swear, it's embarrassing—he's always covered in dirt. Do you want a tour, Mom? I don't think you saw everything the day you dropped us off."

"I'd love one. Are your parents coming, Lauren?"

"Yeah, in a while. They're always late for everything." She added an eye roll for emphasis.

They began to ascend the hill, with a few other parents straggling behind them. Jack must not be here yet, she thought looking around, or Amy would have mentioned it.

"Are you looking for Dad?" Amy said, reading her thoughts in that uncanny way of hers.

"Is he here?" Lake asked, trying to sound casual.

"No, he's not coming now," her daughter said.

"What?" Lake said, stopping in her tracks.

Amy shrugged and let her shoulders droop.

"The counselor told us," she said glumly. "She said Dad called the director and told him he's not going to be here. He said something came up."

10

THAT MADE NO sense, Lake thought. Why wouldn't Jack come? Maybe it had something to do with the Boston trip he had alluded to. Or was he trying to avoid her? Her mind flashed back to Smokey. *Had* Jack shaved him—or sent someone to do it—and now he didn't have the guts to look her in the eye? Was he trying to screw with her mind in general? There'd been that call in the middle of the night, too. If Jack was responsible for what happened to Smokey, he might have been behind the call as well.

"*Are* you, Mom?" Amy whispered, breaking through Lake's thoughts.

"Am I what, sweetie?"

"Are you upset? About Dad not coming."

"Oh no, honey, I'm not upset. I—I was just curious."

The three of them finished the climb to the main grounds of the camp. There were dozens of parents and kids up there, already congregated on a grassy expanse worn bald in spots from endless use. Will was there, too, dressed in swimming trunks and devouring one of the many doughnuts that had been laid out on a weathered picnic table. He spotted Lake, waved like he was trying to flag down an airplane, and then ran over, flashing his crooked grin. She almost cried when he wrapped his dirty arms around her.

"You're already suited up, huh?" Lake said, tousling his silky blond hair.

"It's probably because he's lost his camp shorts," Amy said.

"Shut *up*, Amy—you don't know anything. Mom, I'm swimming in all four categories. There's this kid who's better than me in the freestyle but I think I'm gonna win the butterfly. And maybe the backstroke."

"That's awesome," she said.

"Did you bring Smokey?" Will asked.

She nearly winced. "No, Will, Smokey had to stay at home."

"But you said you'd bring him," he said, furrowing his soft, luminescent brow.

"I did? When did I say that?"

"The day we *got* here. You said when you came for parents' day, you would bring Smokey."

"Oh, I'm sorry, honey. It's just so hot. He wouldn't have liked being cooped up in the car. But you'll be home in a few weeks— you'll see him then."

What would she tell them, she wondered, when they saw him still without most of his fur?

The morning was a blur of events—swimming races, soccer, archery, a lunch of soggy sandwiches and lukewarm lemonade— and she was grateful that little was demanded of parents beyond being herded from one spot to another. Her mind where it was, she couldn't imagine what it would have been like to have to participate in some tug-of-war game or three-legged race. It was all she could do to make inane small talk with the other parents.

By the time the talent show started, she was feeling even more anxious. She was desperate to pick up Smokey and clear out of the house, and yet the thought of leaving the kids made her ache. As the show ended and the campers congregated with friends by the make-shift stage, her eyes searched until they found the camp director.

"Hi, I'm Lake Warren," she said, approaching him. "I'm so sorry I had to wake you the other night."

It took him a moment to connect the dots. "Oh, not a problem," he said, remembering. "Did you figure it out in the end?"

"It must have been a wrong number," she said. "But it did frighten me. I thought something had happened to Will."

"You mustn't worry. We take excellent care of the kids here—they're never out of sight."

"And at night?" she asked.

"At night? Everything's locked up tight. We even have a night watchman. Why? Is there some reason—?"

"No—that call just made me a little edgy. Could you ask the coun-selors to keep a special close eye on my kids? I'd really appreciate it."

"Of course," he said graciously. But she could tell by the way he narrowed his eyes that he thought she was being paranoid—or else hiding something.

As she walked away from him, she bit her lip, thinking. The mystery call had come twenty-four hours before Keaton's death. Therefore it wasn't related to the murder and might not be related to anything at all. Still, if someone *was* after her—if Jack wasn't the one responsible for Smokey—it meant her kids might be in jeopardy, too. Should she take them out of the camp, she wondered, and bring them back to the city? Her instinct was to have them close by, but as her mind grappled with all the possibilities, she realized that the city might actually be the worst place for them right now. At least up here they were off the radar of anyone who might be after her. Plus, she realized, no one but Jack knew exactly where they were.

Friends, even people at the clinic, were aware they were in camp, but fortunately no one had ever bothered to ask the name of it.

At four the events wound down and it was time to go. Both kids acted uncharacteristically with their goodbyes. Will, who she had expected to be clingy, ran ahead with his friends, dragging his swimming medals through the dusty grass.

"Don't I get a hug?" she called to him.

"Oh, yeah, sorry, Mom," he said, darting back and flinging his arms around her. "Tell Smokey hi, okay?"

Amy, however, usually so independent and unflappable, reached for her hand as they walked toward the parking lot and held it tightly.

"What would you like in your next care package, honey?" Lake asked. "I want to send you a really good one."

"I need a new book, Mom. And some Twizzlers. Enough for me and Lauren." .

"Got it . . . Oh, I nearly forgot. You got a letter from that Save the Tiger organization."

She rooted through her purse for the envelope and as she looked up to hand it to her daughter she saw that Amy's face was pinched, fighting back tears. Had she been troubled all day about something, and had Lake, overwhelmed by her own fears, not even noticed?

"What is it, honey?" Lake asked, squeezing Amy's hand.

"It's nothing, I guess." Amy looked as if she were both anxious to unburden herself but reluctant to trouble Lake.

"No, tell me," Lake coaxed. "Do you . . . do you feel sad about Dad not coming?"

"I guess. I wanted him to hear me sing that song in the show."

"They were taping it, I think. He can get a DVD."

"Okay," Amy said sadly. Lake could see, though, that Jack's no-show wasn't the issue.

"There's something else, Amy, isn't there? Tell me, sweetie."

"Mom," Amy asked, almost in a whisper. "Is everything okay?"

"What do you mean?" Lake asked. Her body tightened in alarm.

"I don't know. You seem different today. Like—I don't know."

That was so typical of her intuitive daughter, Lake thought—she had sensed the terror coursing right beneath her mother's skin.

"I'm sorry if I gave you that impression, sweetie," Lake said. "No, nothing's the matter. I'm still getting used to doing things on my own again. But I'm fine. Really."

"Okay," Amy said haltingly. She sounded completely unconvinced.

"You know what I think?" Lake said, enveloping Amy in her arms. "I think parents' days are both good and bad. Everybody gets together for a visit, which is really nice, but it makes us all a little homesick. I'm sad about leaving you, and I think you're a little sad about saying goodbye to me. But as soon as you find Lauren and do something fun with her, you'll feel good again."

"But what about *you* tonight?" Amy implored.

"Oh, I've got plans with a friend," Lake lied. "Now, listen, I want you to run back up the hill and wave to me from the top, okay." Lake wanted to make certain Amy was up in the main part of the camp before she left.

They hugged each other tightly once more, and then Lake watched Amy scamper up the hill. At the top she turned and waved forlornly. Lake waved back, fighting a sob. It wasn't until she pulled out of the parking lot that she allowed the tears to stream down her face. Why was all this happening to her? She should never have gone to Keaton's that night, she cursed herself again. Never should have given in to her pathetic need to be desired.

She drove faster than she should have, often exceeding the speed limit on the twisting roads. When she finally reached the house, she saw two people—a man and a woman—sitting on one of the benches on the green, holding soda cans and chatting casually. Were they who they *seemed* to be? Lake eyed them surreptitiously as she hurried up the front steps of the house.

Inside, the house was deadly still. She walked warily through the ground-floor rooms, making sure nothing had been disturbed. When she reached the kitchen door, she stopped short for a second, listening. Then she pushed the swinging door slowly open. The room was just as she left it, except for the late afternoon sun spilling over the wooden floorboards. And Smokey was there, curled on the loveseat in the little den next to the kitchen. He raised his head and meowed plaintively as she entered.

Gently, Lake eased him back into his carrying case. As she was zipping up the case, the house phone rang, making her jump yet again. It's got to be Molly, she thought. But when she answered, a male voice she didn't recognize spoke her name as a question.

"This is she," she answered, her heart picking up speed.

"Hi, Lake, it's Harry Kline."

"Oh, hi," she said, taken aback. She had left her number with the clinic but of everybody there, the therapist was the last person she'd expect to hear from.

"I hope I'm not disturbing you."

"No—uh, not at all," she said. She knew she sounded flustered, but she just needed to hang up and get out of there.

"Maggie sent an email around telling us how to reach you, and I thought I'd try to catch you this afternoon. From the area code, I guess your place is upstate."

"Yes—in the Catskills."

"That's great. Do you go most weekends?"

"It depends, you know, on the season, things like that." As she spoke, her eyes raced over the kitchen windows, checking outside. "Actually this time I'm only here for half the weekend. I was just about to head back to the city."

"Don't let me keep you, then. If you're going to be back in town tomorrow, would you be up for grabbing a cup of coffee?"

Now he was really catching her off guard.

"Um, sure. Is—is something up?"

"No. I just wanted to chat about a few things—out of the office."

"That sounds kind of ominous," she said.

"I didn't mean it to. It's just so hard to talk in the office with patients around."

"Oh, okay. Sure. I'm free most of the day."

"How's eleven? I know you're on the West Side, so we could meet at Nice Matin—that bistro at Seventy-ninth and Amsterdam."

"Sounds good. I'll see you then." She hung up and grabbed the pet carrier and hurried out of the house.

As she made her way out of town, her eyes kept flicking toward the rearview mirror. The only vehicle behind her was a red pickup truck, which soon turned off onto another road. Whoever had hurt Smokey was clearly long gone—in fact had probably been gone since last night. She suddenly recalled another sound she'd heard—the light slam of a car door when she was in her backyard. It might have been the person fleeing, after drugging and shaving Smokey.

Would the person strike again, she wondered, this time in the city? And would *she* be the target, not just her cat? A brush fire raced across every nerve in her body. I *have* to do something, she thought.

The weekend doorman, Carlos, was on duty when she arrived at her building, and he let her leave her bags in the lobby while she parked the car in the garage. But she kept Smokey with her. When she returned she saw that Carlos had loaded everything onto the brass rolling cart for her. They were alone in the lobby.

"I've got a small favor to ask, Carlos," she said, fumbling for the right words to use.

"Of course, Mrs. Warren," he said.

"I do consulting work, you know, and one of my clients has had some trouble lately. I mean, one of their partners—a doctor—was murdered."

"Oh my goodness," he said, his brow wrinkled. "That's *big* trouble."

"I know—it's horrible. And I'm kind of on edge about the whole thing. I just want to be really careful."

He stared at her, waiting for her to continue. She could see he had no clue what she was driving at.

"I mean, I'm being a bit silly but I want to be extra cautious about the apartment. I don't want to let anyone up until you've seen their ID. And will you let me know if anyone comes by and asks for me?"

He lifted his chin slightly and then nodded, catching her drift.

"Do you think you may be in danger, Mrs. Warren?" he asked.

"No, no. I'm just a little paranoid and hoping you'll humor me."

"Of course," he said. "We always take precautions, but I'll be extra careful, Mrs. Warren. Of course I will."

"And will you tell the other doormen?"

"Most certainly."

As soon as she was in her apartment, she turned the dead bolt on the door and put the chain on, too, something she never did during the day. She'd always felt safe in her apartment, but nothing felt safe to her now. After unzipping Smokey's case and watching him slink sadly into the living room, she checked each room of the apartment to make sure nothing had been disturbed.

It was close to seven, already dark, and she poured a glass of wine and sat with it at the kitchen table. She had to figure out who had taken Smokey and why. An empty envelope lay on the table and she flipped it over. In her work she was a constant note taker, and she found it helped her to not only remember but also make sense of things. With a pen she wrote one word: *Jack*. And then a question mark. Was it really possible that Jack was trying to spook her so that she was a wreck by the time she met with the court-appointed psychologist—making his custody fight a slam dunk?

Lake scrawled the word *clinic* next. As Harry had indicated, everyone had been informed as to where she was going to be this weekend, and since they'd been given the afternoon off, any one of the staff could have driven to her house that Friday. And someone from the clinic would have access to a syringe.

But if someone from the clinic killed Keaton—and was now taunting her—what had the motive been? Sexual jealousy? *Professional* jealousy? In the few short weeks he'd been with the clinic, had he managed to incite something like that? Maybe Keaton's death was connected to the "snag" he'd mentioned to her. But how would she ever figure out what it was?

And then she wrote an *x*—for *unknown*. There was still a chance Keaton's death was totally unrelated to the clinic. Maybe his gambling problem—if he'd truly had one—was at the root of everything and some horrible thugs had killed him. And now they might have their eye on her. But would they have bothered shaving her cat? Didn't they just pump a bullet in the back of your head and dump your body in a landfill?

Her purse was on the table and she found her BlackBerry in the pocket and punched in Hayden's number. There was a chance, she realized, the PR guru had an update on the police investigation.

"I was *just* this minute gonna call you," Hayden said. "I thought I'd catch you before you and your cute little husband went out for the night. Or you probably have family stuff to do, right? Like, see one of those Narnia movies or something."

Lake almost snickered. "My kids are away at camp," she said. "And that cute little husband no longer lives here."

"Oh, phooey—I hadn't heard."

Lake got right to the point, in part to change topics.

"How are things going with the clinic?"

"It's been intense—and getting more so. Levin's okay to deal with, but I can't stand the posse, especially that Brett or Brie chick. She acts as if she's got a stick up her ass—and she looks like it, too."

"So I'm not the only one she seems to despise?"

"No, and she's really ticked at me now. When I found out that Levin was going to send the troops home on Friday, I told her she had to stay and handle the phones. I needed her to keep track of all the vultures from the press who called and refer them to the cops. She was totally annoyed and made the receptionist do it."

"You can hardly blame the press for their interest."

"I know. But Levin says that since 'octomom,' they're just aching for a negative angle to pursue with these clinics. There's some TV reporter named Kit Archer that makes him apoplectic, and Levin wants to make sure he doesn't come anywhere near this mess."

Archer. That had been the name on the file Levin had grabbed from her.

"Can you keep them at bay?" Lake asked.

There was a pause, and Lake could hear Hayden take a sip of something. Lake could almost see her long fingers, nails painted plum, holding the stem of a wineglass.

"No, not now. That's why I was about to call. There's been what you might call a disturbing development, and the shit is gonna hit the proverbial fan."

Lake's whole body tensed. "What is it?" she asked.

"Levin called me this morning. Apparently Keaton had given a set of his house keys to one of the nurses a few days before he was killed. They were sitting in an unlocked drawer all week—and anyone could have used them."

"WHO?" LAKE ASKED, her voice nearly strangled.

"*Who?*" Hayden said. "You mean, who could have used them to get into Keaton's apartment and kill him? I have no fucking clue, and if Levin does he's not sharing that info with me."

"No—what I mean is, who at the clinic had the keys? Whose desk were they in?"

Lake had known that someone from the clinic could have killed Keaton, but this made the idea *real*, not just her own suspicion.

"Oh. Let's see." The sound of rustling papers. "Maggie Donohue."

"Was she seeing Mark—Dr. Keaton?" Lake asked. Involuntarily her stomach clenched at the thought of Keaton in bed with Maggie.

"No, nothing like that apparently. Levin said she'd agreed to pick up Keaton's mail and water his plants when he went back to California next week to tie up loose ends. And she's got an alibi.

She was apparently celebrating her brother's birthday at his house in Queens and spent the night on his couch."

"But why didn't she say anything before now?"

"According to Levin, it never crossed her mind that someone at the clinic might have done it. From what I gather now, there was no forced entry—but the police didn't share that little tidbit last week. Maggie's brother's got cop friends. They told him and then he passed it along to her. She called Levin late on Friday hysterical."

"But the keys aren't missing?"

"No. Levin went into the office and found them right where she said they'd be. Obviously there's a chance someone used them to slip into Keaton's apartment and kill him—and put them back right after the murder. As you can imagine, if the killer works at the clinic, it's gonna make crisis control a *tad* more challenging."

Lake was silent as her mind grappled with the news. If the killer did indeed work at the clinic, there was a good chance he—or she—had also shaved Smokey as some kind of warning.

"I told Levin he had to call the police," Hayden said, filling the silence, "but I could tell he didn't like the idea. His bet is that Keaton's death was an outside job related to the gambling problem—and that's my hunch, too. But in the end he knew he had no choice. Maggie's brother was going to spill the beans if he didn't."

"And so did he? Did Levin call the police?"

"Yup. Tell me—you know some of the players there. Could one of them actually be a murderer?"

"I really don't know anyone there very well. Except for Steve Salman, one of the associates—and I can't imagine him hurting anyone."

"Well, even if someone there *did* do it, I'm sure you're not in any danger. So stop worrying."

"Worrying?" Lake said defensively. "What do you mean?"

"I can hear it in your voice. If the murderer works at the clinic, it obviously involves some internal conflict. You're perfectly safe."

That's funny, Lake thought sarcastically. She was actually less safe now than she'd ever been in her life.

"Hold on, will you?" Hayden said before Lake could comment. "Oh shit, this is a client. I'll call you back when I have more news."

As soon as the call had ended, Lake fell back into the chair. It was clear now that someone from the clinic could have easily gained access to Keaton's apartment, and thus killed him. Her mind want back to the "snag" Keaton had mentioned. A snag might refer to an uncomfortable situation that had suddenly flared up between him and someone on staff. She thought of how Keaton had called Levin a fertility rock star with a trace of mild disdain in his voice. Maybe there was a rivalry between them, one Keaton finally realized couldn't be tamped down. But would Levin kill Keaton just because he had decided not to join the practice?

Later, as she lay in bed, wide-eyed and wired, she wondered if Harry had asked to see her so he could fill her in on the news about Keaton's keys. Or could he possibly suspect her of something? When it came to deceit, shrinks were like truffle hounds—they could *smell* it. She squeezed her eyes tightly and tried to will herself into unconsciousness. But in her mind's eye she suddenly saw Will and Amy lying in their bunk beds, the camp cabins engulfed by the black night. What if I've endangered them? she thought in anguish. It was hours before she finally felt her thoughts fray around the edges and she slipped into a fitful sleep.

The next morning, she forced herself to review all the notes she'd taken on the clinic. She'd promised Levin she'd make an initial presentation next week, and she needed to have the first batch of ideas ready. She'd come up with a few marketing concepts so far, but she needed more—and stronger ones. As she worked she wondered how she would pull it off with her mind as crazed as it was. Maybe Levin would suggest an extension. Surely he himself couldn't be in much of a mood to discuss a marketing plan in light of everything that had happened. She plugged away and lost track of the time, realizing with a start that she was ten minutes late for her meeting with Harry.

Harry was already at the restaurant when she arrived, skimming a folded section of the *New York Times*. Though he wore the same basic uniform she'd usually seen him in at the clinic—dark slacks and a cobalt-blue dress shirt open at the neck—he seemed different to her today as she approached. More relaxed, she thought. Weekends were likely when he allowed himself to unwind from the stress of counseling couples in the depths of despair.

When she reached the table, he looked up, and smiled. It was impossible to tell from his expression what his agenda was. Be friendly, she told herself. But volunteer nothing.

"I thought we might be the only two people in Manhattan this morning," he said, rising. "But apparently seven other people decided to stay in town, too." He lifted his chin to the half-filled tables behind her.

Their bistro table was small, and for the first time she had a chance to take in his face up close. He wasn't classically handsome— the small bump on his nose got in the way of that—and yet his face was appealing: soft brown eyes, smooth skin, and the wry smile he often wore. His black hair was longish, a little wavy, and brushed back along the sides of his head.

"Do you usually stay in the city on weekends?" she asked.

"Sometimes I do—I love how quiet it is," he said. He pushed his dark-rimmed reading glasses up onto his head. "So you only managed a *half* weekend in the country, huh?"

"Uh, yeah," she said. She was completely disinterested in small talk but she knew she had to play along. "I needed to get back here. I still have a lot of work to do on my presentation."

"How's that going, anyway?" he asked.

Could he sense her discomfort? she wondered. He had that shrink way of watching neutrally as you spoke, never tipping his hand.

"Pretty well, I think," she said. "But it's challenging. It's one thing to plan a marketing campaign for a spa or a new brand of body butter. This is so different. The people who need the procedures are vulnerable, and I don't want to hit the wrong note."

"I know. And some of what's happening today is just so crazy," he said. "I hear there are clinics that actually promise money-back guarantees if you don't conceive. Can you believe that? And some of the egg-donor stuff is absurd. There's one clinic down near Washington that offers 'doctoral donors.' You don't just get a baby. You get one with a shot at becoming an astrophysicist."

This can't be why he asked to meet with her, she thought—to discuss issues in the fertility business.

"Do you wish the clinic hadn't decided to become more aggressive about promoting itself?" she asked.

"I certainly see the need for *some* marketing. It's a business, after all, and things are getting much more competitive out there. I'm just not sure where you draw the line."

The waitress interrupted then, wanting to take Lake's order. Lake asked for a cappuccino.

"It must be heartbreaking dealing with the patients," Lake said.

"It can be, yes. The worst part is that they often blame themselves. They sometimes talk about feeling cursed."

"I saw one patient in the hall last week and she just broke down, sobbing," Lake said. "I felt so bad for her."

"I wasn't in that day but I heard about it. Apparently Rory convinced the woman to make an appointment with me, but then she canceled it. Unfortunately I can't force someone to come in to talk to me."

"She looked fairly young. I assume she'll keep trying."

"Maybe," he said, shrugging a shoulder.

"Why only maybe?"

"She's already been through eight IVFs—that's part of the reason why she's so wrung out."

"*Eight?* Wow, that's a lot. It must be tough on her body."

"You sound like Mark Keaton."

The comment took her completely aback.

"What do you mean?" she said, trying to keep the defensiveness out of her voice.

"He didn't seem to like how many rounds she'd been through, considering her situation. When I was looking through her chart, I noticed some comments from him that suggested that."

"Do you think it *was* too much?"

He twisted his head and rested his cheek on his fist, turning the question over in his mind.

"I'm the guy who figures out what's going on in their heads, not their bodies," he said. "What I do know is that the clinic does good work. They help a lot of women get pregnant—and that's why patients come to us."

"I know you also have a private practice," she said. "Why do this kind of counseling on top of that?"

"My sister-in-law had fertility problems, and she just unraveled. My poor brother was clueless about how to deal with her. I could see how counseling would have helped them."

"What ended up happening?"

"After lots of treatment, they gave up. They're still together fifteen years later, but their childlessness is the proverbial eight-hundred-pound gorilla in the room. It didn't help that I'd had no trouble myself."

"You have children?"

"A daughter, nineteen. She's a sophomore at Bucknell."

Lake felt her face betray her surprise. She'd pegged Harry for early forties, but he had to be older than that to have a child in college.

He grinned, reading her. "I was only twenty-two when she was born—in my first year of grad school. Not the best way to start a marriage, needless to say, and in the end we didn't make it. But Allison is great, and I've got no regrets."

"That's wonderful," she said. Where is this *going*? she wondered again.

"I should ask you the same question you posed to me. Any particular reason you decided to work for a fertility clinic?"

For a split section she felt the urge to explain the weird connection she felt between the patients and herself—because they'd all been betrayed by their bodies. He was such a good listener, and how soothing it would be to unburden the thoughts she never really shared with anyone. But she didn't dare show anything of herself to him.

"When Steve mentioned the project it just sounded interesting. I've had friends who've struggled with fertility, but I was lucky."

"Your kids are young, right?"

"Nine and eleven. They're at sleepaway camp right now, up in the Catskills—near where I was when you called and asked if we could get together."

She hoped her mention of the call would serve as a nudge. Harry stirred in his seat and she saw he'd taken the hint.

"Well, I appreciate your meeting me on such short notice, especially with all the work you have on your plate."

"What was it you wanted to see me about?"

"To be honest, I just wanted to see how you were doing."

"How I'm *doing*?" she asked. She felt herself bristle.

"I may be wrong, but I sensed the murder really disturbed you. I thought you might want to talk about it. Even if stuff like this doesn't affect us directly, it can still have an impact."

She'd been right, she thought anxiously. He'd picked up on her panic. If she tried to deny what he was intuiting, he'd know she was lying. Her mind fumbled for a way to force him off track.

"The murder *was* upsetting," she said after slowly taking a breath. "But there's actually something else that's been troubling me. I guess I've worn my heart on my sleeve without meaning to."

"Do you want to talk about it?" Harry asked as the waitress returned with Lake's cappuccino.

No, I don't, she thought. But she might not convince him if she didn't cough up something. She took a sip of her drink before speaking.

"I was in the process of what seemed to be a fairly amicable divorce, and then out of the blue, my husband filed for full custody. It's been very stressful."

"What a creep," Harry said. He started to shake his head in dismay but stopped and smiled. "That's my professional opinion, by the way."

Lake couldn't help but smile back.

"Thanks," she said. "I'm so used to having to suck it up and speak neutrally about him in front of the kids; it's nice to hear someone make a nasty comment about the man."

"I'm sorry to hear you're going through that. Let me know if there's anything I can do."

"I will, thanks."

Harry glanced at his watch.

"Are you getting hungry?" he asked. "We could grab a bite of lunch here if you'd like."

"Um, thanks—but I need to get back to my presentation. Maybe some other time."

He said he would stay and have his lunch at the café. She took a last swig of her cappuccino. When she set the cup down on the table, Harry reached over and lightly touched her hand with the tips of his fingers.

"I hope that doesn't hurt," he said. When he withdrew his hand, she saw that he meant the marks Smokey had made when she'd tried to pull him out from behind the chair.

"Oh, no," she said. "It's just—a scratch. I can't even remember how I got it."

Flustered, she picked her bag up and rose to go.

"Good luck with your presentation," he said. "I'm sure it'll be brilliant."

Hurrying home, she replayed the conversation with Harry in her head. She hoped her confession to him about the custody situation had quieted any suspicions he might have.

As she opened the door of her apartment, she also considered the comment he'd made about Keaton questioning Levin's judgment about the patient they'd discussed—the one who'd had eight rounds of IVF. She wondered for the first time if the snag that had developed for Keaton didn't involve a problem with one of the staff but rather with the clinic itself. She stopped in the hall and closed her eyes, trying to recall Keaton's exact words that night. He'd said something about the clinic not being the best place for him right now. Perhaps Keaton had stumbled onto something that had alarmed him.

Lake had never witnessed anything the least bit suspicious at the clinic, but with her lack of medical expertise, how would she really know if something wrong was going on? There had to be a way to consider what the possibilities were. She thought suddenly about the reporter Hayden had mentioned, the guy who made

Levin apoplectic. He'd written an article on the fertility business, one that Levin clearly didn't want her to see. Maybe the truth lay in that article—or at least a hint of it. Lake dreaded going to the clinic in light of all that was happening but she knew she needed to read that article. The one sure way to save herself—and her custody of the kids—was to figure out who might have killed Keaton and somehow point the police in that direction, and away from her.

She told herself she would hunker down and work straight through until evening. But rather than light a fire under her, the newest developments seemed to paralyze her. Plus, she felt a growing dread about going into the clinic the next day. If the killer *did* work there, she was putting herself right in the line of sight. But she had no choice. She had to get her hands on the article; it was the only thing she had to work with. And if she could find the chance without being too obvious, she wanted to talk to Maggie about the keys.

She was at the crosstown bus stop by eight-thirty the next day and at the clinic by just after nine. After nodding hello to the receptionist, Lake made her way down the main corridor of the clinic. As she passed by the empty nurses' station, her eyes found the top drawer of Maggie's desk, and she fought the urge to stop and open it.

"You're in early today," a voice said behind her as she plopped her bags down on the small conference room table. She spun around to find Rory standing behind her. Great, she thought. She didn't want to appear to be acting out of the ordinary.

"I have an appointment in midtown later," Lake said, "and I thought I'd swing by here first."

"Did you have a nice weekend, Lake?"

"Um, yes—it was good to get a chance to just decompress. How are you feeling?"

"Better, I guess," Rory said, though to Lake she looked tired. There were small bluish circles in the pale skin under her eyes.

"I'm just trying to make sure the stress doesn't affect my baby in any way."

"That's so important. I haven't even thought to ask you—do you know what you're having?"

"A boy," she said, cupping her round belly with one hand. "I'm so happy."

"That's wonderful—congratulations."

"I read that couples who have a boy are more likely to stay together," Rory said. "Because men secretly want boys."

"I've never heard that," Lake said. "But I could see where it might be true. I guess you could call it the Henry the Eighth factor."

The last comment seemed to fly over Rory's head. She looked off to the side, her brow furrowed in concentration.

"I hope it's true," Rory said. "It's so important for kids to grow up in a stable home. Don't you think so?"

Had Lake never mentioned to Rory that she was separated? she wondered. On any other day the comment, however naïve, might have rattled her, but Lake was already too rattled to care.

"Well, I think you just do the best job you can," Lake said.

"What a perfect way of putting it," Rory said smiling and turning to leave. "Have a good day."

As soon as Rory was gone, Lake slipped out of the conference room and zigzagged along the short corridors toward the storage room at the back of the clinic. When she glanced down the hall that shot off toward the OR, she saw a cluster of four people in blue scrubs and hair caps—Sherman, she thought, and Hoss, too—but they were too engrossed in conversation to notice her.

Once inside the storage room, she eased the door closed behind her and tugged open the drawer where she'd discovered the Archer file. It wasn't there. Hardly surprising, she thought. Levin didn't want her to see it and so he hadn't put it back.

In case he'd simply relocated the file, she rifled through the rest of the drawers, but there was no sign of it. She realized that the file was probably tucked away in Levin's office. Would she dare sneak in there and search for it?

And then she realized she didn't have to. She'd more than likely be able to find the article online by searching the reporter's name—she couldn't believe she hadn't thought of this sooner. She hurried back to the conference room and turned on her laptop. She Googled Archer's name and the titles of six or seven articles popped up. They all seemed to be meaty investigative articles, published in a variety of magazines. It wasn't hard to figure out which one had been in the file Levin had grabbed from her: "Brave New World: Behind the Closed Doors of Fertility Clinics." She clicked the link to it.

She'd only gotten through the first paragraph when she caught a glimpse of Maggie's black curly hair bouncing past the doorway. Recognizing that this might be her only opportunity to talk to her alone, Lake lowered the lid on her computer so that the screen wasn't visible and followed Maggie down the hall.

"Hey, Maggie," she called out quietly as the nurse entered the empty kitchenette. Maggie turned around, and Lake was startled to see how drained her face was.

"Hi," Maggie said listlessly.

"Listen, I heard about the keys," Lake said quietly. "It must be so upsetting."

"I shouldn't have ever left them in the drawer," Maggie whispered plaintively, clearly glad to have a confidante. "Do you know what this *means*? It means someone here may have killed Dr. Keaton."

"But it's not your fault. Plus, it doesn't necessarily mean that—"

"I can't really talk now—Dr. Sherman is waiting for me."

"Do you want to meet for coffee after work?" Lake asked.

"Tonight's not good. But I could meet you for lunch, I guess.

My break is at twelve-thirty. I always go to the coffee shop over on Lex and Eighty-first."

After agreeing to meet Maggie there, Lake hurried back through the labyrinth of corridors. She nearly collided with Brie as she once again entered the small conference room. Brie was obviously just leaving.

"Good morning," Lake said, trying to sound friendly.

"Hello," Brie said coolly. Her lips, painted a glossy plum color today, barely moved as she spoke, and Lake noticed that the tip of her nose was pink, as if flushed with blood. "Are you going to be in here all morning? We really need to use this room later."

"I'm leaving shortly," Lake said. "And I'm always happy to work my schedule around the clinic's."

"I actually thought you were going to be *done* by now. Aren't we supposed to be getting your report?"

"As Dr. Levin knows, I'm exactly on schedule."

Brie just stared at her for a moment and then walked briskly from the room. Lake shook off the encounter and sat down. Immediately she could see that there was something different about her laptop. She'd left the lid only partly lowered, but now it was completely closed.

Brie had been snooping. And she'd clearly seen what Lake had been looking at.

WAS THIS MORE than simple nosiness on Brie's part? Lake wondered. Lake knew Brie was a control freak and rigidly protective of the clinic, but maybe it had gone beyond that. If Levin was the killer and suspected Lake knew something, he might have asked Brie to keep an eye on her. And now Brie would report back on what Lake had been up to.

Though she was desperate to read the article, she didn't dare do it here. She needed to find a café with wireless and read it there. And then at twelve-thirty she would meet Maggie.

After stuffing the laptop into her tote bag, Lake zigzagged back to the front of the clinic. Today, every door seemed to be closed. From inside one of the examination rooms she heard low moaning, followed by a choked scream of anguish. She'd heard how uncomfortable some of the procedures could be—such as when they filled the uterus with a solution to better examine it during X-rays.

Passing Levin's office, she held her breath, wondering if Brie was in there now, tattling on her. Suddenly the door swung open. Levin was standing in the doorway, not with Brie but with a striking girl who looked to be nineteen or twenty. Her long straight hair was the color of butter and her face was tanned. Levin extended a hand, palm side up, indicating the front of the clinic.

"Reception is just around the corner to the left," he told the girl, his charm fully on. "We'll see you Monday, then."

The girl bit her lip and shrugged, as if she wasn't sure.

"Okay," was all she said. Her flip-flops slapped on the carpet as she headed down the hallway.

"Oh, you're here already," Levin said, spotting Lake. "Have you got a minute? I'd like to speak to you."

"Of course," she said, an alarm going off in her head. His tone seemed crisper than usual. When she stepped into his office, she found Hoss standing in the room, dressed in a sleeveless blue dress, sans lab coat.

As Levin opened his mouth to speak, Brie stuck her head in the door. The sight of her made Lake's heart jump.

"Dr. Levin, Dr. Sherman needs you stat," she said. "He's in 4."

He sighed, clearly bothered by the interruption.

"I'll be right back," he said to Lake. "I'd appreciate your waiting."

Again crisp, very no-nonsense. But Lake figured Brie couldn't have blabbed to him yet—Levin had been behind closed doors with Hoss and a patient.

"Certainly," Lake said, letting him pass by her.

"Lovely-looking girl, don't you think?" Hoss said to her.

"Brie?" Lake asked, unable to contain her surprise at the comment.

"No," Hoss said dryly. "Kylie—the girl who was just in the office."

"Oh, yes. She's so young to be a patient here."

"She's not a patient," Hoss said. She raised her chin in that haughty way of hers so that it was practically pointing at Lake. "She's one of our potential donors."

"Oh," Lake said, surprised again. She knew that the clinic regularly used donor eggs, and sometimes even donor embryos. It was the last option for women who wanted to become pregnant but whose eggs were too old, too few, or too damaged from something like chemo. Donors received a minimum of eight thousand dollars, sometimes much more, depending on their pedigree, though as far as Lake knew, this clinic didn't go to the extremes Harry had alluded to—like mining for PhD donors. For several years the clinic had relied on eggs from special agencies and brokers but had recently decided to begin its own database of participants. Hoss was supervising the project.

"I thought you weren't going to start with that for a few more months," Lake said.

"We're getting a better response to our ads than we expected. That means we can probably begin sooner."

"That girl Kylie looked like she might still be on the fence."

"We never know for certain until they show for the first procedure. Many of them drag us through a bunch of preliminary interviews and then get cold feet."

"It's a lot to put your body through, isn't it?" Lake said. "I could see why some women might have second thoughts."

"It's one month of hassle, and they're paid brilliantly for it," Hoss said disdainfully. "But girls are spoiled these days. They want the money, and yet they can't bear the idea of any inconvenience."

She elaborated on the selfishness of Gen Y, and as she did, Lake studied her. As she'd noted at the restaurant, it was almost a Jekyll and Hyde kind of thing. Out of her lab coat and black-framed glasses, Hoss was no longer the nerdy scientist; instead she was a handsome alpha female. Her arrogance seemed to spring not only from whatever wealth or social clout she possessed but also from her conviction that she was generally the smartest person in any room.

"All right, thanks for waiting," Levin announced, rushing back in. His hands looked damp, as if he'd washed them after examining someone and then dried them in a hurry. "Catherine, you may as well stay—you might have something to contribute."

Levin slid into his desk chair and flung out his hand, indicating that Lake and Hoss should sit as well. Lake studied him as he glanced down at his desk, his pale gray eyes roving the surface agitatedly. Something was definitely up, Lake thought. She wondered if Brie had intercepted him in the hall.

"I had several conversations with Hayden Culbreth over the weekend," Levin said, looking up and locking his eyes with Lake's. "She clearly knows what she's doing."

"I'm glad you're satisfied with the recommendation," Lake said—though she sensed a "but" coming.

"The problem is that there have been some new developments in this dreadful situation with Keaton, and no matter what we do to protect ourselves, we're going to be exposed on certain fronts."

"Can you be more specific?" Lake asked. He's got to be talking about the keys, she thought.

"I'd prefer not to at this moment," he said. The quick look he shot Hoss made it clear that she was in the know. "It's a police matter, and for the time being, the less said the better."

Obviously he hadn't realized Hayden would keep Lake informed.

"Understood," she said, playing along.

"That said, we need to be proactive on other fronts. We're likely to be scrutinized, and though Hayden will help us do damage control with the . . . situation, we need the clinic to *shine*. How are you coming on your proposal? I think we need to begin implementing things ASAP."

His comment totally threw her.

"We'd agreed I'd present you something next Monday," she said. "I'm on your calendar to do that."

"*Monday?*" he said, as if this were the first he'd heard of it.

"Can't we pick up the pace? We're in a very precarious situation here."

She couldn't believe he was suddenly pressuring her this way. It was the absolute last thing she needed.

"Well, I'd—I'd have to take a look at my schedule," she said. She felt disconcerted and annoyed but she didn't dare show it. "I gave you my original date based on other obligations I have."

"You've certainly had time to get to know us," Hoss said, ignoring Lake's explanation. "I can't imagine you'd need to do any more research."

Lake forced a tight smile, fighting off the urge to strangle Hoss. "I'll certainly see what I can do. But, you know, this isn't the best moment to launch a big marketing campaign anyway. You should probably lay low for a few weeks and concentrate on following Hayden's strategy to keep attention *off* the clinic. Then, when the dust has settled, we can initiate some of the ideas I have."

"I get your point," Levin said, "but there have got to be *some* ideas worth implementing now—like the new website."

"At least let us hear what all the ideas are," Hoss said. "It would be good to have something else to focus on besides this horrible business."

"As I said, let me check on my other obligations," Lake said. "I have to leave now, but I'll be in touch later."

She hurried from Levin's office, and out through reception. As soon as she was outside on Park Avenue, she wiped the fake smile from her face. Surely Levin remembered that the deal was for her to present her ideas *next* week—they'd discussed it several times, and she'd confirmed the date with Brie. She wondered if there was some ulterior motive behind his pressuring her to present them sooner. Maybe this was another way to discombobulate her—even though it wasn't in the same league as nearly skinning her cat. Regardless of his intentions, she had to play along and try to seem nonchalant. And she had to find a way to concentrate and bolster her presentation, which was so meager at this point.

It was hot and sticky outside, but she barely noticed as she hurried toward Lexington Avenue. At the corner she took a right and headed south until she located a Starbucks several blocks away. She bought a coffee, found a table, and after sweeping it clear of spilled sugar, popped open her laptop. Once again she pulled up the article by Kit Archer.

The piece wasn't pretty. It described how fertility clinics had become a big business these days but were still unregulated. Although the CDC required clinics to report their success rates, there was no way to enforce that or audit what *was* reported. That meant there was room for abuse. Archer also reported that some clinics had been accused of encouraging patients to try procedures that had low success rates but high price tags.

Lake had read through articles on fertility clinics when she first took on the project, but she'd never seen this particular one. She kept waiting for the name of the Advanced Fertility Center to pop up—because otherwise why would Archer be such a thorn in Levin's side? But the article was from a Washington, D.C.–based magazine and most of the clinics mentioned were in the Washington area.

So why hadn't Levin wanted her to see this piece? Perhaps one of the doctors at the clinic had once been affiliated with one of these D.C. clinics. Lake dug through her tote bag for the folder with all of the doctor bios and thumbed through them. None of them had ever worked near Washington.

But the article had to be significant. Maybe Archer was working on a follow-up piece and Levin had gotten wind that his clinic was going to be highlighted. Or maybe the article referenced dubious practices that Levin's clinic was engaged in, too, and Levin didn't want to arouse Lake's suspicions.

Lake Googled Kit Archer himself. He was an award-winning journalist who had segued back and forth between print and television. He was now working as a correspondent for *Reveal*, an investigative news show. It was possible that *Reveal* was looking into the clinic as part of a story and that was why Keaton had gotten cold feet about joining. No doctor with a good reputation would want to find himself suddenly mired in that situation.

Lake touched the fingers of both hands to her forehead, thinking. She had sensed from the beginning Levin's ferociousness about the clinic—in their initial meeting he had boasted of its record, dismissed some of the other East Side clinics, and said he was hiring her to get the attention they deserved. If Keaton had challenged Levin—about excessive rounds of IVF, for instance—or stumbled on abuses and threatened to expose him, Levin would have been livid and quick to defend his empire. Who was Keaton, after all, to get in the way of his glorious mission? She closed her eyes and tried to imagine Levin sneaking into Keaton's apartment and drawing a knife across his throat. She couldn't picture it.

But he might have *hired* someone to do it. And Levin had just enough arrogance to keep up pretenses during a dinner in Keaton's honor, playing the gracious host while knowing that Keaton would soon be dead.

Next Lake went to the *Reveal* website and clicked on Archer's bio there. Archer looked as if he was in his early fifties, with the rugged, square-jawed good looks associated with guys who covered wars in safari jackets. What was different was his hair. Rather than the brown shellacked helmet head TV guys generally sported, it was totally white and long enough to be brushed behind his ears. Lake watched a video of one of his recent stories and scrolled through the site to see if he'd reported on fertility clinics, but there was no indication that he had.

There was only one way she was going to learn if Archer was

looking into the Advanced Fertility Center and that was to call and ask him. She had no idea if he'd even talk to her, but she had to try. Her gut kept telling her that Keaton's death was related to something going on at the clinic. She had to figure out what that was and make sure the police knew about it, too.

Lake raised her head and surveyed the café. There wasn't anyone within earshot of her. No time like the present. After calling the main number listed for the show, she spoke Archer's name into the automated system. Three rings later a deep voice announced, "This is Kit Archer." The cadence sounded so natural that it took her a moment to realize she was listening to Archer's voice mail message. She didn't leave a message. She knew she'd be better off catching him off guard.

She still had an hour before she was due to meet Maggie and she felt ready to jump out of her skin. She gathered up her bags and stepped outside in the heat. For the next forty-five minutes she meandered up and down side streets, letting her mind toss around the little she knew, ticking through the staff and trying to imagine if someone other than Levin would kill to protect the clinic's reputation. Sherman was a partner and would also feel threatened by any kind of accusations. So would Hoss; even though she wasn't a partner, she was at the epicenter of the clinical work there. And then there was Brie. She was nothing more than support staff, but she seemed as fierce as a Doberman about both Levin and the clinic.

The blistering heat made Lake consider how ragged she must look. Her hair had begun to fall from its topknot and her back was damp with sweat.

At eleven forty-five Lake changed direction and headed back toward the coffee shop where she'd agreed to meet Maggie. She wanted to find out exactly where the keys had been and who might have known their whereabouts. Maybe those answers would tell her something.

Maggie wasn't yet at the restaurant. Lake took a seat in the back so there was less chance of them being spotted, and she positioned herself so she could watch the door. Though the AC was groaning loudly, it barely made a dent in the heat. Her iced tea arrived with the ice cubes already no more than slivers.

She scanned the menu without seeing it. When she glanced at her watch it was twelve-forty. She's not coming, Lake realized. She's changed her mind.

But as she looked up to wipe her damp forehead with a napkin, she spotted Maggie in the doorway of the coffee shop.

She lifted her hand to get Maggie's attention and when Maggie finally spotted Lake, she edged toward her through the tables. As she came closer, Lake saw that Maggie's face was still slack with worry.

"I'm sorry I'm late," she said. "We were doing a procedure and it took longer than Dr. Sherman had planned."

"Don't worry about it," Lake said. "I'm just glad we could get together."

Maggie's eyes suddenly misted.

"I so appreciate your talking to me," Maggie said. Her brogue seemed more noticeable, as if the stress she was under had teased it out of hiding. "I don't dare talk to anyone at the clinic. Dr. Levin wouldn't like it, and besides . . ." Her voice trailed off but it was clear what the unspoken words were: there was no one at the clinic Maggie could trust.

"I'm happy to listen," Lake said quietly. She knew she had to stay casual, not seem too grabby for information or else she might scare Maggie off. "This must be so hard for you."

"I just feel so guilty," Maggie whispered.

"You shouldn't, though," Lake said. "How could you have possibly known something like this would happen? Plus, those keys might not be connected to the murder at all."

"It's not just about the keys," she said. "It's what happened *before*. I should have known something wasn't right with Dr. Keaton."

13

"WHAT? WHAT DO you mean?" Lake asked. All around them diners droned in conversation and waiters plowed brusquely between tables. Yet none of it mattered. What did Maggie know? Lake wondered. She held her breath, waiting.

Maggie bit her plump bottom lip so hard it looked like it would burst. "Maybe I shouldn't be blabbing like this," she fretted. "My mother always says I talk out of school too much."

Damn, Lake thought. Maggie had sensed that she was pouncing and pulled back. She had to be careful.

"This must be such an overwhelming time," Lake said, keeping her voice easy. "You must feel so confused about what to do."

"I do," Maggie said, shaking her head. Her dark curls bounced.

"So Dr. Keaton wanted you to water his plants while he was in California?" Lake asked. Maybe she would have luck, she thought, getting Maggie to start at the beginning.

"Yes, the trees on his terrace," she said. "And he wanted me to bring in his mail so his mailbox wouldn't get stuffed."

At that, Maggie's eyes brimmed with tears and she dabbed at them with a paper napkin.

"But why give you the keys so far in advance?" Lake said.

"He had his spare set on him when he asked me, so he said he might as well give them to me then. I should have kept them in my purse, but the one I use in summer is really tiny and I didn't want to lug the keys around all week—so I just stuck them in my desk drawer."

As Maggie spoke, her eyes fell to her purse on the Formica table. It *was* small—a tiny white bag of quilted leather.

"Do you think anyone saw him give you the keys?" Lake asked.

"I'm not sure," Maggie said. "We were in the hall down by the lab when he asked me. Someone might have seen us, I guess—or maybe overheard us from the lab."

"How about when you put the keys in your drawer?"

"There were probably people around, but I don't remember who."

Maggie's desk was in an open area that people walked by all through the day. It would have been easy for anyone to sneak the keys out of the drawer—especially during the busy hours of the day when most of the staff were engaged in the exam rooms or in the OR. Or at the end of the day, when staff had begun to leave.

"Did you ever have the sense that the keys had been moved in your drawer?"

"No," Maggie said, almost as a moan. "I almost never use that drawer. I don't think I even looked in there once after he gave me the keys. Oh God, what if I'm responsible for his death?"

"But you're not, Maggie."

The waiter approached and asked for their orders.

"Were you surprised that Dr. Keaton asked you to do such a big favor?" Lake inquired after he'd walked away.

"It wasn't that big a deal. I live in Brooklyn and his place is right off the same subway line I take home. Plus I was getting paid. The last time he gave me a hundred dollars."

"The *last* time?" Lake asked, perplexed.

"In March. I did this in March, too."

"I'm not following," Lake said.

"Dr. Keaton consulted with us once before, back in March, for about a month. Toward the end he went to the Bahamas for a long weekend and I checked on his place for him."

"Got it," Lake said. It seemed odd she hadn't heard about Keaton's earlier stint, and yet she realized there would have been no reason for anyone to bring it up. When she redirected her attention to Maggie, she saw that tears were now streaming down her face.

"Maggie?"

"That's when it happened," Maggie said in another whisper.

"The thing you mentioned before?"

"Yes."

"Why don't you tell me about it."

"It was Friday night—the weekend in March that he went away. A friend and I were going to meet in SoHo after I stopped by Dr. Keaton's. I was running late so I called her from the apartment, and later, at the restaurant, I realized I'd left my cell phone on his counter. I felt so stupid. My friend said she'd go with me to get it and when we went back there after dinner, I had this—I don't know— this creepy feeling someone had been in the apartment. There was a light on in the bathroom but I know I never turned it on."

Lake felt her stomach twist. She remembered the light *she* had seen in Keaton's bathroom—and her fear that the killer might be hiding in there.

"Do you think someone was there?" Lake asked.

Maggie's eyes widened in alarm.

"Omigod, I don't know," she said. "I mean at the time I just thought someone had come in after I'd been there and then left. I even thought Dr. Keaton might have come back early and gone out. But when I called him, he was still at the Ocean Club."

This could mean that someone had been after Keaton long before last week, Lake thought.

"So you told him? Was he concerned?"

"At first he did sound concerned. He asked me some questions—like what time had I been there and when did I go back—and then he said not to worry. He'd been having a problem with the bathroom drain and he said the super had probably checked on it. That's why I forgot all about the whole thing. Because Dr. Keaton had just dismissed it. But now I wonder if it might mean something."

"It would be easy enough to check—the police could ask the super. You told them about this?"

"Not yet. I just thought of it on the way over here. But I will, I swear. I feel so dumb. When I told them about the keys, I could tell they thought I was a total idiot."

"Had you just forgotten about the keys when you first talked to them?" It did seem like a stupid oversight to Lake.

"*Forget*'s not really the right word. When we were being called into the conference room that day to hear the news about Dr. Keaton, Brie whispered to me that he had been murdered. Dr. Levin had told her right before we walked in. She said someone had broken into his apartment. I knew he had a terrace so I figured the burglar had gotten in that way. It was only later, when I was talking to my brother and he said that Dr. Keaton had either let the person in or the murderer had used a key, that I remembered."

"Do you think someone from the clinic *could* have done it?" Lake asked, her voice a whisper now, too.

Maggie's elbows were on the table and she rested her face onto her fists, squashing both cheeks. Then she wiggled her head back and forth in a no.

"I just can't believe that's possible," she said mournfully. "What would the reason be? People seemed happy that Dr. Keaton was joining the clinic.

"Maybe it's all a coincidence, then," Maggie added, lifting her head. "I mean, me having the keys and someone getting into the apartment. If you add it up, Dr. Keaton was only at the clinic for about seven weeks total. How could anyone get to hate him in such a short time?"

"Yes, it's probably just a coincidence," Lake said, smiling wanly. Despite her reassurance, there was every chance someone from the clinic *had* swiped the keys. Seven weeks *wasn't* a very long time, but it was long enough for Keaton to have stumbled onto unscrupulous doings and confronted the person responsible. And that would have given the person reason enough to silence him.

They ate their sandwiches without enthusiasm, though Lake forced herself to ask Maggie a few benign questions about her background and how she'd ended up in reproductive medicine. She listened to the answers without hearing them. When Maggie said she didn't have time for coffee Lake asked for the check.

"You know, I can never look at one of these without thinking of a story a patient once told me," Maggie said, gesturing toward the untouched pickle on her plate. "The day after her transfer, she developed this incredible craving for pickles. She ate an entire jar one night. And then half of another jar. She thought it meant she must really be pregnant. But it turned out it was all in her mind. And now she says the sight of them makes her sick."

Lake imagined the woman forking spear after spear from the jar and devouring them. That's like me now, she thought. Half crazy in desperation.

They paid the bill and walked out of the restaurant. Lake glanced quickly around, making sure no one from the clinic was in sight.

"Are you going back to the clinic now?" Maggie asked her.

"Uh, no. I have some other appointments," Lake said.

"Well, thanks for listening," Maggie said. "I feel a little better. I still can't believe that someone from the clinic did it."

As they stood listlessly on the sidewalk a new question surfaced in Lake's mind. "I'm just curious—how complicated was it getting into Dr. Keaton's apartment?" she asked.

"What do you mean?" Maggie said.

"I'm just wondering if someone might have gained access to the apartment *without* the key. Could they have jimmied the lock easily, do you think?"

"I don't know," Maggie said. "There were just two keys in all, not counting the mailbox key—one to the lobby of the building and another to his apartment door. They *were* easy to use. Then again . . ."

She paused, thinking.

"What?" Lake urged.

"He had a different lock this time," Maggie said. "And it was a little tight. He said I'd need to jiggle the key a little."

"Wait," Lake said. "You're saying that since you were there in March, Dr. Keaton had his lock changed?"

"Yes."

Maybe Keaton had been far more concerned about the light in the bathroom than he'd let on and had his lock changed because of it. But Maggie seemed oblivious to this connection.

"You need to mention that to the police," Lake said.

"You think it means something?"

"It's just good for them to have every piece of info," Lake said, not wanting to say more.

"Oh, okay." Maggie smiled at Lake. "It's great that you're so concerned about this."

"Well, of course," Lake said, trying not to sound defensive. "I care about the clinic—and the people there."

"You just seem to care more than some of the others. Like Dr. Hoss. She's just charging around as if everything's absolutely normal. You've only worked here for a few weeks and you're way more concerned than she is."

Let it drop, Lake thought. The last thing she wanted was for Maggie to tell everyone how involved she was with the murder.

"I better let you go," Lake said. "Take care, now—and let me know if I can help in any way."

As Maggie walked away, Lake turned and headed north on Lexington. The heat normally would have been an incentive to take a cab, but she needed to walk and think. She felt stunned by what she had learned—about Keaton changing his locks, about the light left on in his bathroom once before. Had someone actually been after Keaton for a while? Maybe it was all connected to the gambling problem—a light left on by the intruder as a warning to pay up or else. Keaton may have instantly known what it meant and that's why he'd had his lock changed.

She wondered if there really *had* been a gambling problem. What if Levin had made that up as a form of misdirection? Which led her back to the clinic. It was entirely possible that someone had overheard Keaton's conversation with Maggie, swiped the keys, had copies made overnight, and returned them to the desk drawer first thing the next morning.

Lake had to figure out why Keaton had changed his mind about joining the clinic. If only she could talk to Kit Archer.

She tried his line again but again got voice mail. She considered he might be someone who screened all his calls. She tossed her phone in her bag in frustration. When she looked up she saw that she was almost face-to-face with Steve Salman and his wife, Hilary. They were headed south, in the direction of the clinic, their expressions blank, as if they'd been walking without talking to each other. Hilary, always pretty and bubbly, seemed undone by the heat today. Her cheeks were blotchy and her shoulder-length brunette hair looked as if it had frizzed and then been beaten into some kind of chunky submission.

"Oh, hi," Steve said, spotting her. "Are you done for the day? Someone said they thought you'd left."

"Yes, I'm done for now," Lake said. "Hello, Hilary. Were you guys having lunch together?"

"Lunch?" Hilary said, sounding mildly annoyed. "Please—we all know doctors don't have time for lunch."

"We were doing some quick tile shopping," Steve said. "For a new master bath we're putting in. I was looking for you earlier, by the way. Everything okay?"

"What do you mean?" Lake asked. Why was he always putting her on the defensive?

"I heard you were behind closed doors with Levin."

"Actually, he did throw me a bit of a curveball," she admitted. "He asked me to give my presentation this week instead of next. Maybe you could reason with him. It's not so much that I need the extra time. I just don't think it's such a great idea to launch any kind of marketing and PR blitz right now. We should wait until the clinic is out of the eye of the storm."

"Let me see what I can do," Steve said. "I'm running late right now, but I'll call you later, okay?"

As she said goodbye to the couple and turned to walk away, she wondered if Steve had heard about the keys in Maggie's drawer. She wished she could talk candidly to Steve about the clinic, but after what he'd told the police about her, she wasn't sure he could be discreet.

She took a cab the rest of the way home, and when they reached the corner of her block she saw that the street was nearly deserted. Families had decamped to the Hamptons or the Poconos or upstate New York. Even the afternoon doorman, Bob, was taking a break from the heat, reading a tabloid newspaper in the small, dim room just off the lobby. His head snapped up as he heard her walk by.

"Afternoon, Mrs. Warren," he said, folding the paper over and walking to the lobby. "By the way, I spoke to Carlos. He told me your safety concerns."

"I appreciate that," she said.

"That wasn't the guy who was killed downtown, was it? The fertility doc?"

"Yes. Yes, it was."

"Sounds like a bad situation."

Oh God, she thought. She didn't want to be getting into this with him.

"It is. I just want to be super careful."

"We always take precautions, as you know. But we'll be extra careful."

"Thanks, Bob," she said and hurried past him.

As soon as she entered the apartment, she went through the rooms again, looking for anything askew, her new ritual. Then, after scooping up Smokey, she flopped on the couch and shut her eyes tightly. She needed to turn on the AC but wanted to sit and collect herself for a moment. She felt like she was in some horrible limbo without any sense of what to do next. Smokey nuzzled her hand with his nose, urging her to pet him. His furless body looked unbearably sad to her. Who *did* this to you? she wondered for the umpteenth time. And why?

The intercom buzzer pierced the silence, making her body jerk. She scooted Smokey off her lap and hurried to the hallway.

"Yes," she blurted.

"Mrs. Warren?" the doorman said.

"Yes, Bob, what is it?"

"The police are here to see you."

14

"*WHAT?*" **LAKE ASKED.** She'd heard him, but his words had nearly knocked her over.

"Two policemen. Detective Hull and . . . um, Detective Mc-Carty. Oh, and I checked their IDs."

She stood frozen in place, terrified. Had they managed to place her at Keaton's apartment? she wondered. Were they going to arrest her? Then she remembered the keys. They would want to follow up with everyone at the clinic about the keys in Maggie's desk. Please, please, let it be that, she begged silently.

"Uh, you can send them up, Bob," she said.

Her legs felt like lead but she forced herself to the living room and let her eyes sweep over the room. It was essential, she knew, for her to come across as perfectly normal—a homebody, even hopelessly dull. But since the kids had been away at camp, many of the trappings of family life had been tucked away, and with its melon-colored silk drapes, ceiling-high bookshelves, and wood-framed landscape paintings, the room looked like it might belong to someone sophisticated and perhaps even posh. Quickly she pulled several books down from a shelf and tossed them onto the bare coffee table. Through the doorway into the family room she could see a Uno box on the card table. She darted in there, grabbed the box, and went back to drop it next to the books. She tossed one of the throw pillows onto the floor and scattered the others around the sofa.

What else? she thought frantically. But just then she heard the doorbell sound. It was too late for anything else.

She walked out into the hall, bracing herself. Suddenly she felt something soft on her bare calf. She glanced down to find Smokey wrapping himself around her leg. Lake clasped her hands to her mouth. She'd forgotten all about him.

She grabbed the cat and raced down to her bedroom.

"Good kitty," she whispered, dropping him on the bed.

She was shutting the bedroom door when the buzzer rang again, insistent, irritated by the wait. As she made her way back down the hall, she closed her hands into fists to keep them from shaking.

When she opened the door, she almost didn't recognize the two detectives. Hull had worn his hair slicked back today, maybe because of the heat. McCarty's face was coated with a sheen of sweat—and there were wet half-moons under each arm of his khaki suit jacket.

"Sorry to disturb you at home," McCarty said. "But we have a few more questions we'd like to ask you."

"Of course," she said, as friendly as she could muster. "Please come in. Can I get you some water—or something else to drink?"

"That won't be necessary," Hull said brusquely. His tone implied her friendliness was wasted on them.

She led them to the living room and gestured for them to sit down. They each took an armchair, which left her the couch. As she perched on the edge of it, she saw McCarty take in the Uno box. Did it look calculated, she wondered, like a prop in a play?

"You mentioned the other day that you'd been with the clinic for just a short time," McCarty said, flipping open his notebook. "How long exactly?"

She lowered her eyes, trying to calculate. It should have been easy to remember, but she was so distracted she could barely think. As she struggled she could hear Hull's breathing grow louder, as if he were prodding her with a stick.

"Um, sorry," she said. "Sometimes one day just seems to blur into the next. This is my fourth week."

"Have you got a calendar here?" McCarty asked. "To double-check it?"

"No, I'm sure of it—I've been there just over three weeks. I've never worked a whole day there, though. I usually go in for a few hours in the morning—to interview the doctors, read through material, that sort of thing."

She caught herself overexplaining. Stop saying so much, she scolded herself.

"Anyone there you've gotten to know very well?" McCarty asked.

"Not really. I've chatted a bit with Maggie, one of the nurses . . . and the medical assistant, Rory. Also Harry Kline, the therapist. We grabbed a cup of coffee together the other day."

She felt she should tell them that—they might learn about it from Harry and it would seem odd for Lake to have omitted it.

"What about the doctors?"

"Well, like I said, I've interviewed them, and there was the dinner—but that's all."

"What's your impression of Dr. Hoss? Have you spent much time with her?"

Why were they asking about Hoss? she wondered.

"No more than anyone else," Lake said. "We talked for a few hours one morning about embryology and some of the procedures she's been doing in the lab."

"So you haven't gotten to know any of the doctors personally?"

"No. Oh, wait, I'm forgetting Dr. Salman," she added clumsily, as if she'd just knocked over a glass of water. "He's the one who suggested me for the job. His sister and I are old friends from college and I'd known him for years, but not super well."

Hull sighed, not bothering to hide his annoyance.

"Is that it, then? You're not suddenly going to remember that someone there is your long lost cousin?"

"No," she said. She wished she could have walked across the room and squashed something in his face.

McCarty cleared his throat, directing attention back his way. She remembered then that she hadn't yet switched on the air conditioning and the apartment was warm, almost stifling. The sheen on McCarty's face was practically glistening now. She wondered if she should jump up and turn it on now—but that might only encourage them to stay longer.

"I'm not sure if you've heard the news," McCarty said, "but it turns out that Maggie Donohue had a set of Dr. Keaton's keys in her desk drawer. We're trying to determine if anyone saw them there and took them."

"Yes, I heard. It's so upsetting."

"What is?" Hull asked.

"That someone might have taken them," she said. "That someone from the clinic could be . . . the killer."

"Does it surprise you?"

"Well, yes. I didn't have much contact with Dr. Keaton, of course, but Maggie told me that everyone seemed to like him."

"What do you mean, 'of course'?" Hull asked bluntly.

"Excuse me?" she said. Her heart seemed to stop in her chest.

"You said *of course* you didn't have much contact with him."

"Well, like I mentioned, I never worked a full day there. And . . . since he hadn't officially joined yet, I hadn't interviewed him."

"Did you ever see anyone other than Ms. Donohue going into the drawer?"

"No, not that I recall."

Hull eyed her as if he found her idiotic.

"Well, if you remember anything, will you let us know?" he said. There was the hint of a smirk on his face.

"Of course," she said, forcing a polite smile.

"And you never saw Keaton have a confrontation with anyone there?" McCarty asked.

"No."

If only she could reveal what Keaton had told her about the snag—but she didn't dare. They would know instantly that she'd been more familiar with him than she had let on.

"How about several months ago?" Hull asked.

"What?" she asked.

"In the late winter. When Dr. Keaton was at the clinic before."

"But I've only been at the clinic for a few weeks," she said, carefully.

"You weren't consulting when Dr. Keaton was there back in March?"

"No." Her head was spinning. It seemed like they were trying to lay traps for her, leading her to the edge of a cliff.

"Let's switch gears a minute," McCarty said. "You mentioned the other day that you and Dr. Keaton had spoken about the clinic he'd worked at in L.A. Did he say anything particular about it?"

Where was this going? she wondered fretfully.

"We only spoke about it for a few moments. He said that they had some great marketing strategies."

"No complaints?" McCarty said. "Nothing negative?"

"No, nothing like that."

The heat was starting to get to *her* now. She could feel trickles of sweat running down the back of her neck, one chasing the other. But she just sat there, her posture as straight as possible, waiting for the next question. None came. McCarty thumbed back through endless pages of his notebook, perhaps for the notes he'd taken when she was first interviewed. Was he trying to find a contradiction, some new way to trip her up? Hull just sat there, staring at her. She'd heard about this technique. It was called the pregnant pause, wasn't it?—or the let-them-stew-in-their-own-juices-and-then-see-what-they-spill strategy? Give it time and she would confess to anything, like operating a terrorist cell out of this very apartment.

"You have kids?" Hull said finally.

"Yes. They——" She was about to mention they were away at camp but realized it would be insane to reveal that they hadn't been around last week. "They're nine and eleven."

Hull rose then without a word, as if suddenly bored. McCarty closed his notebook and stood as well. She couldn't believe they were actually going. She followed them out into the hall, letting a breath finally escape from her lungs.

"Is there anything else?" she said. She regretted the words as soon as she'd spoken them, but relief had left her light-headed.

"Actually, yes," said Hull.

She almost smiled at how damn stupid she'd been to ask.

"Someone at the clinic mentioned that you've been awfully upset since the murder," Hull continued. "Not yourself. I'm surprised the murder would have disturbed you that much—I mean, since you hardly knew Dr. Keaton."

Her legs felt suddenly deboned, too soft to stand on.

"Who—who said that?" she asked weakly.

"I'm not at liberty to say," Hull said.

She remembered the ploy she'd used with Harry and decided she had no choice but to try it here, too.

"I *have* been upset—but not just about the murder. I found out last week that my ex is going to fight for full custody of our children. I've been beside myself about it."

Both detectives looked at her without saying a word. She could feel that the entire back of her cotton blouse was soaked now—and there was perspiration above her lips, too. She had to resist the urge to wipe it away.

"That's gotta be tough," McCarty said finally.

"Yes. It is."

Just then a long meow emanated from her bedroom. Followed by another. And then the sound of claws scratching at the door. In unison the two men jerked their heads in that direction.

"Someone doesn't sound very happy back there," McCarty said.

"Oh, it's . . . my cat. I put him back there when I heard you were coming up."

"You didn't have to do that," McCarty said. "We aren't allergic, are we, Scott?"

"No. In fact, we're real kitty lovers," Hull said with a smirk.

She held her breath. Were they just going to stand there and wait until she let the cat out?

"Maybe you could put the AC on for him at least," Hull said, shrugging and turning toward the door. "I bet he's hot as hell."

A minute later they were gone. She watched through the peephole to make sure they boarded the elevator and then she let Smokey out of the bedroom. He shot down the hall as if his tail had been set on fire.

Lake felt completely spent, and yet frantic, too. She tore off her wet blouse and let it drop in a heap on the bedroom floor. After flicking on the AC, she hurried to the kitchen and rifled through a drawer for a pad and pen. Then she began to scribble down notes. She didn't want to forget a word the cops had said.

It was clear from the questions that they were seriously focusing on the clinic—obviously in light of Maggie's revelation about the keys. But they'd also asked about Keaton's work at the clinic in L.A. That seemed to mean that they were pursuing other theories simultaneously. And surely by now Levin must have told them about the gambling issue. As she scratched down these notes, Lake recalled their question about Dr. Hoss. What had that meant? she wondered. Did Hoss have a short fling of her own with Keaton—and was it possible she murdered him because he'd dumped her? She didn't look like the type to accept rejection easily.

But the most disturbing thing had been what they'd said at the end: that someone had reported that Lake had seemed upset since the murder, not herself. The only person who had appeared to pick up on that was Harry. She couldn't understand why he would have betrayed her. Did he really suspect her? Had he just been pumping her on Sunday, not really concerned about her well-being? She wondered if the cops had bought her explanation for her display of nerves. Or did they already suspect her of having been the one in Keaton's bed that night? They'd seemed intent on rattling her, going in circles with their questions.

She had to reach Kit Archer. If there was something going on at the clinic, there was a chance he knew what it was. And who else could she ask? She reached for the phone but this time she knew she had to leave a message and pray he called back. So it was a total shock when after three rings, a smooth, deep voice said, "Archer."

"Mr. Archer," she said, caught off guard. "My name is Lake Warren. I read the piece you wrote on fertility clinics. Do you have a minute?"

There was a pause as he digested what she'd said.

"Okay," he replied. "What can I do for you?" He sounded mildly receptive, like a reporter who knew that sometimes leads came from cold calls like this one.

"I was hoping to speak to you—about the same topic."

"Are you a patient at a clinic?"

"No, I work at one—as a marketing consultant."

As soon as she said the words, it hit her. She was violating the trust of her employer. But she had no choice, not if she wanted to learn the truth.

"Which one?"

"I—I'd rather not say over the phone. I was hoping we could meet in person."

"But what exactly do you want to talk about? You've got to give me a little more to go on here."

She hadn't thought this far ahead. What *did* she want to talk about? Simply the fact that she'd come across his article in a file? That would sound silly.

"You brought up some interesting points in your article," she said, scrambling. "I'm just worried that there could be irregularities at the clinic I'm working at."

"What kind of irregularities?"

"Again, I'd prefer not to get into it over the phone."

"Well, we'd be happy to hear what you have to say. Can I have my producer give you a call and she can arrange to meet with you?"

Damn, she thought. She had to keep trying.

"But I'd really prefer to talk directly to you—and as soon as possible."

"Why the rush?"

"There's a certain urgency. I can explain when I see you."

"Why don't you tell me the name of the clinic? Otherwise we're going to be just pussyfooting around."

"You won't be going anywhere with it at this point, right?"

"Nope—we're just talking."

"It's called the Advanced Fertility Center—on Park Avenue."

There was a pause, and she could almost hear him thinking.

"One of your doctors met a pretty ugly death last week," he said.

She caught her breath. Of course, she thought. Because of Keaton's connection to a fertility clinic, Archer would have found the murder particularly noteworthy.

"Yes," Lake said quietly.

"I'd be willing to talk," Archer said, "but I've got some scheduling problems. I leave town on Wednesday for a story, and I'm not sure how long I'll be gone. Maybe just a couple days, maybe more."

"Is there any way you could meet today, or tomorrow?"

"Today's totally out," he said. "But I could probably meet you tomorrow. I've got an event in the early evening but I should be able to steal a few minutes right before then."

Archer suggested they meet at five-thirty at the Peacock Alley bar in the Waldorf-Astoria, right before his event, which was in the ballroom there. He rattled off his cell phone number; and she offered a brief physical description of herself and gave him her own cell phone number.

This is a start, she told herself as she hung up. Please, please let something come of it.

She made coffee, carried a mug of it into her office, and opened her laptop. No matter how distracted she felt, she knew she had to generate more ideas for her presentation. She emailed both the Web designer she had recruited and the person she had in mind for day-to-day PR, asking them for a few ideas by tomorrow. She'd originally given them a deadline of two weeks from now, thinking she wouldn't need their input for her initial presentation to Levin and Sherman. But she was desperate now.

Later she sent one fax to both Amy and Will. She'd drawn a

little picture of herself and Smokey looking draggy from the heat. When she first started writing the kids, earlier in the summer, she'd been struck by how dull her life was. Now she would give anything to have all that dullness back.

As she slid into bed that night she thought she might fall asleep instantly from sheer mental exhaustion, but it was clear after thirty minutes of thrashing in the sheets that sleep wasn't going to arrive. She tossed and turned a little while longer and then finally dragged herself out of bed, leaving Smokey still draped over a pillow. In her white cotton nightgown, she paced the long hall of her apartment like a ghost. The apartment was deadly quiet, except for the drip of a faucet somewhere—in Will's bathroom, she guessed.

At one point during her lonely, restless prowl, she stopped in the foyer and studied the silver-framed photos on the hall table. There were shots not only of her kids but of friends, too—sitting on the porch in Roxbury, celebrating a birthday, laughing together in Riverside Park. If only she could turn to one of those people now, she thought. But since her split with Jack, she'd let her friendships drift, out of embarrassment, or, in the case of people like Steve's sister, Sonia, because their coupled-up lives now seemed out of sync with hers.

Suddenly, out of the corner of her eye, she registered movement on the ground to her right. She jerked her head in that direction, thinking it was Smokey, but there was no sign of him. As her eyes swept around the foyer, she realized with a jolt what she'd seen. On the parquet floor by the door, the narrow strip of light from the outside corridor had just been broken. There was a shadow in the middle now. Someone was standing on the other side of her door.

It was after two a.m. Who could possibly be there? she wondered anxiously. She stood frozen in place, staring at the slightly ragged strip of shadow. And then the doorbell rang.

15

THE SOUND MADE her reel backward. Who would come to her apartment at this hour? And why hadn't the doorman rung up first?

"Who's there?" she called out from where she stood.

The doorbell rang again. This time longer, more insistent.

"Who is it?" she called, louder now. After a few seconds she forced herself toward the door and squinted into the peephole. There was no one in view.

Tiptoeing backward, she saw that the shadow was gone now. She put her ear to the door, straining to hear. She thought she could hear the faint sound of footsteps moving away. She waited for the deep purr of the elevator but it never came.

She stabbed at the intercom button. While she waited for a response, she pressed her ear against the door one more time. Silence.

"May I help you?" a sluggish male voice answered.

"This is Lake Warren in 12B. Someone just rang my bell. Did you send someone up here?"

A pause followed, as if he had to think about it.

"No—no, I didn't. No one has gone up for a while."

"Well, who do you think it could have been?"

"What did the person look like?"

"I didn't see," she said in frustration. "When I looked through the peephole, no one was there."

"Some people went up a while ago to a party on eleven. Maybe someone got off on the wrong floor. Do you want me to come up?"

"No, that's okay."

She wondered if it was like he said, someone just ringing the wrong bell. Or had the doorman fallen asleep at the front desk, allowing a stranger to slip by in the night? Had it been Keaton's killer standing on the other side of her door? Someone from the clinic, or a person paid to stalk her? Whoever it was, maybe they'd started with her cat and were now proving they could get even closer.

She stared at the door. There was a security chain but it seemed so flimsy now, like popcorn strung on a piece of string for a Christmas tree. After setting the pictures on their side, she dragged the hall table in front of the door. Still, she felt too anxious to go back to bed. She fell onto the couch in the living room and pulled a throw blanket over her. The dull light of dawn was seeping through the windows when she finally drifted off to sleep.

She woke feeling achy, with the back of her throat raw. I can't get sick right now, she told herself. Scenes from the previous night flooded her brain. For a few moments she wondered if the ringing doorbell had been just a dream. She lifted Smokey from his perch on top of her feet and stumbled toward the front door. The hall table jammed against the front door told her she hadn't been dreaming.

She dragged the table back to where it belonged and opened the door, with the chain still in place. She could see her *New York Times* lying on the mat. After taking the chain off, she opened the door more fully and checked the hall. It was empty.

As she was scooping up the paper, she heard the locks being unbolted on the door catty-corner from hers, the apartment belonging to the Tammens. From what she knew, the wife and kids were out in the Hamptons for all of August, and the father, Stan, was commuting out on weekends. It was Stan who stepped out in the hallway now, stifling a yawn.

"Morning," he said. "You guys aren't on vacation this month?"

"No, not this year. Listen, I'm a little concerned about something that happened last night."

"What is it?" he asked.

"Someone rang my doorbell around two this morning. And when I called out, the person just left. I didn't see who it was."

Stan scrunched his mouth and slowly shook his head.

"Can't help you with that one," he said. "I mean, I was here, but I didn't hear or see anything."

After closing her door, she popped three ibuprofen and gargled with salt water. Then she made coffee and forced herself to eat a bowl of yogurt. She hadn't eaten right in nearly a week.

Staring out her kitchen window, as the summer air shimmered around the gray and red brick apartment buildings to the north, she thought of the day ahead. Her plan was to stay home and scramble to finish the presentation—until it was time to meet Kit Archer. It was a relief not to have to go into the clinic today—and wonder if the killer was watching her every move. But she needed to call in, at least. Levin was waiting for an answer about when she'd give the presentation. At eight-thirty she picked up the phone, knowing that most people would be in by now.

She asked the receptionist for Steve first, hoping that he'd somehow managed to buy her more time.

"I'm sorry, I tried," he said when she reached him. "But Tom seems to be on a tear right now and thinks we need to see the plan ASAP."

"No problem," she said, not wanting to give even a hint she was agitated. "I'll set up an appointment for the presentation."

"I hope you don't feel like he's bullying you. I think this murder has him really on edge."

Because he might have been the one who orchestrated the whole thing, she thought to herself.

"I'm sure he's worried about all the police scrutiny," Lake said. She waited, wondering if Steve would mention the keys.

"Of course. We all are," he said, sounding suddenly distracted. "Wait—before I let you go, I've got a proposition for you. Ever since last week, I've felt things have been a little awkward between us. I'm really sorry about that situation with the police. Sonia would strangle me if she knew I upset you."

"Why don't we let it go, Steve," she said, bristling at the memory. "It seems the police accepted my explanation."

"Okay, but here's my proposition: Hilary and I would love you to come by for a drink tonight. You haven't seen our place since we redid it—and you haven't seen Matthew since he was a baby."

"Tonight's not good," she said, almost too quickly.

"How about tomorrow night?"

"Um . . . okay, sure." There would be no way to put him off indefinitely without him sensing something was wrong.

He reminded her of his address and suggested she stop by at seven. Then she asked to be transferred to Brie. When Brie picked up her line Lake got right to the point.

"I want to schedule my appointment to present to Dr. Levin and Dr. Sherman," she said. "Is Thursday afternoon good for them?"

Thursday bought her another two days. She would have liked to stretch it to Friday but she knew Levin would not be pleased.

"Thursdays are usually insane around here," Brie said. "It's going to have to be Wednesday. Or even today."

The woman was clearly a graduate of the Be a Better Bitch Academy, Lake thought.

"Unfortunately, as I mentioned when he suggested moving it up, I have several long-standing appointments with other clients," Lake lied. "Thursday is the first day I can do it."

Brie sighed audibly and began tapping into her computer, checking the calendar.

"Six-thirty on Thursday might work," she said brusquely. "If you don't hear from me, plan on doing it then."

Lake wanted to talk to Maggie but rather than ask to be transferred, she hung up and called the main number again so Brie wouldn't know. She worried Maggie might start to find all her attention odd—but she had to know if there were any new developments. She would express concern for Maggie's state of mind and hope Maggie would fill her in on everything.

It was Rory who ended up picking up the phone.

"Oh, hi, it's Lake," she said. "I was looking for Maggie."

"Maggie took the day off," Rory said in a low voice.

"Is everything okay?" Lake asked, her concern piqued.

"From what I hear, she said she needed a day off to de-stress."

"Oh . . . well, how are *you* doing?"

"To be perfectly honest, I'm worried about my baby. Last night I thought I was having contractions and I ended up going to the ER. It turned out it was just Braxton-Hicks, but it scared me."

"Oh, Rory, I'm so sorry. You can't take some time off?"

"Unfortunately that isn't possible, especially if Maggie's going to call in sick. It's important for us to keep things together here, even if we're upset. Emily thought Maggie was being silly for acting so scared, but now that she heard about the keys, even *she's* wigged out."

"Do you think someone could have taken those keys and then put them back?"

"That's what the police were asking. Those detectives were back here yesterday for, like, an hour—after you left. The creepy thing is, I sit right next to Maggie—our desks actually *touch*."

"And you never saw anyone going into her desk drawer?"

"No, not that I recall. Sometimes people—"

She paused then, as if interrupted or lost in thought. After a moment Lake wondered if she was still on the line.

"Rory?" she asked.

"I better go," Rory said.

"But what were you going to say?"

"Um, nothing. I need to go. Dr. Levin is waiting."

Lake hung up reluctantly. She couldn't tell if Rory had been distracted or had just remembered something and was holding back on it. Lake tried Hayden next, anxious to connect to someone else who could update her, but the call went to voice mail.

After popping one more ibuprofen, Lake glued herself to her desk in her home office, her laptop opened in front of her. Both the PR person and the Web designer had come through for her, emailing their initial ideas. Neither batch was so dazzling that they'd scorch anyone's corneas, but at least she had a few decent items to add to her list. She tapped away at her computer, shepherding her bullet points into categories so her PowerPoint would be easier to create. Generally this was the part of her work that she loved—organizing all her ideas and in the process tweaking them to be even better—but today she had to constantly force herself to concentrate on her task. Her mind relentlessly found its way back to a new tangle of worries: Rory's unfinished comment; the doorbell last night; and the police visit yesterday. Did Hull's surliness toward her *mean* something? Was she a suspect in the case?

Just once she got up to make tea. Though her throat felt less raw, the achiness all over her body had intensified.

At eleven, Hayden returned her call, though her attention had already been diverted by the time Lake answered.

"I don't care if he sends the damn *love train*, I'm not attending," Lake heard her yell to some underling.

"Oh, hi," she said, turning back to Lake on the line. "You know, I must be getting old. My idea of a good time these days is staying home with an ice-cold bottle of Pinot Grigio and a bag of rosemary-scented potato chips."

Lake had no time right now for Hayden's chatter. "Anything up?" she said, trying to move the conversation along.

"We're in a holding pattern at the moment. Levin called last night to report that the police had been there *again* yesterday. They're clearly concerned by the fact that Keaton's keys were sitting in a drawer where anyone could have put their little hands on them. So far that fact hasn't leaked out, but it's not an easy nugget to contain. The police may even leak it themselves to see what they flush out. And of course if they do arrest someone from the clinic, all hell is gonna break loose."

"Do you think Levin has any ideas?"

"About what to do?"

"No, I mean about the keys—who from the clinic might have used them to get into Keaton's apartment."

"If he does, he's sure not telling me. My sense is that his wheels are constantly spinning but I can't always detect what's going on in there. Maybe he's just thinking about ordering a new batch of four-hundred-dollar shirts."

Lake wondered if it had occurred to Hayden that Levin himself might be the killer. But she wasn't going to raise that point.

"Well, I won't keep you," Lake said. "Will you let me know if you hear anything? I just want to be aware of what's up—you know, as I plot out the marketing."

They promised to stay in touch and hung up. After forcing herself to eat lunch, Lake began to design the actual PowerPoint. When she worked she often found herself in what people called "the zone," the experience of being so engrossed in a task that it felt blissful. Today every step seemed like agony. At three she began to check her watch. She needed to allow herself plenty of time to get down to the Waldorf.

As she opened her closet door, mulling over what to wear, she pictured herself in the same exact spot almost a week ago, clothes heaped on her bed as she sought the perfect outfit to intrigue Keaton. If only I could take it all back, she thought. If only I'd never gone out that night.

She chose a lavender cotton suit with three-quarter-length sleeves. It was a little dressy, but she needed Archer to take her seriously.

After the cab dropped her off, she entered the Waldorf from the Park Avenue side. The lobby was cool and quiet and almost empty, like the inside of a medieval church on a hot summer day. A few groups of tourists milled around the concierge desk or made their way sluggishly to the elevators, lugging black suitcases on rollers and shopping bags from the Disney store. Most were dressed down in cutoffs and T-shirts that said things like NIKE and VEGAS 2005 and BLASTED PARROT PUB AND SHOT SHACK.

Peacock Alley was a bar and small restaurant in an open area that spilled out to the left of the lobby. Though Lake had been to the Waldorf ballroom for events, she'd set foot in that bar only once—years ago, on a night not long after she'd moved to New

York. She and a girlfriend, both new to the city, had made a list of things they might do for fun, and "Visit famous hotel bars" had been one of them. She had a vague recollection of it being decorated in peacock blue, but now it was all honey-colored wood and black marble.

According to the gilded clock in the lobby, it was only five-twenty and there was no sign yet of Archer. She lifted herself onto a leather bar chair and ordered a sparkling water. The bartender slid a small dish of olives in front of her. She rehearsed in her mind what she intended to say.

The lobby clock had just chimed on the half hour when she looked up and spotted Archer. He was better-looking in person than in the video she'd seen, perhaps because his face wasn't caked with foundation. He had on a tux, which he wore easily, not like one of those men who complained of having to wear a "monkey suit," but like someone who'd worn tuxes all his life, who'd been thrown into pools wearing them in his twenties and had probably never had to rent one.

Her face opened up as she recognized him, causing him to make his way purposely to her.

"Lake Warren?" he asked, his hand already out to her.

"Yes," she said, taking it. His handshake was firm, and he gripped her hand almost without moving it. "Thanks for coming."

"Is there an actual Lake Warren someplace in the world?" he asked, his eyes curious. They were a soft blue, Lake noticed.

"Probably," she said. "But I haven't heard of it. And as far as I know I wasn't conceived there."

He kicked his head back and smiled.

"Well, even if you were, it's nice of your parents not to tell you. Kids hate hearing that kind of stuff." He looked at her glass. "What are you drinking? I'm going to have a beer."

She hesitated and then said she'd have one, too. She needed

Archer as her ally and wanted to get in sync with him. After snagging the bartender's attention with just a lift of his chin, Archer ordered their beers and turned his attention back to her.

"I wish I had more time," he said. "I'm supposed to be up in the ballroom for some kind of photo op in fifteen minutes. But until then I'm all yours."

"Then I'm going to be perfectly honest with you," she said, holding his gaze. "I don't have much to go on. But I have a vague sense that something weird might be happening at the clinic."

"Weird how?"

Lake's left shoulder shot up instinctively.

"I'm not sure."

He raised his beer bottle to his lips, not bothering with the glass. She sensed his impatience, though he was doing his damnedest to contain it.

"Was it something you saw—or overheard?" he said after taking a long drag of beer.

"As I said on the phone, I'm a marketing consultant for the clinic. While I was doing research there last week, I found a copy of the article you wrote about the fertility business. I was carrying it around, planning to read it later, and one of the partners saw me with it. He grabbed it away from me—like he didn't want me to see it."

Archer raised his eyebrows. They were white, like his hair.

"Is that it?" he asked.

She hesitated and looked off to the side. Her concerns were also based on the "snag" Keaton had mentioned. But she couldn't tell Archer that. She watched him take another swig of his beer. His hands were large, huge really, and slightly ruddy, like his cheeks. No wedding band. When he set the bottle down, he looked directly at her.

"Yes," she said. "Like I said, I don't have much to go on. I just thought if you could tell me what irregularities *might* exist, it would help me figure out if something was actually going on."

Her whole body had begun to prickle with anxiety. She'd not only just betrayed the clinic but suddenly she had the sense that she'd left herself exposed.

"What's the matter?" he asked, clearly picking up on her discomfort.

"I'm worried I've opened a can of worms—perhaps for no reason."

He watched her for a moment and then shook his head.

"I don't think so," he said. "Because you're not the first person to suggest there's something bad going on there."

16

HER MOUTH PARTED in surprise. It was a validation of what her gut had been telling her and yet his words were still a shock.

"Who else told you that?" she asked.

"First tell me about this Dr. Keaton," he said. "Did you know him?"

At the mention of Keaton's name, she could feel the blood rush recklessly to her face. She reached for her beer bottle, which she'd left untouched so far, splashed a little into her glass and took a sip. The coldness soothed her raw throat.

"Just in passing," she said, avoiding his glance as she set the glass back down. "I've only worked at the clinic for a few weeks."

"Do you think someone from the clinic might have killed him?"

Lake was slightly surprised by his direct question, but also relieved not to have to beat around the bush.

"It's possible," she said. "We learned yesterday that he'd

given one of the nurses a set of his apartment keys and she'd left them in her desk. Someone could have swiped them and made copies."

"Do you think there could be a connection between his death and the suspicions you've had about the clinic?"

"I've definitely worried about that. Though this all could just be a coincidence," she said.

"You know what I'm going to say, of course," he said with his eyebrows raised. "As a reporter, you learn there are few coincidences."

"Can you *please* tell me what you've heard about the clinic?" Lake urged.

"Okay. About two months ago a woman called my producer Rachel out of the blue. She'd come across the same article you saw while she was doing a search online. She'd been a patient at the Advanced Fertility Center—of Dr. Daniel Sherman specifically— and said that we ought to do an investigation of the clinic. She claimed they were exploiting innocent patients and they needed to be exposed. My article was on Washington area clinics—I was living there at the time—but the subject overall interests me."

"What did she mean by exploiting?"

"She refused to go into it on the phone. She set up a meeting with Rachel but Rachel had to reschedule because of some breaking news. Then, the day before their appointment, the woman called to say *she* had to reschedule and would get back in touch. That was a few weeks ago and we haven't heard from her since."

"What do you think she could be referring to?"

"Take a guess. You're the one who works there."

"I've never seen anything suspicious, but then again I'm not involved with the patients in any way. Plus, the fertility world is pretty new to me. Something could be going on right under my nose and I wouldn't know it." She paused. "You mentioned in your article that some clinics encourage procedures people don't really need. That may be a possibility."

"They could also be inflating their success rates," he said. "That's a big factor when someone is choosing a clinic."

"I read that in your piece, that some clinics do that. I can't believe there isn't outside auditing done on those numbers."

"I know. It's a three-billion-dollar business with lots of competition and very little government regulation."

Was the clinic capable of such things? Lake wondered. Overcharging desperate couples? Pumping up their success rates? Both Levin and Sherman—and Hoss, too—were certainly arrogant, and arrogant people often played by different rules.

"So there's a chance this woman could be right?" Lake asked.

"It's possible—though Rachel said she sounded like a bit of a nut job. Some high-maintenance Manhattan type who's never been denied anything. I called the clinic myself and talked to Sherman. That's probably why they had my article on file—they must have checked me out. He told me that this woman had emotional difficulties because of her failure to conceive and that her claims were baseless. I'd caught him off guard and he was pretty pissed. Said if I had anything further to say, I should speak to his attorney."

"Is that why you haven't tried harder to connect with her— because she might be unstable?"

"Partly. I've also been swamped with stories lately. But in light of Keaton's death—and then your call—my interest has shot way up. Something could be going on there that needs to be exposed."

Lake picked at the wet label on her beer bottle as her mind raced. Maybe Keaton *had* stumbled onto the fact that the clinic was involved in wrongdoing and had threatened to expose them. If the doctors there were engaged in unethical activities and the truth was brought to light, everything would be lost—not just the clinic, but people's reputations and careers, even their medical licenses. That offered a perfect motive for murder.

But one detail still didn't jibe. According to Maggie, Keaton had changed his locks since the late winter. If he'd uncovered something negative about the clinic then, and was concerned for his safety, why return this summer? Unless he decided it was his duty to dig up more evidence.

When she looked up she saw that Archer had slipped a credit card from a weathered brown wallet and was laying it on the bar.

"I hate to split," he said, "but the publicist for the show is going to have my head if I don't get up there on time."

"I understand. Can I get this? I appreciate your taking the time."

"No, it's on me. But there *is* one thing you can do."

Of course, she thought. Reporters like him were relentless.

"What?" she asked.

"Why don't you nose around a little bit at the clinic?"

Lake caught her breath. "You want me to *spy*? I—"

"Hear me out. These clinics are like fortresses—it's going to be impossible for anyone to get in and investigate without real proof of wrongdoing. Having you on the inside gives us a big advantage."

"What exactly would I be looking for?" she asked tentatively.

"Tough to say since this woman didn't give specifics. I'd see if you could find out what their real success rates are and compare them to what they tell prospective patients. I'd go through as many patient records as you can and make a note of what procedures people are having. Does anything seem *excessive*?"

She stared at the wooden bar, trying to decide what to do. The idea scared the hell out of her. She could barely handle Brie snooping. And as far as Lake knew, the killer could be watching her, too.

Archer studied her, clearly sensing her hesitancy.

"Look, I know this might put you in an awkward situation. But this could be an important story that needs to see the light of day. And time is of the essence. If Keaton's death is related to any wrongdoing, they may try to destroy the evidence."

"All right," she said finally. "I'll see what I can find. What's the name of the woman who called you? I should start with her file."

"Alexis Hunt," he said, scrawling his signature on the credit card receipt. "Would you have a legitimate reason to be going through patient records?"

"No. Technically I don't have the right to look at them."

"Be very careful, then. And call me if you find anything."

She withdrew a business card from her purse and as she handed it to him, the tips of her fingers touched his.

"My home number is on there, too."

"Have you got kids yourself?" he asked.

"Two—they're away at camp right now." The thought of them flooded her with worry all over again. "How about you?"

"A twenty-three-year-old stepson from my former marriage. I kind of think of him as my own, though. Are you walking out now?"

"I'm going to finish my beer," she said.

"Okay. Good luck—and call me if you run into any trouble."

She watched him leave, threading his way confidently through the tables, seemingly oblivious to the out-of-towners who trailed him with their eyes. As she picked up her glass, she caught a man sitting solo focus on her and then quickly glance down. Women alone at hotel bars were always slightly suspect, she knew, but she didn't want to leave until she had made sense of all the thoughts colliding in her head.

She'd probably been foolish to let Archer tap her as a spy. For him it was all about the story and making a major splash on *Reveal*. But for her it was a whole different game. She was already in a precarious situation, and this could make things even worse. Right now there were warning signs that the killer suspected she knew something about the murder. If Keaton's death was tied to wrong-doing at the clinic and she learned what that wrongdoing was, the killer would have a concrete reason to harm her. And if there was wrongdoing that *wasn't* tied to Keaton's death, her spying would expose her to danger from a new front. It was double jeopardy.

And yet, she also knew that learning the truth could ultimately help her escape from the nightmare she'd found herself living through. The police would focus on the clinic and not on her.

She massaged her temples, thinking desperately. She was done with her research at the clinic, but she'd have to show up to-morrow pretending she still needed to do more—and she'd have to be careful not to make anyone, especially snoopy Brie, suspicious. The patient files were in the same storage room as the files she'd been researching, so at least she'd have a reason to be in that room. But *what* would she be looking for exactly?

An idea suddenly gurgled up in her mind: What if she spoke to Alexis Hunt directly? That way she might have a clearer sense of what she needed to search for. She'd need to talk to her soon. Lake rifled through her purse for her BlackBerry and called 411. There was an A. Hunt at 20 East Seventy-eighth Street. Archer had called the woman high maintenance. Well, that fit with the Upper East Side address.

Lake eased herself off the bar stool, deciding to make the call then and there—but outside, where there'd be less noise. As she strode from the bar, she thought she caught the man alone at the table checking her out again—this time above a folded newspaper. Did he assume she was an aging hooker?

Spilling out of the revolving door on Park Avenue, she saw that the sidewalk was churning with tourists, all eager for cabs, so she turned onto Forty-ninth Street and found a quiet spot midway down the block. She held her breath as she waited for someone to pick up the phone. After four rings a woman offered a blunt hello.

"Alexis Hunt?" Lake asked.

"Who is this?" the woman demanded.

"My name is Lake Warren. I—I know you have some concerns about the Advanced Fertility Center. I'd really like to discuss them with you."

"Are you a patient there?"

"No, but—there's a chance I may be able to help you. Can we meet and talk?"

"How did you get my name?" No nonsense. Not the least bit friendly.

"Kit Archer." Lake hated having to use his name but she could tell if she didn't, Alexis was quickly going to hang up.

"Do you work with him?"

"No, but I spoke with him. I have some concerns like you do."

A few seconds of silence followed.

"All right," she said. "I'm just off Madison on Seventy-eighth. How long will it take for you to get here?"

"You want me to come *now*?" Lake asked, startled.

"I don't do lunch, if that's what you had in mind."

"Okay, I can come now," Lake said. "I'm about ten minutes away."

Lake hailed a cab and collapsed against the backseat. She couldn't believe she'd done this. Calling Archer was one thing; meeting with a patient was definitely crossing the line. It felt like such a bold move, one that might even annoy Archer if he found out. But she'd already set it into motion, and it was too late to turn back now.

Alexis Hunt's apartment was in a pricey-looking prewar building. The doorman rang up and then directed Lake to 14B, which turned out to be one of only two apartments on the fourteenth floor. From the voice on the phone and the tiny bit Lake knew of her background, Lake had formed a picture of Alexis in her mind: someone older, hardened and bitter from what she'd gone through, perhaps even furious at the world that boxed smart, ambitious women into marrying late and thus trying to conceive when the odds were against them. So Lake was startled, then, when the door swung open and she was greeted by a fairly pretty, composed woman who seemed no older than thirty-two or thirty-three. She had blond hair styled in a plain, preppy bob, green eyes, and a tiny mouth dabbed with berry-colored lipstick. Though she was slightly overweight, she wore a green-and-white wrap dress that flattered her figure, the kind you often saw on well-heeled suburban women who still dressed to go into town. She didn't look like a nut job. She looked like someone who was about to share her recipe for spinach and artichoke dip.

"Come in," was all she said. Lake stepped inside and followed her into the living room.

The apartment was what you might expect in that building—classy but blandly decorated in muted blues and greens. Lake could see a small library off one end of the living room and a dining room at the other, and she guessed there were probably two bedrooms off the long hallway. There was something oddly unlived-in about the space—no mail or keys scattered on the hall table, no magazine left open on the couch.

"I'm still not clear who you are or why you called me," Alexis said bluntly. She took a seat on an antique straight-back chair, the least comfortable-looking piece in the room. Maybe she doesn't *want* to get comfortable, Lake thought. She chose the blue chintz couch but perched just on the edge of it.

"I've been looking into fertility clinics," Lake said. "I came across Kit Archer's article and tracked him down. He told me about his producer's discussion with you."

"So you're an investigator of some kind?"

"No, not that. I—"

"Are you writing a book or something?"

"No—not a book. It just happens that I have a reason to be researching the Advanced Fertility Center clinic. Mr. Archer told me you have some issues with them."

A smile suddenly formed on Alexis's face, a surprising move given her coldness so far. It was a tiny, wicked smile that suggested she was about to dish on a bad boy they'd both known in college. The composure had all been a front, Lake realized, just a thin, fragile coating for the woman's fury.

"Not issues *plural*," Alexis said. "Just one. They completely destroyed my life."

"How?"

"Excuse me for seeming dense, but I'm still a little confused," Alexis said. There was a real edge now to her voice, as if a screw had been tightened. "What's your motive in all of this—and why do you expect me to cooperate?"

"Another person—someone familiar with the clinic—has raised concerns about them," Lake said. "If they're guilty of wrongdoing, they need to be exposed."

"Aren't *we* the concerned citizen," Alexis said mockingly.

I'm losing ground, Lake thought anxiously. She had to try a different approach.

"Do you mind my asking what kind of procedure you underwent with Dr. Sherman? Was it in vitro?"

"Oh, we'd be here all night if I described everything," Alexis said. She was forcing such a hard, fake smile it looked as if her cheeks would burst. "At first I did intrauterine insemination, sometimes fondly known as the turkey-baster method, except they really use a plastic catheter to shoot the sperm up inside you. Then there were the hormone cocktails I had to inject in my belly. And let's not forget the progesterone suppositories. Lovely. *Then* we proceeded to IVF."

"You're so young. What was the problem?"

"I had cysts on my ovaries—which came as a complete and utter shock. Not only had there never been any symptoms, but I'd gotten pregnant easily several years before. As it turns out, my first pregnancy had pretty much defied the laws of probability—and the chances of it happening again *naturally* were next to nil."

Instinctively Lake's eyes flicked around the room, searching for a sign of the child. On top of a mahogany side table at the far end of the couch was a silver-framed photograph of a toddler, about fifteen months old. From where she sat Lake couldn't make out the child's features, but it was impossible to miss the halo of hair so blond it was nearly white.

"Yes," Alexis said, catching the movement. "My daughter Charlotte."

"And she's about three now?" Lake said. But as she spoke the words, an eerie feeling enveloped her. There was no other evidence of the child anywhere.

"No," Alexis said. "She died of meningitis when she was eighteen months old."

The words hit Lake like a punch to the stomach.

"I'm terribly sorry," she said.

"Do you have children?"

"Two."

Alexis stared at Lake, her eyes suddenly wide and blank. For a brief moment she looked like a character on a horror-movie poster, a mother whose children have been abducted by aliens or lured away forever by gremlins hiding in the cracks of the floorboards.

"Then you can at least imagine what it would be like," Alexis said. "Honestly, a few people actually suggested that my grief must not be so bad because Charlotte wasn't really a person yet."

"How terrible," Lake said. "I—I assume you were never successful in having another child?"

"Very good guess," Alexis said, flashing the evil grin again. "Oh, Dr. Sherman insisted I would be. I had plenty of eggs—in his words, a virtual plethora of healthy eggs—and it was just a matter of time getting one of our test-tube embryos to implant in my uterus. After the fourth attempt I was ready to try another clinic but Sherman practically insisted we stay. He just *knew* it would happen. So I stupidly gave him one more chance—and then another. It was all an utter failure."

"But why not try another clinic *now*? They each have different areas of expertise. Maybe you'd have luck at one of the bigger ones affiliated with a medical center."

"I *was* going to start someplace else—at Cornell, as a matter of fact. But then my husband ran for the hills. He didn't find fertility treatment all that fun, though it's hard to imagine why. Stabbing a needle in my ass every night, watching me fatten up like Jabba the Hut on the drugs and then turn into a screaming maniac. What's not to like?"

Lake almost winced.

"What about having a child without your husband?" Lake asked. "Did the clinic freeze any of your embryos?"

"There *were* extra embryos—plenty of them—but Brian wouldn't give me permission to use them. He found someone else. So the last thing he wanted was a baby with me."

Lake bit her lip, thinking. She needed to nail down Alexis's specific complaint.

"When you told Archer's office that the clinic was exploiting people, did you mean because they pushed you to have treatments that had little chance of working?"

Alexis eyed her guardedly. The wariness was back.

"Partly," she answered.

"Was there anything else? Did they ever—um—overcharge you, for instance?"

Alexis stared at Lake quietly for a moment, her whole body still.

"I've shared an awful lot of information with you," Alexis said finally. "And I don't have anything else to tell you."

Then she shot up from her chair, indicating that it was time for Lake to leave.

"But I want to help," Lake said, rising too. "I really do."

"You say you want to help, but you refuse to tell me your real agenda," Alexis said, marching out of the living room with Lake in tow.

Lake started to protest, but she could see that it was hopeless. Alexis had said all she was going to say. When they reached the front door, Alexis swung it open.

"Have a nice evening," Alexis said flatly as Lake stepped into the hall.

"Thank you for seeing me. I just wish I knew—"

Alexis flashed the tight fake smile again.

"As the French say, '*Cherchez la femme.*'"

And then she shut the door in Lake's face.

CHERCHEZ LA FEMME.

Translation: *Look for the woman.* What had Alexis meant by *that?* In old detective novels the phrase was uttered to suggest that a woman was the root of the trouble, but Lake doubted Alexis had used the cliché literally. Rather, the remark seemed to be her cryptic way of saying there was something else, a secret she hadn't been willing to divulge. As Lake rode down in the elevator, she let her body sag against one of the walls. She'd been within arm's reach of that secret but Alexis hadn't trusted her enough to share it. Lake would have to look at Alexis's file for a clue.

It was nearly dusk when the cab let her off in front of her apartment building, the time of day she'd always loved best in summer. Tonight, though, it filled her with dread. She'd have to go to bed soon, and potentially face the mystery doorbell ringer again. Before stepping into her building, she looked quickly up and down the block. The only people in sight were two preteen boys whipping a wiffle ball back and forth in front of the building next door.

"Is everything okay, Mrs. Warren?" Bob the doorman asked her as she stepped into the lobby. He must have seen her glance furtively down the street.

"Yes, thanks, Bob," she said. "I'm just a little nervous about what's happening. You know, the murder of the doctor I worked with."

"But is everything okay with the police?" he said.

Great, she thought. All she needed was for Bob to mention the police visit to Jack.

"Oh, they were just interviewing everyone who works at the clinic. For background. It's all very routine."

Bob stared at her, his face pinched. He drew a small business card out of his jacket pocket and handed it to her.

"They were here again today," he said solemnly.

Lake forced a smile as she reached for the card.

"Oh, it's just a follow-up visit," she said. "They just need to learn everything they can about the doctor. . . . Well, have a good night."

Hurrying to the elevator, she stole a look at the card. It was McCarty's business card, with a cell phone number listed. In ball-point pen he had scribbled, "Please give me a call."

Is this how they get you to confess? she thought as she rode to her floor. They show up at your home again and again, asking bewildering questions that leave you feeling as if you're about to blow. Or, she wondered, was there some new development—something linking her to Keaton? Suddenly she could barely breathe.

As soon as she had locked the door to her apartment and dragged the hall table back against it, she poured a large glass of white wine. She took two huge swigs before punching McCarty's number into her BlackBerry.

She got his voice mail. Natch, she thought, part of the torture. Let her simmer in her own terror until he finally called her back.

She wanted more wine but she didn't dare—it was critical to keep her wits about her. After microwaving one of the frozen mac-and-cheese dinners she kept around for the kids, she carried it to her office and opened her laptop to the PowerPoint presentation. It needed more work and she was running out of time. But after skimming the first page a few times, she realized she was too frazzled to concentrate.

By the time McCarty called back, twenty minutes later, Lake was walking in circles around her office.

"Lake Warren?" he asked. Her name sounded foreign when he said it, as if he were inquiring about a complete stranger.

"Yes," she answered nervously.

"This is Detective McCarty. I take it your doorman told you we dropped by?" There was a sudden surge of traffic sounds behind him. He might actually be in her neighborhood, she realized, coiled and waiting for the chance to come by.

"Yes. He did. I'm sorry I missed you."

He said nothing back.

"Um, how can I help you?" she asked.

"We were wondering if you thought about what we discussed."

What the hell was he talking about? Was he implying that they were waiting for her to come clean about something?

"I'm not sure what you mean," she said haltingly.

"Now that you've had a chance to think, do you recall seeing anyone go into Ms. Donohue's drawer." The volume of his voice dropped as if he were glancing down and reading something.

She checked her relief. This might be a trap, she told herself.

"Uh, no, I didn't. I work in a small conference room in the back and I'm rarely near Maggie's desk."

There was a long pause. She pressed her lips together tightly, commanding herself not to fill the silence.

"All righty, then," he said finally. "Thank you for your cooperation."

"You're welcome. I—I'm happy to help."

"Great. I'm sure we will be back in touch."

As she ended the call, she felt tempted to hurl her BlackBerry. What had his last comment meant? Did they definitely have her in their sights as a suspect?

She barely slept that night. Her body seemed gripped with tension and her throat ached again. At around three, as she tossed back and forth in her tangled sheets, she realized that she'd neglected to fax the kids earlier. The thought of Amy lying in her bunk bed sad and worrying made Lake's heart ache.

It was drizzling outside when she dragged herself out of bed at six the next morning. Her sore throat seemed slightly improved but her heart had begun to race at the mere thought of the espionage mission ahead. She'd been so cavalier with Archer, jauntily agreeing to his suggestions, but now, as the time approached, she was nervous as hell.

She made coffee and noticed the message light blinking on the kitchen phone. She'd never checked when she'd returned home yesterday. The first call was from Molly, asking if she'd like to grab lunch today. The other was from Jack, saying he needed to talk to her. Go away, she wanted to scream at him.

She waited until ten to hail a cab to the clinic. The smartest approach, she knew, was to try to search through the files when everyone was preoccupied with patients. If she was lucky, she might even be able to avoid Brie altogether.

But she wasn't lucky. After passing through the packed reception area, filled today with men, too—their sober faces made her think of soldiers being shipped off to war—she immediately came face-to-face with Brie outside her small work alcove. She was wearing crisp white pants and a long-sleeved white shirt, and with her cropped red hair she looked to Lake like a giant matchstick.

"Morning, Brie," Lake said, trying to keep their exchange light.

"Can I help you?" Brie asked flatly, as if Lake were a stranger who'd pulled up alongside her to ask directions.

"No, I'm just dotting the *i*'s in my research. There are a few more things I need to read through."

"Really?" Brie said in mock surprise. "I would have thought you'd be done with that part by now. I mean, your presentation's *tomorrow*."

"I guess I'm just a stickler for detail." Lake knew sarcasm wasn't the best approach with Brie, but she hadn't been able to resist.

From there she threaded the maze of hushed corridors toward the small conference room. All the office and exam room doors were closed again today; behind some of them she could hear murmuring voices. She nearly jumped when Dr. Sherman emerged from one, closing the door quickly behind him. He nodded distractedly at Lake, his face flushed. She watched as he hurried down the hall and slipped into the lab.

In the conference room she dumped her purse and tote bag onto the table. For a moment she just stood there, deliberating. There was no reason to wait, she realized. She had to do it *now*. She took a pad and a pen with her in case she needed to write anything down.

As she turned the last corner toward the file room she nearly collided with Harry Kline.

"Oh, hey," he said genially. "How goes it?"

"Fine," she said as pleasantly as she could summon. She was still pretty sure he was the one who'd ratted her out to the cops—

telling them that she'd seemed upset since the murder—and she
had no interest in spending any time with him.

"I hear you're doing your presentation tomorrow."

"Yup. I'm just here to pick up a couple of files. Nice to see
you."

She could sense him following her with his eyes as she walked
away. Just wait, she thought—he'd probably tattle to the cops that
she was guilty of failing to engage in idle chitchat.

To her relief, no one was in the storage room—or in the kitchenette catty-corner to it. She had decided in advance that if someone
came in after her, it would seem odd for the door to be shut all the
way. So she shut it halfway and then dragged a small stepladder
behind it. That way if someone pushed the door open further, she'd
have a little warning.

She moved to the wall of patient files. Taking a stab at where the
H's might be, she pulled open a middle drawer. On the tabs
of the hanging files were last names beginning with *J* and *K*. She
slid the drawer shut and pulled open the one just to the left of it. The
first name she spotted was Havers—this was where she needed to
be. She flicked quickly through the row of hanging files. There it
was: Hunt, Alexis and Brian. She pulled the file from the drawer.

It bulged with papers. She skimmed quickly through them—
test results, more test results, details of the procedures per-
formed, including the IVFs. With her limited knowledge, it was
impossible to know if some of the procedures had been unnecessary. Alexis's situation had been complicated and she may have
truly needed all of it. Despite what Alexis had told her about
having plenty of frozen embryos on reserve, it appeared only two
were banked.

Lake laid the file on top of the open drawer, withdrew another
file at random and flipped through the contents. It wasn't as full
as the Hunt folder but just as impossible to interpret. She realized

that the only way to tell if something was wrong would be to photocopy some of the pages and get the objective opinion of another doctor. But the photocopy machine was adjacent to Brie's alcove and she couldn't risk it.

What if she could talk to other patients? she wondered. If something were going on, Alexis probably wasn't the only disgruntled person out there. She thought of the woman she'd seen Rory comfort—the one she'd discussed with Harry Kline. Though Harry hadn't mentioned the name, she'd heard Rory say it. Mrs. Kastner. Lake slipped the Hunt file back in its place, and after checking quickly behind her, pulled open the drawer to the right. There was a file for Sydney and Ryan Kastner, and it was even thicker than the Hunts'. As Harry had revealed, Sydney had undergone eight rounds of IVF. The most recent IVF had resulted in ten embryos—with three being transferred—but no pregnancy had resulted.

Eight did seem excessive. Maybe Sydney had been encouraged to do too many, pressed like Alexis to continue with the process despite the fact that it wasn't working.

Considering how distraught she'd seemed, she might be open to talking. Lake flipped back to the front of the folder, to the basic information form patients filled out before their initial consultation. The address listed was on East End Avenue. As Lake finished jotting it down, along with the various phone numbers, her eye caught something odd. Next to each name, in pencil, was a series of letters: *Rb* next to Sydney's, *BRbr*, by her husband's. Lake had no idea what they could mean.

Lost in thought, it took her a moment to hear the alert being signaled in another part of her brain. Her head snapped up. There were soft footsteps on the carpet in the hall. Someone was headed toward the storage room.

She clapped the file shut and crammed it into the drawer.

She had just slid the drawer shut and stuffed the paper with the numbers into her pocket when she heard the door knock against the stepladder. Slowly she turned, trying not to seem startled. To her utter dismay, Brie was standing in the doorway.

"What are you doing?" Brie asked roughly.

"What am I *doing*?" Lake asked, trying to sound mildly indignant. "As I told you, I still have a bit more research to take care of."

"But those are patient charts in there," Brie said.

Lake turned around and pulled her upper body back, as if scrutinizing the drawers in front of her.

"Oh, right," she said. She crossed the room, let her eyes roam for a moment and then pulled open the drawer with the press clippings. The whole time she could sense Brie's eyes boring into her.

"What's going on with the stepladder?" Brie asked.

"Excuse me?" Lake said, tugging a press file from the drawer. She turned and faced Brie again.

"Why was the stepladder against the door?"

Lake glanced casually in that direction.

"It was in the middle of the room," she replied. "I just moved it out of the way."

Brie didn't say anything. She just stood there, watching, as Lake walked past her out of the storage room.

Lake's heart was still pounding as she reached the small conference room. She'd played indignant with Brie, but she doubted she'd deceived her. And to make matters worse, Lake had left evidence behind. If Brie opened the drawer Lake had been standing in front of and saw the Kastner file stuffed haphazardly in the wrong spot, she'd realize that Lake had been rooting through there—and clearly on a mission.

Lake knew that the best move she could make now was to just get out of the clinic. She grabbed her bags, leaving the press file on the table as she fled.

Out on Park Avenue, she hurried north along the wet, glistening sidewalk. She would catch the crosstown bus on Eighty-sixth Street and escape to her apartment. It had stopped raining and people were out again—nannies pushing strollers; thin women toting yoga mats and shopping bags; doormen lolling in front of redbrick apartment buildings. How could everything seem so sane, she wondered, when her own world was a nightmare? By now Brie had probably figured out that Lake had been checking out a patient chart. And she had more than likely squealed to Levin. If asked, Lake would have to say that she had grabbed a file before realizing she was in the wrong drawer and hastily stuffed it back in—as unconvincing as that sounded.

The irony of her busted spy mission was that she had absolutely nothing to show for it, though it had given her the idea of reaching out to Sydney Kastner. Without allowing herself time to deliberate, she dug her BlackBerry from her purse and called Sydney Kastner's cell number. She was greeted by a soft hello.

"Ms. Kastner?"

"Yes?"

"Good morning. My name is Lake Warren. I'm a consultant with the Advanced Fertility Center and I'm trying to touch base with some of the patients—for, um, background research. I'd be so grateful if we could meet for a few minutes to talk."

"Meet? What about?" she said. She sounded hesitant but not put out.

"I'd like to learn your impressions of the clinic—what your experience has been like."

"Are you doing some kind of opinion poll?"

"No—not exactly. We just want to better serve patients in the future. And present the clinic in the right way to the public."

"Hmm, well, my husband and I are going away for ten days, but I could do it when I get back, I guess."

Lake's body tensed. She *had* to see her before she left.

"Is there any chance you could squeeze me in today? I'd love to complete my report this week."

"I suppose you could come by my shop at six tonight. I have plans after work, but I could talk for a minute after I close the store."

"Perfect," Lake said, relieved. "I really appreciate you finding the time."

"Not a problem. You see, there *is* something I'd like to tell you. Do you need directions?"

Lake's heart skipped as she scribbled down the shop's address. Don't get too excited, she warned herself. But she couldn't help but wonder if she would hear a revelation that could help her.

As soon as she hung up, she emailed Kit Archer. "Nothing to report yet but still looking."

She'd no sooner dumped her BlackBerry in her purse when it rang. She dug nervously for it again, wondering if Levin had been briefed by Brie and was tracking her down. But the screen showed it was Molly calling.

"Did you get my message about lunch?" Molly asked. "I feel like I haven't talked to you in days."

"I'm sorry," Lake said. "I've just been so busy . . . finishing my presentation."

"Can you meet today? I bet you need a break."

A small part of her longed to say yes, just to have human contact unrelated to the clinic. But she dreaded the idea of having to fake chitchat and pretend that her life was perfectly normal.

"How about a rain check? I've just got so much to do."

"Are you sure? What if I told you I have some interesting gossip about your old pal, Dr. Keaton?"

"What do you mean?" Lake said carefully.

"Just a little something I picked up from another friend; I think you'll be intrigued. And I'm right in your neighborhood."

"The West Side?"

"No, the Upper East Side. Aren't you working for that fertility clinic on Park Avenue? I'm at a restaurant off Madison, near Sixty-second."

"Um, okay," Lake said. "I guess I could do a quick lunch." She had to find out what Molly was talking about.

The restaurant was a French café twenty or so blocks south, so Lake decided it would be easiest to walk. The whole way there she fretted about what the "gossip" was. Had Molly heard something about the police investigation?

Molly was sitting just inside the café, beside the open floor-to-ceiling windows. She was dressed in a sleeveless celadon-colored dress that flattered both her coloring and her well-toned body, and her thick red hair was half up, half down. She looked stunning but also happy, as if life today was especially delicious.

"Great dress," Lake said as she slid into her chair.

"Thanks. You, of course, can wear *anything*. There are three colors that go with my hair and I have to work them to death."

All Lake wanted was to pump Molly for the news about Keaton, but she held back. Molly had a nose for trouble, and Lake knew that if she appeared overeager, it would only arouse suspicion.

"Was it nice to be in the Catskills again?" Molly asked, fiddling with a slice of baguette but not eating it.

Lake didn't dare say a word about Smokey. Molly would begin probing, asking all sorts of questions.

"No, not so great," Lake said. "It's going to take some getting used to—being in a house I once shared with someone else."

"Speaking of Jack, he hasn't dropped by again, has he?"

"No—thank God." She was getting tired of always having to provide Molly with a Jack Warren status report.

A few minutes later, after their salads had been ordered, Molly twitched in her chair, signaling she was ready to dish.

"*Sooo?* Don't you want to hear my news?" she asked.

"News?"

"About Mark Keaton. Don't be coy. That's how I got you here."

"Do tell, then," Lake said. She could hear how stilted her voice sounded.

Molly wetted her full lips and then pursed them together. Damn, don't make me beg for it, Lake thought.

"Do you remember me mentioning a woman named Gretchen Spencer? She's a stylist I've known for years. We both worked at *Harper's Bazaar* and went freelance around the same time."

"I think I do," Lake said. *Just tell me*, she felt like screaming.

"Well, she apparently spent the entire weekend with the good doctor two weeks before he was murdered."

18

LAKE FELT A rush of shame. Yes, she'd suspected Keaton was a total player, but she'd also allowed herself to believe that he'd seduced her because she was special and intriguing, not just another warm body to explore on a boring weeknight. How stupid and naïve of her, she thought.

"*Interesting*," Lake said. She widened her eyes, playing the voyeur.

"Of course, needless to say, Gretchen is in a total tizzy about the whole thing," Molly said. "She was even grilled by the police."

"*Really?* How did that go?" Lake asked.

"Not very pretty. At first she figured they were just talking to everyone who knew him. But they actually asked her if she'd been *with* him that night."

It was no surprise that the cops had concluded Keaton had been with a woman right before he died. She'd known evidence would have pointed them in that direction. But Molly's words were verification.

"So is this Gretchen woman a suspect?" Lake asked, trying to keep her voice gossipy.

"No. She has the proverbial airtight alibi. Besides, Keaton had more or less dumped her by then—which completely chapped her ass. They'd had a few dates and a hot weekend in Saratoga, and then nada. He didn't even return calls from her. The next thing you know, she sees his picture splashed across the *Post*."

"Saratoga?" Lake asked.

"Yup. They stayed at one of those fabulous turn-of-the-century hotels. I hate to tell you this, Lake, but Gretchen claimed he fucked like someone who should have taught a master class, so it's a shame you missed out on that. Though considering the way things turned out, it's probably best you did."

Lake couldn't bear any more of this, so she pretended to lose interest and awkwardly changed the subject. For the rest of the meal, as they discussed Molly's work and her upcoming trip, she had to force herself to smile, to talk, to eat. When she reached for her purse, Molly insisted on picking up the check since she'd been the one who'd suggested lunch.

Out on the sidewalk they hugged goodbye.

"You're not in love, are you?" Lake asked, gazing at Molly's face.

"No—why do you say that?"

"You're glowing. And I've been wondering about your mystery dinner party."

"What dinner party?"

"The one you were picking up food for when we talked last weekend."

"Oh, that was just for an old friend." She glanced at her watch. "I better dash—I'm prepping for a shoot tomorrow. Take care, okay?"

"You too."

"And, Lake, try to make some time just for yourself, will you? I know things are crazy right now, especially with the custody case—but you look exhausted. I've never seen you like this."

It felt like a slap in the face.

"Thanks for the *concern*," Lake said, with a hint of sarcasm.

"I'm just worried, that's all. You're clearly under a lot of strain."

"Okay, thanks," she said, softening. "I'll talk to you later."

In the cab home Lake wondered if she was being overly sensitive about Molly, who was just being her typically blunt self. And yet Lake was sure she detected a snide tone in some of Molly's comments today, suggesting some subterranean resentment. Perhaps Molly was annoyed because Lake had been so unavailable lately. As she replayed the conversation in her mind, her phone rang. To her chagrin, she saw it was Jack.

"Didn't you get my message?" he asked brusquely.

"No," she lied.

"Since I couldn't make parents' day, the camp director said I could stop by one afternoon this week. Will wants me to bring a few books—that sci-fi series he's reading."

"I take it something came up," Lake said.

"If you must know, I had a work emergency."

Or, she thought, he raced back to the city after shaving the fur off Smokey, loath to come face-to-face with her.

"Are you still there?" he demanded when she gave no reply.

"Yes. But I'm not understanding what you need from me."

"I need to get the *books*—they're on Will's bookshelf. He hasn't read the last two in the series."

"All right," she said, cringing at the thought of seeing Jack. "I have to be somewhere at six. Why don't you meet me in the lobby at five-thirty."

"That's not the best time for me."

"I'm sorry, but that's the only time I have today."

He accepted with an irritated sigh.

As soon as she was back in her apartment, she opened her laptop and pulled up what she had so far in her PowerPoint presentation. To her relief, her recommendations seemed stronger now that they were in a kick-butt font against a color background. Over the past day she'd toyed with the idea of suggesting that Levin become the public face of the clinic and be used more on television, so she added a slide spelling out the concept. That, she figured, should at least earn her points with his ego.

It took all of her effort to focus on adding the finishing touches. Her thoughts were constantly jolted back to her conversation with Molly and to the news about the investigation. Lake kept picturing McCarty and that pit bull Hull staring at the report from the forensic lab and wondering who'd been in bed with Keaton. If they discovered it was her, how could she ever prove she hadn't murdered him?

But something else from the conversation gnawed at her—the part about Keaton having sex with that woman, Gretchen. Was it the idea of having been just another lay to Keaton? Yes. But it was more than that: the trip to Saratoga Molly had alluded to. People went to Saratoga in August to see the thoroughbred racing. And to bet on the horses. Perhaps Keaton really *did* have a gambling problem. As suspicious as Lake now was about the clinic, Keaton's gambling issues might still be the reason he was dead. And that could mean some nasty mob type coming after her.

At four-thirty, her brain fried, she gave up on the presentation and faxed the kids. She wrote long notes this time, to make up for forgetting yesterday, and added little poems and cartoons. When she finished, it was almost time to leave for the meeting with Sydney Kastner—and then for drinks at Steve's. Of course, first there would be the encounter with Jack, which she dreaded.

Before heading to the lobby, she went to Will's bookshelf and grabbed the last two books in the sci-fi series.

Jack was ten minutes late, which was typical. When he finally arrived, without apology, she rose from the cushioned bench in the lobby and handed him a small shopping bag with the books inside. He rifled through the bag, inspecting the contents.

"Wait," he said. "One of these is wrong." He rattled off the name of a different book.

"You told me the last two books in the series."

"If I did, I was wrong."

As she met his hazel eyes staring back at her, she felt nothing but disgust. I don't love him anymore, she thought. Not even the tiniest bit.

"Okay, please watch my things," she said, plucking her keys from her purse. When she returned minutes later, she thrust the book in his hand, grabbed her purse, and left Jack without saying goodbye.

Sydney Kastner's shop was on York Avenue, on the other side of Manhattan, and in rush-hour traffic the taxi only managed to crawl in that direction. On East Eighty-sixth Street the cab came to a complete halt, caught in an obnoxious knot of cars. When the driver laid on his horn for the tenth time, Lake felt like bounding from the backseat and running the rest of the way. If she missed Sydney, it would be days before she could learn what she had to share. Finally they began to move and she arrived at the shop ten minutes after six.

It was the tiniest of florist shops but totally charming, the window filled not only with plants and flowers, but quirky garden knickknacks. As she stepped in closer, Lake saw to her dismay that it was dark inside. Damn, she thought, I've missed her. Anxiously she pressed the bell. To her relief a few seconds later she heard footsteps make their way to the front.

She almost didn't recognize Sydney Kastner. In place of the drawn and rattled woman she'd seen Rory console the other day was a calm, ethereal-looking creature. She was wearing a pale-blue sundress and her reddish-blond hair was worn loose now, with just the front part pulled from her face with a dainty barrette.

"Thank you for seeing me," Lake said as Sydney ushered her into the store and locked the door behind her.

"I just don't have much time, unfortunately," Sydney said. She studied Lake's face for a moment. "You were there the other day, weren't you? When I was having my meltdown."

"Yes. And I totally understand."

"Would you like to sit for a second?" Sydney gestured toward two wrought-iron garden chairs close to the cash register.

"Thank you," Lake said. "What an enchanting store."

"It's pretty much a labor of love. I barely cover my overhead, but I adore it. Ironic, isn't it? I'm all about making one's garden grow, but I can't produce a baby."

"You've had quite a few rounds of IVF. That must be very draining."

"Yes. The drugs have been nearly unbearable. The funny thing is that unlike some women, I usually have no trouble producing viable eggs and embryos. They just don't implant."

"But since you have extra embryos, you won't have to be subjected to the drugs for the next round."

Sydney tilted her pretty face and eyed Lake quizzically.

"I don't know who told you that. I don't have any extra embryos. They implanted all three that were produced this time."

"Oh, I'm sorry," Lake said awkwardly. That was odd, she thought. She was sure the chart had indicated ten embryos had been harvested.

"Besides," Sydney said. "There isn't going to be a next time. That's the thing I wanted to tell you."

Lake paused, considering the news. "Why? Have you decided to try another clinic?" she asked.

"Actually, my husband and I have decided to adopt," Sydney said, smiling. "I haven't even told Dr. Levin yet."

"That's wonderful," Lake said. "Congratulations."

"Deep down I think I've always *wanted* to adopt. My younger brother is adopted and I completely adore him."

Lake felt a rush of joy for the woman followed by a surge of disappointment. So *this* was the revelation Sydney had hinted at on the phone? Lake had hoped for so much more to help her case.

"In hindsight, how do you feel about the clinic? Were you satisfied?"

"Yes. . . . Yes, I was."

Lake sensed reluctance in the answer, like an undertow. Maybe there *is* something else, she told herself.

"Did—did you ever feel pressured to keep going?"

Sydney lifted her pale, freckled shoulders as if she had something to say but didn't know how. Here it comes, Lake thought.

"No, never," she said, shaking her head. "Initially I wanted to do whatever it took to get pregnant. If I seem hesitant it's only because the experience turned out to be worse than I imagined—not the clinic per se. Like I said, I hated the drugs. And I despised feeling so desperate and going to those awful support groups. When someone in the group would get pregnant, the rest of us would want to howl like wounded animals."

"So there was nothing about the clinic that troubled you?" Lake asked. She had to force herself not to look crushed. "Something you wish they'd done differently?"

"Why do you keep asking that? I thought you work for them."

"I do," Lake said brightly. "But part of growing and improving is hearing honest criticism."

"That's smart, I guess." Sydney glanced at her watch. "Look, I really do have to dash. I can't say I'm sorry never to be going back to the clinic, but I wish everyone there the best. They do good work."

Sydney stood up and grabbed a purse from near the cash register and began guiding Lake back to the door.

"What finally made you decide to pursue adoption?" Lake asked. She was grasping at straws, she knew.

"It sounds crazy," Sydney said. "But it was that doctor's murder. Dr. Keaton."

It was chilling to hear his name spoken here in this quiet little shop.

"But what . . . I don't understand. How could that influence you?" Lake asked.

"I was Levin's patient but Keaton came in on the day I was having my last procedure. I told him that if it didn't work, I was thinking about bagging the whole thing. He surprised me by saying that would be okay, that sometimes we just know in our guts what the right thing to do is. Right after I found out I wasn't pregnant, I heard he was murdered. I just took it as some kind of weird sign."

Lake fumbled for a response but none came. Instead she thanked Sydney for her time and wished her luck with the adoption pursuit. As she hurried down the sidewalk, she could hear the shop's steel security gate lowering with a rackety clang.

She hailed a cab going west. *Now* what? she wondered despondently. There had been no big revelation from Sydney. And yet there'd been that odd discrepancy. Her chart had said ten viable embryos had been produced, whereas Sydney Kastner thought there were only three. Levin may have lied to her so that she'd agree to another round of ovulation-stimulating drugs, ratcheting up her bill. It was certainly a possibility, but Lake wondered how she'd ever prove it.

The last thing she wanted to do right now was to have a drink with Hilary and Steve. And yet she knew that it would be good to see Steve away from work. He had the inside track there and maybe she could get him to talk about the clinic and see if he inadvertently revealed something worth knowing.

She'd been to their apartment just once before, when Sonia, Steve's sister, had been in town several years ago. It was all the way back on the West Side, in one of the luxury high-rises just north of Lincoln Center. Tonight when Hilary greeted her at the apartment door and Lake stepped inside she saw that "fixed it up" had been a gross understatement. The rooms had been reconfigured and redecorated within an inch of their lives. The furniture was sleek and modern—lots of white leather—and the walls displayed huge abstract paintings with designs that seemed to actually throb.

"Wow, you've done an amazing job," Lake said.

"We had help, of course," Hilary said. "I have a wonderful decorator. I'd be glad to give you her number if you're interested."

"How do you prevent all these white surfaces from getting smudged with little fingerprints?" Lake asked, thinking of Matthew, who had to be close to two now.

"Oh, this room is off limits to little boys," Hilary said.

"When do I get to see Matthew, anyway?"

"In a few minutes. The nanny is giving him his dinner right now. Would you like some white wine?"

They'd wandered to the far end of the massively large living room with sweeping views of the Hudson River and New Jersey beyond. On the coffee table was a bottle of white Burgundy chilling in a bucket, a huge wedge of soft cheese, and tiny cloth cocktail napkins. Hilary gestured for Lake to sit on the couch and poured them each some wine. Her white capris, Lake noticed, were as perfectly pressed as the napkins. On top she wore a sleeveless white tunic embellished with stones that matched the bronzy color of her sandals. Vanished was the beleaguered look she'd had Monday.

"Where's Steve?" Lake asked.

"Oh, he's running late—there was a problem at the clinic."

Lake tried to keep her face straight. "Oh?"

"A patient had a reaction to one of the drugs," Hilary said, to Lake's relief. "I'm just glad I never had to deal with any of that."

"Me, too. I feel so bad for those women, especially the ones who go through round after round of IVF."

"I guess," Hilary said, shrugging a tanned shoulder.

"What do you mean?" Lake asked, puzzled by her reaction.

"It's really their own choosing. No one is *forcing* them to do it. And it's such a drain on insurance companies. I don't understand why these people can't be more accepting of their situation—or why they don't adopt, like Angelina did. There are millions of needy children out there."

Lake felt at a loss for words. Hilary had always struck her as shallow, but Lake couldn't believe her insensitivity. She wondered if she'd have the same disdain for someone who used insurance dollars to have a birthmark removed.

"The desire to carry a child can be pretty intense in women," Lake said.

"Well, then, why don't they start earlier? It's not as if there aren't plenty of articles saying that, duh, your fertility drops after thirty-five. In a way I think fertility clinics encourage women to wait longer to conceive because they know they can fall back on procedures like IVF."

"Steve doesn't have any regrets about his career, does he?"

"No. But I think he'd be better off if he'd stuck to his original plan: plastic surgery. It's not so *morose*, if you know what I mean."

Lake could hardly stand listening to her. "But is he happy at the clinic?" she asked. If Steve was involved in anything unethical, it might translate at home as nerves or discontent.

"Well, he's certainly not thrilled with what's going on *now*."

"What do you mean?"

"The murder, of course," Hilary said. "How creepy, right?

"You know what I think?" she continued. "A woman did it."

"Oh?" Lake asked, wondering what was behind this specula-
tion. "Why is that?"

"He was a horrible flirt," Hilary replied, looking straight at
Lake. Her gray eyes were as cold as two river stones. "I bet he finally made one woman jealous enough to kill him."

Was the comment loaded? Lake wondered. She remembered
Hilary catching the look she'd exchanged with Keaton at the dinner
that night. She had to fight the urge to look away. To her relief, a
Latino woman dressed in a white uniform suddenly appeared in
the doorway.

"Matthew's ready to say goodnight, Mrs. Salman," she announced.

"All right," Hilary said. She turned to Lake, all smiles again. "I
can't wait for you to see him. Bring your wine if you want."

Lake followed Hilary through the dining room into a sleek
white-and-stainless-steel kitchen. Matthew was sitting in a high
chair, banging on the tray with a spoon. He'd grown from a gorgeous chubby baby with huge brown eyes to an exquisite toddler.
Lake felt a visceral rush of pure delight at the sight of him.

"Matthew, what a big boy you are," Lake gushed. He offered a
gummy smile back. Lake turned to Hilary. "He's just so precious."

"He is *now*," Hilary said, folding her arms across her chest. "He
just started throwing temper tantrums, and you should see him
then. She turned to her son. "You're Mommy's little terror, aren't
you?"

"Steve must be on cloud nine," Lake said.

"Oh, he is. I just wish he were around a little more to help. Jenny,
you can wash him up now—and then you can put him to bed."

"Can you show us how tall you are?" the nanny asked him

sweetly. Matthew's arms shot up. The nanny grinned back and pulled him out of the high chair and left the kitchen.

"Oh, let me show you his playroom," Hilary declared. "The decorator did an amazing job on it."

"All right," Lake said. Her head was beginning to pound. She wasn't sure if it was the wine.

Hilary led her down a long hallway, past both the master bedroom and Matthew's. At the end was a small, carpeted room lined with bookshelves and painted with murals. As they stepped inside, a phone rang in another room.

"Excuse me a sec," Hilary said. "The murals were all painted by a children's book illustrator," she called as she hurried away.

Lake ran her eyes around the room. So this was where Matthew was parked so he couldn't mess up the living room. How ironic, Lake thought. The woman who'd had no trouble conceiving could barely be bothered with her child. Suddenly Lake felt overwhelmed with the urge to just get the hell out of there.

"That was Steve," Hilary said, reentering the room. "He's really sorry but he won't be home for at least an hour." She rolled her eyes.

"No problem," Lake said, relieved for the excuse. "We'll do it another time."

"You certainly don't have to rush off," Hilary said.

"Why don't we just reschedule. I'm sure you have stuff to do."

"Is something the matter?" Hilary asked almost petulantly.

"No, no. I—I've just been fighting off a cold lately."

The two women walked back to the living room and Lake grabbed her purse and said goodbye. Her apartment was within walking distance but she didn't have the psychic energy to get there on foot. She found a cab and climbed gratefully into the back. She wondered if Steve's excuse had been legit. Or maybe he was trying to avoid her. Her snooping may have been reported to

Levin, and in turn to Steve. For the past few days she'd felt she was up to her neck in water but still able to breathe; now she felt close to drowning. Her only hope had been to find evidence she could take to Archer, but she'd come up with nothing.

As Lake massaged her temples, she realized that her face was wet with sweat. She dug in her purse, searching for a tissue. Just beneath her patent-leather wallet she felt something unfamiliar—round and made of rough cloth. She pulled it from her purse. For a second she just stared, confounded. It was a small burlap pouch, about the size of a plum. The neck was closed with twine and the insides were filled with something twiglike that poked through the fabric in places. My God, she thought—is it marijuana? Had someone stuck it in her purse?

She noticed a tag attached to the twine, blank on the side looking up at her. Slowly she turned it over. On the back was a single word: *Catnip.*

19

SHE'D BOUGHT CATNIP once for Smokey ages ago—but she certainly hadn't stuffed it in her purse. No, someone else had placed the bag there. It was obviously supposed to remind her of Smokey and what had been done to him. Was it a message? *I was in your backyard. This time I got even closer to you.*

A word shot like a bullet through her mind: *Jack.* She'd left her purse with him when she had to dash back up to the apartment because Jack had told her the wrong books on the phone. His whole visit may have been a ruse just so that he could slip the catnip in her purse. If that was true, it meant he'd also shaved Smokey.

Maybe Jack *was* trying to unhinge her, to make it appear that she was an unfit mother. But was Jack really capable of such sick behavior?

Another thought barged through her brain: If Jack was her stalker, then there was no reason to believe that Keaton's killer was watching her after all. In fact, Keaton's death might have no relation to the clinic at all. All the stuff she'd been doing to save herself—going through files, talking to patients—may have been pointless, and the real threat was the man she used to love.

But, she realized with a start, her purse had also been out of her sight at the *clinic*. She'd left it on the conference room table while she'd searched for the files. Anyone at the clinic could have dropped in the little sack of catnip. Which would mean that the killer *did* work at the clinic, knew of Lake's involvement with Keaton, and was sending her another warning. But a warning to do *what*? she wondered. To shut up or else?

Lake searched in her purse for a tissue and wiped the perspiration from her face. There was something else to consider: She'd left her purse in the living room at Steve and Hilary's when she'd gone to the kitchen to see Matthew, and Hilary had scurried off alone for a minute or two when Lake was in the playroom. What if Hilary had been having an affair with Keaton? Lake remembered how flirtatious Hilary had been with him at the restaurant. And then there was the fight in the car Steve had alluded to. Perhaps Hilary had gone to Keaton's apartment later and discovered he'd been in bed with another woman that night. In a rage she'd killed him. Now Hilary suspected Lake was the other woman but wasn't sure and was trying to flush her out.

And yet that idea seemed as farfetched as Jack hurting Smokey.

"Is this it?" a voice said.

Startled, Lake looked up to see that the cabdriver was speaking to her through the Plexiglas divider. She hadn't even realized that they had stopped in front of her building.

After climbing out of the cab, she glanced furtively up and down the street. The block was empty except for a woman pushing a stroller. As soon as Lake was in her apartment, she dropped the catnip into a plastic bag and shoved it in the back of a kitchen drawer. She couldn't stand the sight of it, but she knew it wouldn't be smart to throw it away.

As she slammed the drawer shut, her eye caught the calendar on the door of the fridge. The kids were due back in the apartment in just a few weeks. She couldn't imagine how she could allow them to live here with the killer possibly closing in on her and the police breathing down her neck. Perhaps she could ask Jack to keep them longer in the Hamptons than planned. She could say she was swamped with a project and needed to work on it 24/7. But if Jack was the stalker, wasn't this exactly what he was trying to do: create the impression of a mommy who was coming unglued?

I have to get a grip, she told herself as she stripped off her top. It was essential to keep her wits about her so she could watch her back at all times. That also held true with the police. She needed to keep a cool head if they showed up sweating at her door again. And if *Jack* was behind all the cat madness, she had to outsmart him, too. It all seemed overwhelming, but she had to do everything she could to save herself. If she didn't, she would lose Will and Amy—and perhaps much more.

She showered and then forced herself to microwave and eat another frozen mac and cheese. After stabbing at the dregs of it in the plastic container, she paced the hall of the apartment. The one sure way to save herself, it still seemed, was to figure out what was going on at the clinic. The discrepancy about Sydney Kastner's embryos bugged her. It could very well point to attempts by the clinic to jack up profits. And she couldn't ignore the odd Keaton connection. He'd consulted on Sydney's case and encouraged her to do what was right for her. Perhaps right before the celebratory dinner, Keaton had figured it all out and confronted Levin.

But how do *I* figure it out? Lake wondered. She thought again of the odd letters on Sydney's information sheet. Even if she summoned the nerve to look through files again, she didn't know what she was really looking for. Her thoughts rushed back to Alexis. There was clearly something she hadn't told Lake, something she'd been close to revealing. It seemed Lake's only hope was to convince Alexis to share what she knew. Lake glanced at her watch. It was almost ten. She would phone Alexis in the morning. And she would try to learn what she'd meant by *cherchez la femme*.

She slept with the table once again propped against the door. All through the night, Smokey paced up and down the bed as if he sensed how tense she was. The last time she remembered looking at her clock it read 2:27.

The late summer sun nudged her awake just after six. For a moment she luxuriated in the soft feel of it on her face until, with a jolt, she remembered everything. She sat up against the headboard and ran her hands through her hair. She didn't want to wake Alexis—she sensed she'd have the phone slammed down in her ear if she did—but she didn't want to miss her if she went to work someplace. She decided to call just before eight. Until then she would rehearse her presentation.

After dressing and making coffee, she opened her laptop. Client presentations were the part of her work she'd always liked the least, and in the early years she had positively dreaded them. She'd felt so exposed, at times even wondering if the shadow of her birthmark was actually darkening and pulsing as she spoke. But she had worked with a speech coach and learned to feel more at ease.

As she went through her presentation out loud, she seemed to stumble over every other word. It would be even worse at the clinic, she knew. Levin had been so cool to her the other day, and Brie may have since gone running to him about finding Lake poking through the files—hardly the makings of a receptive audience. To say nothing of the fact that the killer might very well be one of the people sitting at the conference table during the presentation. She couldn't imagine how she'd ever manage to appear confident and professional.

At twenty of eight, unable to wait any longer, she phoned Alexis. The same blunt, unhappy voice said hello. A male voice—from the TV or radio—yammered in the background.

"Alexis, this is Lake Warren. I came by to see you—"

"I remember."

"Of course. I—"

"What do you want?"

"You said the other night that you were reluctant to share more with me because you weren't sure of my agenda. It's true that I wasn't very clear. You see, I'm actually working at the clinic—as a consultant. I was afraid to tell you that because I was going behind their back."

"And your point is? I'm not sure why you're confessing this now."

"Because I want the chance to speak to you again," Lake said. "I'm really concerned that something wrong might be going on there. If you tell me what to look for, I may be able to find evidence."

There was a very long pause. If Lake hadn't still heard the background voices, she might have thought Alexis had disconnected the call.

"You actually work there. At the Advanced Fertility Center?" Alexis said finally.

"Yes. I'm sorry I was reluctant to tell you before."

"All right. I'll speak to you again. When?"

"As soon as possible. I'm finishing up my work there, so if I'm going to try to get any proof, I have to act immediately."

"All right—come now, then."

Lake was in a cab in ten minutes. The whole way to the East Side, she warned herself to handle Alexis delicately, to resist pouncing. She couldn't come away empty-handed this time.

Alexis was wearing another wrap dress, this one in pinks and browns. Her apartment looked exactly the way it had two days before, like unchanging scenery for a play.

"So you work at the clinic," Alexis said coldly as they took the same seats in the living room they had on Tuesday. "What an interesting detail to have left out of our previous conversation."

"I'm sorry. Like I said, I was afraid of making trouble . . . until I knew it might be justified."

"Is business booming these days?" Alexis asked sarcastically. "I read the other day that the average age of marriage is increasing for women. That kind of news must make Levin and Sherman positively *gleeful*."

"I know they want to build their business—that's why they hired me. I'm a marketing consultant."

"*Marketing?* So you're not in the lab or anything like that? Do you have any medical expertise at all?"

"No. I've had other clients in the health-care field, but—"

"Damn." Alexis shook her head hard to the left, as if she were flicking water from her hair. "I need someone in the lab."

"Why?" Lake asked, surprised. "Is that where you think the problem is?"

"Look, I really don't see how you can help me," Alexis snapped.

Lake could feel her own anxiety starting to balloon. She couldn't walk out of there without the truth.

"Please let me try," she urged. "You can tell me exactly what to look for. If there's something less than kosher going on, I want to help you expose it."

"*Less than kosher?*" Alexis said. The testy tone was back, like a tiger that had suddenly slunk out of the bush. "Excuse my eyes from bulging out of my head, but considering what they did to me, that has to be the understatement of the year."

"What do you mean?" Lake asked. "What did they do?"

"They stole my baby."

Lake played the words back in her mind, trying to decipher them.

"Your baby?" she said. "But I thought you weren't able to conceive?"

"I *did* conceive—in a petri dish. And when I was denied future access to my embryos, they gave them to someone else."

Involuntarily Lake's hand flew to her mouth.

"My God," she said. "How—how did you find out?"

"I saw the baby with my own eyes."

"At the clinic?" Lake asked.

"No. At a store on Madison Avenue. I'd been running errands and had gone into this little gourmet food store to grab a sandwich. They have a few tables in the back there where you can eat lunch. And then this woman—*Melanie's* her name—came in with a toddler in a stroller. And the baby was the spitting image of Charlotte."

Okay, Lake thought, so this is the nut-job part that Archer had mentioned.

Alexis smiled wickedly with her tiny pink lips.

"You don't believe me, do you?" she said.

"No, it's not that," Lake said. "I'm just digesting what you said."

At that, Alexis shot up and for a brief second Lake wondered if she was going to walk over to the couch and slap her. But she hurried out of the room, leaving Lake alone. When she returned a moment later, she was carrying a small piece of paper in her incongruously slim fingers. On her way back across the room, she picked up the silver-framed photograph of Charlotte.

"Here," she said, thrusting both things toward Lake. Lake saw that the piece of paper was actually a slightly blurry photo of a toddler in a stroller, perhaps taken with a cell phone. The two toddlers looked almost identical.

"Are they . . . *twins*?" Lake asked, her voice catching.

"Interesting thought, isn't it?" Alexis said, smirking. "But, no, you can't produce identical twins with an IVF procedure. Brian and I look alike, though, and a sibling of Charlotte's would look very much like her. Think of those Olson twins. They're fraternal twins and yet people can barely tell them apart."

"You took this photo of the child?"

"Yes. When I saw the baby, I changed tables to get closer and took some pictures when the woman was busy blabbing to someone on her cell phone."

"Did you say something to her about it?"

"Good God, no," Alexis said. "I may be crazed but I'm not *stupid*. If this woman had known what I'd just put together, she would have left skid marks on her way out the door."

"How did you figure out her name, then?"

"She used a credit card to pay. After she left, I asked one of the clerks for her name—I said I thought I might have known her in college and wanted to double-check. I'm a regular there and the clerk didn't think anything of it. I'm not sure what this woman was doing on the Upper East Side that day. She lives in Brooklyn. In that area they call Dumbo."

She'd said the word disdainfully, as if it was synonymous with *dung heap*. But it was a hip, trendy part of Brooklyn—Down Under the Manhattan Bridge Overpass—that Lake had visited several times with friends.

"How . . . ?"

"How do I know where she lives?" Alexis asked, her voice edgy again. "She and her husband are listed. . . . Oh wait, how do I know she'd been a patient at the Advanced Fertility Center? That was as easy to find out as her address. I called the girl at the front desk, pretending to be Melanie, saying I needed to review some of my dates for insurance reasons. She'd had two rounds of IVF, starting two months after I'd been told Brian wouldn't release my embryos to me. I didn't want the embryos destroyed, in case Brian changed his mind. But they knew I'd never be back. So they gave them to her."

Lake let out a long breath. The story was horrific—and almost too crazy to believe.

"But why would Sherman have to resort to this?" Lake asked. "If this woman couldn't conceive with her own eggs, why not use eggs from an actual donor? The clinic has even started its own donor program."

"She probably didn't *want* a donor," Alexis said. "She looked like she was in her early forties and she was probably hoping she could still have her *own* child. And I'm sure Sherman encouraged her just like he did me. He and Levin like to tell women, 'You *will* get pregnant,' as if they're the Baby Makers. When Sherman found her eggs were useless, he was stuck. So he just used my embryos— without ever telling her."

Over the past few weeks Lake had read enough about in vitro fertilization to understand the challenges faced by patients over forty. As part of IVF, a woman underwent hormone therapy to encourage the ovaries to release multiple eggs. Those eggs were then collected and placed in a petri dish with sperm from the woman's partner—or, for an additional fee, even injected with sperm to facilitate fertilization. But if the woman was close to forty, or older, like Melanie, the chances for successful fertilization were slim. By that point in a woman's life, her eggs had not only declined rapidly in number but also in quality—in fact, by the time a woman was forty-three, only about ten percent of her eggs were viable. The older the woman, the poorer the chances of harvesting enough viable eggs to fertilize and transfer back to her body. That's why some clinics didn't even take women over forty.

"And you never signed any kind of permission allowing them to share your eggs?"

"Never."

"Have you confronted Sherman about this?" Lake asked.

"Of course. I called him after I'd figured out Melanie was a patient. He was totally patronizing. He told me I should talk to a psychologist who specializes in—quote—'women like you.'"

"Did he suggest you talk to Harry Kline?"

"The psychologist they have on staff? No. I guess they only use him for the women they feel haven't gone completely off the deep end yet and they can still milk for procedures."

"Is there any way of getting a DNA test?"

"Not that I've found so far. Believe it or not, in these cases, the law protects the custodial parent—which is despicable. That's *my* baby and she's supposed to be with *me*."

Lake glanced down at the photos again. It *was* uncanny how alike the two little girls looked. If Alexis was right and the clinic had done this to improve Melanie's chances of conceiving, it likely wasn't the first time—or the last.

"Do you think this woman, Melanie, has any suspicions that the child may not be hers?"

"I doubt it," Alexis said. "If you've been desperate for a baby, you don't allow yourself to question these things. And whether it was intentional or not, Sherman did a brilliant job of matching the coloring. This Melanie woman has light coloring like mine. And her husband's probably fair as well. His name is Turnbull, a snooty English name."

Lake felt her skin turn cold. *Melanie Turnbull.* She'd heard that name before—and recently.

And then she remembered. It was the name written on the scrap of paper she'd seen in the black bowl in Keaton's loft.

20

"DO YOU *KNOW* her?" Alexis asked. She was studying Lake intensely and had seen the flicker of discomposure.

"No—of course not. I'm just trying to absorb everything."

"So what are you going to do to help me?"

"What?" Lake asked distractedly. She could barely concentrate. In her mind she kept seeing the slip of paper in the bowl. Why did Keaton have Melanie Turnbull's name? Had he stumbled onto something suspicious about her pregnancy? Maybe this was the reason he'd decided not to join the clinic. And maybe *this* was the reason he'd been murdered.

"You wanted the truth and I told you," Alexis said fiercely. "Are—?"

"Let me ask you one more question," Lake said, trying to find her footing again. "The day you spoke to Sherman—you didn't talk to another doctor there, did you? Mark Keaton?"

"No," Alexis said, annoyed, it seemed, at having been driven off topic. "I've never even heard of him. So are you going to be able to get into the lab or not?"

"I definitely want to help, but what would getting into the lab do? I'm not sure what I'd be able to discover."

"You could see what the people there are up to," Alexis said. "You might overhear something important."

"I seriously doubt they'd say anything incriminating in front of me, even if I did manage to spend any time in there. But look, I do have access to the charts—I actually looked at yours before. Now that I know about the Turnbulls, I can see if there's anything in their chart linking the two of you."

"Like what?"

"Well, they must have made some kind of notation in Melanie's file indicating who they got the embryos from. With both files in front of me, I may be able to spot it."

Alexis eyed her skeptically. "Maybe," she said. She glanced away, thinking.

"There's something you should be aware of," Lake said. "Your chart indicated that you had only two embryos left. You told me there was a good amount."

Alexis shook her head back and forth angrily.

"Those bastards," she said. "So if Brian ever relents, they'll just say I had fewer than I thought—or that some deteriorated."

Unexpectedly, tears welled in Alexis's eyes. It was the first time Lake had seen her look truly vulnerable.

"I'm going to do my best to help," Lake said. "I'm headed to the clinic later today and will try to see the files. I'll let you know if I find anything."

As Alexis walked Lake to the door, she grasped her arm so hard it hurt.

"I have to get my baby back," Alexis said. "There has to be a judge who will give her to me, if you can prove what Sherman did."

When Lake hurried out of the building minutes later, she saw the doorman study her curiously and she realized how rattled she must look. Halfway down the block toward Fifth Avenue she sank onto a stoop. Could Alexis's story really be true? she wondered. It seemed so farfetched. And yet it couldn't be a coincidence that Keaton had Melanie's name.

If doctors at the clinic really were stealing embryos, they weren't doing so just to make their patients wild with joy. It was obviously to improve their success rates and enhance the clinic's reputation as a place that was expert at making older women pregnant. And that guaranteed greater profits.

This had to be why Keaton had been killed. He'd figured out somehow that Melanie had received someone else's embryos and had decided to contact her.

Or what if Melanie had begun to have suspicions and reached out to *him*?

Lake dug her BlackBerry from her purse and called 411. There was a listing for a Steve and Melanie Turnbull in Brooklyn. She started to punch in the number and then paused. It was one thing to cold-call Alexis because she'd already approached Archer's producer with her concerns, but what could Lake possibly say to Melanie? Your baby may not belong to you and we need to chat?

No, she would have to find something in Melanie's file linking her to Alexis. Lake rose from the step and glanced at her watch. In nine hours she was due to give her presentation. She dreaded the idea of being back at the clinic, especially in light of what she now knew. She also dreaded the idea of going into the file room again. But she had to. Since there'd be no chance of going through the records after the presentation, as the clinic was closing, she needed to arrive early.

Back home she rehearsed her presentation several more times. She knew the only way to get through it tonight was to focus totally on the slides and not on the people in the room. How utterly ironic it will be, she thought, when she reaches the slide about capitalizing on the clinic's success with older women.

Melanie Turnbull flashed in her mind again. Lake started to worry about her plan to search the files once more; she had learned nothing from going through the patient charts so far. What, if anything, would she find tonight? She reconsidered talking directly to Melanie.

At around two she made a salad—just canned tuna and an onion so old it had thick green sprouts shooting from one end—and ate it listlessly. She felt stalled—marooned, really. She had told herself before that she needed to take action, to outsmart Levin as well as Jack, but she was just sitting here, betting on some paper files.

Without giving herself time to think it over anymore, she grabbed her BlackBerry from her purse and punched in Melanie's number. A woman answered, sounding unhurried, pleased with the day, and in the background Lake could hear classical music playing and the babbling of a child. What a contrast, she thought, to Alexis Hunt's sad apartment.

"Is this Melanie Turnbull?" Lake asked.

"Yes," the woman said. "Who's calling?"

"My name is Lake. I—I'm a friend of Dr. Mark Keaton's. You two spoke, right?"

"What?" Melanie asked, sounding mildly irritated now. "I have no idea what you're talking about."

"Dr. Keaton—with the Advanced Fertility Center. He was murdered last week. I know that there were some—well, confidential things you needed to discuss with him. About your baby."

The woman didn't say anything for a moment, though Lake could hear the baby fussing in the background.

"Like I told you," she finally said, all the softness gone from her voice. "I don't have a clue what you're talking about. Do not call here again. Do you understand?"

A hard click followed. Damn, Lake thought. She'd blown her chance. She should have talked to Archer first and plotted out a clear strategy. Now everything rested again on what she could find in the files.

Feeling drained, she wandered into the living room and sank onto the couch. The drapes were pulled and the room was dim. She swung her legs up on the seat and closed her eyes. The last thing she remembered was Smokey hopping up next to her and nuzzling her face.

When she woke, she felt sticky, and her mind was fuzzy. She glanced nervously at her watch, worried about how long she'd slept. It was just after four. She had the odd sensation that a noise had woken her, though Smokey was nowhere in sight. She listened carefully. Then she heard the sound of her BlackBerry, ringing softly from the kitchen, where she'd left it. She shot up awkwardly from the couch and hurried to answer it. Maybe it's Archer, she thought. But the screen said "caller unknown."

"Lake," a woman said.

"Yes," Lake said quietly. She didn't recognize the voice.

"This is Melanie Turnbull."

Lake nearly gasped in surprise.

"Hello," she said.

"I've been thinking about your call," Melanie said. "And actually I do think we should talk."

"Thank you," Lake said, still taken aback. "As I said before, Dr. Keaton—"

"In person, though. I don't want to do this over the phone. And as soon as possible."

"Of course," Lake said. "You tell me when and where."

"Tonight. I want to get this over with."

Lake winced. She wouldn't be done with the presentation until at least seven.

"I have a little hitch tonight. I have to work until around seven."

"That's not a problem. I don't want to do it until I've put my daughter to bed, anyway. At around nine?"

"Okay. Where should we meet?"

"I can't come all the way into Manhattan so it's going to have to be in Dumbo." She gave the name of a restaurant on Front Street and said she'd meet her at the bar.

"Uh, that's fine," Lake said, jotting down the information. Melanie told her that she was tall with shoulder-length blond hair. Then she brusquely ended the call.

Lake felt like sobbing with relief. The fact that Melanie had called *her* had to mean something.

There were some logistics to work out. As long as she left the clinic at around seven-thirty she would reach the restaurant in time. Taking the subway there would be a hassle, though, involving at least one transfer, and it would be tough to find a taxi at that hour, and then again when heading back home. The smartest approach, she realized, would be to take her car. That meant driving to the clinic. She needed to get moving.

By the time she parked her car in a garage on the East Side, Lake felt fried. Traffic had been awful and the trip had taken longer than expected. She was wearing a black skirt and a pink jacket, and they both already looked rumpled, as if she'd picked them from a pile of worn clothes on the floor. But as she hurried down the street she knew she had bigger concerns tonight.

There were a few patients bunched at the reception desk and she skirted around them, heading directly toward the back. No one was at the nurses' station, indicating that the staff was involved with patients. As she turned one corner she saw the backs of two people in scrubs emerging from the OR—Sherman and Perkins, it looked like.

As soon as she entered the large conference room, her stomach began to roil. The last time she had been in this room was when Levin had announced Keaton's murder and Hull and McCarty sat there like predators anxious to pick up a scent.

After unpacking her tote bag, she hooked up her laptop so that it fed into the flat-screen TV on the wall. Next she distributed pads and pencils around the table, a touch that a former boss had always insisted on. When she was done, she ran through the PowerPoint presentation.

"You're early."

Lake spun around and saw that the comment had come from Brie, who was standing in the doorway. Great, she thought. Brie had probably been sent to watch her like a hawk.

"I just wanted to run through my slides on the big screen," Lake said, hearing the defensiveness in her voice and hating it.

"No problem," Brie said, weirdly chipper for her. She was wearing a slim black dress and her lips were painted a nude color that made them almost recede into her face. "Everyone's still finishing up with patients, so six-thirty is the earliest we can start."

"Perfect," Lake said, trying to smile. "Excuse me, you said everyone—who do you mean? Isn't it just Dr. Levin and Dr. Sherman?"

"Dr. Levin asked a few others to join them. He thought it would be great to get their feedback." Still that unnatural cheeriness. "Did you figure out how to hook up your laptop okay?"

"Um, yes, thanks," Lake said.

"Well, just let me know if you need any help. I'm going to be in Dr. Hoss's office going over a few things."

As Brie left, closing the door behind her, Lake pressed the tips of her fingers to her lips, thinking. Why was Brie acting so helpful?

Was it because Lake's work was almost done and she'd soon be out of Brie's hair—or was something more sinister afoot? Maybe the geniality was an offshoot of devilish glee because Brie knew Lake was in trouble. In any case, Lake couldn't worry about that now. She had to focus on sneaking into the file room, which she had fifteen minutes to do. The good news was that it sounded like Brie would be ensconced in Hoss's office.

Lake slipped out of the conference room and looked both ways up and down the hall. No one was in sight. Quickly she made her way to the file room. This time she didn't bother with the step-ladder ruse. It hadn't worked before anyway and she needed to make dead certain no one saw her this time. She shut the door firmly behind her.

She went to the drawers and quickly found the Turnbull chart. It wasn't as thick as the Hunt chart, and as she thumbed quickly through the pages she saw that Melanie had indeed undergone two IVF procedures, the second resulting in a pregnancy. Though it was difficult to completely decipher the doctors' notations, it seemed that only six eggs had been harvested the first time and only one embryo had made it to day three, which Lake knew was the first point it was viable to transfer embryos to the uterus for implantation. The low number wasn't surprising if Melanie was in her forties, as Alexis had suggested, but it also meant that the chances of a pregnancy were very slim. The next IVF, however, produced eight eggs and six viable embryos. What a nice surprise, Lake thought mockingly. If Alexis was right, this was when *her* embryos had been used because Sherman realized Melanie had little chance on her own.

What Lake didn't see was any notation that seemed to link this chart to another. She would have to pull Alexis's chart and compare them side by side. But first she flipped to the front of the file to check Melanie's age. According to her birth date, she'd been forty-one at the time of her first in vitro. As Lake started to lay the file down on top of the open drawer, she noticed several letters, written in pencil, by Melanie's name on her information form. *BLb*. It was similar to what she'd spotted in the Kastners' file, but with different letters, she thought. Her eyes jerked toward Melanie's husband's name. *BLg*. Was this the code that linked one couple to another?

She glanced at her watch. To her shock, it was 6:28. She needed to look at Alexis's file again, but she'd run out of time. Suddenly, from behind the door, she heard the muffled sounds of conversation. She froze. But the sound soon receded and she dropped the chart back into place. Lake eased the door open, peeking cautiously into the hall—no one was there—and quickly slipped from the room. Her heart was thumping so hard, she could hear the sound it made. As she hurried back to the conference room she could feel that the inside of her jacket was sticky with sweat.

Steve was the first to arrive for the presentation, only seconds after Lake had returned to the room. Lake felt a momentary rush of relief. Surely she could count on him to be supportive tonight.

"I'm so sorry about yesterday evening," he said quietly. "There were some complications with a patient."

"Did everything turn out all right?"

"Yes, thankfully. Hilary said you weren't feeling well."

"Oh—it was just a very bad headache. I'm better now."

"Lake, I—"

Hoss had just entered the room—followed by Perkins—and Steve took a seat without finishing his comment. Sherman came in next, along with Brie. Finally Levin appeared. He greeted Lake politely but his eyes slid quickly off her face.

"Okay, let's get started," Levin said as people eased into their chairs.

Lake took a deep breath and pulled her laptop closer to her.

"These past few days have been extremely stressful," she said, "but it's important to press ahead with the marketing plans. You do wonderful work here, and more women need to know about it."

Her voice, she knew, sounded strained. She cleared her throat.

"This is the first of several presentations I'll be making," she continued. "Today I'm going to share some of my initial ideas. I've also included some of the first concepts from the person I retained to do regular PR for the clinic as well as the terrific Web designer who will be redoing your site. They'll develop more extensive ideas after I share the feedback I get from you."

Everyone was looking at her but their faces were expressionless. Except for Dr. Hoss. Her lips were pursed, as if she'd found Lake's introduction oddly confusing. Lake tried not to let that rattle her even more.

The actual presentation took her about thirty minutes. As the slides came up, they looked foreign to her, as if she'd never seen them before. But she read the words aloud and then expanded on each point the way she had rehearsed, often giving examples. When she discussed her community-outreach ideas, she described the halo effect those would create for the clinic. Finally she got to the part where she encouraged a more public role for Levin. She smiled as she described making him a media star, a la Dr. Oz, and forced herself to look at him. All he did was nod.

Finally it was over. Her hands were sticky and she slipped them into the pockets of her jacket to try to absorb the moisture.

"So that's it—round one," she concluded. "There's much more to come, of course."

Though people had maintained a decent amount of eye contact with her during the presentation, most of them now glanced down. All the pads, she noticed, were absolutely blank. From one of the two small windows that faced the alley between the clinic's building and the next, she heard the distant, muted honk of a horn. She felt as if she were in some kind of alternate universe.

"Well," Levin said finally. "You've given us lots to think about."

Lake was stunned by his comment. Was that *it*? All he—or anyone else—was going to say? She grabbed a breath and forced herself to smile.

"Are there any questions?" she asked.

"Not at the moment," Levin said. He gestured toward a stack of papers in front of her. "Is that the hard copy of your presentation?"

"Yes. I have a batch of copies."

"Why don't we take a look at those later and digest what you've done. Then we'll get back to you with our thoughts."

"Um, okay," she said awkwardly. "I'll pass them out."

The next few minutes were nearly unbearable. People collected the hard copies and left silently, with just Perkins muttering a thank-you. Steve refused to catch her eye. The last person to leave was Levin, and when Lake turned and saw him hanging by the doorway, her stomach knotted. What's he thinking? she wondered desperately.

"Do you need any assistance?" he asked. His words were polite but his tone was without any warmth.

"No—I'm set, thank you," Lake said.

"All right, then," Levin said and then walked out of the room.

She unplugged her computer and stuffed her things haphazardly into her tote bag. She wanted to run out of the clinic, but she knew she had to do her best to seem nonchalant. As she passed by the desk of the receptionist, the girl stared hard at her without saying a word.

Lake didn't give herself a chance to think about the presentation until she was safely out the door and halfway down the block, hurrying to the parking garage. Something was definitely wrong. From her perspective the presentation had gone decently enough—her strategies were hardly brilliant, but, as she'd decided last night, they were more than adequate. So it was bizarre that no one, especially Levin, had made a single comment. She'd been dismissed, practically rushed out. Why? If Levin was in any way connected to Keaton's murder and sensed she knew something, he might have initially wanted her around, to keep an eye on her. But if he'd been recently told by Brie she was snooping, he may have changed his mind.

Traffic was heavy but not gridlocked and within fifteen minutes Lake was on the FDR, headed south. To her left, in the fading light, the East River throbbed with activity—speedboats and sailboats and small "dining" yachts with tourists hanging over the rails. As disturbing as the evening had been so far, she tried to focus on her meeting with Melanie Turnbull. Melanie surely wouldn't do anything to jeopardize her situation as a mother, and yet she had agreed to talk. Maybe, Lake thought, she would actually come away with something tonight that could help her figure this all out. From there, she'd reach out to Archer.

She crossed the Brooklyn Bridge and drove the few blocks into Dumbo. With its cobbled streets and nineteenth-century warehouses—and the Manhattan skyline as a backdrop across the East River—the area had always seemed to Lake like a cross between old New York and *Blade Runner*. Using her GPS, she located the restaurant Melanie had suggested. Parking was problematic, and the best she could do was a parking place three blocks north on Water Street.

She stepped out of her car and locked it. It was cooler over here, probably because of the proximity to the East River. Walking south along Water Street, she pulled her jacket tighter. To her right, the waterfront was partially hidden by trees. She glanced at her watch. She wasn't supposed to meet Melanie for another twenty-five minutes. She turned west instead and made her way closer to the water. There was a small park, its entrance nothing more than the mouth of a narrow path. She began to follow it. Within a few yards the winding path opened onto a large open area. Off to the left, along the East River, was a small, pebble beach, with water lapping gently over the rocks. It looked more like the edge of a lake than a river. To the right were large terraced steps made out of pavement where a dozen people sat, scattered about and enjoying the view under the streetlamps. Lake stared across the water at the glittering island of Manhattan. For a moment she wished she could just pick the kids up from camp and drive away from here forever.

She retraced her steps and turned onto Water again and then walked up Dock to Front Street. The restaurant was like a tavern, with old wooden tables and twinkling lights strung across the windows. She picked a table that gave her a view of the door and ordered a glass of wine.

Once again she replayed the presentation over in her mind. How ridiculous those pads and pencils had been, she thought. No one had taken a single note. She drained the last of her wine. It probably wasn't smart to have more, she realized, but if she didn't she'd be in danger of jumping out of her skin, thinking about the clinic. She flagged the waiter down and ordered a second glass of Bordeaux.

This time she sipped slowly, trying to calm herself. She looked up at one point and surveyed the restaurant. When she'd first come in she had noticed a table of five boisterous women clearly celebrating something, but she saw now that they had paid their bill and gone. She glanced down at her watch. It was nine-thirty.

She'd been so consumed by her thoughts that she hadn't noticed that the time for her appointment had come and gone. With a start she realized the truth: Melanie Turnbull wasn't coming.

21

OH GOD, SHE thought, tell me this isn't happening. After checking with the restaurant's hostess just to make certain she hadn't missed a tall blond woman coming in alone, Lake dug her BlackBerry from her purse and called the number Melanie had phoned from. Voice mail. She left a message saying that she understood Melanie might be running late and that she would continue to wait for her—that Melanie should just get to the restaurant whenever she could. But it was obvious what had happened: Melanie had developed cold feet and decided not to come.

Lake ran her hands through her hair. She'd been banking so much on this meeting, believing that she was close to extricating herself from the horrible mess she was in. But she should have known from Melanie's skittish tone that there was a chance she'd be a no-show. Lake decided to hang around for another twenty minutes just in case Melanie heard her message and changed her mind. But deep down she knew it was hopeless.

"Would you like to see a menu?"

It was the waitress, a pretty girl with an Australian accent. Lake had drunk nearly two glasses of wine without having eaten. Not only was her stomach growling but her head felt light, buzzy. And yet the idea of eating had no appeal. She smiled wanly and shook her head.

As she waited, she calculated what her next move should be. Certainly Archer would be interested in knowing that Melanie had asked for a meeting. That had to be significant. And he'd also be curious about the odd letters Lake had seen on the Turnbull and Kastner charts. Maybe Archer could tip off the police that there *might* be something fishy at the clinic to force them to take a closer look. But with nothing more than a hysterical woman's word to go on, they'd never be able to gain access to patient records. Lake's head began to throb, as if someone were squeezing it. She'd figure this out at home.

At nine-fifty she paid the check and slipped out of the restaurant. As she made her way down Front Street, the dull roaring and clacking of cars above her on the Brooklyn Bridge seemed to echo how agitated she felt inside.

At Dock Street, she turned left and headed down to Water. The block was deserted except for a young couple pulling their car out of a parking space. As enchanting as the area was, there didn't seem to be any services along its streets—no delis or coffee shops or laundromats—and at this hour pedestrian traffic was nearly nonexistent. She thought she heard a sound behind her—the scuff of a shoe—and she quickly twisted her head around. There was no one there.

At Water she took a right. She wished she'd been able to find a parking space closer to the restaurant. Across the street an old brick warehouse with carved arches ran the entire length of the block. On her side of the street was a gallery, closed for the day, with an oversize carousel inside. The horses were paused in mid-gallop, their eyes blank in the small spotlight. The building after that, at the intersection, had apartments on the upper floors, and though some of them were lit up, there was no visible activity inside. It was as if she'd found herself in the back lot of a Hollywood studio after closing time. All she wanted was to be in her car heading home.

She heard a sound again, and this time she was sure it was a footstep. She spun around. Halfway down the block she saw a man walking alone at a steady clip. He was dressed in tight dark pants—jeans, she thought—and a sweatshirt and sneakers, and he wore some kind of trucker cap with the beak pulled low on his face. Her pulse jumped and she started moving faster.

Right away she heard the man pick up his own pace. His foot-steps sounded louder and more urgent behind her. Still hurrying, Lake jerked her head around to look. He was walking with long, smooth strides, and though the cap hid his eyes, she could tell he was looking straight at her face.

She was in danger—there was no doubt about it. She turned back and started to run. Behind her she heard the man begin to run, too. The car was a block and a half away and it seemed impossible to reach it without the man catching up to her. "Help!" she screamed—and then again. Her voice was drowned out by the distant roar of subway cars passing over the Manhattan Bridge.

The last block toward the car was completely dark. To her left, just before the river, she could see a small café and she zigged in that direction, her heart nearly ramming against her chest. But as she sprinted toward the café, she saw the tables were stacked along the sidewalk and the inside lights dimmed. Gripping her aching right side, she turned back again. The man was gaining on her. Her only choice was the park. There would surely be people there still, looking at the water. She plunged into the same entrance she used earlier and raced along the path.

"Help!" she screamed again.

But the park was empty. Frantically she scanned the area to the right of the terraced steps for an exit but she saw only a chain-link fence. So she flew down the steps to the pebble beach and began to scuttle across it.

She could sense the man right behind her like a force field, and she yelled, "Get away from me!" Across the East River, Manhattan throbbed with lights, and cars streamed down the FDR Drive, but she knew that no one in the world could hear her.

Suddenly her whole body was being jerked backward. The man had grabbed her pink jacket, twisting the fabric in his fist. She couldn't see him but she could smell him—the reeking scent of aftershave. Struggling, she twisted around. The man let go of her jacket and yanked her arm tightly. Her brain seemed oddly separated from her body; she was thinking and assessing the situation even as her body felt limp with fear. I have to fight him, she thought. Her purse was on her free arm and she let the strap slide from her shoulder. Before the bag could drop, she caught it and wrapped the strap once around her hand. Then she swung the purse as hard as she could at the man's head.

It caught him by surprise and he staggered backward. At the same time his cap flew off, and in the glow of the streetlamps she saw his face. It was a face she had seen before but couldn't place in her frantic state. She screamed "Help" again but no one came.

She tried to dart around the man but he shot to the right, blocking her path. She dodged the other way, but he blocked her again, and this time an evil smirk took shape on his face. In desperation she looked behind her. There was only the river. As she turned back around, the man charged at her with his full force, toppling her to the pebbled ground.

He'd knocked the wind out of her, too, and she struggled to get a breath. As he lunged toward her again, she hurled her purse at him with all her strength. It caught the edge of his shoulder and then bounced onto the rocks. He smirked again and drew something from his jacket pocket. The light caught the object and she saw that it was a knife—long and glinty and terrifying.

Then there was a sound behind the man, coming from near the trees in the park. He jerked his head back to see. In those few seconds Lake scooted back on her butt a few feet across the rocks and then staggered to her feet. Grabbing another breath, she turned around and stumbled to the river's edge. She could hear the man scrambling over the rocks right behind her, ready to grab her again, but before he could catch her, she took a huge step and waded into the river. She dragged her legs a few more feet and then suddenly there was no bottom. She dropped into the dark river water and it swallowed her up to her neck. Behind her she heard the man gasp in surprise.

The water was cold and all her muscles clenched in shock. She paddled a few more feet out from the shoreline and then twisted her body so that it faced the shore. The man was at the water's edge, his hands clenched in frustration. She could still see the knife shooting out, the blade an extension of his right hand.

Would he come after her? she wondered. Treading water, she kicked off her sandals and worked her way out of her jacket. Then, with long, firm strokes she began to swim, parallel to the shore. She was going south and she could feel the pull of a sure, steady current—or rather the outgoing tide, she suddenly realized, because the East River was an estuary of the Atlantic Ocean. Her terror ballooned. What if she was dragged down the river into the harbor? She would drown surely—or be sliced in two by a freighter. The trick would be to stay as close to the shore as possible.

Just ahead she saw an area of large jagged black rocks on the shoreline, almost primordial-looking, and then, not far beyond them, wooden pylons beneath another small park that jutted out over the river. If she could make it there, she could hold on to one of them. After about twenty strokes she flipped her body around and peered back toward the shore where she'd started. In the glow cast by the park lights, she saw the outline of the man still watching her, his arms outstretched tensely by his sides. But suddenly he turned and sprinted across the pebbles toward the entrance and disappeared into the darkness. Was he going to try to catch up with her farther south along the river?

She continued to swim, passing the rocks. Finally, exhausted, she reached the pylons. They were slimy and reeked of a horrible snail-like smell, but she flung her arms around one and held on as tightly as possible. It was such a relief to rest. Though she hadn't swum far, it had been hard to maneuver in her clothes. Farther out on the water a red tugboat steamed along, pulling a black-and-white freighter with Russian-looking words painted along the side. I can't believe this, she thought in despair. I'm floating in the East River. What was beneath her in the bottomless water? Fish and snakes and garbage? Worse?

Where was the man? By now he might be trying to get into the park above her. She had noticed earlier that a chain-link fence surrounded it, one he could easily scale. At that moment she thought she heard a noise on the walkway above the pylons. She pulled herself farther underneath.

The noise quieted after a moment. If it had been him, he would have seen that there was no way to reach her from where he was. But *now* what? she asked herself. He may have gone back to the park to wait for her. She had no choice but to stay where she was and pray that he didn't return there. Then she could swim back to the park and flee this place.

As she waited, she pictured the man's face in her mind. Where did she know him from? It was recent, she knew, very recent, but she couldn't think of where she'd seen him.

She shivered. Though the water wasn't extremely cold, she knew that if she were stuck in it long enough she would develop hypothermia. She dragged her legs back and forth through the water, trying to make her heart pump harder.

The next few minutes were endless. Far out in the river she could see freighters moving along almost soundlessly, pulled by tiny tugboats. She clung to the pylon as tightly as possible. Don't let me die here, please, she begged. She imagined Amy and Will, living their lives without her.

After about twenty minutes, she let go of the pylon and paddled a little back upriver, fighting the tide, until she could get a better look at the park again. There was no sign of the man. But she didn't dare go back so soon. She swam back to the pylon and grabbed hold again. Her arms ached and warm tears ran over the cool wetness of her face.

When roughly ten more minutes had passed, she knew she had to go back. She had started to shiver and her arms were trembling from grasping onto the pylon so tightly. She took a breath and began to swim, quietly as she could, back to the pebble beach. The tide was still going out, and within a minute she felt exhausted from fighting it.

Suddenly, she heard noises coming from the shoreline. With a rush of fear, she dropped her arms and treaded water. The sound was definitely emanating from the park. Was the man back? After a few seconds, she figured out the sound was laughter. She raised her head and peered through the darkness. There were four or five dark forms sitting on the terraced steps, talking and laughing. It sounded like a group of teenagers.

She began swimming harder, fighting the tide as best she could.

Finally she was at the beach. She didn't try to hit the bottom, just propelled herself onto the rocks like some kind of otter.

"Hey," she heard one of the people on the steps call out, then "Oh my God." As she pulled herself into a standing position, her wet clothes sucking at her body, five people scrambled down the steps in unison and ran toward her. As they drew closer she saw that they were all probably in their twenties—three guys and two girls.

"Are you okay?" one of the girls called out. "What happened to you?"

"I—I was chased into the water. By a man," Lake said.

All five of them stared at her in disbelief. It would probably have made just as much sense, she thought, to say she'd been on a reconnaissance mission for the U.S. government and had been diving in search of foreign submarines.

"He was attacking me," Lake added, wringing out her skirt. She scanned the area behind them, looking for the man.

"We should call the police," the same girl said. She pulled a cell phone from the pocket of her jeans skirt and flipped it open.

"No!" Lake said, startling them all. "I mean—I will, but I can't now. I have to get out of here in case he comes back. You—you should leave, too. It may not be safe."

A few of them looked around nervously.

"Yeah, we better go," one of the boys said.

"Could you walk me to my car?" Lake asked. "It's just a block away."

"Sure," the same dark-haired guy said. But no sooner had she said the words than she realized that she didn't have her purse. Her eyes raced over the rocks. There it was—still lying where it had landed when she'd thrown it at her attacker. Barefoot, she made her way gingerly over the rocks and grabbed it. Though a small notebook had slipped out onto the rocks, everything else was safely inside—her BlackBerry, her car keys, her wallet. Turning back around, she found all five people staring wide-eyed at her, clearly still dumbfounded by her entire existence.

She urged them again to leave and together they all hurried out of the park. One of the girls nervously grabbed the hand of the dark-haired guy, though the guys looked more perplexed than worried. They think I've had a fight with my boyfriend, Lake thought, and done a drama jump into the river. She didn't care. She was shivering and her stomach was cramping and she just wanted to be safe in her car.

As she hurried down the street with them, trying not to stub her bare toes on the cobblestone, she constantly surveyed the area. There was no sign of the man anywhere. Ten feet away from the car, with the strangers trailing behind her, she hit the unlock button on her car key and nearly flung herself inside. Before slamming the door shut, she thanked the five strangers for their help. Somewhere in the backseat was her gym bag, where she kept a pair of athletic shoes, but she didn't dare take the time now to find them. She fired up the engine and pulled away. In the rearview mirror she saw one of the guys shrug, as if asking, What the hell was *that* all about?

She could barely think straight as she drove. After making a right on a nearly deserted street, she sped out of Dumbo. When she finally reached a busier street, she pulled the car over and punched her address into the GPS so that she could find her way back to the Brooklyn Bridge.

But then she realized that she couldn't risk going home. What if the man was waiting for her there? Plus, she couldn't let the doorman see her this way. She could just imagine it turning up in a report in the custody case: "Doorman reports that mother once arrived home sopping wet and smelling of tanker oil and raw sewage."

Still shivering, she flipped on the heater and tried to focus. Molly's name flashed in her mind. She would go to her friend's apartment in Chelsea, she decided. Molly would take care of her and help her decide what to do. Maybe now she would even tell Molly the whole story. She clearly had to start getting some help.

Once over the Brooklyn Bridge, Lake took the FDR around the tip of Manhattan and then headed north. Every few seconds she checked the rearview mirror but it was impossible to tell if she was being followed—all she could see behind her were swirling globes of light. At a red light she rooted through her purse for her Black-Berry and called Molly. She got only voice mail.

"Molly," she said plaintively. "I—I need to talk to you. Please call me back, okay? As soon as you can." She tried Molly's landline next, but when there was no answer she just hung up.

Where *is* she? Lake wondered. Though Molly had a busy social life, she'd often told Lake she liked to be in bed before midnight. Lake checked her watch: 11:34. Knowing that Molly should be home shortly, or at the very least return Lake's call in a lather of curiosity, Lake decided to drive to Molly's apartment building. She'd wait outside until she finally heard back—and then she'd crash on Molly's couch for the night. She considered the small chance Molly was on a hot date and wouldn't be coming home tonight. But Lake had no other options.

She proceeded to West Twenty-first Street, frequently checking her rearview mirror. For one whole block there wasn't a single car behind, so she was pretty sure she wasn't being followed. The man who'd attacked her had obviously given up and left. She saw his face again in her mind's eye. Finally, with a start, she remembered where she'd seen him. He was the man in the bar at the Waldorf, the one who'd checked her out after Archer left. He'd been watching her for days, then. Had someone at the clinic hired him? Had he killed Keaton with that knife?

She was so distracted that she missed Molly's block and had to go around again. Once she was finally there, she double-parked just a few yards ahead of Molly's apartment building so she'd be able to see her come in. She craned her neck, checking nervously behind her. A few cars came down the street but they all shot past her.

Lake had stopped shivering but she felt miserable in her wet clothes. Still watching the building, she fumbled in the backseat for the bag with her gym clothes and pulled out the shoes and a T-shirt. She scrunched down in the front seat, peeled off her jersey shell and bra and wriggled into the T-shirt. Then she put on the shoes.

Ten minutes passed. She tried Molly's number again. Still no answer. As she eyed her incoming emails, she saw that Archer had sent her a message only a few minutes before. He'd returned from his trip sooner than he'd anticipated and wanted to catch up to-morrow.

Some movement on the block caused Lake's eyes to shoot back up. A woman with long hair, her back toward Lake, was walking toward the building. Finally—Molly. But as the woman reached the doorway and stopped to speak to the doorman, Lake saw that it wasn't Molly after all. What will I do if she doesn't come home? Lake thought plaintively. Should she get a hotel room? She could imagine the face of the front-desk clerk when her stench blew into the lobby.

The doorman nodded a goodnight to the woman and she pro-ceeded into the building. Two men walked past the building but didn't stop. And then a cab lurched to a stop in front. Please let this be Molly, Lake prayed. She could see the passenger leaning forward in the backseat to pay, and after a few seconds Lake could tell that it was a man. He flung open the door and thrust his body out with assurance. The light of the streetlamp caught his face as he paused to stuff the change into his pants pocket.

Lake stared in disbelief. It was Jack.

HE'S AFTER ME. The thought exploded in her mind before she'd
even fully processed Jack's presence. He'd arranged the bungled
attack on her tonight, just as he was behind what had happened to
Smokey and the bag of catnip. And since Jack knew she'd probably
turn to Molly for help tonight, he'd come looking for her here.

But as Lake slunk down in her seat, some other part of her
brain kicked those thoughts away. Jack had a sweater tied nattily
around his shoulders, and the expression on his face was smug
and expectant. No, he wasn't searching for her. That was the
look of a man who had *plans* for the evening. Jack was here to
see Molly.

Her stomach churned at the idea. She hoisted herself up just
enough to peer over the steering wheel. Jack was now in the foyer,
and the doorman was speaking into the phone. He hung up and
nodded to Jack with a smile that suggested familiarity. Then Jack
strode past him and into the building.

Lake's mind raced. How long had this been going on? Was Molly the reason for the breakup of her marriage? The thought of the two of them together, making love, sickened her. At the same time she felt that bizarre rush that comes with clarity. *This* explained Jack's prison-break departure from her life. It also explained Molly's endless questions about the divorce and about whether Jack was interested in reconciling—questions that had begun to go beyond a friend's concern. Obviously Molly had continued their friendship in order to keep tabs, to learn details about the divorce that Jack might not be sharing. How *evil*, Lake thought.

But the affair might be just the tip of the iceberg. She wondered if Molly and Jack were plotting together to get the kids. Molly's former marriage had been childless and she had admitted wistfully to Lake on several occasions that she regretted not having children. Now, with Jack's help, she could have her own instant family.

Thank God, Lake had never confessed to Molly what had happened with Keaton. It would all be over for her then. Quickly she ran through what she *had* discussed with Molly—that she thought Jack might be snooping, that she had engaged in minor flirting with someone at work, that she'd been interviewed by the police along with the other clinic staff. Nothing that could incriminate her.

She needed to get out of here. More than likely Molly and Jack were "in" for the night, but what if they decided to head out for a late drink or supper? She fired up the engine, and after driving several blocks, double-parked on a side street so she could plan her next move. Since she'd avoided her closest friends following her split with Jack, there was no way she could phone them now, out of the blue. She glanced down at the screen of her BlackBerry. Archer's email stared back at her. It seemed crazy to call him, but it was the only thing that made sense now. At the very least he'd be interested in what had happened to her tonight and what it possibly revealed about the clinic.

He answered on the third ring. In the background she could hear the drone of a TV so she assumed he must be home.

"I hope I'm not calling too late," Lake said. "It's Lake Warren."

"Oh, hey. I was going to touch base tomorrow. What's up?"

"I was attacked tonight. And I think it had to do with the clinic. I—I was just hoping I could talk to you. To be honest, I'm scared out of my mind."

"Are you hurt?" he asked, sounding alarmed. "Have you seen a doctor?"

"I'm okay. Just shaken. And I ended up in the East River, so I'm sopping wet."

"The *river*? My God. Where are you?"

"I'm in my car—in Chelsea. I don't really know what to do."

"I'm in the Village on Jane Street, so I'm not far. Will you be able to drive down here? Or should I come and get you?"

She could feel the relief wash over her. He was going to help her.

"No, I'll be okay driving down there."

He suggested a garage near his building, since street parking was next to impossible in his neighborhood.

"Why don't you call me when you get to the garage and I'll come meet you," he added.

"That's not necessary," she said. "Just give me your address and I'll see you in a few minutes. And . . . thank you."

To her surprise he was waiting in the garage when she arrived, dressed in khakis and a rumpled blue-and-white striped dress shirt. As soon as she stepped out of the car, he shook his head in distress at the sight of her.

"I'm just half a block up the street," he said. He put his arm lightly on her back and guided her along the sidewalk. The street was dark, the streetlamps partly obscured by rows of leafy plane trees, and the whole way there she could sense how alert he was, cocking his head back and forth as he checked around them. He had his keys out before they were even at his brownstone. After letting her into his ground-floor apartment, he glanced up and down the street before he shut the door.

"So tell me what happened," he said as soon as he'd ushered her into his living room. It was a large, comfortable space with a big red sofa and books and newspapers strewn all over its surfaces.

"A man attacked me in one of the river parks in Dumbo," Lake said. "He knocked me down and then he pulled out a knife. I know it sounds crazy, but the only way I could escape was to jump in the river. I swam over to an area beneath a park and hid there until I was pretty sure he was gone."

"Are you sure you're okay?"

"Yes—but it was pretty hairy for a while," she said, her voice catching. "I'm a good swimmer but I don't know how long I could have lasted out there. I was afraid I'd get tired and the tide would sweep me away."

Then without warning, she began to cry. Her shoulders shook, and she let out a weird strangled sound. It was partly from relief, she knew—and partly from despair, because though she'd escaped, she wasn't safe at all.

"Hey," Archer said gently and put his arm around her, pulling her toward him. Her right cheek pressed against his soft rumpled shirt. "Everything's okay now."

"I don't think so," Lake said, brushing her tears away. "I think someone from the clinic is after me. They want to shut me up."

"Tell me why you think that," he said.

"Look," she said, "I hope you won't be mad, but I tracked down Alexis Hunt myself. I wanted to find out what she thought was happening there. I figured if I was going to wade through the files, it would help to know what I was looking for."

"Okay," he said, drawing out the word. He'd turned his head and was looking at her sideways, his eyes skeptical.

"What she told me was pretty staggering," Lake said. "She's convinced that the clinic transferred her embryos to someone else—a woman named Melanie Turnbull. Sometimes couples give permission for this but Alexis definitely didn't. She says it resulted in this woman having a baby—and that she probably didn't realize it was from a donor embryo. Needless to say, Alexis is beside herself."

Archer opened his mouth in surprise.

"Wow, there was a case like that years ago in California. But could this have been a mistake? Embryos accidentally switched in the lab?"

"No, it all just seems too suspicious. The clinic likes to boast about how successful they are with older women. I think they're doing this to improve their numbers with women over forty. Plus, there are two instances I know of—Alexis is one—where the patient has fewer frozen embryos than she thought."

Archer placed a hand on his cheek and let out a long breath.

"I clearly hit a nerve with them," Lake continued. "The reason I was in Brooklyn was that I tracked Melanie Turnbull down, too. At first she didn't want anything to do with me, but then she agreed to meet me in a restaurant in her neighborhood. I waited an hour and she never showed. As I was walking back to my car, this man started following me—and then chasing me. And guess what else? He was also in the bar at the Waldorf the night I met you. He must have followed me there, too."

"So you think this woman reported back to the clinic that you'd called her and they arranged for this guy to try to kill you—a guy they'd already hired to keep you in his sights?"

"Yes, it seems that way. Levin obviously had him start watching me after he discovered I was getting snoopy. Then the assignment escalated." Suddenly she felt her whole body sag from exhaustion. "There's so much I've got to tell you. But I'd love to wash up first. After being in that river, I'm worried I'm on the verge of coming down with *cholera*." She managed a smile.

"Of course. How about a shower? I think that would be better than just washing up."

"Yes, great," she said.

"Come on, then. The main bathroom's upstairs." As he started to get up, he caught himself. "Wait, what about the police. What have you told them so far?"

"Nothing," she said quietly.

"Nothing? What do you mean?"

"I haven't called them. Not yet."

"But you need to."

"Th-there's a reason I haven't. I can explain later, okay?"

He eyed her curiously.

"All right," was all he said. He led her back out into the hallway and up a set of stairs to his bedroom.

"Give me a second to find you a clean towel," he said.

As he rustled through a linen closet in the hallway, her eyes scanned the room. Though the space, with its big oak bed and bedside table stacked with books, bore no resemblance to Keaton's sleek, spare room, she felt momentarily unsettled. The last time she had been in a strange man's bedroom, he'd been brutally murdered. And her world had fallen apart.

Archer returned to the room and pointed to the attached bathroom. He said he'd meet her downstairs when she was done.

"Tea or brandy?" he asked before he closed the bedroom door behind him.

"I could use both, if you don't mind," she said, smiling.

Within a minute she was in the shower, with the water as hot as she could stand. She felt off kilter being naked in a strange bathroom, and yet it was good to get the river stench off her. As she shampooed her hair, her eyes ran along the sides of the tub. There was nothing to suggest that a woman currently spent time on Archer's premises. Suddenly her thoughts rushed back to Jack and Molly. She'd been so preoccupied talking to Archer that she'd lost track of that part of the night's horror show. All those months she'd obsessed over what had happened to her marriage and why she'd been abandoned. Had the answer been literally right in front of her?

When she emerged from the steamy bathroom fifteen minutes later, she discovered a sundress lying across the bed. So, she thought, there *is* someone in his life and he's loaning me her clothes. She slipped the sundress over her head, put her sneakers back on, and carried her wet skirt and underwear downstairs in a bundle. Archer was reading in an armchair. On the coffee table was a tray with a pot of tea, an empty mug, and a glass of brandy.

"Better?" he asked, looking up.

"Yes, much. I can't believe how I've imposed on you—without even knowing you. Thanks for the dress, by the way."

"One of my stepson's girlfriends left it here—I believe she's gone off to Finland, so I'm sure it won't be missed."

Tucking her wet hair behind her ears, she settled onto the couch.

"I hope you're not an Earl Grey kind of girl," Archer said, raising his chin in the direction of the teapot. "All I had was English Breakfast."

"That's perfect," she said, pouring.

"Why don't you start at the beginning," Archer said. "I want to hear everything."

He wasn't going to let her just sit there and decompress. He was a reporter, after all. But she'd known that when she came here.

She started with her call to Alexis and then took him through everything else, including her presentation and the way Levin had shut her down.

"I was being dismissed, obviously," Lake said. "And this whole meeting with Melanie—it was clearly a setup, a way to lure me over to some dark street in Brooklyn."

"Are you sure? What if she had good intentions but simply got cold feet? I even wonder if something might have happened to *her*."

Lake hadn't considered that. But after a moment she shook her head.

"It's possible, I suppose, but I don't think so. Though someone could have followed me to the Waldorf, I'm almost sure no one followed me to Brooklyn tonight. I remember that when I parked on the street, there weren't any cars behind me. Melanie must have alerted someone at the clinic when she'd heard from me and they told her to set up the meeting. Though I doubt she knew they planned to kill me."

Archer tapped his fist lightly against his lips, a gesture she'd seen him use before.

"But what in hell do they think you've got on them?" he asked. "All you actually know is what Alexis told you, and there's probably nothing the police could do with that info anyway."

Lake massaged her damp head as her mind tossed everything around. What *could* they think she knew? Did it go back to Keaton? Was Levin aware she'd been with him that night and assumed he'd told her why he was pulling out of his deal with the clinic?

"Speaking of the police," Archer said, tugging her from her thoughts, "tell me why you haven't called them."

She took a long, slow breath. She needed an explanation that Archer would buy—one that wouldn't arouse his suspicions.

"The night Mark Keaton was killed a group of us had dinner

with him," she said. "The police came on strong during the inter-view with me the next day. Keaton had a reputation as a player and they may have wondered if I'd been having an affair with him—and then murdered him. I just don't want to direct their attention toward me. I'm in a bad custody battle and my ex is clearly looking for anything he can use against me."

Archer didn't say a word, just stared at her. Though his face was expressionless, she could see the question in his eyes: *Did* she have an affair with Keaton? The next question would be: Did *she* murder him? She took a sip of tea to break the eye contact.

"But if you don't involve the police," he said after a minute, "this guy won't be apprehended. And he may try to hurt you again. Look what happened to Keaton—this all might be connected."

"I know he may try again—and it's terrifying," Lake said. "But I honestly don't think telling the police will help. It's not like this guy left his fingerprints in the park. They'd never be able to trace him."

"But someone down there may have seen him getting into a car."

She had to get Archer off the police angle.

"Maybe," she said evenly. "But if these two homicide detectives find out I was chased into the East River, they're going to suspect something funny is going on with me. Remember what you said about coincidences? Even if I tell the cops I suspect the clinic of arranging the attack, it still puts too much focus on me."

"But what they might actually do is investigate the clinic. They could end up arresting people—including this thug from tonight."

Lake shook her head. "But as you said before, there's no way the cops can just walk into the clinic and investigate. They need proof, and there isn't any. All we have is Alexis's word, and, as your producer pointed out, she has a tendency to come off as a nut job."

"Okay, let's talk about proof, then," he said, leaning back into his armchair. "You never found anything in the files?"

She could feel her whole body unclench now that he'd stopped pressing her about the cops.

"Nothing that indicated what they're up to," she said. "But when I looked at Melanie's file tonight, there was a funny little notation—something I'd also seen in another patient's file."

From her purse Lake pulled out the scrap of paper on which she'd jotted down the letters. She handed it to Archer, explaining that she'd seen them next to the names on the information sheet.

"Any idea what they mean?" he asked.

"Not a clue."

"Could they refer to the specific infertility problem Melanie had—or the treatment the doctors prescribed?" Archer asked.

"I'm not an expert, but I know a fair amount of the terminology now, and those letters don't correspond to anything I've heard of. I'm wondering if they're a code that indicates Alexis's embryos were transferred to Melanie. Unfortunately I wasn't able to look at Alexis's file again. Brie, the office manager, caught me going through the files the first time, and I didn't want to take another chance."

"She saw you going through the files?" Archer said. He straightened up in his chair. It seemed some bell had gone off in his head.

"Yes. I made up an excuse, but I don't think she bought it."

"Couldn't *that* explain why you were attacked tonight?" Archer said, his blue eyes flashing. "You may not have any real evidence, but they *think* you do."

"Maybe you're right," she said hesitantly. "I've just assumed the attack was connected with Melanie."

Archer stared at the letters again.

"Can you make another attempt to see Alexis's file?" he asked. "If the letters match what's in Melanie's file, we could have something to go on."

The idea made her shudder. She shook her head. "After tonight, I don't know if I'd have the nerve."

Archer raked both hands through his thick white hair.

"There's just so much at stake," he said.

"Even if I wasn't terrified," Lake told him, "I'm not sure I'd be welcome back in the clinic. Levin acted so weird tonight."

"We've got to find a way to expose them. What if Alexis Hunt is really right? And if she's right, she's probably not the only victim."

Lake took another swig of tea. As she digested his words, she realized that it was the first time she'd really thought about the bigger picture. She'd been so consumed with her own cause, trying to save her skin, and her right to keep her kids, that she hadn't focused on how many other lives were being manipulated. What if it were I, she suddenly thought? What if I discovered that another woman had borne my child and was raising him?

"I've got an idea," Lake said. "There's a young nurse there who seems like a really good person. Her name's Maggie. I could try to convince her to look at the Hunt file for me."

"Do you think you can trust her?"

"Yes," Lake said. "If I can manage to contact her."

Lake set down her mug and reached for the brandy. As soon as she tasted it, she felt transported back to Keaton's apartment. She recalled the first sip of brandy she'd taken there, the hint of it later on Keaton's mouth—and then the sight of him dead in his bed. She choked as she swallowed and set the glass quickly back down.

"Are you okay?" Archer asked.

"Yes," Lake said feebly. "I'm just spent."

"I don't blame you." He glanced at his watch. "God, it's after one. Look, why don't I make the couch up for you. You can stay here tonight, and in the morning we'll figure out some kind of plan."

She didn't protest. As insane as it would be to bunk down at his place, she knew she'd at least be safe for tonight.

While Archer went upstairs for sheets and a blanket, she

stacked the kilim throw pillows on the floor. He returned not only with the bedding but also with a long T-shirt for her to sleep in. She offered to help make up the couch, but he insisted on doing it alone. Was he really this good a guy? she wondered as she watched him. Or was it all because of the story she was bringing him?

"You're all set now," he said, shaking out the blanket.

"Thanks so much for this," she said. She offered the warmest smile she could muster. Then his eyes narrowed in concern.

"*What?*" she asked. Something was clearly the matter.

"There's a bruise on your face. Is it from tonight?"

Her hand swooped to her cheek like a falcon. After the shower she'd neglected to put on any makeup and he was seeing the shadow of her birthmark.

"Oh," she said, flustered. "I had a birthmark there once."

"Ah. Well, it only adds to your fascination factor." He smiled. "Good night. Try to get a good night's sleep."

Minutes later, she was lying in pitch-darkness, the sheets cool against her body. For a while she could hear Archer moving around upstairs, getting ready for bed, and then it was quiet—the only remaining sound the light hum from the central air conditioning.

She hoped she'd be able to sleep. Her whole body ached—from the spill she'd taken on the rocks, from gripping on to the bastion for so long—and yet at the same time she felt totally wired. Memories of being in the river began to rush her mind. They made her panicky all over again, and she shook her head on the pillow, forcing them away. I can't relive that, not right now, she thought. And then she felt a surge of something else, something that caught her by surprise. Satisfaction. She had saved herself tonight. A man had attacked her, intent, she was fairly certain, on killing her, and she had outwitted him. She knew she had to hold on to that victory like a talisman. She needed the courage to continue to outwit whoever was after her.

Tomorrow she would connect with Maggie. She'd ask her to check the Hunt information sheet for a series of letters, written in pencil. It wouldn't be easy, but Lake had to convince Maggie and make her see the need to help her.

Finally, she closed her eyes, exhausted. She fell asleep and began to dream—about Amy. She and her daughter were walking by a body of water in a place she didn't recognize. And then someone was trying to take Amy away, saying she wasn't Lake's child after all. But she looks just like me, Lake screamed, terrified of losing her.

Suddenly she was jerked awake, as if she were stumbling off a curb. A thought grew quickly in her mind, like a sponge dipped in water.

She knew what the letters meant.

23

SHE WOKE THE next morning to muffled kitchen sounds—running water, a pan scraping against a stovetop burner. In her foggy state she thought she was hearing Will in the kitchen, using the stove when he shouldn't. But then she remembered where she was—and what had happened.

In the dim light from the living room windows, she located her purse and the sundress, then ducked into the powder room that Archer had pointed out last night. As she ran the water to wash her face, she checked her phone. There was an urgent message from Molly, finally responding to Lake's call for help last night.

"Are you *okay*?" she asked. "Call me." The sound of her voice made Lake livid.

"Hey, you're up," Archer said as she stepped back into the living room. He was standing in the doorway from the kitchen, wearing a fresh dress shirt and a dark suit, no tie. "How about some breakfast?"

"That would be great," she said. She remembered that she hadn't eaten dinner last night and her stomach was grumbling.

The kitchen fit Archer as well as the rest of the apartment did. Though the appliances were ultra-modern, the space was casual, homey—stacks of magazines and mail on the counter, postcards on the fridge, a bowl full of bananas on the round wooden table. There was a garden out back and the door was open so that a light breeze blew into the room.

"I've got English muffins, yogurt—plain or blueberry—granola, and a cereal called banana crunch that my stepson is addicted to but I think may contain massive amounts of sugar."

Lake smiled. "Plain yogurt sounds good. And an English muffin. But you don't have to wait on me. I can get it."

"No, no, sit down. There's coffee on the table."

"Your place is great," Lake said, sliding into a chair. "How long have you lived here?"

"About five years. When I was married, my wife insisted on doing the whole Upper East Side thing, which never really thrilled me. I found this place right after we split, and it's been great. There's a little study upstairs and a room for Matt, my stepson. In fact, he lived here the whole year I was working in Washington."

"What's he like?"

"A real good guy," he said, setting her yogurt down. "Twenty-three. Now at Columbia Law. How about some sliced banana with that? As you can see, I'm flush with those. My housekeeper clearly thinks I'm suffering from a potassium deficiency."

She smiled again and poured a mug of coffee for herself. "No, this is fine."

After toasting and buttering the muffin, he slid the plate in front of her and pulled out a chair for himself at the table. This is all so weird, she thought. He's the only man besides Jack that I've sat across the breakfast table from in nearly fifteen years.

"We need to make a plan," he said firmly. Suddenly the no-nonsense Kit Archer was back.

"I know—and I have to get home," she said. "I need to feed my poor cat." And yet what if the man from the park was keeping an eye on her building now?

"Where's your place?"

"The Upper West Side."

"I thought I'd drive home with you and make sure you got back okay. I'll head to work from there."

"Look, you don't—"

"Stop. There's no way I'm going to just let you go home alone—not after what happened last night."

She felt relieved knowing he'd be with her.

"Thank you."

"That's just step number one. From there you need to call this nurse you mentioned—as soon as possible. But is there any chance she could be involved?"

Lake shook her head. "At this point I don't feel sure of anything, but Maggie seems like a pretty guileless person."

"Okay, then, explain to her what happened to you. Let her know how serious the situation is and that you need her help."

"I'll do my best to convince her."

"Good. How long has she worked there?"

"About three years, I think. She's the one Keaton had given his keys to so she could pick up his mail."

"It's not going to be easy to get her to betray her bosses," Archer said. He tapped his lips lightly with his fist. "I wish we had some kind of proof to offer her—a way to legitimize your story."

"I think I have something," Lake said softly. "Not actual proof, but a strong indication that the clinic used Alexis's embryos on someone else—and is doing it with other patients as well."

He raised his chin, expectant.

"I think I know what the letters mean. "

"You're kidding," he said, astonished. "Tell me."

"It seems so obvious now, but it wasn't until I was lying in the dark last night and saw them in my mind that I figured it out. I think the first letters refer to hair color—*BR* for brown, *BL* for blond, *R* for red, and *BK* for black, maybe, though I never saw that one. The second set is for eye color—*b* for blue, *br* for brown again, *g* for green."

Archer stared at her, incredulous.

"Geez. Because that way—"

"—they do the best job of matching. Keeping track of a couple's coloring isn't necessary for medical purposes, and even if it was, why be so cryptic about it? But if the clinic is stealing embryos and transferring them to other women, it would be important to have that information. You'd want to make sure that the baby had coloring similar to its parents. The first indication that a child might not be yours would be if the coloring were totally off. From what I know it's fairly rare for two blue-eyed parents to have a brown-eyed child—and many people just assume it's not possible at all."

"Right—blue eyes are a recessive trait."

"If the coloring is really off, a couple might start asking questions. They might even get a DNA test for their peace of mind. And if there's a discrepancy, they're going to panic and demand an explanation."

"But what happens when the kid gets older and his features don't fit so well with his parents'?"

"If the coloring works, it may not seem like such a big deal. And by then there's total attachment. Even if the parents have reason to be suspicious, they may not want to rock the boat."

"Yeah, let sleeping dogs lie. And you just figured all this out last night, lying on my couch?"

Lake smiled. "I think my subconscious has been working on

it for a while. When I spoke to Alexis, she made a point of saying that the baby she saw with Melanie Turnbull matched Melanie's coloring perfectly. That comment has been playing in my brain somewhere ever since."

Archer shook his head in disgust. "And all just to improve their success rates. Do you think all the doctors could be in on it?"

She thought of Steve and felt a pang of worry.

"I don't know," she said. She took a sip of coffee. "It's possible that only a few people are involved and doing it without the others being aware. The nurses, for instance, could be totally in the dark."

"Wouldn't they be curious about the codes?"

"They might not notice them because they only appear on the basic information sheet that patients fill out in the beginning, not on the medical forms that get used later. Once a patient is under treatment, the focus would be on notations made about procedures, that sort of thing."

"You need to persuade Maggie to look through a bunch of the files and see how many have these codes. Of course, if she's in on it, this will be the tip-off that you know as much as they suspect you do."

"And if she's not and they catch her going through everyone's records, this could put her in danger," Lake said.

"Warn her that she has to be extremely careful."

"Okay," Lake said. She glanced down at the table, thinking about all of this. What would be the best way to approach Maggie? She would probably have better luck if she did it face-to-face.

"Speaking of danger," Archer said, interrupting her thoughts. She glanced back across the table. He had leaned back in his chair and was studying her intently. "Tell me what you know about Keaton."

Lake's heart jumped. Where was this going?

"Wh-what do you mean?" she asked.

"How do you think his death fits in with all this? Did he learn something he wasn't supposed to know?"

Lake slowly let out a breath in relief.

"I've wondered the same thing," she said. "We know that anyone from the clinic could have gotten into his apartment by using the set of keys from Maggie's drawer."

She wished she could tell him about seeing Melanie Turnbull's name on Keaton's table. Or at the very least that Keaton was going to bail on the clinic. Maybe she could say that Keaton had let that fact slip during conversation. But that would only arouse Archer's curiosity—and she couldn't give him even a hint of the whole truth.

"Possibly," he said. He finished his coffee and set the mug down. "But as much as I don't like coincidences, there's a chance that Keaton's death is just that."

"What do you mean?"

"I talked to some police contacts I have. They've got their own ideas about what went down."

"Oh?" Lake said, almost in a whisper.

"Keaton had a lady caller the night he was killed. There was a torn condom wrapper on the floor next to his bed. Which explains why the cops seemed interested in you. They're gonna look at every woman he crossed paths with."

Lake looked down, running her thumb along the handle of her mug.

"I can see your mind spinning," Archer said. "Got any ideas?"

"No—no, I don't," she sputtered. "I mean, I guess a woman could have killed him. Someone he was seeing. Is that what you think?"

"That's one possibility," Archer said. "*Or* . . . he had sex with this woman and, lucky for her, she left right afterward. And then after she was gone, someone from the clinic—or hired by the clinic—snuck in and did the job. Maybe it was even the guy who attacked you last night."

"There's so much to consider," Lake said weakly. It was all she could manage to say. She wondered if Archer suspected something and was toying with her. She needed to derail this conversation as soon as possible. She quickly drained her coffee mug and announced that she would grab her things from the living room.

They were in her car ten minutes later. Archer offered to drive and she gladly let him. Whatever sporadic calm she'd felt on and off at Archer's apartment was shot now—in part because she was headed home but also because of the breakfast-table conversation about Keaton. The traffic didn't help: the blaring horns on Sixth Avenue made her want to jump out of her skin. She barely spoke to Archer on the twenty-five-minute drive to the Upper West Side.

"I think I should come in with you for a minute," Archer said as they walked up the driveway of her parking garage. "Just to be sure everything is okay in your apartment."

Once again she didn't fight him. Given the mystery doorbell ring from the other night, she knew someone could easily gain access to her floor.

As they approached her building, she looked around. There were a dozen people hurrying along different points on the block, probably all bound for work. Nothing ominous, at least that she could see.

The doorman, Ray, was accepting a delivery of dry cleaning, but that didn't stop him from greeting her and giving Archer a discreet once-over. She worried briefly if having Archer come up might be grist for Jack's case, but she figured it was okay if he only stayed a few minutes.

"Does everything seem all right to you?" Archer asked as they stepped into the apartment.

"Yes—at first glance."

"Why don't I take a quick look around—if that's okay with you?"

"Thank you, I'd appreciate that," she said.

At that moment Smokey shot down the hall toward her.

"Geez," Archer said. "What's happened to this poor cat?"

"Someone did that to him."

"Last night?" Archer exclaimed.

"No, no. Before." Lake quickly told him the story, as well as about the catnip and the night the doorbell rang. Archer listened with his brow furrowed, not interrupting.

"Okay, I need the actual timeline for all of this," he said when she'd finished. "When was the cat shaved?"

"Last weekend."

"And the catnip showed up in your purse . . . ?"

"On Wednesday."

"This isn't making much sense to me. The office manager—her name's Brie?—caught you going through the files a day or two ago. Since then you were given the cold shoulder at your presentation and you were attacked when you were supposed to be meeting with a former patient. *That* makes some kind of sense. But why was your cat shaved last weekend?"

"I—I don't know," Lake stammered. "Levin knew I'd found the file with your name. Maybe he already thought I was beginning to snoop around. Maybe he wanted to warn me off."

"But how were you supposed to guess that having your cat shaved meant to cool it at the clinic? That takes a hell of a lot of translation. No, there's a piece missing here . . ."

He swept a hand through his hair and stared off to the side, thinking. Lake could barely contain her agitation. She didn't want him thinking about this. Because if he did, it wouldn't be long before he saw the full timeline in his mind and realized that the incidents had begun shortly after the murder itself. And that she was somehow deeply connected to it.

"Should we look around now?" she asked. "I don't want to hold you up."

"Sure," he said, but when his eyes caught hers she saw that they were questioning. She could tell he sensed she was holding back.

With Lake leading, they ducked into each room in the apartment. Nothing seemed amiss.

"I can't thank you enough for this, Kit," she said as they left the family room. She realized it was the first time she'd used his first name. "I honestly don't know what I would have done without you."

"I'm just glad you decided to call me. So when do you plan to talk to Maggie?"

"Around twelve-thirty. She goes to the same spot for lunch most days and I think I'll just wait outside for her."

"Call me right afterward, okay?" he said, walking toward the door. "And call me if you feel in any kind of danger."

Their eyes met and he held her gaze for a moment.

"Thanks again for everything," she said.

As soon as she'd closed the door behind him, she flicked the dead bolt and put the chain on the door. It was just after nine. Though Maggie was her priority today, there was someone else she needed to talk to: her lawyer. Hotchkiss was probably already at his desk. She dialed the number and his secretary put her through.

"I'm not sure if this will help my custody situation or not," she told him, "but I'm pretty sure my husband is having an affair with one of my friends."

"Interesting," he said dryly. "How did you learn this?"

"I happened to see him going into her building last night."

"He could have been visiting someone else who lives there."

"Yes—but she's also been unusually inquisitive lately about anything having to do with Jack and the divorce."

"It's worth checking out," he said after a pause. "And we may be able to use it as a bargaining chip. Remember that I said we might want to hire an investigator? I think we should at this point."

Lake sighed. She couldn't believe it was coming to this. She agreed and Hotchkiss said he would have an associate make the arrangements. Then he warned her not to tip her hand.

"This isn't going to be easy," he said, "but you'll have to act the same—to both of them. If they suspect you're wise to them, they'll alter their behavior. And there will be nothing for us to investigate."

As soon as she disconnected the call, the phone rang in her hand. It was Hayden calling. Lake braced herself. There might be some kind of update about the case.

"What's up?" Lake asked.

"Well, it's not pretty," Hayden said. "And I feel awkward as hell sharing it."

"What is it?" she demanded.

"You're going to be getting a letter by messenger from Levin and Sherman. They're terminating your consulting arrangement."

So this explained the coolness at the meeting—they were planning to can her. But maybe it had more to do with what happened in Brooklyn. They didn't dare face her again.

"They told you that themselves?" Lake said.

"Yes—I just got off the phone with Levin. I called him to say that I thought the three of us should go over where everything stood and he broke the news. Look, I'm really sorry about all this."

"I appreciate your giving me the heads-up."

"What's going on, anyway, Lake? Why's he giving you the boot?"

"What did he tell you exactly?" Lake asked.

"Nothing—but he didn't sound pleased. I know you felt rushed about your presentation. I take it it didn't go over well."

"I guess not. I don't think we saw eye-to-eye on things."

"Do you want me to try any damage control? It's what people pay me the big bucks for."

"No, but thanks."

Lake's heart was racing as she hung up. She'd suspected last night that something like this might be coming. They knew she was onto them and, of course, they couldn't allow her on the premises anymore. And yet the news still felt like a hard kick in the gut.

She tried to calm herself. Everything seemed to be closing in on her—but she couldn't let it. She would leave for the coffee shop in two hours. Her only hope at this point lay with Maggie.

24

AS LAKE WAS about to toss the phone down, it rang yet again. It was a cell phone number she didn't recognize

"Lake, hi, it's Harry Kline. Have you got a minute?"

His voice had that familiar soothing tone, but she bristled at the sound of his voice.

"What is it?" she asked. Was he calling to forewarn her about her situation and then ask how she was *feeling*? she wondered bitterly.

"There's something I need to talk to you about."

"If it's about me getting my walking papers, I've already heard."

"No, it's more than that. Can you meet me this morning?"

"You can't tell me over the phone?" she said impatiently.

"No. I'm at the clinic and I'm not comfortable talking here— even with my door closed. I could just hop in a cab and meet you. Are you home now?"

That was the *last* place she wanted to meet.

"Um, why don't we meet in Riverside Park? By the entrance at Eighty-third Street. That would be easiest for me."

He said he would be there in twenty-five minutes. She threw on a skirt and a top and pinned her hair up in a loose bun. Her mind raced, trying to figure out what Harry wanted to tell her. Things must be tense at the clinic right now. Harry may have overheard a heated discussion about her. Or perhaps he picked up on something in the air and began snooping around himself.

She was at the park ten minutes early. On the walk over she'd reassured herself that nothing could happen in daylight on a busy street, but she was still hypervigilant. There weren't many people in the park—an elderly woman tossing birdseed to pigeons, a few mommies and nannies watching toddlers in a sandbox. People were away on vacation. Like she used to be in August.

"Lake?"

She spun around in surprise at the sound of Harry's voice. He'd also arrived early. He was dressed in his standard dark pants and cobalt-blue dress shirt.

"Thanks for meeting me," he said. "Shall we find a bench?"

They walked farther into the park. Across the Hudson the buildings in New Jersey gleamed in the sunshine and through the trees she saw a speedboat slicing through the water, leaving a row of foam. It made her remember last night, holding on to the pylon for dear life in the deep, dark water. Harry motioned for them to take a seat on an empty bench.

"So what is it you need to talk about?" she asked. As she caught his eyes, she was shocked at how troubled they seemed.

"Look, I may be on the periphery of things at the clinic," he said, "but I'm involved enough to know that something isn't right."

It was all Lake could do to keep from shaking the words out of Harry.

"What do you mean exactly?" she said.

"I don't like what's going on with you."

"With *me*?" she blurted out.

"The way they've just suddenly terminated your agreement."

"I told you I was aware of that," she said. "I haven't received the letter but I hear it's on the way."

"But are you aware of what they're saying?"

"No—what?" she said hoarsely.

"As soon as I heard that they'd ended things with you, I asked Levin why. He said that you'd been unprofessional. In fact, he said some of your behavior could even be categorized as unethical."

"*What?*" Lake exclaimed in shock. "Did—did he explain what he meant?"

"He said you'd been caught going through patient records. I pointed out that part of your job is to gather information, but he said he had reason to believe that you were passing confidential details about our procedures on to another clinic."

Lake's eyes welled up in anger.

"That's a lie," she said. "I would never do something like that."

Harry leaned back against the park bench, his face pensive. A light breeze lifted the waves of his black hair. "Do you have any idea why he's claiming it, then?"

"I—no, I don't," Lake said. She wondered why Harry was sharing all this with her. Was he trolling for information of his own?

"You don't know? Or you don't want to share it with me?"

"Maybe I should start by asking what *your* role is in this," Lake said. "Why are you being so forthcoming?"

Harry bit his lip, as if hesitant to say.

"We've only known each other a few weeks, but I like you, and I respect you a lot," he said after a moment. "It's hard for me to buy what Levin said. And I want to help you if I can."

"Help me?" Lake asked. She could feel her anger close to the surface. "Like you helped me when you told the police things about me?"

"What are you talking about?" Harry asked, looking surprised.

"When we were having coffee last Sunday, you pointed out that I'd seemed unusually upset after the murder. And then suddenly the police are at my apartment, telling me that someone told them the same thing."

He took a deep breath and leaned toward her.

"So that's why you were so cool to me the other day. Lake, I give you my word—I never said anything about you to those detectives. For starters, I'm a therapist, and breaking a confidence runs against every instinct I have as a person and everything in my professional training. Secondly, I'd never do anything to hurt you."

She studied his face as he spoke. His eyes, his mouth, his body language—everything suggested he was telling the truth. But as he'd just pointed out, he was a therapist, someone all too familiar with how people could be manipulated and fooled.

"Look," he added. "I can see that you're still skeptical. So I'm going to admit something that seems ridiculous to put out there right now, but it may lend me an ounce of credibility."

He lifted his shoulders and flipped over both palms in an almost boyish gesture. "The reason I asked you for coffee the other day is that I was looking for an excuse to be with you. I'd like to go out with you, Lake. So the last thing I would have wanted is to put you in any kind of weird situation with the cops."

Lake almost laughed at the sheer absurdity of it all. People were trying to kill her, the cops might suspect her of murder, and this guy was confessing a crush on her.

"I don't know what to say," she said. "I mean—"

"There's no need to say anything at the moment. We can cross that bridge later. The thing we need to deal with right now is your situation with Levin and Sherman. There's obviously been some kind of terrible misunderstanding and we should clear it up. I'd be happy to intervene."

Lake shook her head emphatically.

"Thank you, but once I get the letter from Levin and have a chance to digest what he's saying, I'll make my case with him myself."

"Is there *anything* I can do, then?"

Should I tell him? Lake wondered. What if she enlisted *him* rather than Maggie to search through the files? But despite how genuine he sounded, she felt a lingering suspicion about him. And she needed to stick with the plan she worked out with Archer.

She glanced at her watch. She wanted to position herself near the coffee shop at just a little after noon so as not to risk missing Maggie.

"No, Harry, but thank you. Look, I have an appointment and I need to get back."

"I'm off for the rest of the afternoon, but I'll be at the clinic tomorrow," he said. "Let me know how it goes, okay?"

"Will do."

They stood and walked back toward the entrance. Two boys, nine or ten years old, whooshed by them on skateboards, their faces tight with concentration. One made Lake think of Will, pinching her heart. At the same moment she felt a cloud pass over the sun and she glanced up instinctively. She quickly said goodbye to Harry and hurried home.

Back in her apartment, she made coffee and paced. She felt outraged about the approach Levin was taking—telling people that she'd engaged in some kind of espionage for another clinic. Word would get around in her professional circles and the story could dog her for years, perhaps even ruin her business. Was this Levin's backup plan? If he couldn't manage to kill her, he'd destroy her reputation?

If, of course, Levin was the one behind it all. What if someone else at the clinic was the mastermind of the embryo stealing? Maybe it was Sherman, in cahoots with Hoss. Or, if he'd found the right person in the lab to assist him, even Steve might have been able to pull it off. It would be in his interest, too, to keep the clinic's success rate high. If it *was* someone else, that person could have convinced Levin that Lake was stealing information—while also arranging to have her attacked.

She hailed a cab at 11:40 and was outside the coffee shop by 12:05. She felt exposed standing right in the front of the restaurant, so after a few minutes she ducked into the doorway of the shoe store next door, where she'd still be able to see Maggie coming. As she waited, she rehearsed what she'd say to Maggie. She would have to sound very credible, especially if Maggie had been told that Lake was a spy.

By 12:40 Lake started to worry. Based on her routine, Maggie should have been there by now. Maybe, in light of everything going on, Maggie felt the pressure to stay close to base. Lake shifted her position again and again because her body still ached from last night. Please, please come, Maggie, she pleaded in her head.

And then Lake saw her. She'd made the turn onto Lexington and was hurrying up the block, her shoulders slumped and her face blank. She was wearing another pretty dress today and carrying the same tiny summer purse—the reason she'd left Keaton's keys in her desk.

"Hi, Maggie," Lake said, stepping out from the doorway. "I hate to interrupt your lunch today but I was hoping I could sit with you for a few minutes."

Maggie shook her head back and forth.

"That's not—that's not a good idea," she said.

"Could I just talk to you out here for a few minutes, then?"

Maggie looked off, refusing to make eye contact.

"I'm sorry—I can't."

Lake's heart sank.

"But why not, Maggie?" she asked. "What have I done to upset you?"

"It's not me. It's what you've done to the clinic. Dr. Levin told me all about it. He said you've been giving another clinic confidential information of ours—information about the techniques we use."

"Maggie, I need you to understand the truth. Yes, I did look through a few files but not so I could pass the information to other doctors. I think the clinic is transferring some couples' embryos to other women without anyone's permission. That's the real reason they want me out of there."

Maggie's brown eyes flashed with anger.

"That's not true," she said defiantly. "Dr. Levin is an amazing man—he's a miracle worker really. All he wants is to help people."

"I've spoken to a patient whose embryos were probably stolen," Lake said. She could hear desperation beginning to seep into her voice and tried to squelch it. "And last night a man attacked me. I'm almost positive he was hired by the clinic."

Maggie shook her head again.

"I don't believe you," she said. "That's ridiculous."

"But why would I just make all this up? What would I have to gain from it?"

Maggie raised her chin and looked Lake directly in the eye.

"Because Dr. Levin caught you stealing. And you need to cover your tracks." There had been a slight hesitancy in her words, as if a part of her was still weighing what Lake had said.

"Maggie, over the last few weeks you've gotten to know me a little. Do you really think I'm capable of that?"

Maggie bit her lip. Have I made a dent, Lake wondered?

"I *have* gotten to know you a little, but I know Dr. Levin much better," Maggie said. "And he's the one I trust."

She started to turn. Lake couldn't believe it. This had been her chance and she'd blown it.

"Maggie, please," she said. Lake reached for the nurse's arm and grabbed it at the wrist. A man walking by with a bulldog caught the gesture out of the corner of his eye and swiveled his head in their direction. Lake dropped Maggie's arm. "I can prove to you that what I'm saying is true—you just need to do one thing to help me."

"I can't," she said. "I want you to leave me alone."

Maggie rushed past her, started to enter the coffee shop, and then changed course, continuing north on Lexington. She obviously didn't want to take the chance of Lake following her inside and pleading with her further.

Lake glanced around to make sure no one was watching her. Then she hailed a cab.

Now what, she wondered? letting her body sink wearily into the backseat. She'd banked everything on Maggie, which in hindsight was a stupid plan. Yes, Maggie seemed like a decent person, and, yes, Maggie had clearly liked her, but Maggie was also young and naïve. And probably fearful of getting involved in any way.

At home Lake poured a glass of wine and drank it with a piece of cheese—the only edible thing she had in the fridge. As she paced up and down the long hall in her apartment, she mentally ticked through the clinic's other staff, wondering if she dared contact any of them for help.

Steve. He was her friend's brother, the whole reason Lake was at the clinic to begin with. But as far as she knew, he might very well be in on things. Plus, she couldn't ignore the fact that he hadn't called to hear her side of the story or to ask if he could help.

Which made her think of Harry. But she still didn't know if she could trust him.

She glanced down and saw that she had drained the entire glass of wine. I need to get in touch with Archer and come up with a new plan, she thought. As she set her wineglass down, she heard her BlackBerry ring in her purse. Grabbing it, she saw to her shock that it was the number of the clinic. Could it be Maggie, she wondered, having a change of heart?

"This is Lake Warren," she answered.

"It's Rory," the voice on the other end said, nearly in a whisper. "From Advanced Fertility."

"Yes?" she asked. It was the last person she expected to hear from.

"I know something," Rory said. "I think you should know it, too."

25

LAKE CHECKED THE surge of hope that had already begun to build in her. She'd had a similar call hours earlier from Harry. And though he'd disclosed Levin's latest tactic against her, it hadn't been the kind of information she'd needed.

"What's it about?" Lake asked. "I assume you know I'm not with the clinic anymore."

"Yes, I know that. Everyone does. But"—and she lowered her voice even more—"I overheard Maggie talking to Chelsea. I know what you told her."

"Yes?" Lake asked quietly.

"It made me think. You see, something funny happened here recently. Something maybe you should know about."

Lake wondered if this was finally it—the break she had desperately longed for.

"What happened?" Lake asked. She realized she was whispering, too.

There was a pause. Lake sensed that Rory had turned around and checked behind her.

"I'm afraid to talk about it right now. I can't believe I'm even calling you from here—someone might overhear."

Quickly, Lake tried to think of a plan. "Do you want to come to my place? After work. We could talk here."

"No. I can meet you after work, but I don't want to go to your place. Someone from here might see me going into your building."

"Your place, then?" Lake asked. She remembered that Rory lived north of the city; Lake could drive there.

"That's too far," Rory said. "I'm all the way up in Bedford Hills. Oh gosh, I don't know. Maybe I—"

"I've got an idea," Lake said, her mind forming the plan as she spoke. "There's a little piano bar in the Eighties. It's not far from the clinic, but no one on staff would ever go there. Why don't we meet there when you finish up today?"

Rory sighed. Lake bit her tongue, afraid of pushing too hard.

"Okay," Rory said finally.

Lake gave her the name of the bar—a place she used to go with Jack to hear music—and they agreed to meet at six-thirty.

Next she called Archer to fill him in on her conversations with Maggie and Rory.

"Sounds like we might be in luck. When are you going to speak to her?"

"At the end of the workday."

"Call me, okay? As soon as you're done talking to her."

For the next hour she sat in her home office, trying to concentrate on the rest of her consulting business, which she'd almost totally ignored lately. She hadn't read her emails in days, and there were dozens and dozens of them, many of which should have been answered immediately. She responded to the most urgent ones, including one from a prospective client wondering why she hadn't yet received a proposal from Lake, and then she just couldn't concentrate any longer. Her assistant was due back next Wednesday, and she could help get things under control. But Lake couldn't imagine how she'd function normally in front of her with everything that was going on. Plus, would Lake be putting her in danger?

Suddenly she felt overwhelmed with fatigue. But she didn't dare take a nap like yesterday, in case it would be hours before she woke. Instead she showered, turning the water to cold before she finished. As she toweled off, she mentally prepped for the meeting with Rory, urging herself not to seem desperate like she had with Maggie. She winced at the memory of her grabbing Maggie's wrist. This was a different situation, of course. Rory was coming to her. But she could sense that Rory was a reluctant witness and that she'd have to be careful not to frighten her off.

Lake made sure she was at the bar fifteen minutes early. She found a table toward the back, with a view of the door but away from the windows. It was too early for the first piano player of the evening, though people were already gathered at the bar, a few in groups. She ordered a glass of red wine and folded her hands on the table. Let this *be* something, she thought.

When Rory entered the bar, Lake almost didn't recognize her. In her floral dress she looked far more pregnant than she did in her white uniform jacket. Her blond hair was wavy from the humidity and pinned back on one side with a barrette.

As she made her way to Lake's table, Rory searched the room with her eyes and then looked behind her before sitting down.

"Are you sure no one will see us here?" she asked worriedly as she sat across from Lake

"I'm positive. Would you like something to drink?" Lake asked.

"*Drink?*" Rory exclaimed, her pale blue eyes widening. "But I'm *pregnant*."

"I didn't mean a *drink* drink. Do you want a soda—or a sparkling water?"

"No, nothing."

It was clear Lake needed to cut to the chase.

"I really appreciate your coming, Rory," she said. "Why don't you tell me what's on your mind."

Rory looked behind her once more before speaking.

"Like I told you on the phone, I overheard Maggie and Chelsea talking. Maggie usually eats lunch at this one coffee shop and she *always* takes the full hour, but today she went out and came back in ten minutes with just a sandwich from a deli. I saw her go into the kitchen to get something to drink and she seemed sort of flustered. Chelsea was already in there and I started to go in there, too, but then I overheard them whispering. Maggie said that she'd run into you and that you told her that the real reason you were fired was because you'd discovered something bad going on at the clinic—in the lab in particular."

"Did she tell Chelsea what it was?"

"Not that I heard. She just asked Chelsea if she thought it could be true, if Chelsea thought something weird might be going on. And Chelsea told her that you were just trash-talking out of revenge. Of course, I'm not sure how Chelsea would even know, one way or the other. She's really not that smart."

"As far as you know, did Maggie say anything to anyone else?"

"I doubt it. Chelsea's the only one she's really close to." Rory ran her eyes over Lake's face as if she were searching for something.

"Rory, look—"

"Is there really something going on at the clinic?" Rory asked, her eyes narrowed in worry.

"Yes, I think there may be," Lake said. "A former patient told me she believes that the doctors implanted some of her embryos into another woman—without permission from either one of them."

"Omigod," Rory said, instinctively curling her arm around her rounded belly. "They—they could get in so much trouble for that."

"Have you ever witnessed anything that would make you think that they're guilty of that? On the phone you said that something funny had happened."

"I did see something funny," she said after a moment. "But I don't know if it has anything to do with what you're talking about."

"But it might," Lake urged. "Please tell me."

Rory took her arm from her belly and folded her hands on the table. Her hands were large and strong, fitting her body, but also perfectly manicured—with peach-colored nails.

"When I first got pregnant I felt really awful," Rory said. "I have no clue why they call it morning sickness because I was sick all day long. One afternoon I felt so bad I didn't know how I was going to be able to get on the train to go home. So after I'd finished with the last patient, I decided to lie down in Dr. Kline's office for a while—he's got a little love seat in there. It was about five-thirty and I only planned to rest for a few minutes, but when I opened my eyes it was almost seven. I couldn't believe it. I was afraid that everybody had left and I was locked in with the alarm on. I walked down to the reception area and all of a sudden I saw Dr. Hoss standing there with a man I'd never seen before. She seemed really uncomfortable when she noticed me—like I'd caught her at something."

"Maybe it was someone she was dating—and she felt awkward?"

Rory glanced quickly behind her again.

"Well, he had a silver container with him," she said, her voice hushed. "The kind that's used to carry eggs."

"*Eggs?*" Lake said.

"Yes. And embryos."

"Was he delivering eggs?" Lake asked. "From a donor bank?"

Rory shook her head.

"I don't think so. I think he was taking some away."

"How can you be sure?"

"Because I followed him."

"*Followed* him?" Lake asked, surprised. "How did you manage that?"

"I left the clinic first. I could tell they didn't want me there. But I waited down the street until the man came out. Like I said, the whole thing just seemed kind of funny to me, and I thought if I saw what kind of car or van he got into, it would help me figure it out. But he didn't get into a car. He just started walking. I still felt a little sick, but I decided to follow behind. I knew he couldn't be going very far because he had the cooler with him. And then just three blocks away he went into a townhouse. After about five minutes I went in and checked the name on the plaque. It said New Century Research."

"So the eggs may have been donated for research? Isn't that something the clinic does occasionally?"

"Some couples okay it but not very many. *I* certainly never would if I were in their situation. Besides, that's not the name of a company the clinic deals with regularly. And, like I told you, there was something really funny about the way Dr. Hoss acted."

Lake studied the table for a moment. It wasn't the information she'd been hoping for, but it all might fit in. If the clinic had enough reckless disregard for someone's embryos to implant them in another woman, they wouldn't think twice about selling them for research.

But she needed evidence. She had to convince Rory to look through the patient charts. When she glanced back up, Rory was staring at her.

"Rory, I really appreciate your sharing this with me," she said. "But now I need your help. Would you be willing to pull a few patient charts? I honestly think that the clinic is doing things that aren't ethical, and the proof has got to be in the files."

Rory shook her head quickly back and forth.

"Look, I told you what I know," she said. "If there's something weird going on, I want the doctors to be told they have to stop. But I don't want to make trouble."

"Please, hear me out, Rory," Lake said. "First of all, innocent couples are being affected by this. Secondly, I think there are dangerous people at the clinic. A man tried to kill me last night—and I'm almost positive he was hired by a person at the clinic."

"*Kill* you?" Rory said. She drew her body back, startled. "How?"

"He pulled a knife on me in a park. Fortunately I was able to get away."

"But maybe it was just someone trying to mug you."

"I don't think so. He followed me from where I'd gone to meet a former patient—who never showed, by the way. This guy seemed to know where I'd be. Plus, think about what happened to Dr. Keaton."

She hated even saying Keaton's name, but she needed to use whatever she could to elicit Rory's help.

"Dr. Keaton?" Rory said, clearly shocked by the reference. "What do you mean?"

"I think—I'm wondering if he may have stumbled onto some of this information himself. It may be why he was killed."

Rory wrinkled her nose. "But Dr. Levin said he had a gambling problem and some *Soprano*-type probably broke into his apartment and killed him because he owed lots and lots of money."

"There was no forced entry apparently. And his keys had been left in Maggie's drawer for days."

"But Maggie said he had a terrace. The killer probably got in from there."

"That's not possible," Lake said. "There's—" And then she caught herself. She couldn't believe how stupid she'd just been. She watched Rory's mouth drop open and close.

"What do you mean?" Rory asked flatly.

In her mind Lake fumbled for a way to cover her slip.

"Maggie," she said after excruciating seconds. "She told me he lived on a high-up floor. How—how could anyone have gotten access to a terrace so high? Unless they were like Spider-Man."

Rory stared at Lake, her face as frozen as a mask. Lake couldn't tell if she had guessed the truth—that Lake was personally familiar with the apartment—or was simply weighing whether someone from the clinic could have killed Keaton. Lake held her breath, waiting.

After a moment, Rory shrugged. "Maybe you're right. We live in an old gate house, and I don't know anything about city apartments."

Lake relaxed. Rory may have felt a flutter of suspicion, but she'd clearly dismissed it.

"If Dr. Keaton *was* killed because of this situation at the clinic, you can see how important it is that we stop them," Lake said.

"But what exactly would you want me to do?" Rory asked worriedly.

Lake told her about the series of letters she might find in Alexis's file, and possibly others.

"Except for the Hunt file, it's not necessary to comb through drawers in the storage room," Lake said. "You could just look at each patient's chart as she comes in for her appointment. No one should find that suspicious."

"What do the letters stand for?" Rory asked.

"I'm still trying to figure that out," Lake said, not wanting to divulge her theory.

Rory scrunched her mouth, clearly mulling over everything she was hearing.

"Rory, I know it's a lot to ask," Lake said, frightened now that Rory would say no. "But just think if someone had done this with *your* embryos."

"Okay," Rory said finally. "I guess I could try to do it Monday."

Lake smiled gratefully. "That's wonderful. And if you do find those letters on the information sheets—especially the Hunts'—it would help so much if you could make photocopies. But only if you can do it discreetly. I don't want anyone to see you."

"All right." Rory looked off, thinking. "I really should go now. It's not good to be under a lot of stress when you're pregnant."

"I understand completely," Lake said. She reached into her purse for a business card. "My cell is on here, as well as my home phone. If you run into any difficulty at all, please call me right away."

Rory pulled a small note pad from her purse and wrote down her home and cell numbers.

"My husband—Colin—had to go away again today and I'll be on my own this weekend. I'm not telling him any of this, by the way. He wouldn't want me to get involved."

Lake felt a twinge of guilt.

"I can't tell you how grateful I am, Rory. Just be as careful as possible."

"I'm actually glad I can help you, Lake," Rory said, smiling for the first time since she'd arrived. "I hope this doesn't sound silly, but I really admire you. That's why I wanted to tell you what I know. Can I call you this weekend? Just to go over everything again?"

"Of course. And thank you for what you just said."

Lake reached across the table and laid her hand over Rory's. Underneath she could feel Rory twitch in discomfort, as if Lake had cupped her hand over a small toad on the ground. Quickly,

Lake pulled her hand away. Don't push it, for God's sake, she chided herself. Leave well enough alone.

She stayed for a few minutes after Rory left, finishing her wine. Every nerve ending in her body seemed fired up in anticipation. Finally there was someone who could help her dig for the truth. There was no guarantee of Rory coming across anything, but this was a *start*. It felt like that moment when a nightmare begins to disintegrate from feeling utterly terrifying and you sense for the first time that you've been dreaming.

Plus, there was the new information about New Century Research. That might turn out to be a valuable piece of evidence against the clinic, adding to whatever else she turned up. The only thing that worried her about this evening's conversation was the slip she'd made about the terrace, but it appeared to only have aroused momentary curiosity in Rory.

Out on the sidewalk, she checked nervously around and left Archer a message as she tried to find a cab. Ten minutes later she was finally on her way home. As her cab shot west through Central Park, her phone rang. She glanced at the screen, expecting to see Archer's name, but the phone number was unrecognizable.

"Hello?" she answered hesitantly.

"Mommy," a young girl's voice said.

"*Amy?*" Lake asked.

"Yes." There was a stifled sob.

"Amy, are you all right?"

"No, Mommy. I'm not."

"WHAT DO YOU mean, Amy?" Lake asked urgently. "Where are you?"

"I'm in the infirmary."

Involuntarily, Lake let out a moan of distress.

"Mommy?"

"What happened, honey? Tell me."

"The doctor thinks I have strep. They put this stick in my mouth and it made me gag."

Lake almost laughed ridiculously in relief.

"Oh, honey, I'm sorry."

"Mommy, it hurts so much. I can barely swallow."

"Is the doctor there now—can I talk to him or her?"

"No, just the nurse is here. She's in the other room. And I'm not supposed to be using a cell phone. It's Lauren's."

"Okay, as soon as we hang up, I'm going to call the camp and see what they can do."

"But I'll get in trouble for using the phone."

"Don't worry—I won't tell. But I'm going to find a way to help you get better, okay?"

Lake heard the sound of a sob catching in her daughter's throat.

"Mommy, I wish you were here. I feel so sad."

"I'm going to send you a long fax today to cheer you up. And when you start to feel better, you won't feel so sad."

By the time Lake hung up, her panic had quelled, but she could feel anger filling the void. Why hadn't the camp contacted her? She hated thinking of Amy so miserable. Immediately she punched in the number for the director's office. He had stepped away, she was told and there was no one else who could help her at the moment. Lake asked that he call her the moment he returned.

As the cab swung onto West End Avenue, she was relieved to see that there were people in front of her building—a red-haired woman with a stroller, a tall thin, black man, vaguely familiar from the building, and her neighbor, Stan, holding his jacket over his shoulder with a hooked finger. They stood in a group as if chatting. It was only as she stepped closer that Lake noticed the slack faces. Something was wrong.

"Is everything okay?" Lake asked, grabbing Stan's eye.

"The doorman's MIA," he said.

"What?" Lake exclaimed.

"Bob—the one who works afternoons," Stan said to her. "We've called the super and he should be here any second."

"He never showed up for work?" Lake asked.

"Apparently he was here earlier, but now he's nowhere to be found. He seems to have vanished into thin air," Stan said.

"Maybe he's just run over to buy a lotto ticket," the tall man said.

The woman shook her head in irritation.

"This is *so* wrong. The door's been left unguarded for at least half an hour—maybe longer."

"How do you know?" Lake asked her. She could feel the familiar panic begin to balloon again.

"Because he wasn't here when I went out to run an errand earlier. I know he was on duty earlier. I figured when I didn't see him that he was just helping someone with a delivery, which is wrong, too, but some people in this building are just so demanding. But then he still wasn't here when I got back." The little boy in the stroller began to kick his legs hard in impatience. "Don't do that, Cameron. Mommy doesn't like it."

Lake's feet seemed welded to the sidewalk. She hated being out there, exposed, and yet she didn't dare go up to her apartment. What if her assailant from last night had found his way in when Bob had disappeared? What if *he* had something to do with Bob being gone? She clenched her fists, trying to figure out what to do. Then something caught Stan's attention and as he turned his head toward the intersection, she followed suit. The super was hurrying toward them, his belly jiggling as he ran.

The woman did most of the talking, rattling on to the super as her son moved on to banging his head against the back of the stroller like a ball attached to a paddle with a rubber band. Stan touched Lake's arm.

"You going up?" he whispered. "I promise to slay any dragons that may have snuck in."

She smiled weakly at him. "Yes, thanks."

"Well, I'm planning to stay in for the night," Stan said as they reached their floor. "Just give a shout if you need anything."

There was a moment when she considered asking him to check out her apartment, despite how silly she would seem to him, but as she turned the key in the lock she found that the dead bolt was still secured, indicating that no one had entered.

She opened her door and stepped inside. It was utterly still, as if it was a house that had been empty for years.

"Smokey," she called out, heading hesitantly down the long hallway toward her bedroom. She'd left the AC running in there for him, with the door partially closed. As she walked she looked left and right, into the living room and kitchen and then her bedroom, checking. She wished Archer were here now, helping her like he had before.

Pushing the bedroom door the rest of the way open, she glanced toward the bed, expecting to see the cat curled there. But he wasn't.

"Smokey," she called again. "Here, kitty." There was no sign of him. Please, no, she prayed, don't let this be happening again. She retraced her steps to the front of the apartment and slipped into the family room. Smokey suddenly shot from beneath an armchair. Lake jumped in surprise and followed him with her eyes. He stopped in the living room as abruptly as he'd started. Sitting back on his haunches, he licked a paw with his tongue. Lake glanced worriedly around the family room, and then, seeing nothing wrong, approached Smokey. She wondered what had made him hide like that. Was he just angry that she'd been out so much?

As soon as she began to stroke him, her mind went instantly to Amy. In her wigged-out state about the doorman, she'd completely forgotten about her daughter's plight. She raced back to the hallway where she'd left her purse and checked her BlackBerry. No call from the director yet. She punched the camp's number again and this time she was told he was available.

"Mrs. Warren, I was just picking up the phone to call you back," Morrison said. "You got my message about Amy, correct?"

"Your message?"

"Yes, I left it on your home phone. I thought that was why you were calling."

Walking as they spoke, Lake spotted the blinking light on the answering machine in the kitchen.

"Oh, right, yes. Please tell me what's going on."

"Amy is resting in the infirmary today," he said. "Her throat is raw and scratchy and she's running a slight fever. We've taken a culture for strep because we've had one other camper come down with it this summer. We should have the results later today."

"When did this start?" Lake asked.

"She first visited the nurse today but apparently she hasn't felt her best for a day or two. I wish she'd spoken up sooner."

Lake remembered her own sore throat, which had blossomed Tuesday. Maybe she'd passed something to Amy when she was there for parents' day. She felt overwhelmed with the need to be with Amy and comfort her.

"I have a small favor to ask," Lake said. "Amy has been a little down in the dumps this summer—her father moved out several months ago, as I think you're aware. I'm afraid that the combination of being sick and being away from home and everything else is going to make her feel very blue. I know it's against the rules, but I think Amy could really use a visit from me. I'd appreciate it if I could stop by tomorrow."

"Oh dear, I'm not sure what to say," he said. "Parents really aren't supposed to drop by. And I've already let your husband come by one night since he was unable to make parents' day."

"I understand completely. But I want Amy to enjoy her last days at camp—especially since I'd love her and Will to come back next year."

He hesitated, obviously registering the pressure she'd just imposed. "All right, then. We'll just have to be discreet. When you arrive, ask for the infirmary and go directly there."

"There's just one hitch," she said. "I'd like to check in on Will, too. I can't very well come to the camp and not see him. Could one of the counselors walk him down to my car afterward? I'll make sure he doesn't tell anyone."

His sigh of dismay was audible over the phone.

"All right. But I'm just remembering—tomorrow is field trip day, and the kids are going to a water park. Will won't be back until five."

Lake squeezed her temple, thinking. She had to make this work.

"Okay, why don't I get there just before five? I'll visit Amy and then surprise Will with a quick hello when the bus returns."

"All right, then, I'll let Amy know," he said. She could detect from his tone that she'd left him vexed and grumpy. Tough, she thought.

After she signed off, she dragged the hall table in front of the door again. Two photos toppled over as she gave it a final shove. For a moment, she just stood and stared at the scene in front of her. It looked right out of a horror movie—the door barricaded as if she were expecting the arrival of a homicidal doll or a serial killer hoisting a chain saw. Though Jack would be picking the kids up from camp in less than a week and a half and taking them to the Hamptons for another week, after that they would be back here with her. How could she explain the nightly barricade to them? Or what had happened to Smokey? How could she put them in danger?

There was only one way to stop all this, and that was to expose the clinic. Everything—the kids' safety, *her* safety, life as she'd once known it—rested on that. And that, in turn, depended on whether Rory could find the information she needed and if Archer could supply it to the right people. It had been ages since she'd relied on anyone, and now she was banking on two people she barely knew. It felt unfamiliar, uncomfortable.

She faxed the kids, telling Amy she couldn't wait to see her but saying nothing to Will about her visit. For dinner she nuked a frozen French bread pizza that tasted of ancient freezer burn. She ate it with Smokey at her feet while she searched online for the New Century Research company that Rory had mentioned. Nothing came up. It was an organization that clearly preferred flying under the radar.

At eight she tried Archer again. Still voice mail. It seemed odd not to hear from him since he'd seemed eager for an update. Maybe he was on to the next best story. Next she rang downstairs on the intercom. It was the night doorman who answered, having obviously been called in early. He had no news of Bob, he said. She dug the number for her neighbors out of a drawer, thinking Stan might have heard something. An answering machine picked up. Great—so much for his staying in for the night.

Exhausted, she decided to turn in early and bunk down in the living room again—she felt more secure somehow, knowing she could keep an eye on the door. As she tossed a bed pillow and summer blanket onto the couch, she recalled how safe she had felt at Archer's last night—a place where no one could find her.

She was leafing listlessly through a magazine when the phone rang. It had to be Archer, she told herself. But when she picked up the receiver and glanced at the screen she saw that the caller was Molly. She nearly dropped the phone in shock, as if it had morphed into something venomous. And yet she knew it wouldn't be smart to put off the conversation—she had to pretend things were perfectly normal.

"Hi there," Lake said, as a way of answering.

"You *okay*?" Molly demanded. "I got that frantic message from you last night and then couldn't reach you."

"Oh—sorry. I—I was a little worried about how my presentation went—the one at the clinic—and I just needed to talk. Sorry if I made it seem like an emergency."

"Your voice sounded really rattled. So it didn't go well?"

"Actually, I've heard some feedback since then and they liked it," she lied. "Sometimes it's just so hard to know in the moment."

"And there's really nothing wrong? You still sound funny to me."

"No, you just caught me as I was getting ready for bed. Everything went fine."

"If you say so," Molly said. Lake could almost see her shrugging, unconvinced. Molly obviously sensed something was up. How perfectly gleeful she'd be, Lake thought, if she knew the truth and could run to Jack with it: "Here's something for your custody case, darling—her client thinks she was *spying* on them."

"What about that murder?" Molly added before Lake could chase her off the phone. "Has anyone been arrested? I haven't read any news in a couple of days."

Too busy bedding my ex-husband, Lake thought.

"No, not as far as I know. . . . How are you?"

"Not bad. I did a shoot in Central Park today and the model fainted. Granted, the girl weighed four pounds, but I think it had more to do with wearing a faux fur hooded jacket in ninety-degree heat. I hear it's supposed to rain tomorrow and then get cooler by Sunday."

"Really?" Lake said. She couldn't stand this. As she listened to Molly's husky voice droning on about the weather, she kept picturing the green eyes and full mouth and imagining that mouth on the man she once loved and cherished.

"So how about grabbing a drink this weekend? I could even do brunch on Sunday."

"Um, gosh. I wish I could. But now I'm backed up with a new client. I want to use the weekend to catch up."

"Any Jack sightings? He hasn't been lurking around again, has he?"

The abrupt change in topic suggested Molly had been crouched for the past few minutes, waiting for an open moment to spring that question into the conversation.

"Not lately, no. Look, Molly, I'd love to talk, but I should get to bed. I want to—"

"Is everything really okay, Lake? Be honest with me."

Don't keep denying, Lake told herself. Molly won't buy that.

"Okay, honestly you're right. Remember that roller-coaster factor you mentioned last week? I guess I'm just in one of the dip periods right now. Maybe because the weekend is about to start and I'm still getting used to being on my own."

"See, that's what I was talking about. Well, feel better and call me if you just need to vent."

That did the trick, Lake thought. Because Molly loved being right. As Lake hung up and lay back on the sofa she realized that despite how despicable it was that her friend and Jack were lovers, it would be a relief to cut Molly from her life. Deep down she'd begun to grow tired of Molly's smugness and pushiness.

She switched off the light on the end table and closed her eyes wearily. How different her couch seemed from Archer's. There was no hint of wood smoke from the fireplace still in the fabric, no reassuring footsteps overhead.

The phone rang then. It was Archer, as if she had conjured him up.

"How are you?" he asked. "Sorry it took so long to phone you back. I got stuck in an endless, mind-numbing meeting with our lawyers."

"Well, my doorman is missing, which is scaring the hell out of me, but on the other hand I have some good news."

She filled him in on what Rory had shared about the transported eggs and her agreement to help. Archer pelted her with questions and then turned back to the doorman issue.

"Do you want to crash on my couch again? Do you want me to crash on yours?"

For a split second she considered both. But she felt uneasy about leaving the apartment this late, and it wouldn't be smart to have Archer stay there. It was the kind of thing Hotchkiss had warned her about. And she'd already paid too high a price for ignoring his advice once before.

"I appreciate that. But I think I'm okay. I've got the door barricaded."

"Why don't we touch base tomorrow?"

"Sounds good. I may be out of reach for a while, though. I'm running up to my kids' camp and the cell service is spotty on the way there."

She slept restlessly, and kept waking, thinking she'd heard a noise. The next day she was on the road by one, giving herself more than enough time to reach the camp just before five, when Will would be returning. Before pulling onto the highway, she'd driven up and down a few blocks in Manhattan, making sure no one was following her. She couldn't take the chance of anyone discovering where the camp was. By the time she merged onto the West Side Highway, the back of her summer dress was wet with the sweat of pure anxiety.

She tried to calm herself by focusing on her kids. She craved seeing them, if even for a few minutes. She looked forward to making sure Amy was okay and pampering her a little. She also thought of Rory and felt a surge of hope. Finally she had someone on the inside to help her.

And yet for every comforting thought, there was a troubling one to match. What if Rory got cold feet or came up empty-handed? Then what was she going to do about the kids when they eventually returned? How in the world could she protect them?

27

SHE STOPPED FOR a late lunch on the deck of a roadside tavern. It was hot out, but a light breeze tousled her hair. She glanced up. Though the sky had been clear when she'd left Manhattan, big cumulus clouds had begun to herd together along the horizon.

When she rummaged for her wallet to pay the bill, she checked her BlackBerry. This was a stretch of the road where she had service back and she noticed there was a missed call—from Rory.

"Call me as soon as you can," the message said. "It's important." There was an edginess to Rory's tone.

She tried calling Rory back, but an answering machine picked up. "You've reached the Deevers," Rory's voice said. "Leave a message and we'll get back to you. Have a nice day."

Next she tried Rory's cell and got voice mail as well. When they'd met yesterday, Rory had said she might want to talk this weekend to review the plan. And yet the word *important* in her message was a flag. Lake just hoped Rory hadn't changed her mind.

The last leg of the trip was only thirty minutes long. The wind had picked up and the clouds were growing darker and thicker, crowding each other so that they pushed up high in the sky. It was going to rain, and rain hard, probably thunder and lightning. Lake pictured the counselors at the water park, hurrying the kids into their clothes and onto the bus.

The camp seemed nearly deserted when she arrived. There were only four or five cars in the parking lot, and once she climbed the hill and reached the main grounds, she saw just two people—a male counselor collecting an archery board that had toppled over in the wind and an older man dragging a net bag of soccer balls across the parched lawn.

She approached the counselor and asked for directions to the infirmary. He pointed to a small, roughhewn cabin nestled in a cluster of fir trees. As she entered the building, with its row of old-fashioned, metal-framed beds, she saw that Amy was the only patient. At first Lake thought her daughter was sleeping—she lay with her eyes closed and her thick braid of brown hair flopped on the pillow. But at the sound of Lake's footsteps, Amy's eyes shot open.

"Mom," she said hoarsely. She let out small moan of relief.

"Oh, sweetie," Lake said, sitting on the edge of the bed and pulling Amy to her.

"I don't have strep," Amy told her with a weak smile. "I mean, my throat still hurts a lot, but they said it's a *virus*."

"Well, maybe it will clear up faster, then. Is the nurse here?"

"She went over to the mess hall to get me some Jell-O."

"I brought something to cheer you up." Lake pulled a tissue-wrapped package from her purse and offered it to her daughter. Inside was a small, funky bracelet she'd bought weeks ago and put aside for Amy's birthday.

Amy tore the tissue off and beamed when she saw the bracelet.

"I love it. Thanks, Mom. I'm so glad you came."

"Me, too."

A screen door banged and they looked in unison in that direction. The nurse, a fortyish woman with a short choppy haircut, was back. She introduced herself and set a tray down on the little table that swung out from Amy's bed. There was a cup of tea and the promised Jell-O, along with a stainless-steel spoon that was dull and thinned from a thousand washings.

"Did Amy tell you that the strep test came back negative?" the nurse asked.

"Yes. Though that means there's·nothing you can give her, right?" Lake said.

"Only bed rest. But the good news is that it should run its course in just a couple of days."

Lake chatted politely with the nurse for a minute and then turned her attention back to her daughter. Amy seemed needy of her company, and yet it clearly hurt her to talk.

"Why don't I give you a back massage?" Lake offered.

"Hmm," Amy murmured happily.

As her hands kneaded the muscles in Amy's back, Lake realized that her daughter's body had become more muscular this summer, and yet there was still something so girlish about her soft skin and thin shoulder blades. Lake found herself getting tearful, almost fraught. I can't lose you, she thought. I have to make things work.

After a while she glanced at her watch. It was just before five. The bus might already be back.

"I hate to go, honey," Lake said, stroking Amy's cheek. "But I'm afraid Mr. Morrison will slap me in cuffs if I overstay my welcome. Plus, you need to rest."

"Mom, I did one bad thing," Amy croaked. "I told Will you were coming. That was before I saw your fax and you told me not to."

"That's okay. They told me I could say a quick hello in the parking lot when the bus gets back."

"That's good. He was so mad that he might not see you."

Lake said goodbye to her daughter, hugging her almost too hard. She had to be careful, she knew, or Amy would once again pick up on her fear and anguish.

"See you in just another two weeks," Lake said, as lightly as she could. "We'll have fun shopping for new school clothes, okay?"

Outside it hadn't started to rain yet, but the sky was now a mass of dark, angry clouds, and the wind was chasing herds of fallen leaves across the campgrounds. Lake made her way to the administrative office, where she thanked Morrison for letting her come and learned that the bus was behind schedule. She didn't look forward to driving home in the inevitable downpour.

Descending the hill, she checked her BlackBerry. No call back from Rory. As soon as she was in the car, she tried the home number again. This time Rory answered. Her hello sounded anxious.

"What's going on, Rory?" Lake asked. "Is everything okay?"

"Thanks for calling back, Lake. I'm just feeling really nervous."

Lake's body sagged; she couldn't have Rory getting cold feet.

"Are you worried someone will see you looking through the file drawers?" she asked. "Why don't you wait and try to do it when most people have left?"

"I'm afraid it's too late," Rory said fretfully. "I think someone *did* see me."

"What do you mean?" Lake asked.

"I already went through the files. After I met you, I decided to go back to the office. I was anxious about what you'd told me and wanted to see the charts for myself. I knew some of the staff was going to be there for a late procedure and I told them I came back because I'd forgotten something. When I left the storage room, I had the sense someone had been watching me in there."

"Did you see anyone?"

"No—it was just a sense I had. And then this morning I got this weird hang-up. And then another one a little while later. I'm all alone here this weekend and I'm just really scared."

Lake's stomach knotted. She'd put Rory in possible jeopardy and she had to do something about it.

"Is there any way your husband could cut his trip short?"

There was a pause as Rory seemed to consider the option.

"No, I can't ask him to . . . It's—it's a really important client and so much depends on this trip."

"Do you have anyone else you can call? Someone from your family—or a neighbor?"

"No, no one. We only moved here about a year ago, and people haven't been very welcoming. It's not an inclusive community here at all."

"Maybe the calls are unrelated," Lake said, though her alarm was growing. "Just because someone saw you going through files doesn't mean they think you were doing anything wrong. You might have been just checking out some patient info, right?"

"But they probably saw that the files were missing," Rory said, almost pleading. "They probably know what I was up to."

"What do you mean, *missing*?" Lake asked.

"I took some files with me. I didn't dare photocopy them."

"You have the files with you now?" Lake said, incredulous.

"Yes. About ten of them."

"*And?*" Lake asked. "Do they show anything?" She held her breath.

"Yes," Rory said. "They have those letter codes you talked about. Not every file I checked had them, but I took the ones that did."

With her free hand, Lake ran her hand roughly through her hair. This was exactly what she'd hoped for. She had to see those files—and she owed it to Rory to make sure she was safe.

"Rory, why don't I come to your place? I'll take the files so you don't have to worry about them."

"Are you sure? I'm all the way up in Bedford Hills. It's over an hour north of the city. I can make photocopies tomorrow and figure out the best way to get them back in the drawers."

"I'm actually upstate now—a ways north of you, even. I can leave in a few minutes. Just tell me the address and I'll use my GPS."

"Well, if you really wouldn't mind, that would be great," Rory said. "I just feel so nervous."

Rory rattled off the address and Lake said that it would take her at least an hour to get there. She told Rory to lock all the doors and windows and to call her on her cell if she had any problem. And if she felt in danger to call 911.

By five forty-five the bus still hadn't arrived. Lake was torn about what to do. If she split now, Will would be upset, and yet she was anxious to get to Rory's. Finally, at six, just as she was firing up the engine of the car, an old yellow school bus waddled into the parking lot. Will was one of the first to trip down the steps, and after scanning the parking lot for his mother's car, he bounded toward it and climbed in. A counselor waited outside.

Will's silky blond hair was still damp and his cheek bore the crease from a nap on the bus. He seemed more than happy to see her, and also hyper, on a sugar high from the junk food he'd probably consumed at the water park.

"I went on the log ride five times, Mom. My clothes were soakin'."

"It was fun, huh?"

"Yeah, awesome."

"And what about tonight? What's planned for later?"

"We're having pizza. They ordered like a hundred pies."

"Excellent."

"Yeah, we were supposed to have a cookout but it's gonna rain. There's gonna be this big thunderstorm."

As he glanced out of the car window, clearly wondering what he was missing up the hill, Lake stole a nervous look at her watch.

"Why don't I let you catch up with your friends now?" she said. "I just wanted to be sure to say hi."

"Okay, bye, Mom." He offered her a tight hug and flashed his crooked grin. "Tell Smokey I said hi."

She'd been on the road just ten minutes when the rain started, big fat drops that pelted the roof of the car and seemed to explode on the windshield. She needed to call Rory with an update but she didn't dare take a hand off the wheel. At the first chance she pulled off the road and into the parking lot of one of the caboose restaurants Jack had loved to mock. It was growing dark, and through the streams of rain the blue and white lights from the restaurant sign undulated eerily. This was one of the times of year she'd never loved being up here—when the days grew shorter and there was an utter forlornness in the air.

Rory picked up on the first ring. There had been no more hang-ups, she said, but with night coming, she was feeling more and more scared. Lake explained how far behind schedule she was.

As she pulled onto the road again, barely able to see, a sense of dread began to build in her. What if someone *had* seen Rory take the files? What if Levin—or whoever—decided to dispatch the man with the knife to retrieve them? Lost in her thoughts, Lake jumped in her seat when a clap of thunder rocked the car.

The rain was coming down in torrents now and at times she had to plunge the car through huge pools of water that had formed on the blacktop of the two-lane road. Things were better on the interstate, and yet more than a few cars had pulled onto the shoulder to wait out the storm. Lake kept going, feeling she had no choice. As it was, she wouldn't reach Rory's until after eight.

Three-quarters of the way there, the rain stopped as quickly as it had started. She picked up the pace and the GPS recalculated her arrival time. When she was just fifteen minutes away, she peered through the windshield, surprised at what she saw. Rather than the suburban sprawl she'd expected, she was in horse country. The roads were lined with split-rail fences, and occasionally through the dark she caught sight of a huge house set back from the road and lit up like a cruise ship. She remembered that Rory had said she lived in an old gatehouse.

As soon as she pulled into the driveway she understood why Rory felt so afraid. The house was down a long driveway and there wasn't another house in view—not even the main estate house that the gatehouse must have once been a part of.

After turning the car off, Lake twisted her body and surveyed the area. Rory's gatehouse, she saw, was two stories and made of stone. The first floor was brightly lit and a security light above the small garage illuminated the driveway. The garage door was open, showing the front of a small car butting out. There was no sign of anyone outside, and yet Lake knew that with all the trees and hedges on the property, it would be easy for someone to lurk in the shadows.

Before climbing out of the car, Lake called Rory's home phone number.

"It's me out here," Lake said when Rory picked up. "I didn't want to scare you."

"Okay, I'll meet you at the door."

As Lake tore across the yard, the muddy ground sucked at her clogs. Rory flung open the front door just as Lake reached the top step of the porch.

Rory's blond hair was held back in a simple ponytail today. She was wearing stretchy black capris, obviously pregnancy pants, and a matching maternity tunic. It was the first time Lake had seen her without makeup, and on her left cheek there was a patch of inflamed skin that looked as if it had been picked at worriedly.

"I'm so sorry," Lake said as Rory relocked the door. "Because of the rain I had to drive at about fifty most of the way. Are you okay?"

"I just got another hang-up," Rory said. She shook her head back and forth quickly, as if that would make everything stop. "It's like they're trying to figure out if I'm here or not."

"Okay, let's talk about what to do."

"Why don't we go into the kitchen? I can make us some tea."

"All the other doors are locked—and the windows?" Lake asked.

"Yes," Rory said. "Everything."

Lake followed Rory from the hall into a living/dining room. It appeared as if the interior had been gutted to make the space more modern. The walls of the living room were white, with a wall of sleek built-in bookshelves and cabinets. The couch and armchair were covered with white canvas and the only color in the room was from the blue-and-green area rug and the blue throw pillows on the couch. There wasn't a single picture on the wall.

"Like I told you, we haven't been here all that long," Rory said, as if guessing Lake's thoughts. "We're still fixing it up."

Rory led her into a small, pristine kitchen. It was clear from the gleaming pots hanging from the wall and the shelves of spices that Rory liked to cook. Lake remembered Rory saying she'd made jams.

"Do you want milk in your tea?" Rory asked, filling the kettle.

"No, thank you." Lake said. She glanced around, wondering where the files were.

"Let me just get this started and then I'll show you the files," Rory said, as if she'd read her mind again.

"Good," Lake said. "I also think we need to figure out a place for you to stay until your husband gets back."

Rory's shoulders drooped. "But *where*?" she asked. "I don't want to stay with a stranger."

"You could stay with me," Lake said.

"But you said someone tried to kill you."

"At least I have a doorman. I think you'll feel safer there."

Lake peered out the window. They were on the other side of the house from the garage and all she could see was total blackness. There was no way she could leave Rory alone here. Off in the distance, a bolt of lightning sliced the sky. From inside she could hear drops of rain begin to spatter in the yard.

"Do you really think someone was outside the storage room?" Lake asked. She wondered if Rory, in her anxiety, was being paranoid.

"Yes—I could hear that kind of squishy sound people's footsteps make on the carpet."

"Who was still at the clinic then?"

"Dr. Levin. Dr. Sherman was probably in his office but I never saw him, but I did see Dr. Hoss in the lab along with one of the other embryologists. Brie was around. Oh, and Dr. Kline."

"Dr. Kline?" Lake asked, surprised. She'd thought Harry had told her in the park that he wouldn't be returning to the clinic that day.

"Yes," Rory said. The kettle screeched and she flicked off the burner. "He walked out with me and asked what I was doing this weekend. He told me I should probably savor my time alone since I wouldn't have much afterward. Why don't I get the files now? I have to let the tea steep."

Another bolt of lightning lit up the sky and a clap of thunder followed a second later. The cell of the new storm was moving their way. Rory walked back into the living room, and as Lake took a seat at the kitchen table, she saw Rory pull a handful of files from a cabinet.

"I didn't have time to go through very many," Rory said, returning. "But at least I found some." She handed Lake the stack, all still in their hanging files.

The one on top was the Hunt file and Lake slowly opened it. On the basic information form, by both Alexis and Brian's names, was a faint scribble of letters: *BLg* and *BLb*. The other charts, as Rory had promised, all had the codes, too, and it was clear Lake had been right—they all corresponded to hair and eye colors.

"Had you ever noticed these notations before?" Lake asked.

"No, but I rarely look at that page," Rory said. "It's just for basic information—nothing that matters so much in their treatment."

As Lake studied the files, Rory set their cups of tea in front of them. A butter cookie was cradled next to the cup in each saucer.

"I hope you don't mind herbal tea. Once I got pregnant I threw out everything with caffeine so I wouldn't be tempted."

"No, that's fine, I'm wired enough," Lake said distractedly and took a sip. There was honey in the tea, which she hated, but she didn't have the heart to tell Rory.

"Are the letters a code—something that has to do with the embryos?" Rory asked.

"Yes. I can't explain right now, but I will later, once I get more information."

"Do you really think this is why Dr. Keaton was killed?"

Lake tore her eyes away from the files and looked at Rory.

"I think it's definitely possible. If Dr. Keaton learned about this and threatened to expose the clinic, that would be a very big motive."

Rory seemed to look through her, distracted, and Lake wondered what she was thinking. Suddenly she was jostled by a thought. She recalled an odd little pause when she'd spoken to Rory about Maggie's desk.

"Do you have any ideas, Rory?" she asked. "Did you ever see anyone near Maggie's desk?"

"Well," Rory said. She sat down at the table across from Lake and took a long, slow sip from her cup.

"Rory, please," Lake urged. "Tell me."

"I'm sure it doesn't mean anything. But one day—it was just kind of odd. I saw Dr. Kline there. He doesn't usually come by the nurses' station."

"Harry?"

"Um-hm. And he seemed kind of surprised when I came up behind him. He said he was looking for a pencil sharpener."

Lake felt as if someone had shoved her from behind.

"I almost told you the other day," Rory added. "But I didn't want to upset you. I can tell you . . . you know—like Harry."

"What do you mean?" Lake asked.

"I thought you two might even be dating."

Lake shifted her body in surprise. Clearly Rory had picked up the interest on Harry's part and thought it went both ways.

"I like Harry as a person," Lake said. "But we aren't dating."

"Oh, my mistake, then. I think Harry's great, too. I know he had problems with Dr. Keaton, but I can't imagine him ever hurting him."

"What do you mean, 'problems'?" Lake asked. The hair on the back of her neck lifted.

"Because of what happened with his daughter—and Dr. Keaton."

28

LAKE STARED ACROSS the kitchen table at Rory. She'd heard the words but it seemed as if they'd been said out of order and she could barely make sense of them.

"I'm not understanding at all," Lake said. "What does Harry's daughter have to do with Dr. Keaton?"

Rory cocked her head and lowered her eyes, as if she felt qualms about sharing the information.

"Please, Rory," Lake urged.

"Okay," she said, looking back up. "His daughter did a kind of internship during her spring break in March. Her name's Allison. I guess she's a biology major or something and she wanted to learn about embryology and help out—though I'm not sure what help anyone thought she could be. Well, that's when Dr. Keaton was consulting the first time around, and she was very, very flirty with him. You could tell it made him uncomfortable, and when he ignored her she got mad. She told her father Dr. Keaton was the one being flirty and then Harry became very upset with Dr. Keaton."

Lake couldn't believe this. Harry had made no reference to the situation when he'd spoken of his daughter. Why not at least mention that she'd worked at the clinic?

"How did Dr. Kline feel when it was announced that Keaton was joining the clinic?"

Rory lowered her eyes again and took another long sip of tea.

"I don't think very good," she said softly. "I have a feeling it's why he wasn't around that day. It's like Dr. Levin had told him that if he didn't like it, tough luck."

Lake's mind began to reel. Flirting didn't seem like much of a motive for murder. But what if Rory didn't know the whole story? Maybe Keaton *had* been interested in Harry's daughter. Maybe he'd even seduced her. He'd been so slick—it wasn't hard to imagine. And then, in a rage, Harry had killed him. Perhaps this explained why Harry had tried so hard to tune into what Lake was feeling—he'd suspected she'd been with Keaton and knew something that could incriminate him. Maybe he was the one who'd shaved Smokey and put the catnip in her bag. But then who was the man who had forced her to jump in the river? Was the embryo stealing a whole separate issue?

Lake took a quick sip of tea to steady her nerves. "Have you told the police this?" she asked bluntly.

"The *police*? You don't really think Harry killed Dr. Keaton, do you? Just because of what his daughter said?"

Lake didn't answer. She was trying to get a grip on their situation. Harry had asked Rory what she was doing this weekend. He knew she was home alone. She'd have to convince Rory that staying at her apartment was the right thing to do—at least for a night or two.

A bolt of lightning lit up outside again, followed by an instant crack of thunder. The lights in the house flashed off and then on again.

"Oh God," Rory said. "If the lights go out, I'll die."

"You've got flashlights, I hope," Lake said. Her heart was beating fast now. She didn't like being here. And she would like it a hell of a lot less, she realized, without any electricity.

"Somewhere," Rory said. She jumped up and yanked a couple of kitchen drawers all the way open. "I don't see them. Well, I know I have candles—probably in the living room."

As Rory hurried into the other room, Lake pressed her fingertips to her lips, thinking. She doubted she'd have any more difficulty persuading Rory to leave. She took one last sip of tea and poured the rest in the sink, setting the cup there. As she turned, the yard outside seemed to explode in whiteness, as if it was being lit by a strobe. Thunder rolled over the house and the lights flashed off and on again. Lake could now hear that it was pouring hard outside.

Rory scurried back into the room, carrying a smudged cellophane-covered box with two white taper candles inside. It looked like it had been purchased in some other decade.

"This is it? You don't have any more?"

"Yes. I mean, no, I don't have any more."

"All right—I've got a flashlight out in the car," Lake said, digging her key out of her purse. "Have you got a slicker I can throw on?"

"Yes," Rory said, following her to the door. "It's in the hall."

"I'll only be a minute. As soon as I get back, we really need to pack up and leave."

"Okay," Rory said, squeezing her arms tightly around her bulging belly. "There's no way I'm staying here now."

There were just two coats on the hooks in the hallway—a light-weight woman's jacket and a green slicker. Lake pulled the slicker over her head, and with her car key in hand made a dash from the door.

The rain seemed to be coming down in rivers. As she plunged across the muddy yard, trying to scan the surroundings with her eyes, she didn't know what she was more afraid of—being attacked out there or hit by lightning. She unlocked the car with her key from fifteen feet away, yanked open the door, and quickly locked it again once she was safely inside. Her hands trembled as she hit the button on the glove compartment. She felt overwhelmed with a sense of foreboding.

The flashlight was where she remembered it to be—wedged behind the owner's manual—but when she turned it on she saw that the battery was low and the light was a dull beam. Maybe Rory at least had batteries inside.

She pulled the slicker hood over her head again and jumped from the car. As she staggered through the mud, all the lights in the house went off again—and this time they stayed off. Damn, she thought.

"Rory," she called out as she entered the darkened entranceway. "Have you got any C batteries?" She quickly locked the door behind her and kicked off her muddied clogs.

"Did you hear me?" she called out as she felt for the peg and hung the slicker. "I need batteries."

There wasn't any answer.

She trained the flashlight through the doorway to the living room and let it bounce around. It lit up only the first several feet of the room, and beyond that was only darkness.

"Rory," Lake called again. "Where *are* you?" Maybe she can't hear me from the kitchen, Lake thought. And yet something didn't seem right.

She edged her way through the living room, her anxiety mounting. Finally she reached the kitchen. She ran the flashlight in an arc around the room. There was no one there.

From what she'd been able to see earlier, there were only two main rooms on the ground floor—the living room and the kitchen.

But a doorway at the far end of the kitchen seemed to open onto some kind of mudroom. Lake walked toward it and pointed the flashlight into the space. It was actually more of a pantry than a mudroom, with shelves of canned and packaged foods—and a door to the outside. Had Rory fled the house in a panic? she wondered.

I've got to get out of here, she thought desperately. But first she had to find Rory. She turned and inched back into the kitchen. The light from the flashlight seemed even fainter now, and she knew it might be only seconds before it went out all together. She flicked the light toward the table. She could just make out the package of candles. It had been ripped open and one of the candles was missing.

Squeezing the flashlight in her armpit, Lake pulled out the other candle and then turned and squinted at the stove. To her relief she saw that it had gas burners. She fired up a burner and thrust the candle into the flame, lighting it. Suddenly there was a sound behind her. She spun around. Rory was standing there, a burning candle in one hand and a box of matches in the other.

"God, Rory, where were you?" Lake blurted out.

"I'm sorry. I went upstairs," Rory said. "I thought I heard a noise up there."

"What *kind* of noise?"

"It was this sort of knocking sound. It really scared me. It turned out to be just the drapes in the bedroom—they were flapping against the wall."

"What do you mean?" Lake asked anxiously.

"The window was open a little. The wind was blowing them."

"But I thought you said you'd locked all the windows," Lake said. She could barely hide her irritation.

"I know—I thought I had. But I must not have noticed that one because the drapes were closed."

"And you're certain you're the one who left it open?"

"Yes. But it's closed now and locked."

"Fine, okay, you've got to pack now. What do you need besides clothes and toiletries?"

"I take heparin for my pregnancy. I have to get that."

Suddenly Lake felt overwhelmed by a wave of fatigue. She took a deep breath, trying to summon her strength. "It's going to be tough for you to pack with a candle. Do you have any C batteries?"

"I'm not sure. But I remembered where my husband keeps the flashlights—in the basement." As Rory spoke she cocked her head toward a wooden door across the kitchen that obviously led downstairs. "He's got a workbench down there with flashlights in the drawer."

"Good," Lake said. "Take a seat at the table. I'll get the flashlights and then I'll help you pack your stuff. We can be out of here in ten minutes."

"Okay," Rory replied, but she stood motionless in the middle of the kitchen, staring at Lake.

"What's the matter?" Lake said.

"Are you all right?" Rory asked. "You look funny all of a sudden." Rory's face was drawn with concern, her pale skin like a mask in the flickering glow of the candle flame.

"I'm—I'm just tired. And I just want to get out of here."

"Me, too," Rory said.

Lake crossed the kitchen. After opening the basement door, she instinctively felt for the light switch and flipped it up. Dumb, she thought. She stared below. With the light from the candle, the basement looked like an empty black pit that went on forever. At least there was a railing to grasp. With one hand sliding along it, Lake made her way tentatively down the wooden stairs.

As she reached the bottom step she saw that the basement was split in two by the stairs. To the right were a washer and dryer against the wall and a big, stand-alone freezer, the horizontal kind.

On the far left she could see the workbench with just a few tools hanging from a pegboard above it. All I have to do, she told herself, is find the flashlights and get out.

She crossed the cement floor and tugged at one of the two drawers. Her arm felt oddly weak, and the drawer refused to budge. She tugged again, harder, and this time the drawer jerked open. Its bottom was scattered with loose nails, nothing more. She tried the other drawer. Two flashlights lay side by side. They were the long heavy-duty kind security cops carried.

She grabbed one, pushed the switch up and to her relief saw that it worked. She blew out the candle and then grabbed the other flashlight. Now get the hell out of here, she told herself. As she turned, a muffled crash sounded directly above her, making her whole body jerk. Something had fallen hard in the kitchen. Had Rory tripped? Had someone gotten into the house? Was it Harry? Or the man from Brooklyn? She had to get back upstairs to help Rory.

Flooded with fear, she lunged through the near-darkness toward the stairs. Suddenly she felt dizzy and disoriented in the near-darkness. She raised her foot to meet the first step but didn't reach it, and she stumbled, falling. As she landed in a heap, both flashlights bounced from her hands. She heard one roll across the floor to her left. The other, the one she'd been using, was just a few feet away, shooting a beam of light across the hard cement floor. Terrified, she crawled toward it on her knees. Don't let it go out, she begged.

She reached the flashlight and stuck her arm out feebly to grab it. Then she felt an intense, searing pain in her head. A split second later she slipped into unconsciousness.

Pain woke her, forced open her eyes. She was lying in pitch-black darkness, and her head was throbbing, as if someone had smashed the back of it with a chair. There was a weird taste in her mouth—

metallic. I've cut the inside of my mouth, she thought. She tried to find the spot with her tongue, but it was too swollen to move.

Where am I? she wondered panic-stricken. Her heart began to pound in time with the throbbing in her head. She tried to shift her body, but she felt paralyzed.

She forced herself to take a breath. I'm in a nightmare, she told herself, one of those nightmares you can dream and see yourself in at the same time. And I'm going to wake up. As she breathed, she smelled something musty, like mildewed clothes. No, this was real. She tried again to shift her body. Her arms didn't move but she was able to twist her head a little.

A sound slid through the blackness—a long, low groan that she didn't recognize. Her heart pounded harder. It's a motor, she thought finally.

She realized at last where she was. But why? Had she fallen? Or had someone *hit* her? Her mind was so confused, her thoughts choked like a tangle of weeds in a lake. She found the beginning and tried to go step by step from there. The last thing she recalled was trying to reach the flashlight. It must have gone out, though. How long had she been here and why was she alone? And then suddenly she knew. She remembered everything. She let out an anguished sob at the truth.

She realized that the hum of the motor must be from the freezer she'd seen earlier, which meant that the power was back on. She had to get out. She twisted her head back and forth and commanded the rest of her body to move. Her legs felt leaden, like they were metal drums filled to the brim, but she was able to move one of her arms—the right one. She flexed her right hand slowly open and closed, back and forth.

There was another noise—from far above this time. Footsteps. And next a door opening. Terror engulfed her body, squeezing air from her lungs.

The killer was coming to get her.

Lake tried desperately to move again. She managed to drag her hand to her face, but that was it. Suddenly the lightbulb in the ceiling popped on. The light made her head hurt even more but she forced her eyes to stay open. She realized that she was lying just to the left of the bottom of the steps. Raising her pounding head, she saw Rory descending the stairs.

"Rory," she said weakly as her head fell back onto the hard floor. "I must have passed out."

"Of course you did," Rory said, stepping in front of Lake. She smiled down at her.

"What?" Lake asked groggily.

"I know you did. I gave you a little something in your tea."

Lake felt a sudden urge to vomit, tasting it in her mouth.

"I'm really very angry with you, Lake," Rory said. "If you must know, I'm in a rage. But I'm too professional to let it show."

"What . . . have I done?" Lake asked.

"What have you *done*? I think you know, Lake. You're the reason Mark Keaton is dead."

You must stay calm, Lake commanded herself, you must try to reason with her. "That's not true," she said. "I—I had nothing to do with that. I barely knew him."

"But you knew him well enough to fuck him. You were with him that night, Lake. Don't lie to me. You gave it away for sure when we were in that stupid piano bar—you knew about his terrace."

Lake's heart was pounding so hard she could hear the sound in her head.

"I'd called him that night, you know," Rory said. "I'd told him before I left that day about our baby. It was a little bit of a shock for him but I knew he was going to be very, very happy. We just needed to talk it through and work out all the details. But as soon as I heard his voice on the phone I knew he was expecting someone.

I didn't have any choice but to go there—and of course, I'd been smart enough to make a copy of the key."

"And in case you're thinking the police are going to figure out it was me because they have a record of the call, don't. I made a point of telling them that I'd spoken to Dr. Keaton that night. I said he'd asked me to call him to follow up about a patient. But as you know very well, Lake, the last thing on his mind that night was a patient. When I walked in his bedroom, it was disgusting. I could tell from the smell he'd had sex with someone. And I was almost positive it was you."

I have to do something, Lake thought desperately. She raised her head a little, just to see if she could.

"Rory, I—"

"*Hush*, Lake. I'm not some kind of fool. I'd seen you being super flirty with him for days. One night I'd even thought you might have lured him to *your* place. Women are such predators—they won't leave men like Mark alone."

"But—"

"Don't you dare give me any buts. I know all about women like you. I knew I'd guessed right when I saw how petrified you looked when the police came to the clinic. I mentioned to the police how upset you were and I could tell they thought you'd been up to no good as well. At that point I had to flush you out and see how you reacted."

"Did—did you shave Smokey?" Lake asked. She was stalling for time, trying to think.

"Is that what you call that fat ugly cat of yours? You never said a word about it to anyone. That's when I knew you had something to hide."

"I—"

"Oh, shut up, Lake. Don't you see what you've done? Because of you, Mark will never see his baby."

"But why kill him?"

"You'd obviously poisoned his mind against me. He wasn't going to make any time for me or the baby. I'd be all by myself up here with our son and he'd be busy fucking you in the city."

"Rory, I *did* go to Dr. Keaton's place—but it was only to talk to him," Lake said. Her words sounded hollow to her, but a lie was all she had left. "It was about the clinic. He'd been in touch with one of the women—one of the women who was given someone else's embryos. I need your help to expose the clinic. What they're doing is wrong. No one has to know about Dr. Keaton."

Rory just stared down at Lake, her face blank. Lake couldn't even guess what was behind her eyes. Was she possibly considering what Lake had said? she wondered.

"Liar," Rory spat out. And then before Lake even saw it coming, Rory kicked her hard in the side of the head. She was wearing thin ballet flats, but the blow stung and her head was knocked back to the ground.

Involuntarily Lake moaned. Rory was going to kill her. Lake had to get out of the basement somehow.

She sensed she was starting to regain strength in her arms and her legs—probably because she'd only drunk a little of the tea—but she couldn't let Rory know. She had to outsmart her. Instinctively Lake's eyes glanced from Rory's face to her large hands. Would Rory try to stab her—like she'd done to Keaton?

Rory snickered. "No, I don't have a knife, Lake," she said, clearly having caught the movement of Lake's eyes. "I can't have a bloodbath in my basement. Blood does *not* come out of cement, trust me."

In a flash she was on top of Lake, yanking her by the jersey shirt she wore. Rory twisted the fabric around her fist and began to drag her across the floor. She was strong, stronger than Lake could have imagined. Where is she taking me? Lake thought frantically. She let her body go limp, pretending she was still immobilized, but her eyes shot ahead. Then she saw it. Rory was dragging her to the freezer.

29

SHE'S GOING TO lock me in there, Lake realized. She would die from cold and suffocation, and no one would ever know what happened to her. Her kids would spend the rest of their lives haunted by her disappearance.

In her terror, she felt the urge to protest and to struggle, but she fought the instinct. She had to let Rory think she was powerless to help herself. Her eyes shot around the basement, searching. She needed a weapon, something to strike Rory with. But there was nothing.

They reached the freezer. Rory dropped her to the ground, hard, and lifted the lid. Lake could feel a scream forming in her throat, something primitive and terrified, but she didn't let it free. She tried to wiggle her feet. The muscles were weak, but she could move them now.

Rory spun around and this time grabbed Lake under the arms from behind. She hoisted her up and flopped her torso over the side of the freezer. As a blast of cold air hit her from below, Lake reached out her arms to catch herself. Her hands hit something hard and ice cold—packages of frozen food, she thought. With her right hand she grasped one of them. It was slippery and sharp on the edges and she had to hold it tightly. As Rory tried to hoist Lake's right leg into the freezer, Lake twisted around and smashed the frozen package into Rory's face.

The blow sent Rory reeling backward. Her body still weak, Lake took a clumsy step forward and hit Rory again. This time Rory tottered against the basement wall and crumbled to her knees, holding her belly. Lake staggered toward the stairs and, using her hands to help, half-crawled to the top. The door to the kitchen was open. Please, please let there be a lock, she pleaded. Below her she could hear Rory begin to wail in protest. Lake reached the top of the stairs, lurched into the brightly lit kitchen and slammed the door. There was a lock—a bolt. She shoved it into place.

To her relief she saw that her purse was on the table where she'd left it. She threw the strap of her purse over her head and stumbled into the living room. As she made her way unsteadily to the front door, she dug first for her car key and then her Black-Berry. A dull thudding sound echoed through the house. It was Rory banging on the door from the basement.

Lake hit 911 on her phone. The operator answered in two rings.

"Someone is trying to kill me," she said.

"Please tell me your location."

"Uh—Red Fox Road. Two seventy-one, I think."

"Are you in imminent danger?"

Lake swung the front door open with her free hand. It was still raining, a steady downpour that sounded like water pouring over a dam.

"Yes, but I've locked her in the basement."

"Help is on the way. Please stay on the line until the police arrive."

"I can't. I have to get to my car."

She tossed the BlackBerry in her purse and clumsily jammed her feet into her clogs, which she'd left by the entrance. She groped her way down the front steps and around the side of the house. She hit the unlock button on the key and the car lights flashed, beckoning her. She began to stagger across the yard.

Whatever adrenaline had saved her in the basement was used up, and she felt weary again, light-headed. The mud didn't help. It grabbed hard at her clogs, making her feel like she was running in deep water. She had to stop for a second just to catch her breath.

A sound made her jump. It was a crack of thunder—or what she thought was thunder. She spun around and peered through the streaming rain. There was a dim light glowing toward the rear of the gatehouse, along the base. She realized with a start that the outside bulkhead door to the basement had been flung open. And then she saw Rory. She was charging toward her with one hand raised high, carrying something. It was a shovel, the kind with a small pointy scoop.

Lake turned and forced herself to keep running. The car wasn't far, but she could hear panting close behind her to the right, and the slurping sound of Rory's shoes fighting the mud. Lake was almost at the car, almost. Then the blow came. She heard the whack on her head before she felt it and it seemed to echo in her brain. Then a searing pain shot through her.

Lake stumbled forward and tried to right herself, but the blow had knocked the wind out of her and finally she fell forward, landing on her knees in the mud. She was still clutching the car key in one hand and she tightened her fist around it as she struggled onto her back. Rory had the shovel raised, ready to deliver another blow. As she started to bring it down Lake threw her body to the right. The shovel missed her head but the metal scoop landed hard on her arm, making her yelp in pain.

Lake scooted backward in the mud, trying to get leverage to stand. As Rory brought the shovel up again, Lake kicked hard at Rory's shin. Rory lurched backward, instinctively lowering the shovel as she reached one hand to her shin. Lake struggled up. Her clothes were sopping wet now, almost weighing her down. With all the force she could muster, she charged toward Rory, knocking her to the ground. The shovel dropped from her hand. Lake picked it up and flung it across the yard as Rory let out a scream of rage.

This was her only chance now. Lake lunged toward the car, yanked open the door, and flung herself inside. With wet, slippery fingers she fumbled along the door until she found the lock and clicked it closed. At the same moment, Rory threw herself at the car and yanked hard at the door handle. When it didn't open, she began to bang on the window.

Don't look, just go, Lake told herself. Her right hand was trembling and she had to steady it with the other one just to make the key go into the slot. Rory kept banging on the window, so hard Lake was sure it would shatter. She turned on the engine and put the car in reverse. As she pulled away, she could see Rory standing in the headlights, dripping wet, her mouth slack in angry confusion. Then she turned and plunged into the darkness.

Lake began to edge the car backward down the driveway. In the dark, in the pouring rain, she could see next to nothing in the rearview mirror. I can't do this, she thought desperately. She tried to concentrate but she still felt dizzy and her head ached. Within seconds she veered off to the left and her back bumper rammed a post or a rock along the edge of the driveway.

Turn around, she told herself. It was the only way she would be able to get out. In the headlights she saw grass to the right of the driveway and she guessed that there was enough room to swing the

car around. She put the car in drive, tapped the gas and maneuvered to the right. Then she jerked the gearshift into reverse and
cranked the wheel so she could point the back of the car toward
the house. She touched the pedal. The back wheels lurched but
the front wheels didn't move. They're stuck in mud, she realized,
hitting the brake. She gunned the motor but the wheels spun round
and round, shooting mud into the beams of the headlights.

Lake was almost hyperventilating. She breathed through her
nose, trying to calm herself so she could concentrate. Turning
the wheel slightly, she tapped the gas again. This time the car
jerked backward and she positioned it so she was facing out of the
driveway. With a rush of relief, she put the car in drive and eased
down the driveway. She glanced in the rearview mirror. There was
no sign of Rory.

When she reached the road she turned right. She had no idea
where she was going, only that this was the direction she'd come
from. She didn't dare fool with the GPS now. She would just drive
until she could find a town. And then what? She had called the
police and would have to follow up with them. But what would
she say? They were on their way to the house now and would talk
to Rory, of course. Rory would deny everything, would tell about
Lake being with Keaton that night, would even say Lake was the
one who killed Keaton.

The road was treacherously narrow and the rain was even
heavier now, blowing sideways because of the wind. She still felt
weak, dizzy. It'll be okay, she told herself, just drive slowly. Instinctively she glanced in the rearview mirror. Two white headlights had
appeared out of the darkness. Was it Rory?

Gripping the wheel, Lake accelerated, but she was afraid of
skidding or running off the road. The headlights gained on her.
They seemed to be alive, two demonic creatures bearing down on
her in the night.

But all of a sudden the headlights disappeared. It was as if the car had been swallowed up by the night. Then Lake heard the roar of the car. It was coming up the road in the other lane, alongside her. Rory was preparing to ram into her, she realized in horror.

She'd barely finished the thought when she felt the blow to the back left side of the car. As her car fishtailed, Lake was knocked forward into the steering wheel and her head snapped back. There was a curve in the road and she couldn't see what was on the other side of it. Using some old instinct, she touched the brake lightly and steadied the car as she turned the corner.

A second later Lake heard a loud cracking sound, like a tree being split in two by lightning, followed by a cacophony of shattering glass. Rory had crashed her car into something.

Lake eased her foot onto the brake carefully, wondering what she should do. As she finished coming around the bend, she spotted pulsing red lights. They were on top of a white police car, ahead of her at an intersection and about to make a turn onto the road. She had no choice but to stop.

She slowed the car and beeped the horn loud and long to get their attention. The police car pulled up parallel to hers on the road. It said Bedford Hills Police on the side. She rolled down her window, and the police car's window slid down simultaneously. There was just the driver, dressed in a dark blue police uniform. He was about thirty, with a wide face and thick black eyebrows.

"What seems to be the problem, ma'am?" he asked.

"Did you come because of the call—the 911 call?" Her words sounded almost slurred to her.

"Are you the person who made it?"

"Yes—a woman is trying to kill me. She—she's behind us. She tried to ram her car into mine and I think she hit something."

The cop's eyes shot forward, and at the same moment, he grabbed his radio.

"Call for backup," he said. "High Ridge and Red Fox Road." He turned back to Lake, his eyes stern.

"Ma'am, please pull over to the side of the road and put your blinkers on. Do not get out of your vehicle. I will be back to you shortly."

She did as she was told. Once she'd shut off the ignition, she turned around in her seat, but all she could see were the red tail-lights of the police car curving in the road. Lake glanced down. Her entire front was streaked with glistening mud, and she knew her face was covered with it, too. She must look a fright, she realized, like some crazy person. And it would be her word against the word of someone five months pregnant. How would she ever make anyone believe her?

Inside the glove box she found a few paper napkins and used them to wipe as much mud from her face as possible. She felt a welt just above her eye—from the kick. A worse bruise was on the back of her head. She ran her hands roughly through her hair and touched a huge sticky lump. Wouldn't the wounds be proof that she'd been attacked? But Rory would only say she was defending herself.

Lake fumbled in her muddied purse for her BlackBerry. Miraculously it was dry. She needed to call Archer—and she needed to get a lawyer. It would be too dangerous to deal with all this on her own.

To her dismay the call went straight to Archer's voice mail.

"Kit, I'm in a terrible jam. I—Rory tried to kill me. She was the one who killed Keaton. I'm in Bedford Hills, New York. Please call me back as soon as you can."

She tried Hotchkiss next, knowing she'd get voice mail and yet hoping there'd be some kind of emergency number. Though she would hardly expect him to represent her in this situation, she thought he might be able to recommend someone. No luck. She had a few friends who practiced law and she wondered if she should contact one of them. Won't it blow their minds to hear me describe this mess? she thought ruefully.

Then her BlackBerry rang and to her relief she saw that it was Archer.

"Tell me you're all right," he demanded as soon as she answered.

"Physically, yes—just a little bruised. And woozy. She put something in my drink to knock me out. But that's not the problem. Rory's totally crazy and she'll probably try to make it seem like I attacked *her* or something."

"Where *are* you, anyway? I mean, where in Bedford Hills?"

"I'm on the side of the road in my car. There's a cop here, or just behind me. Rory tried to run me off the road and she hit a tree with her car. She may be injured but I don't know."

"Rory killed Keaton, you said? Were they having an affair?"

"More of a fling, I'd say—last winter. According to her, the baby she's carrying is Keaton's—had I told you she was pregnant? But she's such a nut job, who knows if it's the truth? I need to get a lawyer fast—is there anyone you know?"

Her eyes caught something bright on the road ahead, and over the sound of the rain, she heard the wail of a siren.

"Oh God, there's an ambulance coming," she said, peering through the windshield. "She must be injured."

"I do know a couple of lawyers who handle criminal stuff. Let me see if I can round up someone for tonight."

"Thank you. Thank you."

"Do you have any idea where they'll be taking you?"

"A police station, I'm sure."

"Okay, call me back the minute you know which one. And tell

them you need to go to an emergency room first to be tested for the drug she gave you. You'll need that as evidence. Plus it will buy you some time until I can get there with a lawyer."

"You're coming, too?"

"Yes. I'll start driving north as soon as possible. Just call me when you have the exact location."

As she hung up, the ambulance slid by her, slick with rainwater, and moved carefully up the road beyond the curve. It stopped around the bend, and she could see only the flashing lights through the trees.

She had no idea how long she was supposed to sit here. Surely they'd be sending someone back to talk to her. She tried to assess her situation. What would she tell the police? That she had gone to Rory's house to see the files. The files would be there as proof and Archer could back up her claims about the clinic. And her head injury would verify that she'd been attacked. But if she told them that Rory tried to kill her because she believed Lake had been with Keaton, that might be enough for the cops in the city to have her DNA tested. And then there'd be proof that Keaton had bedded her. She pictured the smug expression on Hull's face when he heard the news. And possibly Jack's, too. Then she pictured Will and Amy. I can't lose them, she thought.

She'd have to come up with something to explain everything. But Rory would have her own version. She'd say that somehow, when they were looking at the files, she had realized that Lake had slept with Keaton and killed him. She'd slipped a drug into Lake's tea so she could escape, but Lake figured it out and tried to overpower her. She'd followed her in her car to see where she was headed.

I have to counteract whatever lies Rory will tell, she thought. But *how*? With *what*? She glanced up quickly, realizing she'd been lost in thought. The rain had stopped instantly in that moment, as if a switch had been flicked. She craned her neck around and saw that more lights now twinkled through the trees. Reinforcements had clearly arrived from the other direction. And a police car was backing down the road in her direction.

Inside was the same officer who had spoken to her earlier. He stopped, stepped out of the cruiser, and approached her car again.

"Ma'am, could you please step out of your vehicle."

Though his voice was low and even, there was an undertow of disapproval. She opened the door and stepped into the humid night air. The headlights of the cop car hit the immediate area.

"What's your name, please?" he asked. In the dark, his thick black brows looked like caterpillars sleeping on his face.

"Lake Warren."

"Ms. Warren, my name is Officer Clinton. We're going to need you to come to our headquarters and answer some questions."

"I—I need to go to a hospital first. The woman back there—Rory Deever—she drugged me. And she hit me over the head."

He had been staring at her blankly, but when she twisted her head so he could see the wound, he pulled back in surprise. He turned away and spoke into his walkie-talkie.

"Why don't you come with me," he said, turning back. "Please lock your vehicle."

She told herself not to act fearful with him. She was the victim, not the criminal, and she needed to come across that way.

"Of course," she said. "The woman who attacked me—did she hit a tree?"

"I'm not at liberty to divulge that right at this time."

He opened the rear door of his car and she climbed in. The backseat smelled of old sweat and fried food and it nearly made her gag. She thought they might drive past the accident but the cop turned the car around and headed in the opposite direction. The drive took about twenty minutes and the entire time she could feel her fear throbbing, like a hand that had been slammed in a door. The exam and tests would buy her time but eventually she would have to face the police and their questions. She prayed that Archer had found a lawyer for her.

She was taken to Northern Westchester Hospital, a big sprawling complex with an ER lit up as bright as day. The waiting room was about a quarter full. People who should have been preoccupied with their sprained ankles and palpitating hearts dropped their jaws at the sight of her being escorted inside by a cop. With the cop nearly hugging her side, Lake explained to the triage nurse about the drugging and showed her the blow to her head. Instead of being forced to endure the waiting area of onlookers, she learned she would be sent to an exam room immediately. As she and the cop were led there, everyone's eyes were on her.

"May I ask where you'll be taking me afterward?" Lake asked him.

"Why don't I let one of the detectives explain everything," he said. "He'll be here shortly."

At least the cop didn't come into the room with her—he remained right outside as a nurse directed her onto an exam table. She asked Lake to wait a few minutes and left her alone. Lake lightly tapped the wound on her head and felt that the blood was still oozing.

"Ms. Warren?"

She snapped her head to the right. In the doorway stood a hulking man with a gigantic mustache, wearing a blue-and-green-checked jacket. Clearly not an M.D. She nodded yes.

"I'm Detective Ronald Kabowski from the Bedford Hills Police. I hear the doctor will be in any second, but I'd like to chat for a minute beforehand—if you're up to it."

You're the victim, she reminded herself. Do not act guilty.

"Thank you for coming," she said.

"My officer tells me you suspect you were drugged."

"I don't suspect—I know. I passed out. And this woman—Rory Deever—admitted she did it to me when I came to."

"It sounds like it's been quite a harrowing night for you." His words were slicked with sympathy, but she could see the strategy. It was meant to make her drop her guard.

"Yes. And there's something important that you should know. This situation is connected to a homicide case in New York City— the death of a doctor there, Mark Keaton."

"Why don't you start by telling me what happened tonight."

Instinctively she lowered her eyes and wished she hadn't.

"I want to tell you the whole story," she said, looking back up at him. "But because things are so complicated—I mean, with the other case—I'd prefer to tell you with an attorney present."

"An attorney?" he said. His mouth dropped open, revealing a huge left canine as yellowed as an old refrigerator.

"Are you sure about that? It's gonna make things take forever."

"I realize that, but like I said, this is a very complicated situation."

He stared hard at her, all the fake sympathy gone.

"Suit yourself," he said. "I'll have to see what I can learn from the other party involved."

HER HEART FROZE. Rory had obviously been taken to this same hospital, brought in through the ambulance bay. If she were the first to tell her story, Lake would be on the defensive, forced to try to undo the lies of a psychopath. But she didn't dare say a word to the detective. She might dig herself into a hole.

"Can you tell me where we'll be going after the doctor sees me?" Lake said. "I need to let the lawyer know."

"The Bedford Hills Police station," he said and turned on his heels.

As soon as he was gone, she called Archer back to give him a rushed update and to explain where he could meet her.

"Okay, we'll find the place. I've just picked up Madelyn Silver—she's a terrific criminal attorney. I only gave her five minutes to get ready, so she said you can't blame her for showing up in her pajamas."

Lake felt a rush of relief.

"You may actually get there before me," she said. "I haven't even been seen by a doctor yet."

"Not a problem. Wait, hold on." She could hear him passing the phone.

"Lake, this is Madelyn Silver," a gravelly voice said. "Have the police tried to speak to you yet?"

"Yes—a detective came to the hospital. I told him that the situation was related to a homicide in New York City and because of that I didn't want to say anything until my attorney arrived."

"Good girl. Don't let them intimidate you. Say nothing."

But what do I say when *you* arrive, Lake wondered after she'd hung up. Did she dare tell Madelyn Silver everything? From the little Lake knew, she was pretty sure that a lawyer wasn't allowed to withhold information about a crime. And wasn't leaving the scene of Keaton's murder a crime? If only Lake could find out what Rory was saying to the police—then she would be on surer footing when she talked to Silver.

The next few minutes were interminable. She had begun to feel less woozy but her head and body ached. She thought about the kids and what they would have gone through if Rory had managed to stuff her in the freezer. But if Lake were sent to jail after this, it would be almost as bad.

Two more patrol cops arrived and paced outside the room. The other one seemed to have disappeared. Nurses glanced constantly toward the open door of her room as they passed by. After ten minutes, the cop who'd driven her to the hospital stepped into the room with a camera. He was there to take pictures of her wounds, he said. After snapping six or seven he left, and more minutes passed. She worried that the longer they waited to test her, the less likely they would be able to pick up traces of the drug. Finally a doctor arrived, a tall, elegant black woman with round brown eyes.

"I'm Dr. Reed," she said, her voice flat. "The police said you're asking for a toxicology test?"

"Yes. I was drugged tonight." She tried to sound calm and reasonable, like a totally sane person who'd done nothing wrong, but she knew that in her muddy, disheveled, weary state she looked like someone who'd experienced a psychotic break.

"Can you describe the symptoms to me?"

"My head started to hurt and I passed out—I'm not sure for how long. It could have been just a few minutes or maybe a bit longer. I felt woozy afterward—and very weak."

"Any nausea?"

"A little."

"I'll send a nurse in to draw blood. You'll also have to give a urine sample—with the nurse watching."

"Fine," Lake said, though it didn't feel fine. "And I have bruises on my head where I was hit with a shovel." She lightly tapped the spongy hair just above the cut.

The doctor pulled a pair of latex gloves from a dispenser, snapped them on, and, parting Lake's hair, examined the wound.

"That's nasty-looking," she said after a moment. "I don't think you need stitches but we should get that cleaned up pronto. And you'll need an antibiotic. Have you had a tetanus booster lately?"

"Actually, yes, two years ago."

"Good. Were there any signs of a concussion tonight?"

Lake stared at her blankly.

"Headaches? Dizziness?"

She shrugged, offering a rueful smile. "Yes, but that may have been caused by the drug."

"Are you in any kind of pain now?" Dr. Reed asked.

The comment made Lake's eyes well with tears. How funny, she thought. What an understatement.

"My head's still aching some."

"I'll give you something for that—but we need to wait until after the blood and urine tests." For the first time she saw a trace of warmth in the doctor's eyes.

Things started to move faster then. A nurse came in to draw blood and to accompany her to the bathroom across the hall, where she watched Lake pee, making sure she didn't try to spike her urine. Afterward the nurse cleaned and dressed her head wounds and gave her an antibiotic to take. Lake pretended to focus on the nurse's actions while she eavesdropped on the conversations in the corridor. She was desperate for news of Rory's condition. Had her husband been called? In the background she could hear doctors and nurses asking for things like CTs and portable ultrasounds or requesting that vascular be called right now. But nothing about Rory. And there was no sign of her, either, as the cop led Lake back through the waiting room—with every eye trained on her.

It was just after ten when she was ushered into the back of the police car again, and ten-thirty when the car pulled up to the station house. The space was a blur of gray walls, metal desks, and linoleum. Kabowski appeared suddenly, as if from a mist. She wasn't sure if he had come ahead or simply followed them from the hospital.

"Did my lawyer arrive yet?" she asked him.

"Not that I'm aware of. Why don't we put you someplace where you'll be comfortable until he arrives?"

"Thank you," Lake said—though she knew that the last thing Kabowski cared about was her comfort.

She was led to a small interview room with a metal table and several stacking chairs around it. The uniformed cop who accompanied her didn't ask if she'd like anything to drink. Didn't they always ask you that on cop shows? She sensed they weren't treating her at all like a victim.

Alone again, Lake felt the urge to lay her head on the table, to let tears fall, but she knew they might be watching her through the mirror on the wall. She sat there instead, blank-faced, but churning inside, wondering what was going to happen next—and when Archer would arrive with the laywer.

Fifteen minutes later the door swung open and a woman close to sixty and barely over five feet tall burst into the room.

"Madelyn Silver," she said as she shot out a hand as wide as a mitten and shook her head, indicating that Lake shouldn't get up.

She wasn't wearing pajamas, but Madelyn's black pants and tan cotton blazer looked like they'd been thrown on in a hurry. Her hair was jet black with a fine band of white down the center part, and the corners of her eyelids were so hooded they gave her small brown eyes a triangular shape. The only makeup she wore was a swipe of red lipstick that ran roughshod over the outline of her mouth. At first glance she looked like someone's grandmother, the kind of person you'd see knitting in a train station, but a few seconds after she entered the room, Lake could feel the force field around her.

"How you doing, kiddo?" she said, taking the seat next to Lake and positioning her chair so they were face-to-face.

"Not so great. I'm just glad you're here. Is Kit outside?"

"Yeah, they're making him cool his pretty heels in their cheery waiting area. What's the story on your head there? How bad are you hurt?" As Madelyn spoke, she shrugged off the shoulder strap from her worn leather briefcase, dropping the bag onto the table, then drew out a yellow legal pad. Something about that pad and Madelyn's brusque but maternal style made Lake feel safe for the first time.

"It's cut—but not bad enough for stitches. I might have a concussion, though."

Madelyn cocked her head and parted her full lips hopefully, as if she'd just heard a rumor of a sixty-percent-off sale at Saks.

"Possible concussion. That means we could get this interview postponed. Are you really up to talking to these guys tonight?"

"I—I don't know," Lake said. "Everything—it's all such a mess. I—"

"Even if we decide to postpone the interview, you and *I* need to talk while everything's fresh in your mind. So why don't we start and see how you feel as we go."

"Okay," Lake said hesitantly. She still had no clue what she was going to say to Madelyn. If she said that Rory had accused her of having an affair with Keaton and had lured her to the house because of that, all roads would then surely lead back to her reckless night with him. "Is it safe to talk here?"

"Yes, that's not a problem. On the way up, Archer filled me in on what you'd uncovered at the clinic. He said you drove to Ms. Deever's house because she claimed to have evidence to show you."

"Yes, some files—and she actually did have them. They're probably still on the kitchen table, and the police need to get them as evidence."

"Okay, we'll alert them to that." Madelyn had begun to make notes on the legal pad, using an elegant Mont Blanc pen. With her other hand she pulled the edges of her jacket over her full breasts, as if the fit felt awkward. "Now, why don't you start from the beginning."

Lake just sat there, paralyzed. How much should she *say*?

"Can I ask you one question first?" Lake said finally. "Do you know anything about Rory? Was she injured? Has she had a chance to speak to the police yet?"

Madelyn set down her pen and peered at Lake. The look in her eyes was dark and grave.

"What is it?" Lake asked weakly.

"I have some disturbing news that I didn't want to drop on you the minute I walked in. The police don't know I know this, but . . . Rory Deever was killed in the accident. She died instantly."

Lake's heart seemed to stop mid-beat. She could barely believe the words. She felt a surge of relief. At nearly the same moment, she thought of the unborn baby and winced in distress.

"But she wasn't driving that fast," Lake argued.

"Apparently she wasn't wearing a seat belt, and her head hit the windshield hard."

"How—how did you find this out?"

"Archer has some contacts up this way in the news media."

"Are you absolutely sure?" Lake asked. "The detective who spoke to me—Kabowski—implied that he was about to talk to Rory tonight."

"I'm sure he was just playing you. But, look—I don't want you to worry. This complicates things, I know, but I'm going to make sure you're okay. Got it?"

Lake nodded as her mind fully processed the news. This changed everything, she realized. There would be no version of events from Rory. Lake fought the urge to laugh like a crazy person.

"Got it," Lake said.

"Okay, now tell me what happened."

Lake started with the call from Rory and took Madelyn through everything that followed. As she relived the terrifying minutes in the basement, her voice choked. For the first time she fully imagined what it would be like to end up in that freezer, lying on top of piles of frozen meat and gasping for air until there was no more.

"But *why*?" Madelyn asked. Her eyes were perplexed, not accusatory. "What was the point of trying to kill you?"

"Because . . . she thought I'd figured out that she'd killed Dr. Keaton. And she needed to shut me up."

"But *had* you figured it out? How?"

Lake paused for a moment, her mind racing ahead of her words.

"She had a slip of the tongue," she said. "As we were looking at the files in her kitchen, she said that maybe Keaton had also learned the truth about the clinic and he was killed because of that. I said it was a possibility but that Keaton's death might well have been a coincidence, that it could have been related to, say, a burglary. The nurse who'd watered his plants mentioned he had a terrace and I suggested to Rory that someone could have broken in from there. And then—that's when she made the slip. She said there was no access to the terrace from anyplace. . . . She'd obviously been there."

It had come to Lake in an instant—to turn the slip she'd made with Rory at the piano bar into a lie that could save her. Who could ever know for sure it wasn't true? And it didn't connect her to Keaton in any way.

"That's when you knew? When she made that slip?" Madelyn looked incredulous now.

"No. I didn't make the leap right then. But the comment seemed kind of odd, and that must have shown on my face. I think she *thought* I knew. After that she gave me the tea. And later in the basement, she started railing on as if I *had* figured it out. That's when I knew."

Madelyn pinched her jacket closed again and sealed her ragged red lips tightly together. Lake could tell she sensed there was something off kilter about the story but didn't know what or why.

"So Rory assumed you were going to expose her?"

"I guess so. She acted totally crazy then, like she'd started to break. She said she was pregnant with Keaton's baby and that she'd killed him because he was sleeping around and didn't take her pregnancy seriously. She clearly had psychological problems—maybe borderline personality disorder."

"Okay," Madelyn said after a moment, as if she'd accepted Lake's words despite her instincts. "Take me through the rest. How did you escape?"

Lake told the story exactly as it happened—locking Rory in the basement, being tackled in the yard, Rory giving chase in her car. There were moments when she felt tentative and then had to remind herself: *This part is all true.*

"She tried to run me off the road," Lake said as she came to the end of the story. "The road was slick and she must have lost control of the car."

Madelyn leaned back and sighed.

"Do you feel up to talking to the cops tonight? It will certainly add to your credibility if you do it now."

Lake took a deep breath. The idea was scary as hell but she wanted desperately to get it over with, especially while the story was fresh in her mind.

"Yes," she said. "I want to do it tonight."

Two detectives joined them next—Kabowski and a young female detective with brassy blond hair and a tiny heart-shaped face—though Lake suspected others were in the next room behind the mirror. Madelyn had told her to begin with her work at the clinic and how she'd stumbled onto the embryo stealing. It wasn't hard to figure out why. Starting there would not only calm Lake down but also help undercut the possible nut-job image the cops had of her.

After she took them through all that, she got to Rory. At the point where she mentioned the patient files that Rory had taken, the female detective slipped out of the room momentarily, and Lake assumed it was to make certain they'd been retrieved from Rory's kitchen.

As she reached the part about Rory's slip, and how it related to the death of a Dr. Mark Keaton in New York, Lake had to force herself to look directly at Kabowski and not flinch. He took notes as she spoke, and yet his eyes rarely left hers.

The worst moments of the night—Rory drugging and attacking her and confessing to killing Keaton—were actually the easiest to describe. Lake forced herself to remember being thrust over the lip of the freezer and the terror that had gripped her then. She wanted that fear to leak through as she spoke because she knew it would help them believe her. Then, finally, she was done.

"Well, we certainly appreciate that you took the time to share this with us tonight," Kabowski said. "I mean, considering what you've been through." His tone sounded sympathetic but Lake knew not to trust it. She smiled weakly, wondering what was next.

Kabowski looked down at his notes and stroked his mustache. "I'm a little confused, however," he said after a moment.

Lake's heart sank. Was he skeptical about the slip, as Madelyn had been?

"Yes?" Lake said softly.

"Why do you think Ms. Deever was so interested in helping you about the files? If she'd murdered this Dr. Keaton, you'd think she'd want to just lay low. Why suddenly decide to play whistle-blower?"

The question caught her totally off guard. As she'd obsessed about how to spin everything that had happened, she'd never seen this one coming.

"I'm not sure," Lake said. She clenched her fist, thinking, trying to make her brain work harder. "But—I could make a guess."

"Okay, let's hear it," Kabowski said.

Lake bit her lip instinctively.

"After she overheard Maggie say that I had suspicions about the clinic—and my theory about the codes in the files—she may have decided that exposing the clinic could throw the police totally off track with the murder investigation. They'd assume someone at the clinic had killed Keaton because he'd learned the truth."

Kabowski looked ready to lob another question at her, when someone entered the room with the stack of patient records from Rory's house. He pushed them toward Lake and instructed her to show him where the notations were. She opened the file on top and pointed to the letters, explaining what she thought they stood for.

Kabowski's body language seemed to relax a little, and Lake wondered if he had begun to believe her.

"Detective, as you indicated earlier, my client has had a very tough night," Madelyn announced as Kabowski continued to paw through the charts. "She may have even suffered a concussion. I think it's time I took her home."

Kabowski stood up, placed his hands on his hips, and nodded but made a big to-do about Lake needing to be available for further questioning. Madelyn assured him that Lake would return to the area if necessary. Lake suddenly felt drained, completely spent— not just from the ordeal, but from the stress and strain of lying.

"You handled that very well," Madelyn said as they headed down the hall. "Let's find Kit and fill him in."

Archer was still in his rumpled tan trench coat, sitting on a metal chair in the waiting area with his long legs thrust out in front of him. He leapt up when he saw them approach and offered Lake a sympathetic hug. In the brief second that his arms were around her, she felt that same rush of calm and safety she'd experienced while lying on his couch.

"I want to hear everything," he said, his voice low. "But let's wait till we're out of here."

Lake glanced at her watch as they hurried across the parking lot, where steam rose from the puddles left behind from the storm. It was well after midnight. Lake's car was being held so the police could photograph where Rory had rammed it, so she had to ride with Archer and Madelyn back to the city.

"Do you think I'll really have to be interviewd by those detectives again?" she asked as Archer maneuvered out of the parking lot.

"Maybe," Madelyn said from the backseat. "Maybe not."

"Great," Lake said despairingly.

"But they are going to be less skeptical at that point because your story will have begun to check out. The tests will confirm that you were drugged. There will be evidence related to the cars. And when they obtain the DNA of the fetus, that will prove the baby was Keaton's. I think the worst is over."

"Great," Lake said.

But she knew it wasn't true. The worst wasn't over. She still had to face Hull and McCarty—and make *them* believe her lies.

31

SIX DAYS LATER, on a Friday, Lake hurried down the street in Greenwich Village toward a small Italian restaurant. It was in the low eighties again, after two days of cooler weather, but there was something fall-like nudging the outside edges of the heat. She glanced at her watch. Twelve-twenty. She was early, so there was no need to rush, and yet her feet seemed to have a mind of their own.

She didn't see him inside the restaurant, but when she gave his name to the hostess, the girl said, "This way," and led her outside to a garden lined with a wooden stockade fence and pots bursting with pink geraniums. Archer was sitting at an umbrella-shaded table, working his iPhone. He was dressed casually—jeans and a faded purple polo shirt that looked as if it had been left to dry, over the years, on endless docks and porch railings.

"Hey," he said, lifting his butt briefly off the chair as she took the seat across from him. He smiled broadly at her. "I barely recognize you without the mud mask you were wearing Saturday night."

Lake smiled back at him. "I actually think that did something nice for my pores."

"How's the cut on your head?"

"Better. I had my own doctor check me out and he said I probably did have a mild concussion."

"Well, I hope you're allowed to drink because I ordered a bottle of rosé for our celebration."

Lake nodded enthusiastically. There were indeed a few things to celebrate. As soon as news of Rory's death got out, the lab supervisor at the clinic had panicked and come forward to the authorities, admitting that some couples' eggs and embryos had been transferred to other patients without permission. There was now a full-scale inquiry into the clinic. And there had been good news for Lake as well. Preliminary drug tests had revealed the presence of a sedative in the bottom of the teacup she'd drunk from, backing up her story. And Madelyn had learned from a friend in the NYPD that toll records had shown that Rory had driven into Manhattan in her car early on the morning Keaton was murdered and left the city shortly after four a.m.

Archer pulled the wine bottle from an ice-filled bucket by the table and poured Lake a glass.

"First and foremost, to your survival," he said, raising his glass. "I keep thinking you're going to confess that you're a former Navy SEAL and that's why you've been able to escape raging rivers and pathological killers and . . ."

Lake grinned. "And avoid the world's worst case of freezer burn?"

"Exactly."

"I think I owe it all to pure adrenaline—and to the fear that I'd never see my kids again if I didn't *do* something. Of course every time I think about Rory's baby dying, it makes me so sad."

"I've got something to take your mind off that—another reason to celebrate. I just heard from my producer that Hoss cut a deal. She obviously saw that it was all coming down around her and decided to save her ass. She admitted that Levin had hired that guy who followed you, the one who attacked you in Dumbo. Melanie apparently let Levin know that you'd called and he sent the guy there after you. Hoss is claiming it was only to scare you. Regardless, this ties up some loose ends—and it also means you'll be safe. As soon as the police have him in custody, you can make an ID."

Lake let out a ragged sigh of relief. It meant that there wouldn't be lingering questions or suspicions about what she'd told the police. They would have no reason to ask for her DNA.

"I guess it's no surprise that Hoss was in the thick of it," Lake said. "She oversaw everything that went on in the lab. But what about Sherman? Was he in on it, too?"

"Apparently, yes."

"And the associates and nurses?" she asked, dreading the answer. "I've been worried about the guy who recommended me—Steve Salman."

Archer shook his head.

"No, it doesn't look like it went that far down. At least from what the cops can tell right now."

Though Steve had offered her no support, she couldn't bear the thought of his life being ruined. He was her friend's brother, after all.

"There's one more person I'm curious about," she said. "The therapist, Harry Kline. He wasn't involved, was he?"

Archer scrunched his mouth. "No, I don't think so," he said. "If it's the guy who I think it is, he's been nothing but cooperative. I hear he was pretty shocked."

She thought of the story Rory had told her about Harry and his daughter. On Sunday, as she'd lain in her bed recuperating, she decided that there must have been a grain of truth to the tale. Keaton had possibly flirted with Harry's daughter—rather than the other way around—and Rory most likely saw the daughter as a real threat. She'd probably gone to Harry and claimed Keaton was after the girl. That would have resulted in the daughter being removed. Harry had left a message for Lake this week, but she hadn't wanted to return it until her own situation was more settled.

"The bottom line is that the clinic is being closed," Archer said, interrupting her train of thought. "With the top people implicated, there's no way it can go on right now."

Lake smiled ruefully.

"Of course, that doesn't help Alexis Hunt," she said. "She still has no rights to her child."

"I know. And according to what the technician told the cops, embryos from at least thirty other couples were used fraudulently. And a fair number of embryos were sold for research without permission."

"Once that news gets out, so many former patients are going to wonder and begin to freak out," Lake said. "It's just so awful."

"And yet think of what you did, Lake." Archer said. "You spared countless other people the same fate."

"It was hardly heroic. I just sort of stumbled onto the truth."

"You did more than that and you know it. Speaking of stumbling, here's an interesting tidbit. Apparently part of the reason why the lab technician gave it up so quickly was because Keaton had recently asked him a few probing questions about some of the procedures. This lab guy was already worried the lid was about to blow off."

That could explain why Melanie Turnbull's name was in Keaton's apartment, Lake realized. Something had pointed him in that direction—though Lake would probably never know what it was.

"Anything new from your end?" Archer asked.

"I told you about the drug test. The DNA test on Rory's baby should come back soon."

"Madelyn said you handled yourself really well with the New York City cops."

Just hearing him reference that meeting made her stomach clench. The session with Hull and McCarty had been terrifying—though at least Madelyn had been at her side, looking ready to bite if either one of them stepped out of line.

Lake had relayed her story to them, just as she had to the Bedford Hills police and to Archer later in the car that night. There had been moments when she worried that it sounded rehearsed, overly polished, but if Hull and McCarty had thought so, they hadn't let on. Maybe because they had no apparent interest in all the details about the clinic and the files Lake had been driving up to see—in truth, that part had seemed to bore them altogether. What they wanted was the stuff on Keaton and why Rory had killed him. When Lake reached the part where she had to lie—and skip much of the truth—she had heard her voice catch just a little. Hull had stared at her so hard it hurt.

They fired a barrage of questions at her then, all about Keaton's murder. But there wasn't anything she could add, she told them. Rory had said she was carrying Keaton's baby, that she'd had copies of his keys made—obviously from the set in Maggie's drawer—and that she'd killed him. And nothing more.

Then she told them about the incident in Brooklyn—Madelyn had insisted on it—and they weren't happy.

"You're chased into the East River at knifepoint and you don't bother calling 911?" McCarty said, not disguising how stupid he thought she was.

"I was afraid to," Lake said.

"'Afraid'?" he said, his large brown eyes nearly lunging from his head. "I would think you'd be afraid *not* to."

"It's because of what I shared with you in my apartment that day," Lake said softly. "I'm in the middle of a very difficult custody situation. My husband would use anything against me."

"He's gonna have a field day *now*, isn't he?" Hull said, snickering.

"That's out of line, Detective." Madelyn retorted. "My client was supposed to remain in bed today because of her injuries but volunteered to speak with you. She has been more than cooperative. Now, if there's nothing else, I'd like to see that she gets home."

The two men just sat there, McCarty running his eyes over the last page of notes and Hull flicking a pencil back and forth, back and forth. Finally Hull spoke.

"There *is* one little detail we're having trouble with," Hull said, his eyes glinting. "Maybe you can help us with it."

Lake didn't say anything, just waited, trying to make herself breathe.

"Ms. Deever's phone records indicate that you two talked several times. Can you tell us what those calls were about?"

"Of course," Lake said, relieved to be able to answer. She'd been over this general ground with them before. "As I mentioned earlier, she called me Saturday afternoon to say she'd brought the patient records home with her. That's when I told her I'd drive to her house to look at them. We spoke a few times after that because I was going to be late. I was delayed at my children's camp."

"What about the *earlier* call?" Hull asked.

"What do you mean?" Lake said. Was he back to the mind games?

"She called your apartment the night before Dr. Keaton's murder," Hull said, his voice hard. "At two fifty-seven a.m., to be exact."

Against her will, Lake's lips parted in disbelief. So it had been *Rory* who had called that night, asking about "William." Of course. She had told Lake in the basement that she was worried she and Keaton were already sleeping together.

She felt Madelyn shift ever so slightly in the chair next to her, sensing trouble. Lake's mind ricocheted, searching frantically for an explanation.

"Yes—I did get a call late that night," she said, furrowing her brow. "I was sleeping and it woke me. But—I couldn't make sense of what the person was saying, and then they hung up. I thought it was a wrong number."

"Why would Ms. Deever do that, do you think?"

"I—I have no idea."

She started to say more, to suggest that Rory had just been crazy, and then she held her tongue. Tell only the essential lie, she told herself.

To her surprise they said she was free to go.

"There's another interesting subplot in all of this," Archer said at their garden table, rousing her from her thoughts.

"With the clinic?"

"No—with Rory Deever. There appears to be no husband in the picture at the moment. The police have spoken to Colin Deever, but he split with Rory a few months ago. I'm still trying to find out more, but I wonder if it's because he knew the baby wasn't his."

Lake touched her hands to her lips, thinking.

"You know," she said, "on a subconscious level, I think I realized the husband was gone. There was no sign of him anywhere in the house."

"What really surprises me is that Keaton returned to the clinic. Why come back when there was such a mess there with Rory?"

"Remember? According to Rory, she hadn't told him about the baby at that point," Lake said. She was on dangerous ground talking about Keaton, but she knew if she avoided the subject, it would seem odd.

"But wouldn't he have started to pick up on the fact that there was something crazy about her?"

"That's very possible. Maggie told me that when she was taking care of his apartment in March, there were signs someone had snuck in one night. It may have been Rory, and Keaton probably suspected it. But then he goes back to L.A. and he may have told himself that Rory's obsessiveness had burned off. A short time later Levin asks him to come back, consider being a partner. He puts a toe in the water by consulting again and discovers everything's cool. Rory appears happily pregnant. She certainly made everyone think there was a nice husband in the picture. She may have even planned to put Keaton out of her mind, pretend the baby was her husband's. But after she saw him, she obviously became fixated again."

"Keaton must have panicked like hell when he did hear about the baby," Archer said. "I can't believe he'd want to work there anymore."

"Maybe he didn't," Lake said and then looked away.

She could feel Archer studying her.

"He didn't drop any hints about bailing to you, did he?" he asked.

Oh God, Lake thought. Does Archer suspect? It took all her strength to return her eyes to him when she answered.

"No," she said. "I hardly knew him."

In that split second, she wished she could unburden her secrets to Archer. Maybe one day, she said to herself—and the words surprised her. For the first time she allowed herself to acknowledge how attracted she was to him—his humor, how easy he was in his own skin, even that crazy white hair. He had helped her when she was in danger, but what really intrigued her was that she had felt comfortable *asking* him for help. Would he want to stay in touch after everything was over? Or would he disappear now that he had his story?

"How's your report coming, by the way?" Lake asked, shifting the topic off Keaton.

"Great," Archer said. "I did a few quick items on the show this week as the story was breaking, but we're putting a much bigger piece together. I'm hoping you'll let me interview you. You should get credit for all of this."

Lake smiled and shook her head. "I'm flattered but I think it's best for me to stay in the background—especially in light of everything with the police. Plus, I just want my life to get back to normal.

"Oh, by the way," she said, before he could push further. "They solved the mystery of my missing doorman that afternoon. He thought he was having a heart attack and hopped in a cab for the hospital without telling anyone. Turned out to be a panic attack."

"Ah. And what about your cat?" he asked. "What do you think the story was there?"

"Just a coincidence, I guess," she said, taking a piece of bread from the basket. "I think some teenagers must have shaved Smokey, just to be mean." There was no way she could tell him that Rory had admitted doing it. That would raise the question of why Rory had been fixated on Lake at that point—and the answer pointed back to Keaton. She hoped he wouldn't remember the catnip and ask about it.

"You were also worried about your doorbell ringing late one night."

"Actually, I may have solved that one this morning," Lake said. "There was a girl I'd never seen on the floor, and I think one of my neighbors, Stan, may be having a little fling with her—while his wife is out at the beach for the summer. We may be adding another divorce to the building."

To Lake's surprise, Archer picked up her hand and held it be-tween both of his. Blood immediately rushed to her cheeks, as if it had been waiting in the wings.

"I haven't wanted to pry, but the other night you mentioned that you were in a crazy custody battle."

"Yes," she said, sighing. "But the worst of that may be over."

It was true. Hotchkiss had called her Monday with news. The weekend had provided evidence of Molly and Jack on board the bliss train all around Manhattan, and Hotchkiss had re-ported this news to Jack's lawyer. Then on Tuesday night Molly had shown up at Lake's apartment and broken down, admitted not only to having an affair with Jack during the marriage but also to keeping up the friendship with Lake to stay in the know about Jack's intentions. Lake had filled Hotchkiss in immedi-ately. It was perfect leverage, he'd said, just what they needed. He'd called back the following day to say Jack would accept joint custody.

"Excellent," Archer said after hearing the full scoop. "Well, look, I don't know how you have to play it in a situation like that, but I'd love to take you to dinner one night—in the not so distant future."

The pure pleasure she felt at his words surprised her.

"I'd love that, Kit, but it's still a little dicey until the final agree-ment gets signed," she said. "For the time being, though, would you settle for a series of fun, thought-provoking lunches?"

"Absolutely," he said, smiling.

The waitress arrived then to take their orders. When she'd de-parted, Lake looked back at Archer. She wanted to change the subject completely, to leave behind everything connected with the clinic, but there was still one thing she needed to ask.

"Question," she said. "Do you think the police would have fig-ured out that Rory was the murderer if she hadn't attacked me?"

"Possibly. From what I know, they felt the wound on Keaton had been made by a woman."

She reached for her wineglass and twirled it between her fingers.

"Oh—so then maybe they would have."

"Of course there's still that little mystery," Archer said.

Lake swallowed, raised her eyebrows.

"Mystery?" she asked.

"A woman had sex with Keaton the night he died, and it doesn't sound like Rory Deever took the time to make love to him before she slit his throat. Clearly this person hightailed it out of the apartment just in time. So, as I said once before, there's a very lucky lady out there somewhere."

"Yes, very lucky," Lake said. She met his eyes and smiled.

ACKNOWLEDGMENTS

I want to say a big thank you to those who helped me so generously while I was doing research for the book: Mary Dodge, PhD, associate professor and director of Criminal Justice Programs, University of Colorado, Denver; Caleb White, police officer, White Plains, New York police; Abigail Greene, managing editor, *Cosmopolitan*; Dr. Mark Howell, psychotherapist; David Razner, Esq., partner and co-chair of the Family Law Group at Fox Rothschild, LLP; Deb Shriver, PR guru; Dr. Paul Paganelli, chief of Emergency Medicine, Milton Hospital, Milton, Massachusetts; Chet W. Lerner, M.D., chief of Infectious Diseases, New York Downtown Hospital; Barbara Butcher, chief of staff and director of the Forensics Sciences Training Program at the New York City office of the chief medical examiner; Rachel Hayes, editor in chief, DailyMakeover.com; Bobbi Casey Howell, partner, chief customer strategy officer, Deutsch.

Also thank you to my fabulous editor, Sally Kim, and my killer agent, Sandy Dijkstra.

Read on for an excerpt from the
exciting new thriller by Kate White.

HARPER

An Imprint of HarperCollins*Publishers*
www.harpercollins.com

SOMETHING WASN'T RIGHT. Phoebe sensed it as soon as she began to walk across the quad that night. The weather was practically balmy, weird for late October, and yet the air carried the pungent smell of wood smoke. But that wasn't the reason things seemed strange to her. It was because of how deserted the campus was. Though she wasn't really used to the place yet, she expected to find more than a few people headed across campus at eight o'clock on a Friday night.

She'd just veered left, planning to head out the eastern gate of the campus, when with a start, she discovered where everyone was. There were at least forty people—students and faculty—congregated in front of Curry Hall. In the two months she'd been at Lyle College, she'd noticed that kids often hung around outside this particular dorm, tossing Frisbees or lolling on the slope of the balding lawn, but tonight everyone was standing, their arms crossed in front and their backs stiff, as if poised for news.

As she drew closer, she saw that two campus police, as well as a local town cop, were speaking to an auburn-haired girl who appeared to be fighting back tears. The dean of students—Tom *something*—was there, too, head lowered and listening intently to the girl.

Phoebe's first reaction was to just keep moving. She'd come to Pennsylvania for a bunch of reasons but becoming best buddies with members of the faculty wasn't one of them, and she religiously avoided moments that called for chitchat. Plus, since last spring she'd developed a severe aversion to packs of people—they reminded her of the paparazzi who'd hounded her for more than two weeks last spring, trailing her down the streets of Manhattan and pelting her with the same questions again and again, as if she'd been accused of running a huge Ponzi scheme or stabbing her husband in the heart with an ice pick.

She started to turn and then stopped. She realized that she wasn't going to be able to resist discovering what all the fuss was about. That, after all, had been her career for the past twenty years—satisfying the unrelenting urge to know.

She edged toward the crowd. After a moment she realized that she'd come up right behind Val Porter, whose long, prematurely gray hair gleamed even in the dark. Val was a women's studies professor, with an office just down the hall from the one Phoebe was squatting in this semester, and though on the surface Val was courteous enough, Phoebe had detected a mild disdain from her ever since their first encounter. Maybe, Phoebe had thought wryly, Val thinks I set the women's movement back on it ass by my behavior.

She started to back away, not at all in the mood for a Val moment tonight. But uncannily the woman seemed to sense her presence and turned around. The movement stirred the scent of patchouli from Val's skin.

"Hello, Phoebe," Val said. There was a slightly disapproving tone to her voice, as if Phoebe had burst in late for an event.

"Hi, Val," she said, as pleasantly as she could. Her M.O. at the school was to be as pleasant as possible. Not wanting to create unnecessary ripples, she sucked it up with Val. "What's going on?"

"A student is missing," Val said bluntly. "Her roommate reported it to the campus police a little while ago."

"How awful," Phoebe said. The revelation caught her like the nick from a razor and she felt her heart skip a little. "Do you know her name?" She wondered if it could be someone from one of the two small classes she was teaching this fall.

"Lilly Mack—she's a junior. No one's seen her since last night."

Phoebe processed the name. It wasn't one she was familiar with.

Well, kids this age can be pretty irresponsible at times," Phoebe mused. "Is it possible she's just gone off with a new boyfriend?"

Val gave her what was close to a withering look, suggesting that Phoebe didn't know a damn thing about "kids this age."

"Anything is possible, of course," she said dryly. "But according to Tom Stockton, she's not the type to just go AWOL."

"I take it someone's called Glenda?" Phoebe asked, referring to Glenda Johns, the president of the college.

"Of course. This could get very, very messy."

"What do you mean?" Phoebe asked.

"This girl's boyfriend disappeared last year. He was a senior here and he apparently just took off in the spring. He hasn't been seen since."

"Do they—?"

"Will you excuse me?" Val said bluntly. "I better check in with Tom and see if there's anything he'd like me to do."

It was more than a dismissal. It implied that Phoebe's help would never be needed.

"Good luck," Phoebe said, keeping her voice even. "Let me know if I can help in any way."

Val started to turn but then looked back, giving Phoebe's outfit the once over. That's rich, Phoebe thought. Val's fashion style was high priestess meets seductress—lots of crushed velvet, jangling bracelets and deeply scooped necklines—and yet she always eyed Phoebe's clothes as if her fairly classic style was just too much.

"Doing something fun tonight?" Val asked.

Phoebe was tempted to toss out a comment that would make Val blanch—like "I've got a hot date with the captain of the lacrosse team"—but bit her tongue. Don't make waves, she told herself. It's not worth it.

"Just grabbing a bite," Phoebe said. "'Night. I hope things turn out okay."

Phoebe faded back from the crowd and retook the path across the quad. Lyle wasn't exactly a gorgeous college. The buildings were all non-descript redbrick or concrete, without an inch of ivy shooting up their sides. But there were dozens of big maples on campus, planted when the school was built in the 1950s, and at night, illuminated by moonlight and streetlamps, they looked majestic and almost magical.

As Phoebe hurried toward East Gate, she thought about the missing girl. She also considered the impact the situation could potentially have on both the college and Glenda Johns. Two and a half years ago Glenda had been recruited by Lyle College to boost its lackluster reputation and flabby endowment, and though she'd made progress, it had been tough going. This situation tonight would hardly help. A second missing student in a year—that, Phoebe realized, would be roughly on a par with news that a Lyle professor had been making porn flicks with students as the stars. Phoebe winced at the thought. Glenda had been Phoebe's roommate in boarding school—both of them scholarship students—and ever since then, one of her closest friends. And it was Glenda who had given Phoebe needed sanctuary this year.

Outside East Gate, Phoebe waited for the traffic light to change, crossed the street, and then walked three blocks down the Bridge Street hill to Tony's, a small Italian restaurant she'd discovered after she'd arrived in late August. It was one of those land-that-time-forgot kind of restaurants, with a lamely painted wall mural of Venice, dust-coated plastic ferns and platters of shrimp scampi reeking of garlic, but Phoebe found the small, candlelit rooms to be oddly comforting.

She'd already eaten once at Tony's this week and she hadn't planned to go back so soon, but a psychology professor named Duncan Shaw had more or less forced her hand. The two of them had ended up on an impromptu committee and almost from the start she'd sensed his interest in her. Last night, to her dismay, he'd asked if she'd like to join him and a few friends for dinner. He was attractive, a little mysterious looking, even, with his dark beard and mustache. And engaging, too, with a deep, infectious laugh. But she was on a self-imposed sabbatical from anything romantic and she wasn't going to be stupid and bite. She'd told him she had plans, but thank you, maybe another time, and prayed he'd taken the hint.

She'd decided originally to eat at the bar of a new restaurant at the edge of town, where the food and ambiance were surprisingly upscale, but now she couldn't take the chance of bumping into Duncan there. After her last class she'd picked up the ingredients for a salad with the intention of just staying in. But then, feeling too restless to face a night alone in the tiny house she was renting, she decided she'd sneak off to Tony's. She figured it was the last place in the world Duncan and his pals would be welcoming in the weekend.

When she reached the restaurant, she paused for a moment outside, trying to shake the twinge of melancholy she felt. Metallic chips in the old sidewalk caught the moonlight and sparkled like crazy. From four short blocks further downhill, she could pick up the smell of the Winamac river—muddy, fishy, but rousing in a strange, earthy way. Sometimes from outside Tony's she could hear music wafting up from the taverns along River Street, but it was too early right now. Hopefully, she thought, Lilly Mack had hooked up with a guy last night and spent the last twenty-four hours in bed with him, oblivious to anything but the crazy sex she was having.

As Phoebe entered the restaurant, the short, pudgy Tony greeted her with a bear hug, declaring her his favorite blonde. After her initial dining experience someone had apparently divulged to him that she was a famous author from New York City. Obviously, Phoebe thought, the person had failed to reveal the rest of the story or Tony might have been far less jolly.

He led her to her usual table in the back of the dining room, which ran adjacent to the bar area. She slipped off her trench coat and glanced around the restaurant. It was about three-quarters full. She'd discovered that people ate insanely early in small-town Pennsylvania and most of tonight's patrons were well into their meals. At moments like this she sometimes felt like Alice had after slipping down the rabbit hole: Everything around her was not only disturbingly unfamiliar but it made no *sense*. Seven months earlier she'd been living in Manhattan with her partner, Alec, just off the tour for her latest book—*Hollywood's Badass Girls*—and smack in the middle of writing her next tome. She'd bought herself a pair of diamond studs as big as hubcaps to celebrate the book's tenth week on the *Times* list. Things couldn't have been sweeter. And then it had all come crashing down—with the speed and force of hitting a deer as it bolted across the highway.

It had started with Alec. When she began to clear dishes after dinner one night, he'd held up a hand and asked her to please wait.

"What's up?" she asked, sitting back down again. He's probably miffed, she thought, at how distracted—and absent—she'd been during the last leg of her book tour.

"We need to talk," he said.

"*O-kay,*" she replied, slightly disconcerted now.

"I think the world of you, Phoebe," he said soberly, "and we've had five great years together."

My God, she thought, is he about to *dump* me as we sit here with our dirty plates in front of us? "What's the matter?" she demanded, unable to keep the edge out of her voice.

"I've always known you didn't want to get married. And I accepted that."

"Well, if I remember correctly, you've never wanted to, either," she said.

"I guess. I mean, sure. But . . . I don't know, lately I've wondered if I may have been wrong thinking that."

The comment shocked her but at the same time relaxed her a little. "Are you saying you want to get *married*?" she asked. Then quickly she saw from the panic in his eyes that she had it wrong.

"It's not just marriage," he said quickly. "I think I'd like *kids*, too. And I know that's a deal breaker for you."

"Well, it's a deal breaker *now* certainly. I'm forty-two and there's not much chance of me getting pregnant. But let's at least discuss this. If your needs have changed, I'm willing to listen. I love you, Alec."

But it wasn't open to discussion. He loved her, too, he said, but he'd made up his mind to move on and move out, to try something new in life. No, there wasn't another woman, he said. She had just sat there at the table, reeling from the shock.

"I actually thought you might be relieved," he said after a few minutes. "I've sensed for a while that you weren't all that invested."

"What's that supposed to mean?" she demanded angrily.

Alec had shrugged. "You never quite seem in the— I don't know, in the throes of the relationship."

Six weeks later, he announced in a phone call that he was seeing a thirty-one-year-old woman at his law firm. No, he swore, nothing had happened while he was still living with Phoebe, but "to be perfectly honest," he realized in hindsight there'd been a certain attraction from the beginning. Christ, Phoebe thought, I finally know how Jennifer Aniston really felt.

She took a tiny bit of consolation in the fact that her work was on fire. But in late May her brilliant career went off the rails, too. Her editor, Daphne, had called her at nine a.m., and not even bothering with "Good morning," had asked if Phoebe was near a computer. Of course, Phoebe had told her—she was in her office working. What did Daphne think? Phoebe wondered. That she sat around in her jammies till noon? Breathlessly Daphne told her to go online. A blogger was reporting that sections about Angelina Jolie in Phoebe's most recent book had been lifted from a series of blogs on a Web site in the UK.

"That's utterly untrue," Phoebe had said indignantly. "*What* blogger, *where*?"

"It's on Huffpo. And it's not some random jerk saying it."

"Well, it's a lie. I've never lifted a *thing* from another writer."

But she had. Not intentionally. Over the next weeks, as she began to unravel the nightmare, she discovered that a freelance researcher she'd used had typed up notes from the blogs and stupidly placed them in a file of Phoebe's own typed notes rather than in a research folder. When Phoebe had read the notes months later, it wasn't hard to mistake them for her own work— the writer had actually seemed to be aping a blunt style that Phoebe was known for—and she had incorporated them directly into her book.

On the advice of the best spin doctors she could find, she'd made a statement explaining everything, but the press coverage had been unmerciful and unrelenting, fueled in large part by the glee of people who'd come off badly in her books. *See*, one Hollywood super agent had declared to the world, everything Phoebe Hall has ever said is total fabrication.

Thankfully, the publisher accepted her version of events—or at least seemed to—after the blubbering researcher had admitted her error in the publishing house's conference room. They said they were committed to working with her and had every reason to believe it would all blow over, just as it had for authors like Doris Kearns Goodwin who'd been in her position. But they wanted to push back the next book, let things cool down a bit. The TV gigs—the *Today* show, *ET*—and her own blog on The Daily Beast screeched to a halt.

Her agent, Miranda, the pit bull who snared the big advances, had been as blunt as a tire iron. "This will blow over, Phoebe, but it can't happen twice. You know that, right?"

"Of course," she'd said. "I should never have hired someone with so little training in research. I—"

"If I were you, I'd get out of town for a while. Go somewhere where you can chill, do a postmortem. Cabo. That's where I'd go."

Fat chance on Cabo, she'd thought. With the next payment for the new book delayed, the paperback for the current book in limbo, and the increased expenses for carrying her apartment alone, she had a cash-flow problem. She'd built a nice nest egg over the years but she didn't dare tap into it.

And then Glenda had called. She suggested Phoebe teach a couple of nonfiction writing classes in place of a professor who'd decided not to come back after the birth of her child. It seemed to make all the sense in the world. Phoebe could sublet her apartment and regroup in a sleepy Pennsylvania town away from the prying eyes of the press. And she could finish the new book, which she was seriously behind on.

When the waiter arrived, she ordered the roast chicken with rosemary, one of the few dishes that wasn't up to its eyeballs in sauce. During dinner she made some mental notes about her classes next week. Later, as she lingered over coffee, Tony sent over a plate of zabaglione with strawberries. It was sublimely delicious and she ate the entire thing, wondering if all the sugar would make her feel less morose—or perhaps even more so.

"'Night, Tony," she said as she rounded the corner of the dining room a few minutes later. He was standing at the podium with the reservation book, just to the right of the bar. "The zabaglione was divine."

"For *you*, I use my finest Marsala."

"I could tell—thank you."

There were only three people at the bar—a middle-aged couple and a guy with wavy, dark brown hair, his back directly to her. As she said good-bye to Tony, the guy at the bar turned his head in her direction. She saw recognition in his eyes and didn't understand why. Then she realized: It was Duncan Shaw. He'd shaved off his mustache and beard in the three days since she'd seen him.

Instinctively she dropped her mouth open in shock—at seeing him here, at the change in his appearance. She watched his brown eyes flick to the left, just over her shoulder, checking to see who she'd been eating with. A second later his eyes betrayed his recognition that she was alone—and that she'd lied to him about having plans. Damn, she thought. I am totally busted.

He smiled ever so slightly. Not surprising, she thought. He's not the sensitive type who's going to seem wounded.

"Oh, hello," Phoebe said, flustered. She noticed that in front of him were a half-filled pasta bowl and a nearly empty glass of wine. "What—what happened to your friends?"

"They wanted to drive to Bethlehem for dinner and I realized I wasn't up for that big of a night. So you're a fan of Tony's cuisine?"

"Yes . . . definitely," she said, moving a little closer. "Look, I feel incredibly awkward. I don't want you to think I lied to you."

He smiled again, a little fuller this time so that it made the skin around his eyes crinkle. Though he was in his mid-forties, she guessed, his skin on his lower face was very smooth, perhaps from having had the beard. "Don't worry," he said. "I'm going to have another glass of wine and see if that will take the sting out." The words could have played sarcastically but his tone didn't let them.

"But it wasn't a lie—really. I told you I had plans and I did—to go out to dinner alone. I find I need to do that on Friday nights. It's a chance for me to decompress."

"No need to explain." Not quite as friendly this time. She wondered if he was one of those dark-eyed guys who sometimes got moody or sullen.

"By the way, I like your new look," she told him, at a loss as to what else to say. But she meant it.

His smile returned. "Thanks. Of course about ten people have asked why I would do it just *before* winter was starting."

The bartender sauntered over.

"Can I top off your wine for you?" he asked.

"That'd be great," Duncan said.

"How 'bout you, ma'am? Can I get you something?"

For a split second she thought Duncan would urge her to accept the offer, and to her surprise she realized she would. But he said nothing, his silence nearly palpable. Of course, she realized. She'd made a bit of a fool of him and he had no desire to have her to stay.

"Um, no, thank you," Phoebe said. She turned back to Duncan. "Well, I'd better get back. Enjoy the rest of your evening."

"You too," he said.

What a dope I am, she thought as she made her way back up Bridge Street. I should have stayed in, eaten the damn salad. Well, at least this would discourage Duncan Shaw from asking her out again.

She cut back through the campus. As she hurried along the path, she wondered if there would still be a crowd near Curry, holding vigil for the missing girl. But everyone had dispersed. Up on the quad however, she found a cluster of students gathered around a tree. She realized that they were tacking up a white flyer of some kind. Scanning the quad, she saw that other trees were already plastered with them. She cut across the quad to one of the trees.

The headline said "Missing" and below that was a photo of Lilly Mack. She was pretty, with blond hair falling far below her shoulders and a small cleft in her chin. With a start Phoebe realized that she recognized the girl. She wasn't in either of Phoebe's classes but Phoebe had walked with her in the rain recently, sharing an umbrella.

And the girl had made a confession to her.